THE FALLEN COWBOY

COLDIRON COWBOYS SERIES

The Fallen Cowboy is a work of fiction. Names, characters, businesses, places, events, and incidents are either the products of the author's imagination or used in a fictitious manner. Any resemblance to actual persons, living or dead, or actual events is purely coincidental.

Copyright © 2019 by Mina Beckett

ebook ISBN: 978-1-7327051-4-2

ISBN: 978-1-7327051-5-9

Published by CurtissLynn Publishing

Cover and internal design by Shiver Shot Design

Editing by The Killion Group, Inc.

The Fallen Cowboy is the second novel in the Coldiron Cowboys series from award-winning author Mina Beckett.

Love heals all wounds …

Out of commission saddle bronc rider Jess Coldiron is putting his horse skills to work by serving as the Executive Director of the Promise Point Horse Rescue Ranch.

Jess's gift for taming wild broncos and pretty women has taught him that both can take a man from zero to ninety in seconds, shake him senseless, and damn near kill him if he landed the wrong way. And Jess had. So bumping anything but heads with the beautiful Mallory Montgomery — his sister-in-law's estranged sister — is out of the question.

Mallory came to Santa Camino, Texas, to fulfill her mother's dying wish of reuniting with her sister, not to fall for a cowboy with a Texas-sized chip on his shoulder about the limp in his swagger and the woman in his past. But the ruggedly handsome, once famous bronc rider has a sexy smile and a fiery touch that ignites a spark in her every time they're together.

Mallory knows there's only one way to get Jess back in the saddle, but she wants more than he's willing to give. And seducing the fallen cowboy may cost Mallory her heart.

THE FALLEN COWBOY

COLDIRON COWBOYS NOVEL

MINA BECKETT

CURTISSLYNN
PUBLISHING

CHAPTER 1

THE DULL, ALMOST CONSTANT THROB IN JESS COLDIRON'S right thigh had become such a part of him, he could hardly remember what his life had been like before bad luck and love had tossed him into the air and tried stomping the life out of him.

But he'd had a life before the fall, a life of bucking broncs and trophy buckles, of cheering crowds and adrenaline rushes, and of flinging his hat high into the air when he made eight seconds.

Most days he didn't think about that life. But some days it crept in, and all he did was think.

He snatched his faded brown Stetson – a hat that was older than any of his relationships — from the dash of his truck and let out a weighted sigh as he scrubbed a thumb over the hoof print near the back of the brim.

He and the old hat had plenty in common. They'd both seen a lot of airtime, been knocked around, stomped on, and reshaped.

Nowadays, the hat kept the sun from his eyes, his hair in place, and reminded him of everything he had lost.

Jess's position as the executive director for the Promise Point Horse Rescue Ranch was nowhere near as demanding or rewarding as competing in the ProRodeo circuit, but it was a lot safer.

On a good day, sitting behind a desk didn't bother him, but on a bad one — when his thigh felt as though it were in a vice and under the merciless twist of a vengeful woman — it was hell. A hell he hated because nothing, including the pain pills the doctors liked to throw at him, helped.

After his fall at the National Finals Rodeo eight years ago, he had undergone countless surgeries and months of grueling therapy just so he could walk again.

He'd learned to live with, and to an extent alleviate, the physical pain of his injury. He stayed in shape, worked out regularly, ate well, and was doing daily stretches. But this morning, he'd been in a hurry to get the workday over with.

He was paying for that now.

Jess put in long hours because he enjoyed his job, his locally hand-crafted desk, his well-worn leather office chair, and the embossed stationary set his sister, Louisa, had given him last year for Christmas.

Most of all, he liked his title. He liked seeing his name on the office door. Not because he needed to be some high falutin administrator. That wasn't Jess's style. He hated wearing a suit and tie and having to shave daily. His office attire was his scuffed-up Justin boots, a t-shirt, and faded jeans.

He liked his title because it kept him away from the shit and shovel part of the Rescue. The hands-on, horse, hoof, and halter part.

Holding to the pinch, he set the hat on his head, opened the door, and eased from his truck. He shifted his weight to his left foot and massaged his right thigh until he was sure he could walk before taking a step.

"You're doing it wrong."

"Oh, for God sakes, Logan," Violet moaned and threw up a hand in her brothers' direction. "Will you please shut up and let Ty fix the damn thing."

"Stay out of this, Vi," Logan warned.

On top of the pain in his thigh, Jess would probably have to play referee between two of his best friends and the woman responsible for his daily dose of caffeine.

Logan and Ty would forgive him for breaking up their family row. But Jess wasn't so sure Violet wouldn't punch him in the gut if he got in her way.

The baby of the Gates family could be a hard cup to measure. But Violet wasn't a pistol with a sensitive trigger like his sister Louisa. She was usually a sweet and somewhat callow woman who was often all smiles.

But lately, Violet had a rebellious side that often reared its ugly head when her brothers were too protective or dismissive. The woman could be as mean as a pissed-off grizzly when she was angry, and she was, all the way down to her petite pink sneakers dotted with brown and white drops of caffeinated beverages and high- calorie pastry frosting.

"Why?" she demanded, curling her fingers into fists. "Why do I have to stay out of this? I'm a part of this family, and a third of that rusty heap is mine."

"Hey!" Ty shouted from under the belly of the ranch truck. "Don't disrespect the Green Machine."

"Fine, you stubborn asses!" she threw up her hands. "Do whatever!"

"How many times has this damn thing died?" Ty asked, not waiting for an answer. "And how many times have I been the one to resurrect it?"

3

"Can't help it," Logan said. "Obviously, practice doesn't make perfect, little brother."

Holding back a groan, Jess slammed his truck door and slowly started down the incline towards the brothers.

Violet mumbled a heated curse as she stomped past him on her way to her baby 4x4 parked in front of his truck. "Those dunderheads have been messin' around with that damn thing for almost three hours." She pointed to a stain on her pink Pixies Coffee Shop t-shirt." I have grounds and caramel sauce all over me. I'm tired, hungry, and need a shower. They're all yours."

"Thanks a lot," he grumbled.

"Oh." She stopped in mid-stomp and swung around on a heel, the hard scowl on her face relaxing. "How's Eleanor? I haven't had a chance to call her. Have there been any changes?"

Five years ago, his niece Sophie had arrived without much warning and almost made her appearance on I-35, so his brother and sister-in-law, and every other member of the Coldiron family, were on high alert in anticipation of the couple's second child.

"No," he said, looking at his watch again. "I was on my way to Redemption to check on her when Logan called me for a tow."

His brother, McCrea, had handed over the long-distance rescues to Brody Vance, the horse trainer they'd hired last year, so he could be there when the baby was born. This afternoon McCrea was on his way back from a rescue on the other side of the county but would be home in time for supper.

His parents usually took turns checking in on the expectant mother. But his mom and Louisa were shopping in Houston, and his dad was out of town at a cattleman's meeting in Fort Worth.

If Eleanor went into labor, Jess was flying solo.

"Well, good luck at getting Ty to give up," she said with a blistering glare in their direction before she climbed in her truck. "Maybe you can bait him out with beer and beanie weenies."

Jess shuddered — remembering the atomic cloud that lingered in the air after Ty consumed the two — and started towards the twenty-year-old heavy-duty diesel that should have been hauled to the junkyard years ago. "What's the problem?"

"The problem is," Logan said, raising from his bent position under the hood of the truck, "Ty doesn't know his ass from a hole in the ground."

Predictably, the brothers exchanged derogatory insults about holes and hoses before Jess intervened.

"What's wrong with it this time?" He leaned over the grill to take a look at the motor.

"Hell, if I know," Logan said, fidgeting with the fuel line. "It started choking and sputtering a few yards back. Then it just died."

"Sounds like it's out of fuel." Jess threw in his two cents.

"It's got half a tank," Ty answered from below.

Logan closed his eyes as if he were asking the Almighty for patients. "Is the gauge working?"

Ty rolled out, stood, and dusted his backside. "It's not the gauge."

"Then what is it, genius?" Logan asked.

"I thought it had a fuel leak last week, so I crawled under to see if a line had busted."

"And?" Logan prompted.

"It's not a line," Ty said, walking to the bed of the truck for his toolbox, a thought-filled pull pleating his brow. "I think it's losing oil pressure from a clogged valve."

And just like that, Ty had the problem figured out. Heading back to the front of the truck, he opened the beaten and battered hand-me-down box and started digging through it for sockets.

"You *think* it's losing oil pressure?" Logan asked, sparring another argument.

A clogged valve was going to take longer than ten minutes, and Jess wasn't going to add to Ty's troubles by telling him to hurry.

Logan had that covered.

Ty was an excellent mechanic. Working in the oilfields and on the ranch had taught him how to improvise. And Jess had no doubt the truck would be up and running soon if Logan left him the hell alone.

"Just get in the damn truck and let me tow you back to the ranch," Jess said.

"I've almost got it," Ty said, unwilling to throw in the towel just yet.

"I'm leaving in ten minutes," Jess told them, catching sight of a long grease streak across the middle of his t-shirt. "With or without you."

"I only need five," Ty assured him.

"And a good mechanic," Logan threw in.

Jess snagged the hem of his t-shirt and yanked it over his head. He wasn't going to stand by in the July heat while the brothers verbally duked it out.

He let the tailgate of his truck bed down and hoisted himself onto it. Then he eased around and leaned his back against the inside of the bed, drew his good leg up, and stretched his bad leg out, feeling the tendons and scar tissue in his thigh tighten as he did.

He plucked his hat from his head and dropped it on his knee, then scrubbed a hand over his head, noting he should have made time for a haircut before his date with

Brandi tonight.

The beautiful blonde executive of Winsor Rodeo Productions wouldn't mind the length of his hair, only his performance and stamina after dinner. With that in mind, Jess tried to drown out the sound of the bickering brothers.

But the distant hum of a vehicle brought his head up.

The gravel road, which was off the beaten path, ran through the heart of the Gates Ranch and rarely saw traffic, so whoever was behind the wheel of the dust cloud was either lost or looking for one of them.

More than likely, when the dust cleared, a face similar to Ty's would be staring back at them. But Jess would never let his friend know that he favored Clayton Durant, Ty's biological father, more than he did Emmett Gates, the man who had raised him.

"Yo, Ty." Logan swatted his brother's leg, thinking the same as Jess. "You've got company."

"What?" Ty called out without looking up.

Logan's voice went cold. "Clayton is here."

That got Ty's attention. "What the hell does he want?"

"He's probably a man short for some shit job," Logan said, staring flatly at the road, ready and waiting to face a man he despised, but tolerated for Ty's sake.

But as the vehicle sped closer, the outline of a motorcycle and its rider emerged from the dust.

Jess scooted from the tailgate. "Since when are bikes the vehicle of choice for Durant Drilling?"

"You couldn't tie Clayton to one," Logan answered, cleaning his hands on a grease rag from the floorboard of the truck.

Ty joined them as the bike slowed and then stopped about twenty feet from them. When the dust cleared, the curvy feminine form of the rider appeared.

The woman removed her helmet, freeing a crop of

dark, mahogany hair and a face that looked nothing like the always-frowning roughneck, Clayton Durant: high cheekbones set against an oval face, a straight, elegant nose and lips that begged to be kissed.

A pair of stylish aviator sunglasses added to the mystery and stirred Jess's male curiosity.

The ends of her long locks were tousled and wind-blown from miles of road and sun. She gave her hair a shake and offered them a friendly smile. "Hi, guys."

The coarseness of her voice blew across Jess like a sultry breeze, arousing more than Jess's curiosity.

"Holy shit," Logan murmured.

"Fuck me," Ty whispered under his breath.

"She looks too smart for that," Logan returned without taking his eyes off the woman.

What she looked like was a hot, sexy fantasy plucked straight from the cover of a motorcycle magazine. The sight of her firm thighs straddling chrome and leather were enough to entice the most sainted man. And Jess had always been one step closer to hell than to heaven. Judging from the lustful expression on Logan's and Ty's faces he wouldn't be alone in the descent.

"Boys," Jess cleared his throat. "Remember your raisin'. Let's not act like primates."

"Says the man who has drool drippin' from his chin," Logan murmured.

Ty extended his hand to Jess. "I bet you fifty bucks I can get her number in under five minutes."

Usually, before Jess would have taken a bet like that, he would have upped the ante with, "I can get it in two." Because this woman — sitting astride a bike that alone gave him a hard-on, with slender legs clad in a pair of dark denim jeans and leather chaps, a trim waist and full breasts that pressed tight against her riding jacket — was exactly his type.

But something about *this* woman made Jess err on the side of caution and kept him from accepting that bet.

"She could be a reporter," Logan suggested.

She was relaxed and at home on the back of the fully blacked-out motorcycle. Reporters looking for a story about gold or rescued horses were usually more discreet, more plainly dressed, and never, ever sexy.

Jess swallowed, trying to dislodge the dry knot that had suddenly formed in his throat. "I haven't seen hide nor hair of a reporter in months, and I've never seen one on a murdered out Indian Chieftain Dark Horse."

"Yeah, you're right," Logan said, handing Ty the grease rag. "I don't think she's here for a story. But she could be part of the archeology team."

"No way," Ty disagreed. "She's too pretty to be diggin' in the dirt with those academic needle heads up at Vera la Luz."

Ty was probably right. Over the last two years, Jess had met several of the archeologists and grad students involved in the excavation of the old Spanish Mission atop Promise Point. Not one of them resembled this woman. Her complexion was too evenly colored and smooth for an outdoor occupation.

She tucked her helmet under an arm and glanced over her shoulder at the road as if she were waiting for someone to catch up with her.

Satisfied there wasn't, her eyes went back to them. She shifted her ass to the other side of the seat as her full lips pulled to one side in consideration. "Excuse me."

The cord tightened, stirring lust low in Jess's stomach. It pivoted downward when she lodged the tip of her leather-clad finger between her teeth and slid her hand free. It was an innocent but sensual gesture that made him hard.

"Maybe she's lost and looking for the interstate," Logan suggested.

"Reporter… archeologist." Ty adjusted the waist of his dirty jeans and grinned. "I'm readily available for whatever Beautiful needs."

She lifted her face towards the sun then closed her eyes, momentarily soaking up the rays. The smooth lines of her face were almost angelic. The woman was a tempting mixture of seductive innocence and alluring beauty. It was a combustible combination that caused caution to stir inside Jess's chest.

With a huff of frustration, her eyes opened, and again, she focused on the three of them. "Yo, fellas!" She impatiently slapped the side of her helmet to get their attention and pulled her sunglasses to the end of her nose, giving Jess a view of her dark eyes. "You guys speak English or something similar? I'm not fluent in grunts and scratches, but I'll figure it out."

Jess grinned and held up a hand to signal he was on his way. "A hundred bucks says I can send Beautiful packing in two minutes."

Ty's face contorted with confusion. "Why the hell would you do that?"

"Yeah, man," Logan agreed, speaking from the side of his mouth. "She's a knockout."

Jess had experience lust at first sight more times than he cared to admit. The rodeo had been oozing with gorgeous women willing to share his bed as he climbed the ranks.

Some had been clingy and demanding. Some had acted innocent and accommodating. All of them had intentions of claiming a piece of him after they left his bed.

Only one had come close. But that one had taught him trouble and heartache could come wrapped in a pretty package.

And as sure as there were Texas dirt and sun-fried grass beneath his boots, Beautiful was a biblical proportion of both. "Something's not right about her. She's trouble."

"If she's trouble, give me a double dose," Ty said and started towards her.

"Hold up," Jess said, halting him with a hand to the mid-section. "I'll handle this."

"Oh, he'll handle it," Logan mocked.

"Yeah." Ty laughed. "I know what he wants to handle."

Ignoring the brothers, Jess made his way up the incline to the road. His steps were slow, his gait jerky and stiff. It was hard for a man to feel confident when he could hardly walk, but Jess held his grin.

"Can I help you?" he asked, noticing that her eyes weren't brown but hazel.

"Ah…yeah," she said, glancing at his leg. "I hope so."

Jess was used to drawing pity stares and brief looks of interest. His way of dealing with it was by ignoring it. But Beautiful's empathetic glance was a double punch to his manhood.

"I'm trying to find Redemption. Charlie and Rose Mackenna's ranch."

The Mackenna Ranch was next to his parents' ranch. McCrea and Eleanor had begun remodeling the old house soon after they were married last year. But all that had been put on hold until after the baby was born.

The last few weeks had been stressful for the newly-weds, and Jess wasn't about to add to their problems by giving Beautiful directions to Redemption until he knew what she wanted.

He gave her a flirty wink. "Now what would a pretty thing like you want with that dilapidated old horse ranch?"

"I — ah." Her eyes squinted and her lips did a cute little twist of annoyance. "It's urgent that I speak with Eleanor Mackenna. Do you know her?"

Jess pretended to think. "The name seems familiar."

She motioned towards the bike's instrument panel. "I followed the GPS —"

"Those things aren't reliable out here," Logan interjected, walking up to where Jess was standing.

"A lot of these back roads are nothing but horse trails," Ty added, stuffing the end of the grease rag into his back pocket as he joined them.

She took a deep breath and let it out. "Great."

"Don't worry." Jess widened his grin. "I'll give you directions."

Relief relaxed her shoulders. "You will?"

"Sure," he said, walking closer. "What kind of gentleman would I be if I didn't help a lady in need?"

～

THEY WEREN'T THE FIRST COWBOYS MALLORY Montgomery had seen up close and personal.

La Claire, New Mexico, had been full of smooth-talking, wannabe rodeo champions who thought they were God's gift to women.

But these guys were different from those low-life hustlers. There was an authenticity to them that sank in deeper than their scuffed-up cowboy boots, dusty cattleman hats, and worn Wranglers.

The one walking towards her with a lazy but somewhat halting saunter looked like he would be entirely at home in the saddle.

His jeans were frayed and threadbare in places, but the man had a finesse about him. She tore her eyes from his tanned and sweaty six-pack long enough to notice a tiny scar near the bottom of his stubble-covered chin. "You're familiar with the ranch?"

His lips inched from playful to roguish, giving her a glimpse of his straight, white teeth. That sinfully dirty grin of his was oddly familiar. Maybe she had seen him at one of the rodeos or one of the art festivals in Monterey Bay. Or perhaps she had met him at work. There had been more than one cowboy amble through the doors of the Pallento Fine Arts Gallery.

"Vaguely," he said, stopping a few feet short of her bike.

His eyes were frosty blue, a color that bit into her with the exhilaration of a cold winter's day. A glint of mischief danced across them when the taller cowboy behind him cleared his throat to stifle a laugh.

Despite the heat, Mallory shivered, overcome by a strange sensation pulling at her core.

She had a feeling that underneath his Texas drawl and charming front, there was something downright wicked hiding beneath the surface of this cowboy's cool blue eyes.

Something fun and playful, but not harmful. Having grown up in a place like La Claire had given her a sixth sense about men and her surroundings.

Judging from the handshake Cool Blue and the other cowboy had exchanged before he walked over, she was sure that some sort of wager had been made regarding her.

Typical.

As irritating as their dude bullshit bet was, Mallory knew she had little choice but to indulge in their juvenile ways if she wanted to find the Mackenna ranch.

Cool Blue pointed down the road in the opposite direction she had traveled. "Keep going on this road and at the end, turn left. Follow that road for about eight miles until it forks. Then turn right onto the gravel road and follow it to a green gate."

"Left. Then straight until it forks. Then right on the gravel road. Green gate," Mallory repeated, memorizing the directions. "Got it. Thanks."

She shoved her hands into her gloves and started the bike as he moved a step closer.

"Happy to help," he said, reaching out to loop a strand of her hair around his forefinger.

Mallory recoiled and knocked his hand away. "Whoa, there, Cool Blue."

She could handle herself. Aiden had taught her self-defense when she moved to California, and if all else failed, she had mace in her jacket pocket.

"Look but don't touch," she said, throwing back her head to helmet up.

His eyes narrowed a fraction with humor before he took a step back and surrendered both hands. "I didn't mean any harm. But I was hoping for more than a 'thank you' as payment for those directions."

CHAPTER 2

MALLORY'S STOMACH FLIPPED AND ROLLED AS IF SHE HAD eaten bad sushi. "I beg your pardon?"

The impious play rising in his eyes was wicked. "How about I give you a ride?"

"You?" She pointed at him. "Want to give me a ride?"

"Yeah, you know, a boots—in—the—air…" he gave her a lewd gyration of his pelvis as an example. "Thanks-for-the-directions kind of ride."

A cold wave of disappointment wrapped around her, earning him a short, expiring laugh. "Well," she said, looking directly at his crotch. "Unless you've gotten a horse hidden in your pocket, I doubt there's anything sizeable enough to mount."

"Ouch," the cowboy behind him laughed.

"Yeah," the other one laughed. "Way to go, stud."

Cool Blue's smile widened, and his mouth opened with what Mallory was sure was a comeback. But she didn't wait. She started the bike and peeled out, peppering him with dirt and gravel. Through her side mirror, she watched him cover his head with both arms, stumble backward, and go down on his ass.

After the three cowboys were nothing more than a speck in her side mirror, she let off the throttle and settled into the seat. She focused on the road and the reason she had driven halfway across Texas.

Laying her hand on the leather tank bag, she felt the round contours of her mother's urn. But there were no tears. No matter how hard she tried, they wouldn't come. Years of resentment, loneliness, and neglect wouldn't let them surface.

Mallory had been only six years old when her sister moved to Texas to live with their Grandma Rose in Santa Camino Texas. Her father's controlling personality and abusive behavior became worse after that. Rex wouldn't allow her or her mother back at the ranch. Her mother had numbly complied to his every demand, and Mallory had been too afraid to disobey.

She never saw her sister or grandmother again, and her life with her parents had been hell until Aiden came along.

The grief that wasn't there for her mother wrapped around her heart and squeezed.

It had been thirteen agonizing months since two men in uniform rolled into their driveway and delivered the news of Aiden's death, and the pain was still fresh. It pulsated through Mallory like a broken high voltage wire. It twisted, hissed, spun, and sparked every time she thought about him and the pain Rex had caused them both.

Out of habit, she checked her side mirror for her father's red Dodge truck. He couldn't be far behind her, and she knew he remembered more about her mother's hometown, than she did. He could probably drive straight to the ranch.

Mallory had gotten a cheap hotel room last night and barricaded the door with a dresser. But her sleep hadn't been restful.

She was tired, so damn tired. When she left home for California, she thought the violence and darkness were behind her. But that monster was growling at her heels once again, and it would be until Rex Montgomery was either dead or in jail.

Mallory followed the road, praying Cool Blue had had the decency to at least give her good directions. Left. Right…or was it left and then straight? Jesus, she couldn't remember, and nothing looked familiar.

Hill Country was different from the Western part she had driven through last night. There was dark green grass and trees. Flat pastures that stretched out for miles before rising into rolling hills on the horizon.

Suddenly, a smell of something rancid caught her nose and became stronger as she drove.

She slowed when she saw the green gate. Where were the house, the barns, and horses? A shadow darted across the road, then another and another.

She slowed the bike and put her foot down. Then removed her helmet and looked up as another bird joined the circling wake. The shadows were buzzards. Big buzzards. Giant buzzards that made her swear. The scavengers swooped down and landed on a sign that read Santa Camino Landfill.

"Buzzards." The word came out as a hiss under her breath. "I asked for directions, and the man gave me buzzards."

~

Jess opened his eyes amidst the dust cloud and coughed. He held his hand out to Ty. "Where's my money?"

"I didn't take that bet. I didn't think you were dumb enough to run her off." Ty grabbed his hand and yanked him to his feet. "I guess I was wrong."

"I can't believe you sent her to the landfill," Logan said, shaking his head.

Jess didn't know who the woman was or why she needed to see Eleanor, so he hadn't been keen on giving her directions to the ranch.

"Yeah," Ty made a grunting sound. "That's not going to score you any points when you see her again."

Jess knew he would. Santa Camino was a small town and finding Redemption wouldn't be hard once Beautiful made it out to the main road.

He swatted his dirty hat against his thigh. "I'm not looking for points. I've seen her kind before."

"Her kind?" Ty asked, frowning as he climbed into the Green Machine. "For all, we know she's the reincarnation of Mary the Queen of Scotts."

The engine cranked a couple of times and then roared to life. Grinning from ear to ear, Ty revved it up and shouted, "Hell yeah!" above the noise.

"All he needed was the proper motivation," Logan said, slamming the hood shut.

"This is the second time in a month that rust bucket has quit on you," Jess pointed out. "One day, it's going to give up the ghost, and no amount of motivation will be able to resurrect it."

"That describes most of the vehicles and equipment we have on the ranch. But you work with what you have," Logan said, grimly.

He clamped a hand over his friends' shoulder. "Are you still playing the lottery?"

"Religiously."

The Gates siblings were on a steep climb up a rough and rocky hill. A flash flood last year had wiped out their pack barn and most of their bull stock.

Thanks to the income from Violet's coffee shop, Ty's side jobs, and Logan's talent for stretching a dollar, they'd managed to keep the mortgage on the ranch paid. But without the income from the sale of those lost bulls, they wouldn't be able to hold on much longer.

The south road led to higher ground and the site of their new barn. The brothers had been hauling material in for weeks, hoping to have everything ready for spring breeding next year.

Neighbors and members of the community had organized several fundraisers to help them get back on their feet.

"Things will turn around soon," Jess said, knowing the money from the fundraiser scheduled in a few weeks would help make payments on the bank loans Emmet had taken out before his death.

Logan shoved his hands into his pockets and kicked at the gravel. "Harry called."

"And?"

"He wants to meet with us."

"It's about time," Jess said, annoyed it had taken them over a month to get an appointment with the mayor.

"I guess that proposal you put together got his attention."

Jess had spent weeks working on that detailed proposal because he knew how beneficial the economic impact of hosting a rodeo would have on Santa Camino. "It'll have to be on Monday. I'm headed to San Antonio," he said, looping the neck of his t-shirt over his head as he walked towards his truck.

Logan looked up from the rock he'd been shoving around with the toe of his boot. "Business or pleasure?"

In the years since his fall, Jess had not only sworn off riding, he had also sworn off emotional attachment to the women he dated. He kept his relationships simple. He never brought a woman back to his house, never had sex with her in his bed, and he never dated locals.

He shoved his arms through his t-shirt and yanked the bottom back in place. "I'm meeting with Winsor Rodeo Promotion to see if they can do the staging for us."

"I thought Steve retired last year."

"He did. Brandi took his place."

Logan's bottom jaw dropped open. "You lucky S.O.B."

Grinning, Jess climbed into his truck and started the engine. "Text me and let me know what Harry says."

After making the three-mile trip to Redemption, Jess slowed the truck and turned into the long drive leading up to the main house.

He kept left as the drive split and followed the fenced-in yard. Then he parked in the circle used as a turnaround.

After Rose Mackenna's death, the ranch had fallen into disrepair, and several of the outbuildings along with one of the barns had to be torn down. But after Eleanor and McCrea moved in, new barns had been built, and the old house had undergone a complete makeover on the outside with a new roof, siding, and shutters.

Several shrubs and native plants had been added to the landscape, and the flower beds were alive with vibrant blooms. And of course, McCrea had built an overly extravagant play area for Sophie and her soon-coming baby brother in the back yard.

Jess was ecstatic about his brother's happiness, but at

times, he was a little envious. Because at one point in his life, he had also been in love and ready to settle down.

He tried to mentally switch gears from those years when his life had been turned upside down to the present. But even when the pain wasn't there, the fall was, running in the background of his mind, reminding him of what a fool he'd been.

Easing from the truck, he felt the muscles in his thigh tense. He winced, cursed, and began rubbing the knot that had formed.

When the pain was bearable and the spasm had passed, he limped onward towards the walk, thankful there was no one around to see his crippled ass hobble up the sidewalk.

He composed himself, plastered on a bogus smile to hide the pain and rancor swarming within him, and opened the screen door without knocking. "Anybody home?"

"In the kitchen," Eleanor called out.

Though money had never been an issue for the couple, they had chosen to keep the furnishings and décor simple. His sister-in-law was a practical woman with modest tastes, and McCrea would have been happy living in a tent as long as Eleanor and Sophie were with him.

Jess closed the door behind him and breathed in the pungent smell of something Eleanor had cooking in the crockpot. Was it pot roast, beef daube Provençal with mashed potatoes, or spicy-sweet ribs with beans?

His stomach rumbled.

He hung his hat on the hanger and wiped his boots on the throw rug before walking across the living room and into the kitchen.

A familiar warmth spread through him. The house was inviting and felt more like a home than his own did.

He found Eleanor in a bent position with her hands on the sink. "Are you alright?"

"I'm fine," she said, rising with an exhale. "Just trying to alleviate some of the discomforts in my back."

Alarm made the hairs on the back of Jess's neck stand up. "Discomfort?"

She turned around, lay a hand over her pregnant belly, and leaned her backside against the sink. "I'm nine months pregnant, Jess. Discomfort is my middle name. There's no need to panic. I'm not due for another week."

He wasn't panicking. McCrea had gone over the routine with him at least a dozen times in the last two weeks. Her suitcase was packed and in the upstairs hall closet. And the numbers he needed for the hospital where taped down on the table next to the phone. If anything happened, he was prepared.

Eleanor's lips pressed into a thin line as her face paled. Her nose flared out as she drew in a deep breath and let it out slowly.

"Why don't you go lie down? Put your feet up and rest."

"I don't want to put my feet up," she snapped.

He surrendered, both hands in the air. "Okay, don't bite my head off. I'm just trying to take care of you."

Her face relaxed with remorse. "I know. I'm sorry. I didn't mean to sound ungrateful. It's just McCrea is smothering me to death. He waits on me hand and foot, and when he's not here, he makes sure someone conveniently comes by to babysit me."

"Guilty, but I am a fun babysitter," Jess said, grinning as he made himself at home in one of the dinette chairs. "Where's Sophie?"

She eased into one of the chairs across from him. "Upstairs in her room. She snuck Pocket Change into her room about a half hour ago. She and that dog are inseparable."

His smile widened. "Uncle Jess nailed that birthday present." He had grown quite fond of his new title, but at times, it was hard to believe that he was someone's uncle, partly because that made his brother a daddy.

Eleanor had always been sweet on McCrea. But love hadn't come easy for the two of them. His stubborn-ass brother had refused to give in. And after years of chasing him, Eleanor had seduced him the night before she left for college.

They'd had a bitter falling out and gone their separate ways for four years until Eleanor came back to town to sell Redemption. Learning that he was a father had knocked some sense into McCrea and opened his eyes.

After years of dancing around their feelings, McCrea and Eleanor had finally given in and decided that love was worth the risk. Jess was proud to say that he'd had a hand in making that work by helping Louisa play matchmaker to get the two of them back together.

McCrea had adapted well to fatherhood and wedlock. Eleanor's current condition was proof of that. Love had changed his brother, and Jess was damn happy it had. They were married last fall under the Rescue pavilion with lots of friends and family to celebrate their happy union.

"Since Uncle Jess is here, he can clean up the mess," Eleanor returned before her face tightened again. She closed her eyes, breathing through the "discomfort."

He wasn't an expert on childbirth, but those looked like controlled breathing techniques.

Given the stress level of Eleanor's current state of "discomfort," Jess wasn't sure he needed to mention Beautiful. But her showing up unexpectedly on the doorstep wouldn't be good either.

"El," he said, absently tracing the floral design of the tablecloth with his forefinger. "There was a woman out on the south road asking for directions to Redemption. Logan thought she might be a reporter, but –"

"What did she look like?" she asked, her eyes springing open.

"Dark hair and eyes." He measured her height by referencing a place on his shoulder. "About five-six —"

"Did she have a dimple?" she pointed to her cheek.

"A dimple? Ah…" Caught off guard by her question, Jess tried to remember if Beautiful had the cute little dimple near the bottom of her chin that Eleanor had said was prominent in all of the Mackenna women. "You think she was family?"

She shrugged a shoulder. "I always hold on to the hope that Mom or Mallory might visit."

Jess swallowed. Maybe he shouldn't have made that boots-in-the-air comment. "This woman was too young to be your mother and too… too…" He searched for the right word to describe her. The only one that came to his mind was titillating. "This woman wasn't your kid sister."

"Mallory isn't a kid anymore. She's a grown woman."

The summer Eleanor came to live with Rose, Mallory was all she talked about, and as they grew up, that image of a little girl who played with dolls had been permanently imprinted into Jess's brain.

Beautiful was about the same age as Mallory, but still, she was much too rough around the edges to be Eleanor's sister. "Neither of them would need directions to the ranch."

"Mom wouldn't, but Mallory was only six when Mom and Rex brought me to Redemption. I'm not sure she remembers me or the ranch."

Jess knew the story behind the sadness in Eleanor's

eyes, and he hated that he had caused her to remember the pain of being uprooted from her mother and half-sister at such an early age. The fear of Mallory being left alone to bear her stepdad's temper had given Eleanor more than a few nightmares. "Have you tried contacting them again?"

"I tried when Grandma died but didn't have any luck." She stood, yielding a thin smile, and patted his shoulder as she passed by him. "I think I will lie down for a few minutes."

"Yell if you need anything." When she disappeared into the living room, Jess climbed the stairs.

He quietly made his way down the hall to Sophie's room and peered inside. Sitting with her back to the door, she played undisturbed with her partner in crime. The miniature beagle was perched obediently in one of the toddler-sized chairs, lapping up milk from a plastic plate.

"Your momma will tan my hide if she catches that dog in your room."

Sophie lifted her head with a bright smile, causing the dimple in her cheek to deepen. "Uncle Jess!"

He swung her up and into his arms. "Hey, Dimples. Am I too late for tea?"

She giggled. "Yes."

"Then what shall we do?"

She shoved her little fingers into his hair. "Play dress-up."

Oh, God, he groaned inwardly at the prospect of scrubbing cheap makeup from his face but kept his smile.

"First, let's get Pocket Change out the back door before your momma finds him."

The last thing Jess wanted to do today was clean up pee puddles and dog turds.

Sophie slipped an arm under her tiny companion's front feet and lifted him from the chair. A full belly —

complete with milky white whiskers — made Pocket Change compliant for the journey downstairs. The pup would crawl onto his bed on the back porch and fall asleep.

Chuckling, Jess found a comfortable spot on the floor and leaned against the wall while he waited for his stylist to return.

The brushes Sophie used to apply the makeup to his face were soft and relaxing. But he would have a hell of a time getting the glitter off his eyelids.

"Do this." Sophie puckered her little heart-shaped mouth, and Jess did as she instructed.

After she applied a thick layer of bright red lipstick, he smacked his lips together and reached for the hand mirror lying next to her makeup kit. "How do I look?"

She snatched it from him and held it to her chest. "You can't look yet."

"Why not?"

"I haven't done your hair."

"Of course." He laced his fingers together and rested them across his middle. "How silly of me."

She brushed his hair, snapped a few dozen brightly colored barrettes in, and grabbed a bright pink feathered boa from her bed.

Jess wrapped it around his neck and smiled. "Am I beautiful?"

Sophie clapped her hands. "Yes."

"Jess!" his name was followed by the slamming of the back screen door. "Get down here! Now!"

"El?" he scrambled to his feet, snatching Sophie up as he headed down the stairs. He found Eleanor in the kitchen, gripping the table as she breathed through a contraction. "Oh, shit."

"That's a bad word, Uncle Jess," Sophie scolded.

"Sorry, Dimples." He sat her down and took hold of Eleanor's arm as she breathed through the pain.

When it ended, she looked down at her soaked pajama bottoms. "The dog was whining, so I went to check on him, and my water broke."

Jess reached for the phone. "I'll call an ambulance."

She snagged his arm in a death grip, causing him to stumble sideways. "There's no time to wait for an ambulance!"

"Yeah, ah…okay." He wondered how such dainty fingers could have such brute strength. "It's okay. Everything is fine," he assured, even though his heart was beating in his ears. "McCrea went over everything with me. I know what to do."

"Then do it!" she yelled. "Get me to the hospital, or you're going to be delivering this baby by yourself!"

Fear escalated through Jess when he thought about what that might involve. He'd deliver dozens of calves and a few colts, but he wasn't prepared to bring his nephew into the world.

He jumped into action and ran as fast as he could towards the stairs. "I'll get the suitcase."

"Sophie's car seat is in the crossover. We'll save time by taking it. The keys are in my purse in the dining room and don't forget the baby's diaper bag."

He took the stairs two at a time until he reached the top, yanked out his phone and hit the call button next to his brother's name.

"Yeah," McCrea answered.

"Her water just broke."

"What? The baby's not due −."

"We're headed out the door right now," he said, plowing through his brother's denial as he opened the closet door and reached in for the suitcase. "Damn it, man, tell me you're close by."

McCrea started panting, and Jess knew he was running for his truck. "I just dropped the horse off at the Rescue. Tell Eleanor I'm on my way."

Jess shoved the phone into his pocket, took hold of the suitcase, and was slinging the diaper bag over his shoulder when Sophie hurried past him. "Where are you going?"

"To get my backpack."

"Hurry, Dimples," he said, rushing to the stairs. His boot slipped on the third step, nearly causing him to tumble headfirst down the stairs.

He caught hold of the railing, swung the big yellow diaper bag decorated in ducks to the other side, and blew a feather out of his mouth as he hurried down the stairs.

CHAPTER 3

MALLORY STOPPED HER BIKE AT THE BASE OF THE LONG drive and looked up at the smooth wooden beams holding the iron letters of Redemption Horse Ranch.

After years of being gone, her mother was finally home, and the heavy weight resting on Mallory's shoulders seemed to lighten a little.

Thanks to the bartender at Tub's Roadhouse, she had found the ranch without any trouble. It had only been a short drive from the road she had gotten lost on and was easy to find.

But the road ahead of her was going to be more challenging to navigate. There was no guarantee she would be welcome here or that her grandma or sister would allow her to stay long enough to scatter her mother's ashes.

The relationship between her mother and grandmother had been strained years before Mallory was born. After Eleanor left home, her mother never revisited the ranch, never talked about her childhood or her parents.

Mallory continued up the drive, trying to find something that might jog her foggy memory or tie her to the

Mackenna bloodline. But there was nothing, no familiarity, no connection, and no sentiments.

The fields, hills, and landscape around Redemption were as unfamiliar as the roads she had traveled to get here.

From Cool Blue's description of the dilapidated old horse ranch, Mallory was expecting rickety barns, rotted fences, and overgrown fields. But the barns and paddocks were in excellent condition. The ranch was bustling with cowboys, work hands, and ranch trucks. Several horses grazed in the pasture, swatting their tails back and forth in slow motion.

The L-shaped house was pristine with white siding, brown shingles, and shutters. The long wraparound porch was decorated with hanging flower baskets, rocking chairs and a cozy porch swing at the end.

Her eyes locked on the silver Chevy truck parked in front of the house. It was the same truck Cool Blue had been walking from when she pulled up to ask for directions.

Damn, that man!

He had not only sent her on a wild goose chase, but he had also lied to her. He'd known precisely where Redemption was.

Mallory parked beside it and pushed the kickstand down to secure the bike before she dismounted and removed her helmet.

She wanted to march in that house and plant her elbow in Cool Blue's solar plexus. Huffing, she set her helmet on the seat and unzipped her jacket.

"Mallory?"

The woman's voice jerked her attention from the truck to the blond woman standing on the porch. She hadn't seen her sister in years, but Mallory knew it was Eleanor.

Blinking several times as if Mallory were an apparition she was trying to see clearly, Eleanor moved to the edge of the steps. "Is that you?"

Mallory made her way up the sidewalk, stopping a short distance away from Eleanor. The memories of her sparse visits to her grandparents' ranch here were like clouded snapshots of an old movie. Bits and pieces of a happy time she longed for. But her last visit was vividly clear. It had begun and ended in this exact spot at the bottom of the porch steps.

The sound of her own cries pierced her ears, propelling her back to that awful day when she said goodbye to her sister and grandma. She could feel the steel grip of her father's fingers wrapping around her arms as he snatched her from her Grandma Rose.

It had been a horrible day filled with sadness and weeping.

She prayed today wasn't a repeat. Her heart raced. Her palms became sweaty, and her legs began to shake. This was it. The moment of truth.

With her heart in her stomach, she tried to smile. "Yes, it's me."

When they were children, they had loved each other unconditionally. But as adults, they both knew what kind of man her father was. So many years had passed. Had her sister been able to move past those early days of their childhood? Past the hurtful words and angry slaps delivered by *her* father?

Eleanor's expressive eyes softened. "Oh, it is you." She stepped closer and threw her arms around Mallory. "I can't believe it's you."

In her sister's embrace, years of distance and loneliness came crashing in. Mallory let out a tear-filled sigh, feeling like she had successfully jumped the first hurdle in a long race.

Eleanor tightened her arms. "I thought I'd never see you again. I thought I'd lost you forever."

Mallory had spent months crying herself to sleep and the rest of her life thinking about this exact moment in time. The moment when she would be reunited with her sister.

"I was never lost," she said, laughing. "Only misplaced."

Eleanor dropped her arms, took a step back, and bent forward, grasping her belly with both hands.

Mallory held onto her sister's arm, alarm replacing her joy. "Oh God. Are you in labor?"

Eleanor's face tightened. "My water broke a few minutes ago, and your nephew is about to make his entrance."

With her teeth clenched and her hand gripping the step rail, Eleanor breathed through the contraction.

"Okay, so," Mallory tried breathing too. "There's no need to panic." She glanced back to the silver Chevy. "Where's the cowboy who drives this truck?"

"Son of a −." A loud crash thundered through the screen door. The man inside the house continued to belt out low curses, some of which Mallory had never heard.

"Is everything alright in there?" Eleanor asked in between pants.

The screen door flew open and out lunged Cool Blue with a large suitcase in one hand, a diaper bag in the other, and a purse swung over his arm.

"Yeah," he said. "I had a minor run-in with the table at the bottom of the stairs. Don't worry. I'll fix it." He raised his arm and worked his shoulder. "Damn, that's gonna be sore in the morning."

Letting the screen door slam behind him, he started for the steps but came to a boot-skidding halt when he saw Mallory.

The sexy, laidback, country boy grin he'd given her earlier curved his mouth upward, but this time it was decorated with a thick layer of bright, ruby red lipstick. "Hello, Beautiful." He wiggled his crudely drawn eyebrows up and down. "You here for that ride?"

If Mallory hadn't been so pissed, she would have burst into laughter at the intense pink glitter covering his eyelids.

She pointed her finger at him. "You sent me on a wild goose chase!"

A breeze caught the bright pink feather boa around his neck and whipped it over his face like the tail of a deranged unicorn. "I did not," he defended as he smacked at it. "I sent you to the landfill."

"Jess," Eleanor gritted as another contraction began building. "This is my sister, Mallory."

His grin melted. "Oh, shit."

~

"MALLORY," ELEANOR TOOK IN A BREATH AND LET IT OUT slowly. "This is my brother-in-law, Jess."

"Happy to meet you," he said, handing Mallory the suitcase. "We need to go. Now."

He scooped Eleanor into his arms and headed down the steps.

An hour ago, Mallory would have thrown the suitcase at him and told him to go straight to hell. But there was no way she was leaving her sister with this painted jackass.

She followed him to the crossover, lugging the suitcase behind her.

He opened the passenger door and safely deposited

Eleanor into the seat. Then slipped the purse and diaper bag from his shoulder and handed them to Mallory. "Make sure Sophie is buckled in."

"Don't," she said, stomping her foot for added emphasis, "order me around."

"Okay," he said patiently. "Will you please make sure Sophie is buckled in?"

"That's better. Who's Sophie?"

A slight tug to the hem of Mallory's t-shirt brought her attention to a little girl with big brown eyes. "I'm Sophie."

"Your niece," he added, shutting the door once Eleanor was buckled in.

She had a niece, a nephew, and had regained her sister all in one day? Her heart swelled. "Hello, Sophie. I'm your Aunt Mallory," she said, crouching down eye level to Sophie.

"I'm five," she held up a whole hand, "years old."

"Did you do his makeup?"

"Uh-huh." Sophie's head proudly bobbed up and down. "He's beautiful, isn't he?"

Mallory suppressed a laugh as she helped her into her car seat. "I don't think I've ever seen a more colorful cowboy, Sophie. You did a wonderful job."

Jess started the car and pulled it into drive then reached out to take Eleanor's hand. "That's it. Breathe through it," he coached. "You're doing great."

"Did you call McCrea?"

"He was dropping the horse off when I called him. He's a few miles behind us. Everything is under control. You just concentrate on bringing that baby into the world."

Eleanor nodded. "Okay."

Jess turned onto the main road and according to the road sign, was driving east towards town.

Mallory had taken a first-aid course in high school but

preventing hypothermia and sewing butterfly stitches hadn't prepared her for delivering a baby. "How far is it to the hospital?"

"Nine point eight miles," Eleanor answered, panting through the pain. "My phone is on the coffee table at home."

Jess leaned back in the seat and lifted his hips up. "Mallory, grab my phone out of my front pocket. We need to time the contractions."

"I can use mine…" she said, feeling her pockets for hers but remembered that it was in the bag on her bike.

"Mine has an app for timing contractions," he explained, glancing at her through the rearview mirror.

Mallory wasn't a touchy-feely person. She liked her space, with plenty of room between her and everyone else, so she wasn't up for the daunting task of rummaging through this cowboy's denim even if it was to help her sister. "Pull over, and we'll switch places."

Briefly stopping for a stop sign, Jess gave her an angled grin. "Weren't you the one asking for directions a few hours ago? The woman who got lost on some country backroad?"

"Weren't you the moron who sent the lost woman farther down the country backroad to some godforsaken, buzzard-ridden landfill?" she countered.

"Children!" Eleanor shouted. "Can we save the arguments for later?"

This was not how she imagined her first day in town would be and fighting with Jess wouldn't make a good impression with her sister. "Sorry."

"I was only trying to make a point," he mumbled. "Mallory doesn't know the road or the town well enough to drive."

Though she would never admit it to him, Jess was

right. She had gotten lost out on the back road. Navigating through town to the hospital in time for Eleanor to deliver would be challenging.

"Mallory," Eleanor said patiently. "Please, get the phone."

Suppressing a groan, she loosened her seatbelt and scooted to the edge of the seat.

"McCrea made everyone download the app when they found out they were pregnant," he explained, lifting his elbow so she could get between his arm and the console.

"A lot of good it'll do." Eleanor let her head fall back against the headrest with a breathless laugh. "I can tell you without timing the contractions that we'll be lucky if this baby isn't born right here in this seat."

Mallory leaned forward, ready to dig in. She could do this. It was just a pocket, and he was just a man. A man who obviously cared for her sister. More importantly, Jess was a man her sister trusted.

That should have eased the anxiety brewing inside of her. But it somehow made it worse. Jess was not only a man who was trustworthy and caring, but he was also attractive in a way that made her warm between the thighs.

She gathered her hair into a ponytail and gave it a twist to temporarily keep it out of her face. She reached in, grazing the underside of his defined bicep and recoiled, surprised by the tiny spark of electricity streaking up her arm.

"You'll have to do better than that," he said, shooting her a measured look over his shoulder. "I have deep pockets."

Deep pockets covering masculine thighs that were attached to sensual, gyrating hips...

"It would help if you moved your arm," she groused a complaint to excuse her pause.

Jess propped his hand on the back of Eleanor's seat, giving Mallory more room. "Go on," he enjoined, batting his glitter-covered lids at her. "Don't be shy."

She wasn't shy, just cautious.

Pretend he's Aiden, she told herself and plunged four fingers thumb deep into his pocket.

Nothing.

"Lower and to the left," Jess instructed, watching the light.

When her brain calculated where that course would take her, she jerked her hand to the far right of his pocket. "You really don't know when to stop giving bad directions, do you?"

He answered her with a deep, throaty laugh and spared her a second look. His eyes twinkled with naughtiness. "Don't deviate from the path and you won't touch that horse I have hidden in my pocket."

"God," she groaned, heat rushing to her cheeks. "You're something, you know that?"

His grin widened.

She leaned closer, rested her cheek against his shoulder, and pushed her whole hand into his pocket. He smelled of dirt, diesel, and motor oil with a trace of sweat mingled in. An oddly arousing mixture she was sure would be a best-seller if it were a cologne.

Her fingers moved down the hard planes of his upper thigh muscles to a deep indentation. The cause of his limp.

When she felt him tense and draw in a sharp breath, she pulled back with a, "sorry," then, moved her hand lower. Her fingertips brushed the top of the rubber case. "Wait. I think I feel it."

He hoisted his hips higher to give her better access.

She snagged the phone with two fingers and pulled it free. "I got it."

Eleanor raised her head. "Here comes another one."

"The app is green," he said, reaching to retake Eleanor's hand.

"I found it," Mallory said.

"They're getting stronger." Eleanor made a growling sound as another contraction hit. "I need to push."

"No. No. No," Jess said, his voice encumbered with alarm as he navigated through a four-way stop. "Don't you dare push."

"It's not like I have a choice!" The growl turned into a scream that drew her forward.

Sophie's eyes grew wide. "Mommy?"

"Don't you worry about Mommy," Jess said, giving Sophie a big smile and a reassuring wink through the rearview mirror. "Babies are born every minute of the day."

"Mommy's just excited, that's all," Mallory explained. "I bet you're excited too, aren't you?"

Sophie nodded. "I'm going to have a baby brother."

"Oh, wow." Mallory kept her tone engaging. "I'd be excited too. Brothers are the best."

"I'm going to teach him how to talk and walk and…" she reached into her bag and pulled out a sheet of paper. "How to draw."

Jess flipped on the caution lights and drove faster as Mallory hit the stop button on the last contraction.

"They're less than a minute apart," she told him, fearing her sister might be right about the baby being born in the seat. "How much farther?"

"It's the next street up," he answered.

A minute later, he made a quick turn into the hospital parking lot. He parked near the emergency entrance and came around for Eleanor. He unbuckled her seatbelt, reached in, and picked her up then hurried towards the double sliding glass doors.

Mallory shed her riding jacket, making sure the long sleeve shirt she had on underneath hid the bruises around her wrist. Then she unbuckled Sophie and shoved Jess's cell phone into her back pocket. She looped the diaper bag and purse over her head, slid them around to one side, grabbed the suitcase, and handed Sophie her backpack.

The nurse had Eleanor in a wheelchair and was pushing her down the hall towards the Labor and Delivery Department by the time she and Sophie caught up.

Eleanor held her belly with both hands. "Where is he?"

"He'll be here," Jess said, stopping shy of the doors.

The nurse pointed to the right. "There's a waiting area for the family down the hall next to the nurse's station."

"Daddy!" Sophie exclaimed as a dark-haired man Mallory assumed was Eleanor's husband came running down the hall.

"Hi, sweetheart." He stopped briefly for a hug. "You stay with Uncle Jess. Mommy needs me, okay?"

"Okay, Daddy."

McCrea made a motion towards Jess's face. "Have you been playing dress up again?"

Jess scrubbed his lips and mumbled a curse when he saw the lipstick on his fingers. "You'd better hurry. That baby is coming with or without you."

With an enormous grin on his face, McCrea disappeared through the double doors with Eleanor and the nurse.

Mallory led Sophie to the waiting area. She climbed into one of the seats and began unpacking crayons.

Jess rested both hands on his hips and blew out a sigh,

undoubtedly relieved he had gotten Eleanor here before she could deliver.

A tall blonde nurse popped around the corner and glanced amusingly at Jess's face. "Did you lose a bet?"

"Oh, hi, Angie," he said, a lopsided grin resting on his lips. "No." Slipping the boa from his neck, he let it dangle in front of Sophie's nose. "We were playing dress up when El went into labor."

Mallory didn't expect that there were many cowboys or men in general willing to partake in a glamor makeover by a five-year-old. But Jess had, and without little consideration to what it might cost his manhood.

He had been an ass by giving her wrong directions. But it was hard to stay angry at a man who had shoved his dignity to the side, adorned his pink boa with pride, and smiled through layers of tawdry makeup while amid a crisis.

And Jess had.

Sophie made a grab for the boa. He snatched it up and out of her reach. She giggled, her smile stretching from ear to ear as they played. The relationship he had with her was adorable.

"Jess Coldiron."

The woman's voice straightened Jess's posture and brought him around. He let the boa drop. "Mrs. Hubbard."

"Lord, son." The matronly woman tilted her head to one side as she eyed him disapprovingly. "Tell me that some poor woman wasn't foolish enough to procreate with you."

"No, Ma'am," he answered slowly, his tone flat. "My sister-in-law is having her baby."

"God bless her." She crossed her arms over her belly

and slung Mallory an appraising stare. "One Coldiron brother is as bad as the other."

Coldiron. Coldiron. Why was the name so familiar?

The muscle in Jess's jaw flexed, but he veiled his irritation and remained unmoved by the woman's insult. "As I remember, your daughter didn't seem to think I was all that bad."

Ah-oh.

His remark threw a dart that embedded itself in a sensitive spot near the center of Mrs. Hubbard's spine, causing her to throw back her shoulders. "Sandy has since learned what a real man is."

He let out a laugh. "I'm sure Sandy has."

"She and her husband are expecting their son at any moment."

Jess widened his eyes. "Sandy is having a boy?"

Mrs. Hubbard answered him with a stiff affirmation.

"How about that. A boy." He grinned proudly. "I always wanted a son. I imagine most men do."

Her scathing smirk was accompanied by a snigger. "Don't get your hopes up. I doubt there's a woman alive willing to marry the likes of you."

"You're right about that," he agreed, the edge of something exact biting into his eyes. "I'll never put a ring on a woman's finger. But that doesn't mean I don't enjoy their company."

"Thank God, Sandy found herself an honorable man and not some good-for-nothing like you."

"Oh, Raymond is an honorable man," he agreed, shoving his hands into the front pockets of his jeans.

Her eyes narrowed. "You know Raymond?"

"No, not really. I just know he works on an oil rig somewhere in the Gulf and is gone for weeks at a time. Sandy told me she gets real lonesome."

The extra roll of sagging skin around Mrs. Hubbard's neck jiggled as she gulped and placed her hand over her heart. "You spoke with Sandy?"

"Yep, I paid her a visit about eight…?" He paused, looking up at the ceiling as he thought for a moment. "No, make that nine months ago. She mentioned then that Raymond was out of town."

Mallory clamped a hand over her mouth to keep from laughing.

It took a few seconds for what Jess was implying to register with Mrs. Hubbard's narrow-minded brain. When it did, her face paled, and her mouth fell open. "Oh, merciful Jesus," she whispered and set a course for the Labor and Delivery doors.

"Jess," Gina whispered, fighting a smile. "You didn't?"

"Hell, no," he said, denying everything. "I don't eat from another man's plate and I don't fool around with married women."

His frown split into a grin as he yelled, "Tell Sandy I'll be by later to see the baby!"

"I better go check on her," Gina said, hurrying down the hall. "She's liable to cause a ruckus."

CHAPTER 4

Jess dragged his hat off and started to rake a hand through his hair. But it snagged on a variety of rainbow barrettes. He mumbled out a curse and moved to the decorative mirror over the coffee table. He targeted a yellow one with a hard tug, and winced, taking a few hairs with the small bar-shaped clip.

Mallory unzipped the diaper bag and searched until she found the diaper wipes. "That woman really hates you."

The barrette hit the small trash can with a clink. "The feeling is mutual."

She walked around the chairs and over to where he was standing. "You know every time she looks at her grandson, she's going to see you."

"Damn right, she will," he said, flinching as he yanked out the blue barrette next to his left ear.

She held the wipes out. "Here, these should help with the makeup."

Glancing down as he accepted the container, he saw the bruises around her wrist. "Jesus, Mallory."

She quickly dropped her hand, securing the sleeve over her wrist. "It's nothing."

As a child, Mallory had become a master at hiding her bruises, and as a teenager, she had learned not to get in her father's way. But as a grieving daughter, she had gone full force into the fight. It was a stupid decision. She knew that. Her stubbornness always sent her dad into fits of rage. But she had been too angry to be scared or rational.

Jess gently took hold of her elbow, clasping his hand firmly around it to hold her until he could inspect her wrist. With his other hand, he pushed the sleeve higher get a better look at the bluish imprint of her father's fingers still visible from the argument they'd had over a week ago. "You don't have to hide it from me."

Oh, but she did. No one needed to know about that part of her life.

His fingers brushed over her skin with careful examination, noting each detail of the mark.

Throughout her failed dating experiences, Mallory had felt twinges and urges. But usually, touching was a trigger, an impediment that doused the sparks of desire before they had a chance to ignite.

But with Jess, her fight or flight response was being overpowered by a sublime stir in the pit of her stomach. As his fingers glided higher and higher up her arm, the sensation coiled tighter into a delicious ache.

"Who did this?" he asked, his voice ruinously soft.

His attention was keenly fixed on her as he leaned in closer, ready, and attentive to hear her answer.

But Mallory couldn't vocalize a single syllable.

When his fingers glided over the tattoo of Aiden's name on the inside of her forearm, he stopped. The formidable way his bottom jaw jutted forward thrust his lower lip outward in a vexing yet provocative glower. "Is he the bastard who did this to you?"

Jess's insult to Aiden quarried through her newfound desire and stabbed at her temper. "Aiden wasn't a bastard. He was a kind and caring man who didn't condone violence."

Easing her arm free of his grasp, she secured the cuff around her wrist and added venom to her voice. "Most men don't get a second warning about touching me, so you're lucky I left my mace in the car."

Mallory took a step back and waited for Jess to respond with anger or indifference, the way every other man had when she warned them. But there weren't any signs of pique or apathy on his makeup-covered face. He didn't rebound with snide remarks about her being frigid or irrational. No grinding of teeth nor flaring of the nostrils.

He just stood there, gazing down at her with an intense, thought-filled look.

"I'm not most men, Mallory." His blue eyes were more invasive than his touch. "I don't know why you don't want to be touched, and I don't have to. It's your body and your right. I will abide by your rule."

She rubbed her arm, feeling the impact of his words ripple over her. Her body. Her right. Her rule. No man had ever forfeited his ego to give her that control.

"I won't touch you again unless you want me to."

And that was perhaps the most surprising part of this whole encounter. She *did* want him to touch her. But she would have to make the first move. Again, Jess was giving her all the control.

As the tingling sensation caused by his fingers ebbed, she felt the hollow place inside of her expand.

He gave her a smile to show her that there were no hard feelings on his part. "Are we good?"

She cleared her throat, trying to dislodge the complicated emotions wrapped around her vocal cords. "Ah... yeah." She tried smiling too. "We're good."

He pulled a couple of wipes from the container and set about cleaning his face as if nothing had happened. He scrubbed until most of the lipstick was gone, then went to work on removing the eye shadow and glitter.

Mallory pointed to a speck of glitter just above his eyebrow. "You missed a spot."

He targeted the area, giving it several hard strokes before he gave up and tossed the makeup-covered wipe into the trash. "These things won't take the glitter off." He handed her the wipes. "I need soap and water. Do you mind sitting with Sophie while I'm in the restroom?"

Jess had tossed out a lewd suggestion and given her wrong directions — things she knew he regretted now. But she was beginning to see that he was a man with deep concern and thoughtfulness. A man of patience and reason. A man who respected her body and her boundaries. "No, I don't mind."

"I'll be right back." Tugging at another knotted barrette, he disappeared around the corner to find a restroom.

The bruise was nothing. It wasn't sore and had only caused superficial damage. But her body's response to Jess's touch had been profound.

She had just experienced a crucial moment in her adult life. Attraction and desire without the urge to recoil and run. She wanted to jump and shout halleluiah from the top of her lungs.

But that would not only be weird, it would also bring about more questions, so she celebrated within.

She plopped down in the chair and let out an

exhausted sigh, depleted of energy and astounded at her reaction to a man she hardly knew.

A quick pulsating ping coming from her back pocket brought her bottom up and reminded her that she had Jess's phone. She pulled it out as a slew of texts popped up on the screen.

Mallory wasn't a snoop, but the text might be important.

She hit the text and scrolled to the first text that appeared beside the name Brandi, then, scrolled up to past texts, reading days and days of conversation between Jess and the woman.

Her giddy excitement crashed to the ground.

UNTITLED

~

When Jess saw Beautiful standing on the porch, ready to plant her boot in his ass for giving her bad directions, he had been prepared for an engaging ruckus with a sharp-tongued woman. Because eliciting that sort of a reaction from a petite bundle of lethal leather and fuming female was bound to lead to exciting situations and fun games.

But he hadn't been prepared for the bruises.

He shut the bathroom door behind him and scrubbed a hand over his face. "Shit, shit, shit," he whispered. He had been a major dickhead to a woman who had probably just gone through hell.

Boots in the air? He cringed and flipped the faucet on, then ducked his head under the spout, soaking in the cold water.

With Mallory's hand fishing around in his pocket for the phone, it had been hard for him to think about anything but how close she was to his horse.

49

But when her fingers ran the length of the scar on his thigh, he had flinched and looked down as she recoiled. The cuff of her riding jacket had been pushed up, and he had gotten a glimpse of the dark blue-green band around her wrist.

He shut the water off, raised his head, and jerked a couple of paper towels from the dispenser to dry his face. Then he chucked them into the trash can and rested his hands on the edge of the sink.

He stared down at the residue of pink glitter resting along the edge of the sink bowl. Beautiful wasn't trouble. But trouble wasn't far behind her.

Mallory acted brave and tough, but the wounded look in her eyes when he asked about the bruises told a different story. The guarded way she backed away from him made him physically sick.

Jess raked both hands through his wet hair and grabbed his hat.

It had been years since Eleanor had seen her sister and Mallory wasn't an innocent child anymore. There was a chance she was involved in something dangerous. Questions about who Aiden was and why she referred to him in the past tense made Jess uneasy.

He opened the bathroom door as McCrea came through the Labor and Delivery doors. "How's El?"

"Tired, but good. She was a trooper."

"And the baby?"

"Tucker is perfect," McCrea said proudly.

They had named the baby as soon as they knew the sex, deciding on an old family name that had been passed down to his brother.

McCrea looked around. "Where's Sophie?"

"She's in the waiting room with Mallory," Jess explained.

"Mallory?" He raised both brows. "Eleanor's sister?"

"Yeah," Jess said. "She showed up at the ranch about the time El's water broke and rode with us."

"Why do you look worried?" McCrea asked, his grin giving way to concern.

"I don't think she's here for a simple reunion," Jess confessed. "I think she may be in trouble."

McCrea hooked his thumbs through his belt loops. "Why? What's going on?"

"She's chewing her fingernails, looking over her shoulder and," he hesitated, "she has bruises on her wrist."

The muscles in his brother's jaw flexed. "Shit."

"I had the same reaction. Whoever Mallory is running from might not be far behind her."

McCrea thought for a second and then backtracked down the hall. "I want to let Eleanor know what's going on."

"Have you talked to Mom or Dad?"

"No. Both phones went to voicemail."

"I'll keep trying them." Jess reached for his phone and remembered Mallory had it. He made his way back to the waiting room and found her sitting next to Sophie, who was working on her latest masterpiece. A pink and yellow butterfly.

"Try a darker shade of pink under the wing to give it depth." Mallory colored the underside of the butterfly. "See." With just a few strokes in the right places, the wing of the one-dimensional insect almost fluttered to life.

"Aunt Mallory is an artist too?" he asked.

"I do okay, I guess," she admitted and handed the crayon to Sophie. "Now you try it."

"I talked with McCrea. The delivery went well. El and the baby are doing fine."

Relief caused her to let out a little sigh. "Good."

Jess tossed his hat into a chair. "We got off on the wrong foot earlier. The boots-in-the-air comment was way out of line. There's no excuse for the way I treated you. I'm sorry. I'm not usually an asshole."

She stared at him for a moment, her eyes swaying between doubt and humor.

"It's just that El has had a lot of stress on her lately with the baby and the renovations…"

"I understand," she said. "I can't say I wouldn't have done the same thing." She gave him a side glance. "I wouldn't have made the boots-in-the-air comment but…"

"That comment went against everything my dad ever taught me about how to treat a woman." So why had he made it? Because there was something about Mallory that tripped all his bells and whistles. A foreshadowing in the pit of his stomach that told him to run like hell as fast as he could in the opposite direction. "If he knew I'd said it, he'd kick me in the butt."

Her lips toyed with a grin. "I like your dad already."

Jess moved to the seat across from her. "If I had known you were El's sister, I would have driven you to the ranch myself. She's really missed you."

The warmth of her smile spread through him. "I've missed her too."

"Any chance your mother might come for a visit?" he asked. "She'd love that."

Her smile wavered and then fell away completely. "No. Mom won't be visiting."

"That's a shame."

"It's more than a shame." Bitterness coated her words. "It's a damn tragedy. There are so many wasted years that we three could have spent together."

If she thought that, then why had she waited until now

to reconnect with her sister? Why was she here? He wanted to ask those questions. But he refused to let himself be drawn in deeper with this woman.

"Well," he said, reaching for his hat. "You're here now, and that's all that matters. El's happy you're back." He was going to San Antonio and hopefully by the time he got home, Mallory would be gone. "Do you have my phone?"

"Oh, yeah," she said, quickly reaching into her back pocket.

After taking it, he dialed Brandi's number.

"Hey, handsome," she laughed over the sound of George Straits' "Amarillo By Morning" blasting in the background. "Are you on the road?"

He made his way to the other side of the room, so he could talk privately. "No, not yet."

"Someone better be dead," she joked.

He heard a horn blow and knew she must be driving home. "Just the opposite. My sister-in-law's water broke, and she went into labor on my watch."

"Oh my God!" she squealed and lowered the volume on George. "That's awesome!"

"Yeah." He grinned. "It was."

"So are we still on for this weekend? I completely understand if you cancel on me. I'd trade you for a baby any day."

The Brandi he knew years ago would have never gotten excited over babies. She had been just as free-spirited as he had, never letting her boots stay under the same bed for more than a couple of nights.

"Chubby cheeks, soft skin, cuddles…" Her exhale ended with a groan. "I want a baby so bad."

Oh, hell no. "Can't help you with that," Jess returned coarsely, thinking he might not have known Brandi at all.

"You can. You just won't and even if you would, I wouldn't, not with you anyway —"

"I'm great father material," he interrupted her rant, taken back by her lack in his daddy abilities. "I love kids, and they loved me."

"No. You're great uncle material," she corrected. "Meaning you get all the freedom of a bachelor while enjoying the love and admiration of your brother's kids."

Jess didn't see how that was a bad thing. He scrubbed a hand over his face, irritated by her reaction and the gullible way he had let himself get drawn into this baby discussion. "Brandi, why are we having this conversation?"

"Sorry, I'm rambling. I always ramble when I talk about babies. So," she sighed again. "Are we on or off for this weekend?"

Telling his brother about the trouble Mallory might be in had helped ease Jess's conscience. He had done his part. Mallory would be safe because McCrea would make sure nothing happened to her.

But McCrea already had his hands full with the Rescue and the new baby.

"I — ah," he stammered when he glanced across the room and saw Mallory watching him. "I'm not sure."

"Call me when you know."

"I will."

He slid the phone into his pocket and watched as McCrea walked back into the waiting area.

Mallory rose to her feet, planted both booted feet firmly on the floor, and tightened her hands into fists. If Jess hadn't been watching, he would have missed the subtle way she prepared herself for McCrea's approach.

His brother held out his hand and smiled. Mallory hesitated for a split second then returned his smile but brushed his handshake aside by picking up crayons.

She was a strong, independent woman who was serious about protecting her personal space. But there was frailty hidden underneath all that leather and resilience. A weakness that made Jess want to wrap her in his arms and protect her at all costs.

CHAPTER 5

ELEANOR'S HUSBAND HAD A CARING SMILE, WITH DARK EYES and a calm voice. He made polite conversation about the weather and kept a few steps ahead of her as they made their way down the hall to Eleanor's room.

Sophie sat perched on her daddy's arm, resting her head against his chest.

"Are you sure this is okay?" Mallory asked. "I know she must be exhausted. I can come back tomorrow."

He stopped at the room, shifted Sophie from one arm to the other, then held the door open for Mallory. "She really wants to see you. Now, you two visit for a while. I have some calls to make."

"Can I stay with Mommy and Tucker?" Sophie questioned, her eyes budding with excitement and the hope that her daddy might say yes.

"No." He grinned and tipped the end of her nose with his finger.

McCrea, like Jess, had a rugged but tender way about him. The softness of his strong hands as they lifted Sophie and the gentle tone he used to answer her stirred Mallory's childhood longing for paternal bonds and affection.

"Did you call Ed and Sue?" Eleanor asked him.

"They're at the top of my list, darlin'," he answered patiently and began backing out the door.

"Don't forget your mom and dad," she added. "Oh, and Louisa."

"Jess is giving them a call after he parks the crossover." He winked at his wife. "We'll be back in a little while."

Mallory waited until the door was closed before she whispered, "Your husband is a nice man who clearly adores you. You're a fortunate lady."

Eleanor smiled with the satisfaction of that truth. "I know."

Mallory set the diaper bag and purse near the closet. She approached the bed, tears gathering in her eyes at the sight of the newborn cradled in her sisters' arms. "He's beautiful."

Eleanor's face glowed. "He is perfect," she said, stroking the baby's round head which was covered in hair the color of Sophie's.

"I can't believe you're a momma."

Eleanor smiled up at her, her eyes misty with joy. "Sometimes it's hard for me to believe too." She patted the bed, silently asking Mallory to take a seat. "We have so much catching up to do."

"Yes, we do."

The happiness on her sister's face dimmed. "Grandma passed away. I tried contacting Mom, but the phone number I had was disconnected, and my letters came back."

"We left Santa Fe not long after you moved in with Grandma," Mallory said, not wanting to dive too deep into an explanation.

Eleanor's smile bounced back. "I can't tell you how happy I am that you're here."

"I can't tell you how happy I am that you haven't told me to hit the road."

Eleanor frowned. "Why in the world would I do that? You're my sister?"

Their mother's blood made them siblings, gave them a bond and a kinship. But the blood of her father had the potential to break them apart. "Because I'm Rex Montgomery's daughter."

"Don't ever feel like you have to apologize for that. Do you hear me?" Eleanor took her hand, lifting it with a gentle shake that revealed the bruise on her wrist. "Oh God, Mallory. Did he do this?"

She had been running for the door, running for her life, when her father snagged her wrist. "I don't want to ruin this moment — this day by talking about my bruises," she answered, neither confirming nor denying that her father had made the bruises.

Eleanor wasn't satisfied with her answer, but she was willing to let the question go for now. With concern etched across her face, she nodded. "Okay, but promise me that we will talk about it."

Mallory reached out and touched the baby's head. "I'll get a motel room and come back for a visit tomorrow."

"I won't hear of it," Eleanor said, giving no thought to a protest. "We have a guest room, and it's yours for as long as you want."

"No. I couldn't —"

"I won't take no for an answer." She squeezed Mallory's hand again. "I know you don't want to talk about what happened, but I'd feel better knowing you're safe at the ranch with us."

She was elated to know Eleanor wasn't holding any

grudges for her being Rex's daughter and that she had invited her to stay at the ranch. But she didn't want to endanger them by being there. "How long until you and the baby are released?"

"I'm guessing a couple of days," Eleanor answered, smiling warmly when the door opened, and McCrea and Sophie came in. "That was a short trip."

"Jess finally reached Mom and Dad. Ed and Sue are on their way over," he explained, walking around Mallory to deposit Sophie on the opposite side of the bed next to Eleanor. "I thought you'd want to know."

Mallory eased from the bed and moved back, feeling out of place in the modern-day Norman Rockwell painting the four of them made. Soon, more family would be arriving, and she'd be in a room filled with strangers asking questions.

Thinking she could slip out the door and find a nice, quiet spot in the waiting room to occupy until Jess came back, she took a step back, careful not to make a sound that would let them know she was leaving the room.

Mallory was almost to the door when her heel hit something hard. She looked down to find it was the toe of a familiar, well-worn cowboy boot.

She went to take a step forward, lost her balance and pitched backward into a solid wall of muscles and brawn.

She jerked her head around, and her eyes zeroed in on the chest and followed the neckline of a t-shirt − covered in pink glitter − up to a familiar scar on the tip of an equally familiar masculine chin.

Jess's mouth lifted at one corner. "Just for the record. You're touching me."

Mallory noted that for a man who was practically a stranger, there were a lot of familiars about him. "I guess I am."

There was something about Jess's hard chest pressing against her back that made her want to lean in and snuggle closer.

When she didn't move, he lowered his lips to her ear. "You're still touching me."

The tepid exhale of his breath across her skin as he spoke was so sexy.

"Sorry," she said, taking a step forward.

A trace of humor sparked across his face. "Where were you sneaking off too?"

She swallowed. "Nowhere. You're my ride, remember?"

His smile deepened. "Oh, yeah. I guess I am."

"I was just trying to get out of the way," she explained, wrapping her arms around her stomach. "And make room for the family that's coming."

With a tilt to his head, Jess motioned her back to the bed. "You are family, and you're never in the way when you're with them."

That may have been the case with his family, but it certainly had never been with hers.

Leaning down, he gently grazed Tucker's cheek with his forefinger. "Hi, little man."

Tucker responded with a wide yawn that ended with a goofy smile.

Jess cocked his head back and let out a deep laugh. Then he pointed to McCrea. "That face is all you, brother."

"Yeah," McCrea agreed, giving them a grin mirrored his son's.

Jess's heartfelt apology had moved Mallory, and her opinion of the painted jackass was starting to sway. She stood quietly by and observed the gratifying display of family love and affection. She had never felt anything as moving as what she was witnessing now. Grown men, tough men, rough cowboys had joyful tears in their eyes. Tears they didn't try to hide.

Jess shoved both hands into the front pockets of his jeans with the warmest smile Mallory had ever seen on a man. "He's something, ain't he?"

Mallory choked back a rising tide of emotions and answered him with a headshake. It was overwhelming to think that she had a place in this tender and sacred moment, that she might belong in a family with so much love to give.

Being tossed around from one foster home to the next during his childhood hadn't given Aiden much experience with family bonding or nurturing.

But he and Cassie had done their best. They had given Mallory her first taste of what a real family was supposed to be. They had loved her as best they could, supported her and tried to help her be a typical teenager.

They hadn't succeeded.

"Mom and Dad are going to have him spoiled in no time at all," Jess announced matter-of-factly.

"No doubt," McCrea answered.

As the three of them talked, Sophie dug into her bag for crayons and paper and set about drawing her latest masterpiece.

Mallory stepped to the side. But this time it wasn't to quietly slip out the door. She wanted a better look at the cowboy standing next to her. The one who had made a promise not to touch her.

Jess wasn't long and lanky like most of the cowboys she'd seen. She guessed he was a little over six foot. He was built soundly with sturdy shoulders and arms and was a perfect proportion of muscle and height.

Mallory watched his bicep flex as he lifted his arm to

scratch his jaw. That bicep had felt smooth, hard, and a bit more tantalizing than she thought it should.

After all, it was just an extremity.

There were many more riveting parts of his male anatomy to ponder, like that strong chin. And that hard, sculpted chest of his — bare in all of its muscular glory — had been a sight to behold. His skin, hot and sweaty from the sun, his round pec muscles covered in a scattering of golden hair and those nipples...

Mallory drew in a deep breath. Nipples had every right to be tantalizing.

She quietly fanned her flushed skin, remembering those glossy beads of sweat sliding down his tanned six-pack.

Her eyes moved lower to his hips. Narrow, but sturdy and with a full range of motion. He had demonstrated that with the lewd suggestion.

Jess's thighs were also impressive. The left one was like the rest of him. Firm and powerful. But the right one, the one with the deep scar, was slightly smaller.

Whatever injury he had undergone didn't seem to impair his stamina or strength. He had proven that when he had whisked Eleanor up and carried her as if she weighed nothing at all.

But he did have a limp.

Mallory had noticed it earlier this afternoon as he made his way up the hill to her. She had also seen the way his eyes iced over when he caught her watching him.

He had probably taken her admiration for staring, and after he had made the boots-in-the-air comment, she really hadn't given a damn.

But that was before she had seen this side of him. The concerned brother-in-law, the proud uncle, and the devoted brother was nothing like the Jess that had given her wrong directions.

The softness of his smile and gentleness of his voice was quite a contrast to the man he had been out there on the road.

"Mallory," Eleanor interrupted her appraising review with a fun smirk. "I believe you've already met Jess."

Jess tipped the brim of his hat with an official greeting and smiled wide. "Ma'am."

Feeling more at home and relaxed among her new family, Mallory saw her chance for a little payback. "Yes, we met earlier out on the road. When he suggested I repay him for directions with…" she smiled vengefully at Jess. "What was it you said? A boots-in-the-air kind of ride?"

"Jess," Eleanor gasped. "You didn't?"

Jess's cheekbones took on a fascinating shade of road-rash red.

"Please don't judge the rest of the Coldiron family by this idiot," McCrea said.

Mallory was in no position to judge anyone's family. "To be fair, I didn't tell him who I was, only that I needed to see you."

"It was all a misunderstanding," Jess explained.

"And he did apologize," she threw in, wanting to set everything straight.

"I've invited Mallory to stay in the guest room," Eleanor said, shifting Tucker higher on her shoulder. "Jess practically lives in my kitchen, so don't be alarmed when you hear him roaming around."

"I don't live in your kitchen," Jess objected.

"You're more than welcome to stay at the ranch with us," McCrea said. "But we're about to bring a newborn home. We're going to be up and down all hours of the night, feeding and changing diapers…It's going to be a noisy place for a while."

"You're right," Eleanor grimaced. "I hadn't thought about that."

"There's always the apartment at Promise Point," Jess said, frowning slightly when he looked at his watch.

"Yeah." Eleanor's face lit up. "That would be perfect."

"We own a horse rescue," Jess went on to explain when Mallory shot him a perplexed glance. "We added an apartment over the new stables we had built a couple of months ago. But it's a lot bigger than the spare room at Redemption."

"I appreciate the offer," she said offering her gratitude before she told them that she wouldn't be in town long enough to justify moving into an apartment. "I really do, but—"

"You'd have your own space," Jess cut in.

Her own space, meaning when Rex showed up, she wouldn't have to worry about anyone getting hurt. "On second thought, having my own space sounds nice."

"Good," Eleanor said, with a relieved smile. "We'll get you settled into it after I get home."

"If you're ready," Jess said, looking tense around the jaw as he glanced at his watch again. "I'll drive you back to the ranch, so you can settle in for the night."

Having read the steamy texts he and Brandi had exchanged, Mallory knew he was ready to rid himself of her and be on his way to San Antonio.

She leaned over to give her sister a hug. "I'll see you later."

Sophie thrust her latest portrait of Tucker at Mallory. "Here, I made this for you."

"Oh, Sophie," she gasped, knowing how important praise was for a young artist. "It's beautiful. Thank you."

"Supper is in the crockpot," Eleanor started. "And extra sheets are in the linen closet upstairs."

"I'll show her where everything is," Jess assured her, following Mallory to the door.

∽

"OH, WAIT." JESS PAUSED AT THE DOOR TO LOOK BACK AT his brother. "Did Lester Oaks talk to you about that horse?"

McCrea's expression stalled for a second because Lester had been dead for at least ten years. "No, I — ah… I haven't talked to Lester lately."

Jess knew he should have moseyed out the door, dropped Mallory off at the ranch, and been on his way to San Antonio without a second thought. But he couldn't get those damn bruises out of his head.

He handed Mallory the crossover keys. "Wait for me in the car. I won't be long."

A splash of wicked entertainment flashed in her eyes as she accepted the keys. "My how the tables have turned."

"Don't you leave me," he warned, fearing there was a good chance his ass would be walking back to the ranch.

Smiling, she turned on her heel and headed down the hallway.

"Lester Oaks?" McCrea questioned.

Jess closed the door and went back to the bed. "Sally came by the office today to make a donation, so Lester's name was fresh in my mind. Did Mallory tell you who made the bruises?"

"No," Eleanor answered. "She closed up and wouldn't say anything about what happened."

"My money is on Rex," McCrea said, anger flashing across his face.

Jess knew more than he wanted to about Eleanor's stepfather. He had heard the stories and witnessed the fear in her eyes when she first came to live with Rose.

"But why would she need to run from Rex now?" Eleanor asked. "She's an adult and probably left home the minute she turned eighteen."

"There is another possibility," Jess said, devising a theory that might explain Aiden. "Mallory could be running from a boyfriend or even a husband. Did she mention anything about a guy named Aiden?"

Eleanor thought for a second. "No. She didn't. Why, did she say something to you?"

"No. That name is tattooed on her arm. When I asked if he'd made the bruises, she said no, but…" he paused, thinking about the sorrow in her eyes as she defended the man. "I don't know. Something wasn't right."

McCrea scooted one of the hospital chairs closer to the bed and sat down. "You think this Aiden guy is bad news?"

"Maybe."

"I don't want her left alone. Jess, for my peace of mind, promise me that you'll stay with her," Eleanor said, her voice almost pleading.

He and Eleanor had been friends since they were kids and sparing cold-blooded murder, there wasn't anything he wouldn't do for her. She held a place in his heart that was reserved for baby sisters. A protective place Lou should have occupied, but vehemently refused to be placed in.

Calling Brandi to say he wouldn't be leaving Santa Camino until later tonight wasn't a problem. But staying with a woman who moderately despised him until his brother made it home this evening….

Jess rubbed a hand over the back of his neck. "I don't think your sister would be thrilled about spending the afternoon with me."

"Ah," McCrea cut in, grimacing slightly. "I'm afraid you'll be spending more than the afternoon with her."

"Huh?" Jess asked, not liking the vagueness of his brother's comment.

"I've got another rescue up near Dallam County, so," McCrea gave him a weary smile, "you'll be on your own tonight."

On his own? As in *he* would be spending the night *alone* with a woman who didn't want to be touched in any way, shape, form, or fashion. A woman with trust issues and an angry boyfriend.

He didn't need this kind of shit in his life.

What Jess did need was Brandi, the warm and willing woman waiting for him in San Antonio.

Eleanor's face fell. "I thought Brody was handling the long-distance rescues."

"He is," McCrea answered. "But he had a family emergency and won't be back until Monday."

Brody Vance fit perfectly with the Promise Point family and with their own. Their mother insisted Brody have dinner with them at least once a week because everyone assumed he had no family.

"Since when does Brody have a family?" Jess asked, somewhat irritated by the way he was being thrown into the middle of this situation.

"I'm just as surprised as you are. But with Brody gone, I'm it." McCrea winced, regrettably at his wife. "I'm sorry, darlin'. I got the call a few minutes ago."

Jess clamped a hand over his forehead.

Damn it, he had plans. Plans with a woman who didn't want to permanently blind him with mace and was game for more than a night of awkwardly bumping into him.

How was he going to get out of this? He wanted to growl and kick a dent into the trash can. But then an idea popped into his head. It wouldn't get him to San Antonio, but it would save him from spending the night with Mallory.

"I'll go," he blurted out. "I'll do the rescue."

McCrea's raised his dark brows high. "You've never wanted to go on a rescue before, so why do you suddenly feel the need to volunteer for this one?"

Jess shoved his hands into his front pockets and shifted his weight onto his good leg, ready to bullshit his way out of the situation. "Well —"

"Is it because of Mallory?" Eleanor cut him off, her big blue eyes staring up at him as if he'd just run over her favorite dog. "Because if it is…"

"It's not," he lied.

"I don't want to guilt you into something."

"You're not," he lied again, supporting it with a wink this time.

"Jess, we've known each other a long time," Eleanor said, softly. "I know when you're lying."

He closed his eyes, knowing there was no way in hell he was lying his way out of this one. "El, she's awfully skittish of me. Maybe you could call Violet or Sage. I'm sure they'd be more than happy to stay with her tonight."

"No doubt," McCrea said. "But how can they protect her from Rex?"

Jess's groan was audible because his brother was right. He couldn't put the women at risk.

Eleanor tilted her head to one side. "Mallory doesn't despise you, and the skittish part will change once she gets to know you."

Jess didn't want Mallory to get to know him. He didn't want to care about her or her problems.

"Don't take her jumpiness personally," Eleanor continued her appeal.

He had never given any woman cause to fear him, never raised his hand or voice above a hoot and holler to one. And though Mallory's knee-jerk reactions to his touch hadn't dented his male ego, they had dug into the tender spot of his heart. And he didn't want to experience anything that raw or real with the woman.

Mallory was already on pins and needles, and he didn't want to cause her more distress. "Have you thought about how she'll react to spending the night alone with a man she barely knows?"

"She won't like it," McCrea said, giving Jess an empathetic smile.

Eleanor stroked Tucker's head. "Once Mallory learns she can trust you, she'll be fine."

Something about a vulnerable woman trusting him made Jess uncomfortable. There were so many ways that could go wrong.

He had never met a woman with a Look-But-Don't-Touch rule, so he didn't have any experience to base an argument on.

Not that arguing with Eleanor would do him any good. He *was* spending the night *alone* with Mallory whether he liked it or not.

Damn it.

He sighed, giving in. "And you're sure Mallory didn't drop any clues about who made the bruises or why she's running?"

"No," Eleanor said, looking more worried than ever. "Only that we'd talk about it later. Why?"

He threw up his hands. "I don't know. I guess I'm trying to figure out what I'm up against. An angry boyfriend might be a lot harder to deal with than a coward like Rex."

"Don't bet on it." Eleanor steeled her eyes against old

memories. "Rex is a coward who won't fight fair, especially if he's cornered."

Jess had gone up against more than one man who didn't fight fair and even with only one good leg to support himself, he could still pack a mean punch.

McCrea's face drew tight. "Sophie can spend the night at Mom and Dad's. If there's trouble at the ranch, I don't want her there."

"I hate this." Eleanor shifted positions and tried pushing herself up higher in the bed. "She needs me, and I'm stuck here. Maybe I can get the doctor to release me early."

"Oh, no," McCrea sternly objected. "You'll go home when he says you can and not a minute sooner."

"Don't you worry." Rising to his feet, Jess took a step closer and bent to plant a kiss on her head. "Mallory will be safe with me."

She offered him a grateful smile. "Thank you, Jess."

He stopped at the door. "You take care of yourself and my nephew. I'll check on you tomorrow."

CHAPTER 6

Jess closed the door and headed down the hall to the ER entrance. When the automatic doors opened, he drew in a deep breath and covered his face with both hands.

It was turning out to be one hell of a day.

"Where's Sophie?"

Mallory's voice drew his head around. She was sitting on a concrete bench just outside the entrance, chewing on her thumbnail.

"With McCrea. He's taking her to our parents' house to spend the night because he'll be out of town." He pointed to her thumb. "You're going to gnaw that thing off."

She gave him a tense smile. "It's a nervous habit."

"You don't have to be nervous. I'll be with you tonight, so you can give that little digit a rest."

"Oh no, you won't." She dropped her hand and rose to her feet, ignoring him as she searched the parking lot for the crossover. "Where did you park?"

"Yes, I will," he said, pointing to the left side of the

parking lot. "I promised El I wouldn't let you out of my sight."

Mallory stepped off the curb and started walking towards the crossover. "I don't need a bodyguard and Brandi is expecting you in San Antonio."

"How'd you know…?" He trailed after her, fighting a curse from the pain in his thigh. "You read my texts?"

She used the remote to unlock the door. "You mean those cheesy porno scripts? Yeah, it was kind of hard not to. It was like I was in some kind of weird and smutty trance."

Jess chuckled, surprised by this side of her. "You're just jealous."

She cut in front of him and opened the driver's door. "Of the cheesy porno script or that you're getting laid and I'm not?" she asked before getting in.

Mallory's brash question caught Jess off guard. The toe of his right boot caught on the heel of his left boot, tripping him. Luckily, the backend of the crossover was there to stop him from plowing face first into the pavement.

He hurried to get in before she backed out. Given his present state of pain and stiffness, that wasn't an easy task. But he folded into the passenger side without groaning too much. "You're a pretty woman —"

"Aw…" She smiled sweetly and turned the wheel. "You sweet talker."

"So why aren't you getting laid?" he asked, unable to fathom why a woman like Mallory was having that sort of problem.

"Because I'm very picky about who touches me."

Being selective with men meant Mallory was smart and knew what she wanted. "Nothing wrong with that."

She braked abruptly at the end of the row, prompting Jess to reach for his seatbelt. "Which way do I turn?"

"Oh." He laughed, enjoying the irony. "Now, you trust my directions?"

"You're right." She turned left and gassed it. "I'll figure it out on my own."

He held on to the dash. "Or you could just pull over and let me drive."

She tapped her forefinger against her chin. "Let me think about it... Ah, no. I like being in control."

"That could be why you're not getting laid," he said, grabbing the door handle as she sped down the road. "When's the last time you drove something with four wheels?"

"It's been a while."

"I thought so."

"Are you," she whipped the steering wheel around, slinging Jess against the door. "One of those men who like their women docile and obedient in bed?"

Again, her question caught him off guard.

"Hell, no," he objected. "But I don't like being covered in chocolate and tickled with feathers either. I'm more of a traditionalist when it comes to sex."

"Interesting," she said, narrowing her eyes as she watched the road.

"What's interesting about it?"

"Have you ever been covered in chocolate and tickled with feathers?" she asked, shooting a quick glance his way.

He did a double take. Was she serious? She looked serious, but he couldn't tell. "No."

She arched one dark eyebrow and twisted her lips into a sexy smirk. "Then how do you know you won't like it?"

Beautiful was into chocolate and feathers?

Jess was having trouble pulling air into his lungs because he was thinking about his palm smearing warm chocolate over the smooth, firm contours of Mallory's bare breasts. The light tickle of a feather across her hard nipples…

She braked again for the four-way stop, propelling Jess forward. Then, she hit the gas, and Jess went back against the seat with a *whomp*.

He cleared his throat. "Are you?"

"Am I what?"

"Into chocolate and feathers?"

"Would it shock you if I said yes?"

Damnation. Mallory *was* into chocolate and feathers. "Honestly," he said, attempting a deep breath. "Nothing you say would shock me."

Jess liked a woman who spoke her mind, but Mallory's frank attitude about sexual fetishes surprised him. And this wasn't how he envisioned the two of them getting to know each other.

"Make a right here," he instructed as they approached the stop sign. "I need to go by my place first for a shower and a change of clothes."

"Let me take you back to the ranch." Her tone was much more mellow than before. "You can get your truck and be on your way to see Brandi. My sister never has to know you didn't spend the night."

"I'd know," he said, pointing to the right. "Turn here and then left at the fence."

She let out a long sigh and made the turn. "Okay, fine. Have it your way."

"Don't pout. It'll be like a sleepover. We'll eat pizza, tell ghost stories, and play Truth or Dare."

"I can't wait," she said blandly.

"Turn right. This is it."

She whistled. "Is that your house?"

The rambling design of the cedar log home with a purlin roof design and open windows was nestled into the foothills of the Promise Point Ridgeline. "Yep," he answered feeling the sting of an old memory irritate his mood. He and Hallie had chosen the floorplan for the house together. They wanted plenty of room for children and family time. They had made plans, big plans that all ended the night he fell.

She pointed to the fenced pastures. "And this?"

"I bought the twenty acres where the house is ten years ago. When our granddad died, my sister Louisa and I inherited this section. She owns about fifty acres on the other side of the fence." He pointed to the ridge in behind his house. "It all borders our parents' cattle ranch. McCrea and Eleanor own the south side including Promise Point which boarders Redemption on the north side."

"Northside, southside…how do you keep your bearings out here?"

"How do you keep your bearings at home?"

"There are plenty of road signs in Monterey Bay," she said, grinning. "And most of the horse trails come with guides."

Chuckling, he motioned her up the drive. "Park around back in front of the garage."

Mallory did as he said, switched off the motor, and impatiently drummed her thumbs against the stirring wheel.

"Are you coming?" he asked as he opened the door and climbed out.

"Oh, I get to walk in with you?" she asked with mock surprise. "I thought you were going to handcuff me to the wheel."

"That's not a bad idea," he teased and headed up the sidewalk.

When they reached the front of the house, Mallory

looked up at the open windows of the two-story foyer. "You live here by yourself?"

"Yep." He unlocked the door and held it open for her. "I am a big boy now. I cook, clean, and grocery shop all on my own."

She let her head fall to one side and pretended to glower at him. "I just meant it's so big for one person."

He walked in behind her and shut the door. "You get used to it. Make yourself at home."

She made a face. "Thanks, but me walking around naked would probably be awkward at this stage of our friendship."

Jess never knew what to expect from her. She bounced between quiet and reserved to flirty and audacious.

"Oh!" She pointed to the framed photo of him on a Haflinger gelding. "Is this you?"

"Yep."

"You were so cute."

"I'm still cute," he defended, lightheartedly.

"How old were you when you learned to ride?"

He let out a long burst of air as he thought. "I think I was three when Dad put me on that horse."

"Three?" she questioned incredulously.

"We start 'em young around here." He grinned. "Tucker will probably be ropin' before he's out of diapers."

She laughed and followed him into the den.

"If I had it to do over, I would have built a smaller house." Jess pointed to the first framed photo on the den wall. It was one of him riding Meet Your Maker. "But we poured the foundation when I won state."

"We?" she inquired.

"I was engaged once," he answered and moved a finger to another photo. "The walls were up, and the roof was on by the time I won the National Finals Rodeo. I finally finished the place a few years ago."

Her eyes widened. "Jess Coldiron, the saddle bronc rider." She snapped her fingers. "I knew you looked familiar."

Before the fall, he'd had the privilege of signing his name on everything from hats to breasts. For a short time, he had enjoyed a taste of being a national celebrity and a local hero.

But now people seldom recognized him outside of Santa Camino.

"Are you a fan of the rodeo?' he asked

"I used to be, but I don't follow it much anymore," she said, moving down the line of photos that chronicled his rodeo career. "You looked so different in all these photos. So rough and rowdy." She gave him a dubious grin. "And maybe a little untamed."

He had been totally undomesticated back then, living like he rode: wild, free, and without fear. Winning was all he had cared about. "It's hard to believe I was that kid."

For a moment, he was in the arena. The smell of dirt and livestock filled his nose, the noise of the crowd, his friends, the power of the horse, the rope in his hand…

"You were a lot smaller back then. Not as buff."

He slid a hand over his chest. "Had to be, but I've put on a few pounds since then."

"There's not an inch of fat on you," she said, reaching out to make a pinch at his abs.

He dodged and caught her hand. "Hey, what happened to look but don't touch?"

"Yeah." Her lips twisted to one side with thought. "I think I might retract my warning."

Her small hand nestled securely in his caused a tight,

constricting sensation in Jess's chest. "Why would you do that?"

"I made it in haste," she confessed. "Before I knew you."

"We've only known each other for a couple of hours, Mallory."

"I'm not saying I'm ready for His and Hers bath towels or getting a dog together." The center of her eyes was the color of whiskey cured in virgin oaks. A golden-hued liquid he partook of often. "But my sister trusts you or she wouldn't have sent you to babysit me tonight."

"Ah," he said, taking a step closer. "So your faith in me is based on a sister you haven't seen since you were six?"

"Of course not," she said, her gaze dropping to his chest. "I've watched how you are with Eleanor and Sophie. You're protective of them and have fond affection and respect for her. And…"

"And?" he taunted.

"That you're a rarity among men."

Over the last decade, life had done a damn fine job of kicking Jess's ass. Some days the only thing that got him out of bed was a deeply rooted stubbornness that refused to be whipped.

There were days when he fought the urge to submerge himself in a bottle of bourbon. Days when he looked in the mirror and saw nothing but a broken - down rodeo dreamer. Days when he wanted to mount a horse and ride until he felt whole again. Days when he called up old acquaintances and arranged last minute dates just so he wouldn't have to face another sunrise alone.

Today had been a combination of all those things plus, *this*. A beautiful woman gazing up at him with trust and awe in her eyes, while garnishing him with words of praise.

It was all surreal. How could Mallory look at him and not see what he saw?

"There's nothing rare about me. I'm just a fallen cowboy, crippled and stripped of most of my pride from a ride that should have killed me," he informed her, curtly.

"Gentleness and strength don't often coexist in my world," she said, her regard unchanging.

The brunt of her words hit Jess hard, knocking the hell out of his self-centeredness. Every point he had made was about *his* inadequacies, *his* problem, *his* limp... *his* outward appearance.

"And when you've been through what I have, you become an excellent judge of character."

Jess didn't want to know what she had been through. Not now. Not ever. If he did, he might kill a man.

"And the way a man treats his family speaks volumes about his integrity. You love yours and would do anything to protect them, so yes, you," her mouth tilted up with an admiring smile that made a hollow place inside of him ache, "my fallen cowboy, are indeed a rarity."

Her fallen cowboy?

He wasn't sure how he felt about the possessiveness in that comment.

He hated that Mallory had seen so easily past his shallow self-observances and into the only place in his heart he hadn't fenced off. To the only piece of him that hadn't been damaged by that goddamn fall.

He loved his family without measure or fear. And that's what made him a rarity among men? In Mallory's world, it did. He felt undeserving of such acclaim because in his world that was what real men did.

"This isn't your world. It's mine, and no one will ever hurt you here, in my world." He touched a finger under her chin, keeping her head tilted up as he spoke. "But I need to know about your world."

"My world isn't pretty like yours. It's a dark place."

"Tell me about that darkness. Tell me who hurt you."

Like smoke blown away by the wind, the trust in her eyes vanished, and she was the woman she had been in the waiting room. Cold and shielded.

She pulled her hand free from his and moved away. "This darkness isn't something you can explain. It's not a shade or a color. It's something that stains your soul and something you can never outrun."

Mallory's transformation was disturbing, but something Jess assumed was a necessity for surviving in her world.

"We were in the nosebleed section of the stands the night you fell," she explained, holding tight to a dispassionate mien. "Rex won tickets to the finals in a poker game."

As an eager participant of numerous bar brawls, Jess recognized a defensive maneuver when he saw one, and he knew that bringing up the fall was Mallory's way of blocking the oncoming blow of his questions about who had hurt her and the darkness.

It was a weak defense but nonetheless effective. "Lucky you."

"Hardly." Her laugh was stony and impersonal, and so unlike the woman she had been just a few minutes ago. "Rex lost a lot of money on you. He was pissed for days." She followed him across the foyer and down the hall to the master bedroom. "Is that why you have the limp?"

Pride was an emotion, it wasn't a palpable, living organ inside the body. But Jess envisaged that if it were, it would be housed somewhere between his heart and lungs because right now, his chest felt like a thousand-pound bovine was charging over it. "Nice of you to notice."

"Well, it's kind of hard not to, but you make it work. It adds to your sexy swagger."

He yanked his t-shirt over his head and flung it into the corner of the room. Then he sat on the bed and started tugging off his boots. "There isn't a damn thing sexy about having steel pins in your leg, and you were there, so you know what happened."

"But I don't. After you went sailing into the air, Rex grabbed me by the arm and practically dragged me from the nosebleed section because he knew he'd lost the bet." She leaned against the door jam, watching him undress. "Like I said, he was pissed."

Jess let out a heavy sigh and propped his palms on his knees. "I didn't just get bucked off. I got bucked off and stomped a couple of times by a horse appropriately named Dirteater."

"I — I'm sorry," she stumbled, a flicker of remorse shooting across her face. "That must have been horrible for you."

"It was. But life goes on, and I make the best of this damn thing people call a leg." He stood and began unbuckling his belt. "Now, I'm going to get undressed and take a shower. If you'd like to stay and play twenty questions, that's fine by me. But I will insist that you also be naked. Plus, I'll be asking questions too, and though you may be fine with the naked part, I don't think you're too comfortable with answering my questions. So," he unzipped his jeans and raised an eyebrow, "are we playing or not?"

~

THE TANTALIZING GLIMPSE OF JESS'S BLUE BRIEFS AND THE outline of the slightly jutting mystery that was all male brought back that delicious ache between Mallory's thighs.

Her artistic imagination sprang to life with vivid images of his naked body under the shower spray. She could see the glossy sheen of water hitting the hard planes of his tanned shoulders, roll down the furrow of his spine, and curve along with the firm muscles of his bottom.

Or maybe it would take a more enthralling route over the vast expanse of his pecs, channeling downward through the scattering of golden hair, over the hard v-shaped muscles of his stomach, dipping into his navel and beyond…

Yes. She wanted to stay and play.

What woman wouldn't?

But he was right. She didn't want to answer his question about her world because a man like Jess – a man born and raised in a loving family with devoted parents and security – wouldn't be able to comprehend the darkness in hers.

Mallory wasn't comfortable with the being naked part either, but that would be her little secret.

She cleared her throat. "I'll be in the kitchen raiding your fridge."

"That's what I thought," he said, slipping his belt from the loops.

She turned on her heel and headed for the kitchen then stopped and backtracked a couple of steps to yell, "Which way is the kitchen?"

"Straight ahead and to the right." There was a dullness to his voice now that hadn't been there before.

There were times when Mallory's cold disposition served her well. It could shut off switches, throw up shields, and make her appear less vulnerable. But those self-taught defense tactics hadn't been necessary with Jess. Because this man who had deemed himself a fallen cowboy had been genuinely concerned about her well-being.

She shouldn't have brought up the fall or his limp. But she had panicked when he had started asking questions about the part of her life that was too painful to share with anyone but Aiden.

She would be more sensitive next time. She wouldn't throw up shields or dodge those hard-to-answer questions about the bruises.

Next time.

Mallory groaned.

There would be a next time because Jess wouldn't give up until he knew who was responsible for the bruises.

She didn't want to think about the next time or that she had just turned down an open invitation to shower with a gorgeous cowboy. She needed consolation food and lots of it. She hadn't eaten since this morning, and her stomach was about to riot.

The front of Jess's home was one capacious room that included the den and living room complete with a fireplace built from scree rock and a tribal rug under what resembled a Ralph Lauren sofa and love seat.

Everything was neat, clean and masculine.

He'd been engaged, but his fiancée hadn't been around to add a woman's touch to the decorating. Mallory was curious about the woman and about why the engagement had ended. Maybe she would be around long enough to ask him.

She kept straight down the long hallway, stopping briefly to admire the art he had along the wall. One painting was by River Scott, a highly sought after and well-known contemporary artist, and the other one was by

Jordan Powers, a nineteenth-century realism artist. They were both originals worth thousands of dollars.

She whistled softly. "Jess does have deep pockets."

A few feet past the paintings, she made a right. Then stopped, peering up to the rugged, centuries-old hand-hued wood beams that lined the vaulted ceiling of the rustic kitchen. "Whoa."

There was a long island in the center with a granite top bar that could comfortably seat eight. It was fitted with modern stainless-steel appliances, and the centerpiece was a large copper hood seated above an enormous gas range. "Who's he feeding, Paul Bunyan?"

She hurried across the stone floor and opened the double-doored refrigerator. "Oh, God," she whined when she saw the greens and protein shakes. "He's a health nut."

When she couldn't find anything worth eating, she closed the doors and started rummaging through the cabinets. "Ah-ha!" she said when she saw a jar of peanut butter on the second shelf.

She unscrewed the lid and with her finger, shoveled up a dollop as Jess ambled in. He was like watching Poseidon, the god of the sea and horses, ascend from the water.

He was freshly showered, cleanly shaven, and dressed in a pair of blue jeans with his feet and chest bare. His damp, sun-streaked hair dropped tiny beads of water onto his shoulders.

"Did you find something you like?"

CHAPTER 7

MALLORY CHOKED BACK A LAUGH. OH, YES, SHE undoubtedly had found something she liked. She licked the peanut butter from her finger and tried swallowing. "This will have to do."

"Why will it have to do?" Jess opened the fridge. "There's plenty of food here and in the pantry."

She licked her finger again and joined him in front of the fridge. "That so-called food is an abomination to my taste buds." She pulled out the vegetable drawer and held up a bag of Brussels sprouts. "This is why you live in my sister's kitchen, isn't it? Who the hell eats these things?"

He frowned. "I do. They're loaded in nutrients and high in fiber."

"So is hay, but you won't catch me munching on it either. I bet you get Brussels farts."

He tried so hard not to show his amusement, but the sparkle in his eyes gave him away. He snatched the bag from Mallory and tossed it back in the drawer. "You don't like Brussels sprouts?"

"No," she said, digging her finger back into the jar only to have him snatch it from her.

"Hey!"

"Don't they have spoons where you come from?"

She licked her finger. "Hunger caused me to improvise."

He grabbed a spoon from the drawer next to her, stuck it into the jar, and handed it back to her. "Have you ever tried Brussels sprouts?"

She gagged. "God, no."

His mouth curved towards teasing. "Then how do you know you don't like them?"

Mallory had never met a man who matched her in smartassery or wit, but Jess could shoot back word retaliations with lightning speed.

"Don't you dare compare kinky sex with those little alien heads." She screwed the lid on the jar and set it back on the shelf. "Now, this has been loads of fun, but I need to get back to my bike."

"It's safe at the ranch, and I've been thinking. Since we're here, you could just spend the night. There are four bedrooms upstairs. Take your pick."

"Thanks, but no thanks." She took a step back, ready to make her way towards the foyer. "But you should definitely stay."

He held up the key to the crossover. "It's a long walk back to the ranch, and it'll be dark soon."

Mallory hated being at the mercy of anyone, especially when they were so damn smug about it. She thought for a moment, torn between delivering that punch to his solar plexus and her new commitment to sensitivity. "I can't stay here."

"Why not?" he asked, crossing his arms over his chest.

He made her feel caged and cornered in a way she

hadn't been prepared for. He had promised her safety in his world. It was a vow no man could keep. She knew that. But there was something about Jess that put her cautious mind at ease and almost made her believe she *was* safe.

"Can we just call a truce? Take me back to the ranch. I won't ask you about the fall, and you don't ask me about my bruises."

"My fall is over and done with." He pointed to her wrist. "Whoever did that is still a threat to you, to Eleanor, Sophie, and the baby…"

"Sophie is with your parents, and Eleanor and the baby are at the hospital. Everyone is safe, and he wasn't far behind me, so this should be over by the time they're home."

"Who isn't far behind you?"

Couldn't Jess see that the ugly, horrible truth about her world was like the pins in his leg? A deep scar that made her weak and caused her pain.

No, he couldn't. Jess's world was too perfect and refined for all of that. But he wasn't taking her anywhere until she answered him. "If I tell you, do you promise to drive me back to the ranch?"

He scratched his jaw, deciding if he should agree. Finally, he nodded. "I promise."

Why she trusted him to keep his promise was beyond her, but she knew he would. "My father made the bruises."

A flash of stone-cold fury cut across his face.

"Can we go now?"

He took the few steps separating them and lifted her hand, gently brushing his fingers over her wrist. "Why did Rex do this to you?"

Eleanor had grown up in Santa Camino so it only made sense that Jess and others would know who Rex was.

It was sad that the man's deplorability had reached all the way to Texas.

She gathered up what was left of her dignity and admitted to herself that sometimes brutal honesty was all there was. "I learned a long time ago that a man doesn't have to have a reason to hurt a woman."

Jess rolled his bottom jaw, settling his lips into that sensual moue Mallory found so attractive. "Why is he coming for you?"

"Because I have something he wants."

The faint lines around his eyes creased. "And you're not going to tell me what that something is, are you?"

"I can't. Not yet."

"That something is on your bike?"

"Yes, that's why we need to go now."

A deep breath expanded his chest, but her honesty seemed to appease him for the time being. "I'll take you back to the ranch, but you don't go anywhere without me. Understand."

"Yeah. Yeah. I got it. Let's go, Warden."

AFTER DRESSING, JESS GRABBED THE BAG HE'D HAD PACKED for his weekend with Brandi, dug into his dresser for a faded pair of pajama bottoms he hadn't worn in years, and snagged his laptop from his office desk as he went out the door.

He usually didn't wear clothes to bed, but there was only one spare bedroom at Redemption, so he would be crashing on the couch.

Mallory was waiting in the crossover for him when he opened the door and climbed in. There wasn't a smile lurking on her lips or fun in her eyes. She was solemn, distant, and lost in a world of her own. He knew admitting Rex had made the bruises had taken a piece of her.

He watched her rub her wrist. "Does it hurt?"

"No," she said, tugging her sleeve lower. "Not anymore. It mostly itches. You know how bruises are."

Jess knew. He'd had plenty of them, but none like the one around her wrist.

His parents had always been his heroes and were a perfect team of commitment and devotion. They loved their children and weren't afraid to show it now that he and his siblings were adults.

Correction and discipline had been handled by both of his parents but were never done with violence.

They, along with his grandparents, had supported his need to compete from the first time he had crawled on the back of a horse. His family had encouraged him to pursue his dream of winning a rodeo championship even when the odds were against him. They had been with him through it all. The ups, the downs, the wins, and the loses. They had never let him down or given up on him.

His bruises had come from his own stupid mistakes of riding recklessly, falling face first into the dirt, and being bucked off.

Other ones, deeper ones, had come from trusting the wrong woman, not listening to his gut, and letting himself fall in love. He wasn't sure Mallory had those bruises. But she had referred to Aiden as being in the past, so maybe she did.

"El's one hell of a cook, but I'm not sure what's in the crockpot. We can stop and get you something at one of the fast food places in town, or I can pick up a pizza. They don't deliver out to the ranch."

"No, but thanks for offering." She smiled briefly at his

effort and raised her thumb to her lips to chew her nail again.

"Don't worry about Rex," he said, reaching over to pull her hand down. "I'll be there to protect you."

"I don't need protecting." This time the smile reached her eyes. "But I am glad you're spending the night with me."

That should have bumped up his self-esteem because, since the fall, he hadn't felt useful for more than balancing a budget and creating reports. Instead, her words sparked unbidden images of them engaged in slow, satisfying sex.

Jess moved his hand back to the wheel. "Happy to help."

"Don't lie. You and I both know you wouldn't be here if Eleanor hadn't asked you to be my bodyguard."

He made the turn into Redemptions drive. "Okay, so maybe I'm doing this as a favor to El, but that doesn't mean I'm not enjoying myself."

She arched an eyebrow and gave him a smirk. "You'd be enjoying yourself a lot more if you were with Brandi."

"Maybe," he admitted, shifting from one hip to the other as he guided the crossover up the road. "Maybe not. Brandi is an old friend and the head of a rodeo staging company. I was headed to San Antonio to talk about a business prospect."

She leaned an elbow on the console and propped her chin in her palm. "Like a job prospect?"

"No, I have a job."

"Doing what?"

He parked the crossover under the metal garage. "I'm the executive director for our rescue, the Promise Point Horse Rescue Ranch."

Her eyes widened, and she gave his shoulder a little shove. "No way! Cool Blue is some swanky executive."

"Hardly," He chuckled. "But you can't judge a book by its cover nor a cowboy by his hat."

Mallory's smile softened. "I guess not. By the way," she said, giving the brim of his dirty hat a little flick with her finger. "I have plenty of friends, and none of them talk cheesy porno to me."

She was out the door and to her bike before Jess made it out to his feet. She crouched beside a side compartment and came up with a folded piece of paper. She shoved it into her back pocket and unfastened the saddle back from the gas tank.

Walking stiffly, he reached out to take the bag. "I can get that for you."

She did a split-second glance towards his leg and smiled. "I got it."

His pride roared to the surface. "Just because my leg is useless doesn't mean I am."

"It doesn't look useless to me, and I'm used to packing my own weight," she said, moving around him and up the sidewalk.

He spun around, took a step, and gripped his leg with both hands as the muscle knotted up again.

Glancing over her shoulder at him, Mallory stopped. "Are you okay?"

"Yes," he gritted out.

She let the bag ease to the ground and hurried back to where he was. "Are you sure?"

He massaged the muscles, trying to ease the cramp and didn't answer.

"Put your arm around my shoulders, and I'll help you."

"I don't need your help. Just go in the house and leave me alone."

She rolled her eyes skyward. "That's not happening.

We're a team. Remember? I don't go anywhere without you."

He narrowed his eyes. "You're really testing my patience."

She crossed her arms over her chest and shifted her weight to one leg. "Like you're the first man to ever say that."

Despite his irritation and the pain in his thigh, Jess found himself grinning. "Get in the damn house."

"Not without you, Warden."

He stood, doggedly anchored in place.

She sighed and set her eyes towards the open fields in an audacious display of boredom.

They were at a standoff and odds of his good leg outlasting Mallory's stubbornness were slim to none. They could be out here all goddamn night.

The low rumble of distant thunder sounded off to the south, sparking a tiny shaft of lightning in the distant sky.

She watched the horizon. "A storm is coming."

Jess didn't look at the sky. His eyes were on the tempest standing no more than three feet in front of him with unshakable resolve.

He moved his leg, working out what was left of the cramp, ready to follow her up the walk when she gave in.

But Mallory wasn't going anywhere. "Who called it quits? You or your fiancée?"

Old mistakes quaked to life, jolting him upright. "I did."

"Why?"

In his younger days, Jess had satisfied his cravings for sex with women who he never wanted to know past the bedroom until he had met Hallie.

She had been a dangerous kind of trouble that had almost cost him his leg and his life. He had been too blindsided by love and lust to see the real her until it was too late.

His mind travelled back to the night he'd fallen. One hand was in his pocket with his fingers wrapped around the ring box. The other was on the doorknob of their hotel room.

But that's where he made the memories of what had happened next stop. Not that it hurt him anymore. It didn't. But everything after that did — physically and emotionally.

"Because when I put an engagement ring on a woman's finger, I expect to be the only man in her bed."

"Oh." Her brows lifted briefly before she looked down at the ground. "I see."

"Everyone but me did." He had willfully put blinders on and let Hallie lead him almost to the altar.

She unlocked her arms and let them fall to her sides. "She really hurt you."

Jess didn't flinch. His relationship with Hallie had broken more than his heart and his pride and people close to him knew it. He saw no reason to lie about it. "She did. But that was a long time ago."

Her eyes moved over his face as though she were reading an intriguing novel. "I've heard some broken hearts never heal."

His smile was condescending. "This one did. Falling in love was a mistake I swore I would never repeat."

"I don't think we have a choice about who we fall in love with. I think it just happens and being bitter about love won't stop it."

"I passed bitter years ago." He hobbled closer, snatched the bag from her hand and draped an arm over her shoulders. "Ready?"

She shook her head. "Men are so prideful."

He wanted to say that this wasn't about his pride. But it was. It was always about the mistakes he had made, the fall he had taken…

"What's in that bag is very dear to me, so I wanted to carry it. It had nothing to do with your capabilities as a man. I don't think any less of you because you have pins in your leg or walk with a limp. Like I said before, I think it adds to your —"

"Sexy swagger," he finished her sentence, glancing down at the bag. Maybe he'd had it wrong. Maybe what she had in her pocket wasn't important at all. "Is Rex after what's here?"

"No." Her eyes dropped to her thumbnail and Jess saw her swallow. "He never cared about what's in the bag."

The sorrow in her voice and the timid way she was trying to smile tore a hole through Jess, and suddenly it wasn't about him or his damn pride. It was about this incredibly strong woman, offering to help him — a grown ass man — while trying hard to keep her wounds hidden.

He handed it back to her. "I'm sorry."

She pushed it back to him without rebuke. "No, you carry it. I trust you."

A poignant thought came to Jess's mind as he stood there holding on to her, one he would have rather dismissed, but couldn't. She was trusting him with something precious, something she cherished and loved. Something he might damage if he fell.

"Now," she said, positioning one hand at the base of his back and the other just below his sternum. "Move that big ol' ego of yours out of the way and let me help you into the house."

Her touch burned his skin through the thin layer of his t-shirt. The firmness of her breast grazed his ribs and rousted his dick into a ten-hut position.

She smelled of leather and sandalwood. An unusual combination for a woman and hardly a scent he would have called feminine. But it was.

He hadn't expected that she would ever be this close to him, that he would earn her trust so quickly, or that he would have to resist the urge to kiss her.

Jess was amazed, humbled, and shaken.

He had turned off the part of himself that felt anything beyond desire and physical pleasure. Life was less complicated and safer that way. But Mallory made the dormant parts of him come alive.

He'd wanted to taste those lips from the moment he laid eyes on her. Lifting his hand to cup her cheek, he edged her lower lip with his thumb.

She drew in a sharp breath as if his touch had burned her, but she didn't retreat. Instead, she shifted her gaze to his lips and raised her head.

CHAPTER 8

MALLORY HADN'T ALLOWED A MAN THIS CLOSE TO HER IN A long, long time. Pressed against the hard planes of Jess's body, she had never felt more womanly, safer, or more like this was where she belonged.

The fact that she didn't want to bunch up her fists and fight for her life because she was this close to a man was tear-jerking progress towards her being a normal woman.

With his eyes focused on her mouth, he moved his hand to the base of her head, guiding her closer, feeding the current of longing that made her body ache.

The heat of his breath floated across her lips as his head moved lower and lower. But just before his lips touched hers, something jolted him out of the trance, something from within. A silent alarm triggered by whatever thought had suddenly sprung to his mind.

His head came up, he blinked and focused as the tendons of his neck flexed with a hard swallow. He wrapped his fingers around her hand and removed it from his chest. "You're too trusting, Beautiful."

Shaken by the desire of their near kiss and his abrupt

change, Mallory couldn't summon a response.

Why was there such a battle raging in his eyes? Why wouldn't he kiss her? What harm could come from one kiss?

Still holding the bag, Jess gave her a gentle push back, set his hands on his hips, and bent his head.

She tried breathing through the ache that had settled into her lower body and fought the disappointment of their missed kissed.

After several minutes of silence, he held the bag up. "Is this the only one you have?"

"No," she said, her voice weak and thin. "I have more, but —"

"There's no need to make two trips," he said, rubbing the center of his chest.

Too shaken and disappointed to argue, she turned and ran back to her bike.

Jess continued up the walk, climbed the steps, and punched in the security code on the alarm before he opened the front door. Mallory followed, unable to understand why he had ended the kiss.

"Oh my God," she moaned as the enticing aroma of beef and onions hit her nose. "Supper smells delicious."

"Yeah," he agreed absently as he continued to rub his chest. Whatever was troubling him, seemed to correlate with the spot just over his heart.

"Are you sure you're okay?"

"What?" His eyes snapped to attention, and his brow wrinkled with a frown. "Yeah," he said, turning around to shut the door. "I guess you'd like to grab a shower before we eat."

"That would be nice. Road grime is the worst."

She followed him across the living room. There was a plush couch, and two matching chairs with comfy pillows and cozy afghans tossed onto the back. A toy box over-flowed with dolls and dress-up clothes near the fireplace and coloring books stood stacked under the coffee table. The room had a happily unorganized chaos vibe to it.

He opened the door to the guest bedroom. "They added this section a few months ago."

The bedroom was palatial and open and almost as big as Mallory's apartment over Aiden and Cassie's garage. The wood headboard, made from mismatched planks, had been aged with a tinges of blue-green paint, adding a feminine touch to the bucolic furniture. Four solid teal-colored pillows accented the white bed skirt and duvet, and the cowhide rug near the center of the room gave the room a western touch.

ABOVE THE BED WAS A HAND-PAINTED SIGN THAT READ, Wild Heart. The room was calm and inviting. "It's lovely."

Laying her bag on the bed, he pointed to the bath-room. "There's towels and washcloths on the rack. I'm not sure about soap and shampoo…"

"I have my own,' she said, wishing he would at least smile at her. "But thanks anyway."

"No problem," he said, frowning slightly. "I−ah…I'll be in the kitchen when you're ready to eat."

After he closed the door behind him, Mallory listened to the distinct shuffle of his boots on the hardwood floor as he crossed the living room. The sound tapered off, and there was only the faint echo of his movements. She rubbed her arms, feeling the loneliness of recent months settle into her soul.

She laid her bags on the bed and moved to the window overlooking the front of the house, then drew back the curtain.

The evening sun sat low over the hills and painted the sky a dusty orange. Everything about the ranch was calming and picturesque but Mallory was uneasy.

She wasn't afraid of being along tonight or any other night. But maybe with Jess in the house, she would be able to get some sleep.

She yanked her boots off and left a trail of clothes to the bathroom. After washing the dust of the day away, she squeezed out the last of the travel shampoo to wash her hair. Then she dried off and unpacked the clothes she had crammed into her bag before leaving California.

Three pairs of panties, two bras, two pairs of socks, two pairs of jeans, four t-shirts, a baggy pair of shorts, and her favorite running shoes.

She chose the shorts and an old faded 49rs t-shirt Aiden had given her and shoved the rest back into the bag. Then she towel-dried her hair and let her nose lead her to the kitchen. The dollop of peanut butter she had was doing nothing to fill the giant hole in her stomach. Starch covered in a pound of cheese and pepperoni sounded like heaven. But she had been too anxious about getting back to her bike.

Mallory rubbed her palms together as she entered the kitchen. "So, what are we eating?"

"Beef bourguignon," Jess answered, scooping out a portion into an earth-colored bowl.

"I have no idea what that is, but it sounds yummy."

"It's fancy beef stew," he explained glancing down at her shirt.

"What?"

He filled another bowl. "Is your boyfriend a 49ers fan?"

"Boyfriend?" The word felt weird as it rolled off her tongue. Foreign and well, laughable, because women like her didn't have boyfriends. They had cumbersome dates that ended with embarrassment and disappointment.

Mallory glanced down at her t-shirt, realizing Jess thought the oversized garment belonged to that nonexistent boyfriend. "Oh. No." She laughed and scooted a chair out before she sat down. "How about you?"

"I'm a Texan." He handed her a bowl, took out his phone, and sat across from her. "What'd you think?"

"I think men take their sports too seriously. I'm sorry if my t-shirt offends you," she said jokingly.

Jess kept his eyes glued to the phone and didn't crack a smile.

From the tone of the texts he and Brandi had exchanged, there wasn't anything more profound than sex happening between them. There wasn't the mention of love or even an indication of affection. Their relationship was a quick fix that served their needs. But that didn't make sitting across the table from Jess while he had phone sex with another woman any easier.

She grabbed her spoon and was about to dig into her fancy beet stew when a sharp yelp rang out.

Pressing his lips into a thin line, Jess rose from the table and walked to the back door. She heard the door open and a tiny bark. "Hush," he scolded softly.

The beagle pup bounced through the laundry room and ran straight for Mallory.

"A puppy!" Laughing, she crouched down to give it a rub behind the ears. "It's adorable. What's its name?"

"Pocket Change," he answered, scrubbing a hand over his face before he sat back down.

The pup wagged his tail and hunkered down on both front feet, ready for a game of chase.

"Don't you dare," he warned.

She picked the pup up and nestled him in her arms. "Don't scold him. He's just a baby."

"He's a nuisance who will probably whine all night," he said. "He's lost without Sophie."

As his attention settled back on his phone, the tip of something mean and vengeful embedded itself deep inside Mallory's chest. Something as alien as the word boyfriend.

"Come on little guy, you can share my bed." She held up the pups' paw and gave Jess a wave. "Say, night, night."

"I thought you were hungry."

"I am. But I'd rather not be present for more of your cheesy porno scripts." Taking her bowl, she started to stand. "So I'm taking my fancy beef stew to my room."

"Sit down," his soft command added to her annoyance.

"No," she said tediously. "Your rudeness is giving me indigestion."

Jess looked up in surprise. "How am I rude? I haven't opened my mouth except to eat."

"Exactly. What happened to the nice, talkative man who drove me over here?" That man had vanished with their missed kiss and she didn't know why. "Did he stump his pinky toe or break a nail while I was in the shower?"

He gave her a tiresome frown. "Maybe I'm a man who likes eating his supper in silence."

There were so many unpleasant thoughts that could occupy silence. It made her uneasy and anxious. It opened avenues to her past and prompted memories she kept hidden back to the surface.

She made a disagreeable face. "I hate silence."

Jess shoved the spoon into his mouth and chewed. "I noticed."

"It makes me uncomfortable, and so does your moodiness."

"You don't look uncomfortable."

"Well, I am," she said, digging the spoon into her stew. "Maybe we both should have chosen comfort over manners and come to the table naked." She winced, instantly regretting her words.

His eyes locked with hers. The cool blue color Mallory fancied so much had darkened, giving them the hue of a troubled sky. The heaviness of his lids and the slow glide of his tongue over his lower lip gave him a striking resemblance to a hungry wolf.

The predatory way his eyes raked over her made Mallory think she might be his next meal. "If you came to the table naked, the last thing we'd be doing is talking."

Jess's words reverberated through her, bringing a flush to her face and those naughty images of him naked back to her mind. Mallory wanted to crawl under the table and hide for making that bawdy remark.

A woman didn't cavort around naked in front of this cowboy unless she was serious about having sex.

Mallory was dead serious about sex.

She wanted sex, needed sex, in the worst possible way, but her intimacy issues weren't going to disappear overnight. And even if they did, Jess seemed the least likely candidate for soothing her ache. "That didn't come out right. What I meant to say was…"

What was she saying? That she wanted to see him naked?

Tanned muscle. Smooth skin. Rippling six-pack. Firm ass – *Stop*, she, commanded her brain. *Stop thinking about the man sitting in front of you without a stitch of clothing on.*

Mallory propped her elbow on the table and dug a finger into her temple. The man was making her crazy. "I just don't see why polite dinner conversation is so hard for you."

"It's not." He laid his phone face-down on the table. "I

wasn't trying to be rude or moody as you said. Pick a topic, and we'll talk."

Forced conversation. Great. "No, it's fine."

"I said we could talk," he said, patiently. "So why are you angry?"

She picked at a potato. "I'm not." Resentful that he would rather have phone sex with Brandi instead of talk with her? Yes. Annoyed that he was sitting there looking all in control and confident while she was making puerile remarks about them being naked? Hell, yes, but she wasn't angry.

"I don't want to argue," she said, her stubbornness waning. "So, *it's fine* means it's fine if we sit here in silence."

Jess gave her an unruffled shrug and went back to eating his stew.

But as the silence settled between them, Mallory became more uncomfortable and restless. She started counting the faint clicks of the old clock in the living room.

One, two, three…She tapped her finger against the table. Seven, eight, nine…

Her foot joined in. Thirteen, fourteen, fifteen… "Why do you rescue horses?"

She heard the clank of his spoon hitting against his bowl, and an exhale of impatience escape his mouth. "I don't."

"But you said —"

"McCrea and Brody do the rescues. I handle the business side of things."

That surprised her. "Why?"

"Why what?"

"Why don't you rescue them?"

"I just don't," he said, simply.

Knowing she shouldn't push too hard in the wrong direction given his surly mood, Mallory decided a less intrusive way to pry. "I've always wanted to learn how to ride. Maybe you can teach me, and we can ride together."

Jess pushed his chair back, stood and shoved his phone into his pocket. "I haven't been on a horse since the fall, so I don't see us taking that ride, Beautiful."

He walked to the sink to wash his plate and spoon and then disappeared out the front door.

After setting Pocket Change on the floor, she tossed her uneaten portion of stew into the garbage and cleaned her dishes. The pup trotted along behind her and she was happy that at least she'd have the dog for company. As she started across the living room, she heard Jess's voice. Through the screen door, she saw him sitting on the first step. He rested an elbow on his knee and propped his chin on a fist.

"Something else has come up, Brandi." His voice was low, but she could hear every word. "No, I won't be able to make it this weekend."

The pup's guileless eyes stared up at her. With a tilt to his head, he whined. Mallory held a finger to her lips and tried quietening him with a, "Shhhh…"

"How about next weekend?"

Mallory held her breath.

"North Dakota, huh? No, I understand. You can't cancel that."

She felt a little guilty for the happiness that rippled through her.

"The next weekend?" he rubbed a hand over his eyes. "No, that's not good for me. We're having a fundraising for the Gates Ranch. You remember Logan and Tyler, don't you?"

Gates Ranch had been on the door of the heavy-duty truck his two cowboy accomplices had been working on this afternoon.

"Yeah, I know." His soft laugh was sexy. "I'm disappointed too."

"Oh, I bet you are," she murmured, feeling a gash of envy cut through her happiness.

"No, no," he rushed to say. "I'll call you. Yeah, soon. Okay. Bye."

Mallory had no right to feel jealous over Brandi or angry at Jess for talking to another woman with sexiness in his voice. But she was.

$\sim$

"Don't bust my balls," Mallory groaned, combing a hand through her hair. "I told you I'd call when I got here."

She had been awake all night, thinking about that kiss she and Jess had almost shared last night. It was a little past six now, and the ground, untouched by the sun's heat, soaked her bare feet as she walked from the back deck down to the swing set near the fence.

"I haven't heard from you in three days, Mallory." The growl of a flatbed diesel rolling through the back gate, drowned out Cassie's concerned voice.

"Hold on a minute. I can't hear you." Mallory stuck a finger in each ear and winced as the truck passed by her. When it was gone, she lifted the phone back to her ear. "Okay, I'm back."

"I was worried sick," Cassie continued. "Aiden would have been furious with you."

Mallory had held tight to Cassie's hand through the full military funeral, watched her receive the folded flag and nearly jumped out of her seat when the three-volley salute rang out.

She had gone to the grave with Cassie, dried Cassie's

tears, and stayed awake most nights listening for the sound of Cassie's nightmares. But Mallory hadn't been able to summon a single tear of her own.

Cassie kept her wedding dress in the closet and Aiden's engagement ring on her finger because she couldn't acknowledge that the love of her life was dead. "Aiden isn't here, Cass."

"I know," Cassie choked out. Moments passed, and Mallory couldn't say anything she hadn't already said. Cassie would have to come to terms with Aiden's death on her own. "And I can take care of myself."

She heard Cassie take a wobbly breath before she spoke. "I know you think you can."

"Cass…"

"Have you told your sister?"

"No," she sighed, sitting down in the swing. "I can't find the right time."

Was there ever a right time to tell someone their mother was dead?

"Mrs. Pallento keeps asking me when you'll be back."

"I don't think I'm coming back, Cass. Texas is turning out to be more interesting than I thought." She glanced over her shoulder to the back door, remembering how Jess had looked when she found him sleeping on the couch this morning. Shirtless, sexy, and hard. "The landscape is beautiful."

"Tell me you're joking."

Mallory had never felt desire, and she'd given up on ever experiencing passion. But last night's near kiss had made her hungry.

The mere thought of Jess's lips triggered feelings in her that caused her heart to bat around in her chest like a leaf at the mercy of a squall. "No, I'm done with California and New Mexico."

She moved her feet, twisting the swing around and around. "If things don't work out for me here, then I'll hit the road and ride until I find home."

"Ride until you find home?" Cassie seethed. "This is your home."

"No, it's your home." The charming two-bedroom beach house Cassie had inherited from her grandparents had been a refreshing change from the dingy mobile homes Mallory had been raised in.

The three of them had been happy there. But after Aiden died, the house became a reminder of all she had lost. Everything from the sound of the waves to the color of the sunset had changed.

She wanted a fresh start and a life of her own. She wanted to reconnect with her sister, spend time with her niece and nephew, and make new memories. She needed to feel alive again, not go back to the macabre memories she'd left behind.

Mallory had accepted that she would probably spend the rest of her life without male companionship. But Jess calmed her chaotic mind, brought peace to her soul, and made her think twice about the certainty of her insolated life.

She wanted more of that peace, more of that passion, and more of the man.

Cassie sniffed. "I wish Aiden had never taught you how to ride that damn bike."

The Chieftain had been the one thing the lovebirds hadn't agreed on. "Don't worry about me, Cass. I have plenty of people looking out for me here."

"But I do worry —"

"I'll call you later," Mallory rushed to say and hung up.

She laid the phone in her lap and held her feet up. The chain unwound, spinning her around and around. She closed her eyes and leaned back, letting her cares drift away, the way she had when she was a little girl.

Her childhood visits to Redemption had been few. But sunny, summer days like this one were implanted in Mallory's memories. They had been like colorful ribbons of joy and peace in her bleak and unhappy childhood. When things were bad, she could pull them out and think about how beautiful life could be.

But that escapism hadn't always worked.

She placed her feet on the ground, halting the swing, and opened her eyes to the one night that had changed her life forever. The night the darkness in her mind had been so overpowering that she couldn't find a single pretty ribbon to catch hold of.

Fighting back panic and still holding tight to the chains, she gazed up at the blue sky. She thought about the man inside the house with eyes the same color. How his smile warmed her, how his voice soothed her, and how easy it was for her to trust him.

Jess was a man trying to mend from an emotionally hard time in his life. His fall from grace had left him with a lot of scars, physically, mentally, and emotionally. And he couldn't talk about them. They were all bottled up inside him.

Mallory knew how that felt. She had her own personal bottle of Will Not Share With Anyone safely hidden away.

What had happened to her when she was sixteen would always be with her. The demons of her old life would invariably taunt her with the threat of exposure. They would continue to lash out at her with filthy names and hurl sharp stones that could shatter her into a million broken pieces.

CHAPTER 9

Jess cracked one lid open, then shut it tight when the light from the living room window shot through his skull. With a groan, he lifted his head and tried again. This time, he was able to focus enough to find his wristwatch lying on the coffee table beside him.

Six-fifteen.

He let his head fall back to the pillow and covered his eyes with his arm, dreading the day ahead. He had watched television until midnight and then rummaged through Eleanor's craft cabinet until he found wood glue. Then he had worked until after two o'clock fixing the table he had broken on the way out the door yesterday.

It sat precariously next to the front door, ready and waiting to fall when someone breathed on it.

He sat up, placing his feet on the bare wood floor, and fought the grogginess in his head. Rubbing his eyes with the heel of his hands, he let out a low growlish yawn.

He couldn't operate on four hours of sleep without coffee. Eleanor had given up everything with caffeine in it when she found out she was pregnant, and his morning ritual of grabbing a coffee at Pixies before work would be sidetracked by his current babysitting job.

He glanced down at the afghan draped across his crotch and then to Mallory's open bedroom door. His pajama bottoms were a thin, gray material and comfortable but did little to conceal his morning wood.

Maybe he had shocked Beautiful. A part of him hoped he had. Mallory had knocked him out of having sex and his morning coffee. All the more reason not to like the woman. But he did like her – a lot and not just the arresting parts of her anatomy.

He liked her smile, her determination, her stubbornness, toughness and her unpredictability.

Mallory wasn't like any of the other women he'd dated. She didn't flaunt her body by wearing skimpy halter tops and shorts that revealed her true hair color. Admiring her womanly form through modest t-shirts and jeans that could be – in his opinion – a size smaller, took a little imagination.

She wasn't the leather-clad vixen he'd seen straddling that bike. She was sweet and at times, even shy.

When she had bounced into the kitchen last night — looking breathless and beautiful, smiling and flirting with him — wearing a t-shirt he knew belonged to another man, he had been so damn irritated.

At her for lying to him about that boyfriend and at himself for caring. And that was the root of his problem. His feelings for this woman were growing beyond gentlemanly concern and family duty.

He was starting to care for Mallory in a way that brought up his defenses and intensified the mistakes he had made.

Jess moved his eyes to the twisted sheets and comforter that lay in a giant heap on top of her empty bed. For a second, he let himself entertain the thought of waking up with Mallory in his arms, of her hair cascading over the pillow, of her legs wrapped around his hips, the softness of her warm, wet body as he thrust deep into her...

He groaned and buried his head in his hands.

"You're up."

Mallory's perky voice brought his head around and made his dick do a full, click heels salute.

He silently cursed it for being so happy to see her but didn't bother trying to hide its enthusiasm when he stood.

Her eyes locked on his crotch and grew wide as a splash of pink colored her cheeks.

"Damn, woman." He laughed with the curse, surprised and pleased by her reaction. "Are you blushing?"

Blinking several times, she pulled her eyes away from his crotch and focused on a potted plant near the door. "Is that a crime?"

"No. I just assumed you'd seen a hard-on before and wouldn't be all shocked and bothered by mine."

"I am well aware of how the male body words," she said evenly.

"Then I don't need this," he said, tossing the afghan to her before he turned towards the stairs.

She caught it and took to the couch knee first, crossing her arms over the back to watch him. "So, what's on the agenda for today, Warden?"

He stopped at the bottom step. "I'm going to go upstairs, lock myself in a bedroom, and do some stretches to get my leg working before I shower."

She slid from the couch and draped the afghan over the back. Yawning wide, she crossed her arms behind her head and did a long, lengthy stretch that gave him a glimpse of her gorgeous midsection. The stretch ended with a flip of her tousled hair and a sleepy smile. "And then?"

"I'm going to shower and go to work," he said in a voice that made him feel old and cranky.

"Are you taking me with you?" she asked, excited as a kid at Christmas.

"Yeah, it's Bring Your Prisoner to Work Day," he said, walking towards the stairs. "We have cupcakes too."

She clapped her hands and played along. "I love cupcakes."

"I knew you would," he answered, his pleasant tone overly done.

She followed him to the first step. "When can I see the apartment?"

At the time, suggesting Mallory move into the apartment over the stables had seemed only practical. But now Jess wondered if the self-preservation part of him had been thinking ahead. He never went to the stables, and with Mallory living there, he could carry on with his life, live in Eleanor's kitchen, and go to work in that office he loved so much. "Have your bags packed and be ready to walk out the door in thirty minutes."

Twenty-five minutes later, he watched her throw a leg over her bike and helmet up. By eight o'clock, she was following him through the Rescue gate.

Jess pulled into the empty space next to Kara's silver Fiat. The little car made his crew cab look like a monster truck. But it was the perfect vehicle for the studious teen they had hired last year as a part-time receptionist.

Mallory parked her bike next to his truck and dismounted. She was dressed in a pair of light-colored blue jeans that did nothing to hide her curves and a light V-neck shirt with Monterey Bay written across the front.

She smiled with the same anticipation he had seen earlier. "It's so big and beautiful."

Jess had been here for all the stages of the Rescue's growth and spent most of his days locked inside his office, staring at a computer screen. The new had worn off a long time ago. "I can remember when it was nothing but limestone and trees."

"How many horses do you have here?"

"Seventy-six in all. Seventy-four are up for adoption."

"I'd love a tour," she said, walking behind him up the sidewalk to the main office.

"Sure," he answered, sorting through his key ring for the one that unlocked his office door. A tour would get her out of his hair for a couple of hours. "I'll see what I can do."

He held the entry door open for Mallory and followed her inside.

"Morning, boss." Kara said without looking up from the computer screen.

"This is Kara," Jess said. "Our ever attentive and overly enthusiastic receptionist."

Kara looked up without cracking a smile. "Someone didn't have their latte this morning."

"No, someone didn't," he sighed, shooting Mallory a scowl.

"If it helps, there's a fresh pot of java in the kitchen," Kara returned.

"It does. Remind me to bump up your Christmas bonus this year."

"I will," she said and offered Mallory her hand. "I'm Kara, the boss's underpaid, overworked, and trusty administrative sidekick."

Mallory chuckled and shook her hand. "I'm Eleanor's sister, Mallory."

Kara's smile turned genuine. "Happy to meet you."

"Likewise."

"Oh." Kara reached under her desk and brought up the carburetor he had been waiting for. Wiping grease residue from her hand, she placed it in front of him. "Tom Norton dropped this off on his way to work."

Mallory moved closer to get a better look at the part. "Why do you need a bike carburetor?"

Not only did Mallory ride one of the sexiest bikes on the market, but she also knew what a carburetor was.

Holy hell. He was going to need another cold shower.

Kara started stacking papers into neat piles. "He has a whole garage —"

"Kara," Jess cut in. Mallory had intruded into his past and was now making herself at home in his presence. He didn't want her anywhere near the one place he felt at peace. "Mallory is going to be staying in the apartment over the stables while she's in town. Since you're in charge of the Rescue tours and new volunteer orientation, I thought you could give her a tour of the facilities and then help her get settled in."

"I thought you'd be giving me the tour." Mallory's face reflected her disappointment.

Taking the carburetor from the desk, he walked across the small lobby to his office and shoved the key into the lock. He gave the knob a twist. "I'm swamped with reports."

"Sorry, Boss." Kara stood, grabbed her white-framed sunglasses, and secured the papers in one arm. "I'd love to give her the tour, but I'm helping Pam plan the kiddy tours for the veterinarian clinic today, remember? You signed off on it a month ago."

Jess laid the carburetor on his desk and closed his eyes. Damn it, he had.

"Don't worry about me," Mallory threw in, letting out a forced laugh. "Just point me in the right direction, and I'll find my way."

Jess turned and rested a shoulder on the doorframe, watching Mallory nervously walk around the room. "I doubt that," he murmured just loud enough to evoke a scathing ha-ha smile from her.

"I'd be happy to give you the tour tomorrow," Kara said, pushing the front door open with a hip.

"I might take you up on that." Mallory threw up a hand and gave her a smile. "It was nice meeting you."

"You too."

Mallory flopped down in a chair, picked up an equine magazine, and began flipping through.

Jess knew that would occupy her for about five seconds and then she would be pacing around the lobby, doing acrobatics from the lights, or dancing riotously in the middle of the floor.

He pinched the bridge of his nose and headed down the hall to the kitchen. After pouring himself a cup of coffee, he added three sugar packets, two creamers and stirred it together as he walked back to his office.

As he predicted, Mallory had discarded the magazine and was now standing in front of his desk holding the carburetor.

"Make yourself at home," he said wryly as he took it from her.

"Sorry." Grinning shyly, she slid her palms down her thighs. "It's a rebuild, right?"

"Yeah." He set his coffee down and rolled his chair back. Maybe if he ignored her, she would take the hint and go back to the reception area.

But she didn't do either.

He glanced up to find her staring wide-eyed at the painting behind him.

"That's a J. Kramer original."

"Right again," he said, tersely and clicked opened the spreadsheet he had been working on yesterday. "Jules gave it to me for my birthday last year."

Her jaw went slack. "You know Jules Kramer?"

"She and my mother have been friends for years," Jess said, noticing the wonderment in her eyes. "You're a fan of her work?"

"The woman is so incredibly talented. Her style and technique are so…bold and moving." She slid a finger over the bottom of the wood frame. "When I was a ten, Mom enrolled me in a summer art class at the library. There was a print of one of her originals hanging in the classroom."

She gazed up at the Worrier, her eyes glistening with admiration. "Her ability to capture the human spirit is remarkable. Just look at the depth of his eyes. The pain is almost tangible."

Jules had a unique way of painting, and Jess was a collector of her work, mainly because she portrayed the essence of the West, its people, landscapes, and rich history. But like the Rescue, he had never seen the paintings with the beauty and wonderment Mallory did.

He took a spot on the corner of his desk, seeing for the first time the agony in the proud Sioux's obsidian eyes. "I went to Oregon with Mom when Jules first opened her art school. A lot of her works are on display there."

Her hand dropped disappointedly from the frame. "It's always been a dream of mine to attend, but…"

"Have you applied?"

"No." She laughed with the same nervousness she had when he tried pawning her off on Kara. "I'm nowhere near good enough for something that prestigious."

Her lack of assurance in her abilities annoyed him. "I saw the way you helped Sophie shade that butterfly."

Her cheeks tinged pink. "I'm afraid it takes more than a portfolio of crayon-colored insects to make it into the Jules Kramer Art School."

Jess shook his head. "I didn't mean to compare your artistic abilities to a five-year-old's. You have a gift for seeing the depth and beauty of things and people."

And that was it. The reason why Mallory unnerved him so much. She could see things others couldn't, and she wasn't a bit reluctant about sharing what she saw. She asked too many questions and knew too damn much about the things he wanted to keep hidden.

"I'll let you get back to work." Crossing one foot over the other, she turned around. "Sorry about the carburetor."

When she assumed that self-protective position, she was the saddest thing he had ever seen, and her weak smile nudged at the softest part of his heart.

He set his coffee down and grabbed his keys, switching off his computer screen. "This thing is going to be updating for a while. Are you still interested in that tour?"

Her eyes brightened. "Absolutely."

～

MALLORY WAS ALL BUBBLY INSIDE WITH PRE-TOUR JITTERS. "It's every girl's dream to own a horse. I had a whole shoebox full of little horse figurines and trinkets."

"Stilling holding tight to that dream?" he asked, locking the main office door behind them. "Because I can make it happen. We have an Aztec gelding that's as gentle as a lamb. He'd be perfect for a beginner like you."

"A horse?" she questioned. "Wow. How about we start with the dog and work our way up to the horse?"

She heard him chuckle. "Well, our adoption process is lengthy, and we do require more space than a shoebox."

Mallory had given up on those dreams years ago when Rex burned the box to punish her for talking back.

She followed him around the building. "Then it's a definite pass on the horse."

"Let's start with the stables."

They took a set of pavers across the large lawn behind the office building, and Mallory was excited that he would be giving her the tour.

"When the Rescue started out, it was only equipped to house a couple of horses. It has since expanded to house one hundred. As I said before, we currently have seventy-four up for adoption."

He opened the smaller door, and she followed him inside. The stable had a long hallway that ran the length of the building. A vaulted truss ceiling with skylights allowed natural light to shine in and ventilation to flow. The stall partitions were a combination of tongue and groove pine wood and metal bars.

"Have all these horses been neglected or abused?" she asked, surveying the stalls.

"Unfortunately, most have." He paused by a cream-colored horse. "But sometimes their owners turn them over to us because they can't care for them."

He ran a hand down the side of the horse's neck and was rewarded with a whinny. "Ginger's owner lost his job and had to move to another state to find work. He was happy she would be taken care of, and we were thrilled to have such a good-natured horse in our equine thereapy program."

"She's breathtaking."

"That she is," he agreed, his eyes softening.

Mallory placed a hand on Ginger's neck. Her coat was soft and shiny and felt smooth beneath her palm. The horse was all she had imagined and more. The magnificence of the animal was overpowering. "Tell me more about this therapy program."

"Horses are herding animals, so not only are they highly intelligent, but they're also highly sensitive to sensory data. Sight, taste, smell, touch… They perceive danger and," he pointed to Ginger's ear, "can hear the faintest sounds like a person's heartbeat. They sense happiness, confusion, peace, so what you may be able to hide from a person, you can't hide from a horse."

She withdrew her hand, considering the consequences of that. "That's kind of scary."

"Not in the least," he said, placing her hand back on Gingers' neck. "Horses are also wonderful confidants. They never tell your secrets."

Jess scratched the underside of Ginger's chin, prompting the horse to move her head up and down in a way that said she agreed.

He grinned. "See."

Mallory laughed at his clever puppetry.

"Their heightened sensitivity to a person's physical state makes them perfect for psychotherapy. Some people can't express the grief or trauma they've been through. But the horse can emulate their physical and emotional state, giving therapists a better understanding of what's going on with that person."

"What if the person is very good at hiding what happened to them?" she ventured and then tried backpedaling when she thought about how obvious that sounded. "I—I have this friend…"

Jess tapped the top of the railing with his forefinger as

he thought. "How do you know your friend has been through something traumatic? Has she said something?"

How did she answer that? "No." She folded her arms under her breasts and gave him an aloft shrug. "I just know."

"If you know, then she's not that good at hiding it." His eyes met hers. "Or she wants to share it with someone she can trust but doesn't know how."

She gave him a faint smile. "She doesn't trust easily."

"That often comes with trauma." He held out his hand for her to take. "Trust has to be earned."

Mallory had heard these words before from her therapist and from Aiden. But it was the reticent conversation happening between her and Jess that made her take hold of his hand.

His fingers wrapped around hers, holding her safely, gently, confidently as he led her down to the lower end of the stables to a bay-colored horse. "There are two horses and three donkeys that are permanent residents at the Rescue. Hope is one of the horses. She was a local rescue. She was found at an abandoned ranch on the outskirts of town and was on her way to a slaughterhouse when McCrea rescued her. She was pregnant and so emaciated. It's a miracle either of them survived."

"The foal lived?"

"It was touch and go for a while, but they're both doing well. Filly shows no signs of trauma, but Hope is a different story." Jess held up his hand, letting the horse sniff his palm. Then he cautiously moved his hand to Hope's neck. She flinched and made a weak, whinny of alarming protest. "Shhh…" he soothed, his voice dropping to that calm tone. "You're safe here. No one will hurt you."

Mallory felt those words sink into her soul and wrap

around her heart just like she had yesterday at his house. "She's too scared to trust you."

"That's because she doesn't know me, I haven't earned that trust. But Brody's made great progress with her. She's learned she can trust him and is safe with him." Jess gave her hand a gentle squeeze. "Your friend is a lot like Hope. She's been hurt, and she's learned to be highly perceptive of and sensitive to people. It's how she protects herself."

Those blue eyes of his were holding her in place, peeling back her protective shell with his careful observations.

Her heart began to race.

Hope let out a sharp whinny and stepped back, sensing Mallory's uneasiness. A prickle of goosebumps scattered across her skin, prompting her to let go of his hand.

He took hold of Hope's halter, soothing her again until she quieted. "It's okay, girl."

She watched his large hand make long, gentle passes down the horse's mane, and though he wasn't physically touching her, Mallory felt the calming power of his presence.

Words that weren't there before suddenly sprang to her lips. "I hate Rex," she confessed, her throat tight with anger and resentment she didn't usually let surface. "He made my childhood a living hell. The man destroys everything he touches. I wouldn't lift a finger to save his life." Again, the horse stirred. "How can you work for an organization that rescues horses when one nearly killed you?"

Jess tilted his head to one side, his eyes sympathetic and understanding as he spoke to her. "Horse's aren't evil, Mallory. They aren't malicious by nature, and they don't hurt people for the pure hell of it."

The mystery about why her father was such a loveless bastard had been summed up in two simple sentences.

"A wild horse has more heart and compassion than a coward like Rex." Picking a piece of straw from Hope's mane, he went on to say, "I don't hate Dirteater. What happened to me wasn't the horse's fault. My mind wasn't where it should have been the night I fell. I wasn't focused on the ride." He snapped the straw in half, and it fell to the ground. "I let myself become distracted, and I paid the price."

CHAPTER 10

THEY WERE SHARING INTIMATE THINGS ABOUT THEMSELVES, things that went past standard tour topics and friendly conversation, so it seemed an appropriate time for Mallory to ask questions. "What distracted you?"

"A mistake," he said, dropping his hand from the halter. "Let's walk outside."

His answer spawned more questions, but Mallory didn't ask. She charted a path for the door and followed him out.

He led her to the fenced-in pasture where several horses were grazing. "We started the Rescue with Boaz." He pointed to a chestnut horse with a blond mane near the fence. "He belonged to our friend Colton Ritter. Colton grew up in Santa Camino but moved to Montana to help his dad run the family ranch. He joined the military after he and Lauren married and was badly injured in an explosion." Jess lay an arm on the fence. "Colton struggled with post traumatic stress disorder for a long time. One day, he couldn't take it anymore."

Mallory listened carefully, hearing Jess's voice shift from informative to pained.

"He mounted Boaz and rode out into the middle of a snowstorm."

"Oh God," she whispered.

"Luckily, McCrea found him before it was too late. He suffered hypothermia and Boaz had a bad hoof injury. After the horse was stable, we brought him here and started nursing him back to health."

"And Colton?" she asked, fearing the worst.

"His recovery took longer. But he's finally in a good place mentally and works with donors around the country to raise donations for the Promise Point Foundation, which funds the equine therapy program and helps veterans and others suffering from mental health issues."

That hit a soft spot in Mallory's heart. Being the executive director for the Rescue wasn't just a job to Jess. The work he did was personal.

She thought about Aiden and the changes that had happened to him between deployments. Combat had made him a different man. He was harder, quieter, and kept to himself a lot. He could have benefited from this program.

Her mind wandered away from the Rescue and into another world. A world where Aiden was alive, and she could call him to share all that she was learning about the foundation and Rescue. She could see him grin and hear him say, "Don't worry about me, Mally Cat."

"Mallory?"

She felt Jess touch her arm. "Sorry, I kind of zoned out. What were you saying?"

Worry laced his eyes. "Are you okay?"

"Yes, I'm fine. I was just thinking about a soldier who could have benefited from the program."

"Could have?"

Mallory trained her attention on the horse. "He was killed in action on his second deployment."

"Damn," he said, his eyes softening. "I'm sorry."

"Me too."

"We can skip this and go on to the apartment."

"No, I'm fine. Let's keep going." She pointed to the large building behind them. "What's that over there?"

"That's the veterinarian clinic. Would you like to see it?"

"Yes."

He filled the short walk to the clinic with lots of details. "We have several local volunteers that help keep the place running smooth. For the sake of posterity, we try adding new activities to educate children and adolescents about what it is we do here and how they can help. We host community picnics in the pavilion." He pointed to a large pavilion sitting in the middle of the facility. Four enormous oak poles held up the vaulted ceiling. "Horse rides when the weather is good, and Kara and Pam are adding the kiddy tours she mentioned."

"It's all very efficient," she said.

"We've helped over fifty veterans and their families this year thanks to donations and devoted partners." He opened the double glass doors to the clinic. "So we must be doing something right."

The pristine white walls and blue-colored floor tile gave the clinic a clean and airy feel. Stainless steel light fixtures and countertops reflected the florescent lighting and the smell of lemony disinfectant infused with the aroma of horses.

There was a large reception area with an adjoining conference room where Kara sat behind a long table. "I see the boss gave in."

"He's been very hospitable," Mallory answered, smiling up at Jess.

"He's almost human after his coffee," Kara added.

Jess ignored her light-hearted insult and pointed to the adjacent building. "Those are the equine therapy offices. We have fifteen staff members; that doesn't include the veterinary staff."

"There are three of us in the main office," Kara cut in. "Me, the boss, and Brody, though Brody is rarely in his, so it's usually just me and Mr. Grumpy."

"Watch it," Jess cautioned with a threatening glare in Kara's direction that made her grin. "We added the clinic two years ago. It's complete with a surgical facility and adjacent to the stables and apartment where you'll be staying."

"It was built for Brody, but —"

"I prefer the view from the cabin," a deep male voice echoed through the waiting room, swinging Mallory around to a large man standing between her and the exit.

A black t-shirt stretched tight over his broad chest and shoulders. Dark hair curled up from under the brim of his black hat, and a pair of steel-gray eyes stared back at Mallory.

The man was huge.

～

"BRODY? WHAT ARE YOU DOING HERE?" JESS ASKED, watching Mallory take two steps back as Brody walked by her on his way to the table.

"I work here, remember?"

"McCrea said you were out of town this weekend," he added, suspicious of Brody's sudden arrival.

Brody pulled out a chair and sat down across from Kara. "I came back late last night."

"Eleanor had the baby," Kara rushed to get a jump on the news.

Brody's face broke into a smile. "Yeah, I called the proud papa this morning to let him know I was back at work."

"Did he say when *he'd* be back?" Jess asked.

"No." Brody picked up one of the flyers Kara had printed off.

"They're for the kiddy tours," she explained.

"About time we do something for the little ones." He laid the flyer back on the stack and looked at Jess. "Why? Is there a problem?"

"No," Jess answered because really there wasn't. At least not one he would admit to. "I think we were all just surprised to know you had family somewhere."

Brody frowned using his whole face. "Hell, Jess, I wasn't hatched under sagebrush."

Kara snorted a laugh. "That was a good one. Oh, by the way." She pointed her pen at Mallory. "This is Mallory, Eleanor's sister."

Mallory tried smiling. "Hi."

Brody was a damn fine horse trainer. He was quick to notice idiosyncrasies in people and the animals he worked with. He had been watching Mallory since he walked through the door. Her wide-eyed, two-step-back reaction to his appearance had let Brody know that she was fearful of strangers and that he shouldn't attempt physical contact.

"He's our horse trainer," Jess explained.

Brody stayed seated but raised the brim of his Stetson a notch higher on his forehead. "McCrea mentioned you'd be staying here."

Mallory tried to smile but kept her arms securely

locked around her stomach. "I hope that won't be a problem."

"It's not for me." His voice remained even and mellow.

Mallory's shoulders relaxed. "Jess tells me you've made great progress with Hope."

"I'm lucky." Brody smiled lazily. "Horses respond to me better than women."

Jesus, Jess cursed silently.

"Do you ride?" Brody continued his soft approach.

"No," Mallory said, shooting Jess a quick look. "But I've always wanted to learn."

Jess wanted to kick his own ass for handing Brody that opportunity.

"I'd be happy to teach you. I'm free after five every day of the week and on most weekends," Brody informed her. "Stop by anytime."

Sonofabitch.

"If I'm not here," Brody kept on talking, "I'm usually at home in the cabin behind the lake."

"Oh, okay," Mallory said, absorbing every ounce of the bullshit. "I may be knocking on your door."

Brody capped it all off with a friendly smile. "I'm lookin' forward to it."

Jess couldn't take it any longer. "Are you done talking?"

Brody's smile never wavered. "Maybe."

Kara cleared her throat loudly and scooted her chair back. "I'm going to lunch."

With a hand at her elbow, Jess steered Mallory out the door. "You didn't fall for the bullshit Brody was dishing out, did you?"

"What bullshit?"

"The man was coming on to you?"

She squinted her eyes, her mouth gaping open. "Brody was being nice."

"Nice is a 'Hello, Ma'am.' Not a 'come to my cabin anytime.' "

She stopped dead in the center of the walkway. "So what if Brody was coming on to me? What's it to you?"

Jess gritted his teeth so hard his jaw hurt, but he would be damned if he stepped into that trap. "Beautiful, if you want a ride from Brody Vance, don't let me stop you."

"I won't."

"I'm just trying to look out for you." He stepped around her and continued up the walk, expecting her to follow. But when he reached the office door, she was nowhere to be found.

He went back to his office and tried to keep his mind on work. Three hours later, he hadn't been able to do anything except stare at his computer screen and think about Mallory.

The Rescue was fenced, and the only way in or out was through the main gate. Letting her wander around might have helped her burn off some of the annoying energy she had. Or give her plenty of opportunity for those riding lessons.

Jess hadn't felt jealousy in years because he hadn't cared about a woman enough to worry about another man taking his place.

He rose from his office chair and went to the window. Mallory had found a seat under the pavilion. Her head was tilted slightly to the right allowing the late afternoon sunlight to filter through her dark hair.

She wasn't his in any way. He didn't have a place in her life or her bed, so if Brody or any other man wanted to give her riding lessons, it wasn't any of his business.

But that didn't mean he had to like it.

He pulled out his phone and hit the number beside his brother's ID.

"Hello," McCrea answered a little winded.

"Where the hell are you?"

He grunted and cursed before answering. "A few miles outside of Lubbock."

"What's going on?" Jess asked.

"We had a blowout and almost lost the damn trailer."

He could hitch up one of the other trailers and drive up to Lubbock. But he wasn't too keen on leaving Mallory at the apartment with Brody now that he knew she was interested in riding lessons. And the time it would take the two of them to drive to Lubbock and back was too long to be confined in a truck with Mallory. "You want me to send Brody up?"

"No." Jess heard the tire iron hit the ground. "It's fixed. We should be back on the road in a little while. How's it going? Any sign of trouble?"

Jess went back to his desk and sat down. "No. Everything has been quiet so far."

"We're going to grab a bite to eat before we get back on the road. But I'll have to take it slow. I won't be home until tomorrow."

His brother was halfway across the state, away from his family, rescuing a horse, and he was complaining about protecting a beautiful woman.

That put things in perspective and made Jess feel like an ass for being selfish. "Don't' worry about anything here. I'll stop by and check on El before we go home."

"Don't bother," McCrea said with a chuckle. "I just got off the phone with her. She's had a lot of visitors today. She's exhausted and is probably already asleep."

After Jess hung up the phone, he grabbed the key to the apartment from his top desk drawer and headed out the door.

It was now close to four and the few weekend staff

members they had would be leaving soon. He would get her settled into the apartment and be on his way home.

He locked the office doors and walked around back to the pavilion.

When she saw him, she smiled and patted the bench. "Have a seat." She wasn't holding any grudges about what had happened earlier.

With the apartment key in his hand, he sat beside her and stretched his leg out. "McCrea won't be back tonight."

"Well, there are cameras everywhere, and I'm assuming you lock the gate at night, so I won't need a bodyguard tonight."

"Yeah," he said, warring between wanting to leave her at the apartment and making sure she was safe. "But spending another night together probably wouldn't have been so bad."

"No, not really," she said, a brief smile at her lips. "You could have told me those ghost stories, and we could have made popcorn."

He stood, shoving the key into his pocket. "I thought you were more of a s'mores person."

"I am, but I'm not about to turn down food."

It hit him that he hadn't offered her lunch after they left the clinic. She was probably starving. "I had other things on my mind and didn't think about food. You should have said something."

"You were already pissed at me," she said, dusting crumbs from her shirt. "I didn't want to disturb you."

"I wasn't pissed." He positioned his hat on his head, tugging the brim low to hide his eyes. "Just concerned."

She pointed to the empty potato chip bags in the trash can. "I could have ridden out on my own for food, but I made do with the vending machine."

"Come on," he said, taking her hand to pull her up. "I'll at least feed you before I take you to the apartment."

"You are a saint," she said, pausing to snag her boots from under the table.

He look down at her bare feet. "Why are you barefoot?"

"My feet were wet when I put my boots back on. They started rubbing a blister on the side of my foot, so I pulled them off." She lifted her foot for him to see.

The red patch near her big toe had indeed bubbled into a blister.

"Why were your feet wet?"

"Because I dipped them in the lake."

There was something strangely erotic about Mallory's feminine feet gliding beneath the surface of the lake. The water lapping at her shapely calves, the arch of her neck as she tilted her head back and drank in the sunshine.

He wanted to ask if that was on her way to or from Brody's cabin but didn't. He wouldn't let jealousy browbeat him into looking like an ass. "You should know that Brody and my sister are involved."

"Will you please let that go," she returned, resting a hand on her hip.

She was a gorgeous display of disheveled beauty. An annoyed hot mess of sexiness and unsophistication that brought a grin to Jess's lips.

"Why are you grinning?" she demanded.

"I was just thinking about how pretty you look," he said, laying his thoughts out.

"Are you kidding me?" she asked, with stark surprise. "I'm sweaty, dirty, and have blisters on my toes."

She'd loosely twisted her hair over her left shoulder, but long tendrils had escaped and blew freely around her flushed face and neck.

Her reaction to his complement was refreshing and arousing.

"Still pretty," he insisted, reaching out to rake back those loose strands of hair. "But you should have come inside in the air conditioning. The heat is dangerous."

The sensual contraction of her throat drew his eyes to the soft shallow cleft at the base of her neck. "The water," she said, the slight hitch in her breath lifting her breasts up. "K— kept me from overheating."

Beautiful was hot and aching just like he was, burning for something they both wanted but couldn't have.

And why was that? They were both adults. Both willing to satisfy their needs and move on after. Right?

She crossed one leg over the other and nervously twisted her hips, trying to soothe her growing desire. She was so easy to read.

Her reactions to his touch evoked cravings inside of him. A deep hunger that he longed to satisfy. He needed to taste the saltiness of her skin and fill his nose with the sweet fragrance of her passion.

Acting on impulse, he reached down, grabbed her boots, and lifted her into his arms.

She let out a yelp. "What are you doing?"

"Helping you to the truck."

"I don't need help," she said, kicking her feet. "It's a blister. Not a broken leg."

She could have made it all the way across the parking lot with a broken leg. He knew she was that damn tenacious. But he also knew he needed to justify why he had picked her up. "It sucks having to lean on someone, doesn't it?"

"So this is payback for me helping you yesterday?"

"Maybe," he answered, walking around the main office. "Or maybe this is me returning the favor."

"Oh." She relaxed against him and circled an arm around his neck. "Well, maybe this is me letting you return the favor."

He wasn't sure why he had picked her up. It damn sure didn't help his throbbing dick. He just knew it felt great to have her this close. The weight of her soft, warm body resting against his. It made him feel good in ways he couldn't explain.

"You do know there are snakes in the lake, don't you?"

"Snakes?" She tightened her arm around his neck, bringing her breasts closer to his face. She glanced down at the ground, fearful one might be slithering around his ankles. "What kind of snakes?"

He mimicked a chomping sound with his teeth. "The kind that bite."

Her hazel eyes were loaded with doubt. "Are you trying to scare me?"

They had almost reached the truck. A couple more steps and Jess would have to let her go. He should have walked slower or faked a leg spasm. "I'd never try to scare you, just pester you a little."

She grunted softly and smiled, giving into the teasing. "Is that why Mrs. Hubbard hates you? Because you teased her daughter with snakes?"

Jess set her down and opened the door. Using his body, he corralled her between him and the truck. "Mrs. Hubbard hates me because she caught Sandy and me in the hayloft together," he said, lifting her up and into the seat.

She raised her brows high, adopting an innocent face, and hooked her front teeth into her bottom lip. "Were you playing with snakes?"

He propped his forearm on the top of the cab and leaned closer, enjoying the juvenile way they were flirting with each other. "We were fifteen, and she *was* curious about snakes."

Her shoulders shook with silent laughter, and her eyes were bright and frisky. Holding back a smile, she asked, "Your snake or snakes in general?"

"My snake." He gave his brows a quick wiggle and grinned. "It was bigger than all the other snakes."

"Oh God!" Mallory cringed and gave his chest a light smack. "Stop! Just stop! That's so," laugher overtook her. "Bad!"

"Yeah." He grinned and patted her knee. "That was bad. Sorry."

As her laughter tapered off, her eyes met his, and at that moment, Jess had never been more tempted to lean down and take a kiss.

He wanted to feel those soft lips against his and explore the sweetest parts of her mouth. But kissing her would only fuel those cravings of his. He would want more, much more.

He stepped back, letting his arms fall and the moment pass. "There are snakes around here, so be careful about walking barefoot."

Mallory let out a shaky breath. "I'll be more careful next time."

Jess closed the door and headed around the truck, thinking he should do the same.

CHAPTER 11

MALLORY DREW HER BARE FEET UP TO THE EDGE OF THE truck seat and rested her arms over her knees. Jess had given her a Band-Aid to cover the blister, but she hadn't put her boots back on.

She like walking barefoot. She liked the freedom of wiggling her toes and feeling the grass under her feet. But his warning about snakes hadn't gone unheeded. She hated snakes.

She let out an immature giggle. Well, not all snakes.

And after seeing Jess strut around this morning all aroused and proud, Mallory could see why Sandy had been so curious.

Her heart was still racing from that near kiss a few minutes ago, and she was more than a little curious about what would happen if they did kiss.

Maybe the strange attraction could be satisfied with a kiss. Perhaps the fire would spark and burn or simply fizzle and evaporate.

She let her head rest against the seat and flipped the visor down to look at herself in the mirror.

How on earth could he think she was pretty?

She'd had all sorts of complements ranging from vulgar to extravagant from men who wanted to get her into bed. None of those comments had ever hit home, they never stuck, and she never believed any of them.

She rubbed a finger over her cheek.

But pretty was different. Pretty was unique and feminine. Dainty and a little frail like the petals of a flower.

"Pepperoni and black olives with extra cheese," Jess said, startling her back to attention.

She licked her lips and accepted the pizza box through the open window. "Yes, please."

He climbed in and buckled his seat belt before backing out of the parking spot.

Positioning the box on her lap, she opened the lid and inhaled the smell of garlic and Italian spices. She peeled a pepperoni from the thick layer of steaming cheese and held it to her lips. "You should let me pay you for the pizza."

He made sure traffic was clear before he pulled onto the road. "I'll let you buy my supper sometime."

She popped the pepperoni into her mouth and chewed. "I doubt I'll get the chance. Once Eleanor and the baby are home, you'll probably run and hide somewhere until I'm gone."

He watched her lick the grease from her fingertips until the truck's tires hit the rumble strip. He corrected the wheel and gave the road his attention. "You're El's sister, so we'll probably be bumping into each other from time to time."

He didn't seem happy about bumping into her accidentally or otherwise. But it was a tempting prospect to her. The thought of her body colliding with his stirred an alluring fire deep in the pit of her belly. "Do I still get the ghost story?"

"You really want a ghost story?" he asked.

"I do, but you should know that I'm a fan of scary movies. So," she devoured another pepperoni, "I'm hard to impress."

"Oh, well," he said, smiling. "Now, I'm obliged to deliver."

Mallory wasn't sure what she had started or where his plans for a scary ghost story would take them. And she didn't care. She had a greasy pizza in her hands and a sexy cowboy as a chauffeur.

Her life hadn't been this perfect for a long time.

Jess drove back towards the Rescue and slowed as they neared a dirt road just past the main gate. Then he turned left. "Hold on to your pizza."

She gripped the box as the truck bumped and heaved up the rutted-out road. Jess was quick, dodging large holes that could swallow the cab as they climbed the hill behind the Rescue.

She grasped the handle above the door. "You did it."

"Did what?" he asked, smiling.

"I'm terrified."

"Oh, Beautiful," he laughed and shifted the truck into four-wheel-drive. "We're just gettin' started."

Closing her eyes, she held on tight and braced for another hole. The front tire hit, jolting the pizza box out of her lap and opened her eyes in time to see it flying into the air. "No!" She made a grab for it and caught it before it landed face down in the floorboard.

The truck bounced and pitched a few more times, then rolled smoothly up to a flat place near a grove of juniper trees. He brought the truck to a stop, causing the dry, rocky ground to heave up a cloud of dust.

"We're here," he said, smiling more widely than before. "Safe and sound."

"Where is here?" she asked, shoving her feet back into her boots.

"You'll see." Jess reached over the seat to a cooler he had in the back floorboard and came back with two bottles of water.

He stuffed them into his back pockets and hurried around to her side as she opened the door. "Grab the pizza." He held out his hand out for her to take and she did, feeling her pulse quicken when his hand contacted hers.

He led her up a path thick with shrubs and pebbles. "Watch your step. Some of the bigger rocks are loose."

The path widened, and the shrubs and trees thinned as they walked, giving her a better view of the Rescue below. But the trail ended at the base of a rocky ledge. "You can see everything from up here."

"There's a better view at the top."

With her hand, Mallory shielded her eyes against the sun to look up at the rocky expanse above them. "Too bad we aren't monkeys."

Jess handed her the bottles of water and jumped to take hold of the rock ledge above him. With one hand, he swung back and forth, grinning boyishly.

"You aren't seriously thinking about climbing that, are you?"

"It's just a small ledge, no more than seven or eight feet. It's easy." To prove his point, he latched hold with the other hand and lifted his body.

The muscles in his shoulders and back flexed tight under his gray t-shirt, giving Mallory a visceral display of his rugged strength and athletic agility.

When the ledge was at his waist, he hooked his boot

onto the side and pushed up. Then he sprang to his feet, threw his head back, opened his mouth, and let out a wolfish howl of triumph.

Her jaw dropped with a shocked-spectator expression. There was nothing crippled about this cowboy.

His lips took on that cocky, country boy grin that fit his roguish personality. "It's easy."

"For you maybe, but not for me."

He sat down on the ledge and let his boots dangle over the edge. "Toss me the water."

One, by one, she threw them up. "Now what?"

He pointed to the rock beside her. "Climb up here and give me the pizza."

After finding her footing at the base of the rock, she stepped up and held the box up to him.

"Now," he scooted closer to the edge, wedged his boot against a massive rock near the base of the ledge and held out his hands. "Give me your hands."

She dried her sweaty palms on her jeans and extended her arms. "Please don't drop me."

His large hands wrapped around hers, kindling a rush of warmth through her arms. "I thought you trusted me."

"I do," she answered without hesitation.

His hands tightened. "Then let's do this."

He lifted her up, and her feet left the rock. For a second, she dangled in mid-air, wholly in his hands. The distance between her and the rocky ground below was hardly enough to kill her, but if she had misjudged Jess, if he let go, if she fell, there was a chance something would break.

But his hands stayed firmly planted around hers, hauling her up and back to land safely on top of him.

The force of her body meeting his jaunted his hat side-ways and allowed a hank of sun-streaked hair to tumble across his forehead. He was a sublime temptation of muscles and maleness.

The tendons of his neck flexed with a hard swallow. "That landing was a little rough. Sorry."

Their bodies were a marvelous contrast of soft and hard that was fascinating to her. Mallory couldn't move much less offer words to reassure him that the landing was quite all right with her.

Letting out a shaky breath, Jess carefully rolled her to the side and secured his hat back on his head. Snagging the tops of the water bottles, he headed up the path without a word.

Mallory breathed through ache and dragged herself to her feet.

She dusted the seat of her jeans and grabbed the pizza box, irritated by the abrupt end of such a close encounter. Cold pizza, cold cowboy... cold shoulder.

The short path to the top wasn't as hard to climb, and they were at the top in minutes. The hills were nothing in comparison to the mountains Mallory had hiked in California, but the view was beautiful.

She could see the stables and office buildings of the Rescue, the green pastures, and the horses grazing in the fields. "I'm not disappointed, but this isn't exactly scary stuff, Jess," she said, looking behind her to find him gone. "Jess?"

"I'm down here."

She followed the sound of his voice down to a small grove of junipers. He was sitting on a log near the base of a large rock looking out. This side of the hill was matted in tall grass, thick shrubs and thorn bushes.

She huffed and puffed her way along the path, annoyed he had left her at the top and tossed the pizza box onto a smaller rock near his boots. "Thanks for leaving me."

He handed her a bottle of water. "Stop complaining and sit down."

"I'm not complaining," she said, snatching the bottle from his hand. "Okay, maybe I am, but I'm hot, hungry, and ready to go."

This hike wasn't going to produce anything except more blisters and frustration.

"We can't go," he said, taking her hand to pull her beside him. "I haven't told you the story."

She sat down and sighed heavily as reached into the box for a slice of pizza. "Well, get on with it."

"In a minute." Leaning his elbows against the rock behind them, he kept his eyes on the horizon. "When the lighting is right."

Mallory stopped in mid-chew. "What lighting?"

He pressed a finger against his lips and pointed down the hill. "Be patient and keep your eyes on the vista of rocks."

She followed his finger to the horizon to where the blue sky met the jagged landscape of deep crevasse and rocky limestone. Slowly, the sun rode the blue-gray skyline down. It met the earth and transformed the rocky view into the shape of a wall. "What is that?"

"That," he said. "Is what remains of Vera la Luz, an old Spanish Mission. There are dozens of stories about its inception and dark past."

"Such as?" she questioned, her teeth deep in a piece of crust.

"On dark nights when the sky is clear and bursting with a million stars, it is said that the fires of hell open up. Allowing the spirits of the unconverted souls who perished here to walk the earth."

"Oooo," she mocked teasingly and twisted the lid off the water bottle. "Scary."

He smiled at her doubt. "It is elementary at best. But most ghost stories are based on a tiny truth. With time, they're embellished and regurgitated to serve the needs of the storyteller."

"You're the storyteller this time." She wiped her mouth. "What needs are you serving?"

"None," he said as he stared out over the rocks. "I just wanted you to you have a good time. But you're obviously not."

Guilt slammed into her. "I am," she assured Jess. "I'm just frustrated and achy from…"

"The climb," he supplied, giving her an unreadable look.

"Yes. The climb." She saw no reason to tell him the real reason she felt all hot and bothered. What happened earlier didn't seem to have fazed him at all. "It's nothing a hot bath won't cure."

"I prefer a stiff drink," he said, rising to his feet. He moved a few feet down the hill to where the trees thinned.

She made her way over to where he was and gazed down at the ruins.

The long nave that once housed the altar and sacristy was oriented from east to west. The cross foundation was all that remained of the Mission.

Smaller foundations of what once were Native American jacals, the granary and storage structures, sat along the outer edge of the wall. The walls of two larger structures near the back of the sanctuary – she assumed they were once the private living quarters for the monastics – were mostly intact.

She could picture the Mission in its original beauty. Limestone and mortar walls with hand-hewn timber beams and a three-tower belfry. A retable of saints above the altar, a wooden crucifix, the smell of incense, and the sound of bells echoing through the land below

With its adobe façade and fortressed walls, Vera la Luz would have been a beacon of safety and hope for those seeking salvation and refuge.

Jess shifted his view from the Mission to a campsite a few hundred feet from the ruins. "McCrea brought in a team of archeologists a couple of years ago to excavate the site."

Tents, campers, and all-terrain vehicles swarmed the land adjacent to the Mission.

He pointed to the cemetery sitting off to the left. "Those are my people. I have great-great-grandparents buried there. Some great aunts and uncles too." He moved his finger to the right side of the sanctuary where dig grids were laid out. "Last month, they uncovered several unmarked graves over there."

"Who do they think they are?" she asked, moving closer to him. Rising on her tiptoes for a better view, she lost her balance and bumped into him.

He closed a hand around her arm to steady her, then stepped away. "Some speculate that they're the bodies of the legendary Walker Gang," he explained, adopting a smooth narrating voice. "A notorious band of cutthroat outlaws who terrorized Hill Country after the Civil War and made Ravorn Caverns their hideout. That's about the time the Legend of the Wayfires Gold started showing up in the history books."

"Gold and outlaws," she mused. "This is Texas."

"Eva Walker, a.k.a. The Lady Outlaw, was the daughter of the gang's leader." He dropped one lazy lid her way. "She's described as impetuous, beautiful, and deadly. She captured the eyes and hearts of many men and then led them to their death."

"She sounds like a real catch," she said, laughing.

"My great-great uncle was one of her lovers. He died in the fire that destroyed the Mission."

Mallory looked down at the sanctuary and imagined it engulfed in flames. "Really?"

He squinted against the brightness of the sun. "Why do you sound shocked?"

"It's hard to believe a man with Coldiron blood was lured to his death by a woman."

"Why is that?"

She studied his profile against the backdrop of ruins. His prominent brow, straight nose, and square jaw was an iconic description of the American Cowboy. Durable, rugged, and utterly unmovable.

"You and McCrea seem so solid and level-headed," she shrugged. "And immune to the wiles of a woman. I guess I thought your uncle was the same way."

His face became placid as he stared out over the ruins. "Love and trickery are often dealt with the same hand. Maybe he was in love with Eva Walker and didn't know what kind of woman she was until it was too late."

Mallory knew Jess wasn't talking about his uncle and that what she said had hit a raw spot in his past. She wanted to reach inside of him, latch hold of all that pain and bitterness entwined around his heart and yank it out. But she didn't want to be confrontational. And she didn't want tonight to end the way last night had.

She wasn't dreaming of exchanging rings or naming babies with the man, though one day that might be nice. She could see him bouncing kids on his knee and settling into domesticated life if he ever allowed himself to fall in love again.

But Jess was attractive in ways she couldn't describe. He was indeed a rarity. A marvel she wanted to know more about. And she knew that if she wanted to get closer to him, she would have to confront the indignation caused by the woman who had dealt him that lousy hand.

"Why do they have a chain-link fence around the perimeter? Do they expect to find gold?"

"No," he said. "There is no evidence to suggest there is any truth to that part of the story. The fence is there to keep looters out."

"If they don't' think there's gold, then why dig?"

"Archeologists have discovered layers and layers of history at the Mission. We want to preserve it and uncover the truth about the people who lived here."

She lifted one side of her mouth in disagreement. "I wouldn't want people digging around in my past. And neither would you." The secrets of her past weren't covered in layers of dirt and couldn't be unearthed by a shovel or brush. They were buried deep inside her under a thick layer of disgrace.

"I suspect that's the case with most people," he said, turning his back to the Mission.

A gentle breeze swept past her, swirling the dry dirt at her feet into small cyclones. The junipers waved from side to side as it passed on down the hill.

She twisted her hair into a knot and with one hand, held it on the crown of her head. The air cooled her clammy skin. "God, that feels good."

The wind was a godsend, but uneasiness crept up her spine as dark clouds rolled across the sky to the east. "The last one passed us by. Do you think this one will too?"

"Probably. More than likely, it's just heat kickin' up a little dust." He walked to the path and waited for her to catch up. "It'll be dark soon. We should be getting back to the Rescue. We'll save some time by taking the paved road back down to the truck.

"There's a paved road?" she asked, in disbelief.

"Yep." He laughed.

Here he was traipsing up the hill as if nothing had happened, and her legs were so shaky she could hardly manage to put one foot in front of the other. "Why didn't we take it?"

"Paved roads are for security guards and archeologists. I thought you might like a little adventure with your ghost story."

Adventure? He thought a bumpy truck ride was an adventure. The man was clueless. Waking up to a nearly naked cowboy on the couch and two near kisses... That was an adventure.

CHAPTER 12

On the way back to the Rescue, Jess kept his eyes on the road. A stern silence had consumed him by the time they pulled back into the parking lot. "Leave your bike here for the night. I'll help you pack your bags to the apartment."

Mallory was too tired and disappointed to argue. Her toes hurt, her body ached, and she was spending the night alone in an unfamiliar place with a storm on the horizon.

Jess removed her bags from the bike and handed her the one she was so possessive of. He led her across the lawn to the stables they had toured earlier and then around back through a door to a hallway with a flight of steps leading to the apartment.

She followed him up the stairs and waited for him to open the door. The floor to ceiling windows in the cozy living room allowed sunlight to spill on to the sleek, white cabinetry of the fully fitted kitchen.

"Wow,' she said, running her hand over the apron sink. "I wasn't expecting this."

"We wanted it to be nice," he said. "But I think Brody feels more at home in the cabin."

"I don't think elegant granite countertops and hanging pendant lights are Brody's style."

"No," he chuckled. "I guess not."

She made room for the leftover pizza in the refrigerator and closed the door. "Thank you for the pizza and for the trip to the Mission. I enjoyed the story and the company."

He handed her the key. "Ah…yeah, me too."

"Well," she said, wishing he wouldn't go. Today had been special for her. Not that they had shared or done anything of great consequence, but that those close encounters and little moments of almost kissing meant something.

"I should be going." He turned, then stopped. "Are you sure you're okay with staying here by yourself?

She wouldn't hold him as a hostage any longer. If he stayed, it wouldn't be out of loyalty to her sister. "I'm sure." Taking hold of his shoulders, she turned him around and pushed him towards the door. "I've imposed on you enough. I'll be fine."

"It's no imposition," he said, stopping at the door. "I'm fine with sleeping on the couch if you need me to."

"Nonsense. I'm safe." She pointed to the cabin up on the hill. "And Brody's right there if I need help."

His face pulled to a tight frown. "That doesn't make me feel better."

The thought of him being a little jealous of Brody made her want to kiss him square on the lips. "Go home, Jess. I'm fine."

He scratched the back of his head. "Okay, then. Goodnight."

"Goodnight," she said, shutting the door behind him.

When his footsteps were gone from the stairs, Mallory

walked around the apartment to familiarize herself with her temporary home. It was a beautiful space, open with an energetic vibe that made her creative juices flow.

There was a set of double doors to the right of the living room that opened to a little balcony over the stalls. She could see Ginger and Hope and a few of the other horses.

The little girl inside of her was in horse heaven.

Another set of double doors near the entry opened into a room without furniture that Mallory envisioned as a studio. Two large windows allowed plenty of natural light. The area was perfect for painting.

There was a hallway past the living room that led to the bathroom and a spacious bedroom with a view of the pasture and main office.

She could see her bike and Jess's truck.

After showering, she carried her bags into the bedroom, pulled out her sketch pad and pencil then settled into one of the plush chairs next to the window.

She needed to create and expel all the emotions running rampant inside of her. Up until today, those had mostly been grief and loss. But somewhere amidst all the darkness and death, an ember of light caught inside her. And she began to see images in her mind.

She took a shaky breath and moved the pencil over the paper, remembering just how Jess's eyes had looked when they were talking over dinner last night. Edgy, dark, controlled, and with a dash of that anger mixed in. The shape of his lips, the slope of his nose, the tiny scar on his chin…The profound transformation of his eyes.

She flipped the paper over and started another sketch with Jess in the foreground of Vera la Luz. She worked adding shading and shape to his face without keeping track of the time or worrying about the storm. Her mind was on capturing the man in her thoughts. The man who had called her pretty and carried her in his arms.

The fallen cowboy who had almost kissed her twice.

When Mallory laid the pencil down, it was dark outside. She tucked the sketch pad back into her bag and rose from the chair, noting how quiet the apartment was.

Uneasiness crept up her spine. She knew Rex was close by and watching her every move. And she knew the time for telling her sister about their mother's passing was approaching. She wasn't sure how Eleanor would take the news or how she would feel about her afterward.

She moved to the window and raised the sash, releasing a gust of night air into the room. It was sweet and warm against her face. The song of cicadas in the mesquite trees and an occasional croak of a frog down from a nearby creek was serene and calming.

The evening had transformed into the night, and the air had cooled, quelling the storm. The security light above the main office reflected off the cab of Jess's truck.

He hadn't gone home, but the office lights weren't on, so where was he?

The stir and whinny of one of the horses in the pasture brought her attention to the shadowy figure sitting under the pavilion. She couldn't see the face, but when a man's leg stretched out into the light, she recognized Jess's boots.

Walking out of the apartment and down the stairs, Mallory made her way across the lawn to where he was sitting in one of the Adirondack chairs. On the table beside him was a bottle of bourbon and in his right was an empty glass. He had the ambiance of a cattle king. Ruling. Confident. Controlled.

"I thought you went home."

"I did." His voice was low and coarse. But his words

weren't slurred. He either had a strong constitution or had just started drinking.

She sat on the edge of the footstool and took the glass from him. Then lifted it to her lips for a drink, wincing as it burned its way down her throat. "Why," she coughed. "Did you come back?"

He shifted forward and landscape lights near the pavilion allowed her to see his face. His lids were heavy, and his lips austerely cocked to one side as he looked at her. "I was worried about you."

"I told you I'd be fine."

He drained the glass and set it on the table next to the bottle. "Did you have your bath?"

A bath and a stiff drink. Ah… so, maybe he had been affected by their near kisses. Was a stiff drink his way of easing the ache?

"Yes. But I'm still achy."

The thick muscle of his jaw flexed tight. "Me too."

"You've fed me and told me a ghost story," she said, reaching in to retake the bottle. "Are we going to play Truth or Dare now?"

He kept a tight hold on the bottle, unwilling to let her have it. "Games and alcohol don't mix."

Confronting what was really happening seemed to be the fastest way for them to move forward with whatever was happening between them. "Are we just going to pretend like you didn't want to kiss me today? Like that's not the real reason you came back?"

He continued to stare at her, unmoved by her blunt questions. "That's exactly what we're going to do."

She knew she was treading on temptation by being this close to him, but this was her chance to see if they sparked or fizzled.

Easing into the scant space between him and the footstool, she caught him by surprise and claimed the bottle. "Do you always drink when you're sexually frustrated?"

He made a growling noise and let his head fall against the back of the chair. "Go to bed."

"I can't sleep," she said, taking a sip straight from the bottle. "I keep wondering if Rex is out there hiding in the bushes, waiting for the right moment to kick open the door."

Jess lifted his head with a sigh. "You don't have to worry. I'm here. The only way in and out of the Rescue is through the front gate, and it's locked and armed with a security code. The only way into the apartment is through those doors."

"How high are the fences around back?" If Rex wanted in, gates and security codes wouldn't stop him.

"High enough," he answered. "You're safe. No one will get to you here."

She swallowed another sip. "I'm just paranoid. Rex won't do anything with your truck in the parking lot. That's not his style. He'll wait until he's sure I'm alone."

"Is that why you wanted me to leave the ranch last night? So you could lure him in?" he asked, taking the bottle from her.

She smiled. "That and I knew you really wanted to get laid."

The corner of his mouth lifted upward. "Jesus, Mallory. I've never met anyone like you."

Her smile widened. "Should I be flattered?"

"You should be cautious," he said, taking a long swig.

"Why?"

He rested the bottle on his knee. "Because the fall isn't half as bad as the getting up."

Okay, maybe he was drunk. Mallory motioned for him to pass it her way. "I guess you would know."

"I guess I would." Moving to the edge of the chair, he handed her the bottle. "If this was Truth or Dare which would you choose?"

"That would obviously depend on the truth."

He stared at her for several seconds. "Tell me about Aiden."

"Why do you want to know about Aiden?"

He traced her tattoo with his index finger, launching a surge of chill bumps over her skin. "That's not how the game is played."

Aiden's passing had ripped apart every piece of her. It had pierced her heart with a poison that had spread to her soul, leaving her hollow and empty inside.

She didn't want to succumb to those feelings now. She wanted to taste Jess's kiss, feel the warm glide of his lips over hers, and fill her heart with something other than death.

"I can't—" She ventured another sip, letting the alcohol settle into her body. "I'm not ready to talk about Aiden, not yet. I may never be, so I guess it would have to be a dare."

He leaned in closer. The blue of his eyes darkened, but not with turmoil as they had before. What consumed them now was desire. A hot, lustful burn that made her body clench tight. "Beautiful, I don't think you're up for one of my dares."

His words dripped with a challenge Mallory couldn't refuse. "Try me."

JESS STARED AT HER PARTED LIPS, WET AND GLOSSY FROM the bourbon, and felt an old sensation stir inside him. This woman was a delectable morsel of sinful temptation that could easily be his downfall if he let her.

The gentle tug of her lips around the end of the bourbon bottle was so provocative that his dick had damn near busted the zipper of his jeans.

If he had any sense at all, he would walk away and leave her and the bourbon sitting here in the dark.

But he craved the taste the smooth oak bourbon mixed with the sweetness of her lips. "I was hoping you'd say that."

Capturing Mallory's chin between his finger and thumb, he lowered his lips and claimed her mouth.

Heaven and hell collided when her soft, yielding lips touched his. They were warm, sweet, and hungry. It was nothing unlike the dozens of other women he had kissed.

With Mallory, there was an exotic ingredient. One that made him ache harder than he ever had. An addictive component that went beyond taste and feel. Something his whiskey-soaked brain couldn't quite identify.

She braced her hands on his knees and leaned in, eager for more. The little drone emanating from her throat as he deepened the kiss was the foreboding sound of a looming catastrophe.

He shouldn't do this. It wasn't right. Mallory was a woman he was supposed to protect. A woman in danger and probably on the rebound from a guy she couldn't talk about. A guy whose name was inked into her skin.

But the longer he kissed her, the more he wanted her. There wasn't a rational thought in him. He wasn't going to stop, and she wasn't pulling away. This was happening. They were about to have hard, rock-your-world-in-the-chair sex, and he didn't care what it cost him.

He drew her onto his lap and parted her thighs. The heat of her aroused body curved over his hardness perfectly. The torturous temptation roused a deep moan from him.

"Holy hell," he swore as his fingers bit into the soft flesh of her bottom, thrusting his hips into her. "You feel so damn good."

With her palms against his chest, she raised her head and moistened the bottom of her swollen lip with the tip of her tongue.

"What?"

"I thought..." Her frown gave way to a smile. "It's nothing."

He cupped the back of her head, bringing her mouth back to his. He deepened the kiss, hooking his thumbs in the waistband of her shorts, ready to strip them away.

She pushed up again. "Did you see that?"

"See what?"

"I thought I—" She tucked her bottom lip between her teeth and bit down as her eyes went back to that spot behind him. "There it is again."

"There what is?"

She braced her hands on the chair arm and started to lift her body from his.

"Don't move," he said, unwilling to let her go. "Just tell me what's wrong."

She swallowed. "I think someone is here."

Alarm bolted through the thick fog of lust, clouding his mind. Brody was the only other person at the Rescue, and he wouldn't be nosing around in the dark.

He eased his hold on her hips, letting her move back to the footstool.

"There was a flash of light." She folded her arms over her breasts. "Didn't you see it?"

A light? Had she ended the kiss for a light? A light that could have come from the main road. "No, I didn't," he said, taking a controlled breath to dismantle the sexual frustration raging through his body. "I kiss with my eyes closed. Like a normal person."

She pointed over his shoulder. "They were really bright like headlights."

"That's highly unlikely. That's the ridge that separates Redemption from the Rescue. The only thing in that direction is the ridgeline, and it's gated off —" The lights flashed again.

She jumped to her feet. "See. I told you."

Jess rose and hurried to the edge of the pavilion in time to see a vehicle just beyond the tree line.

"Can you see who it is?"

"No, but I wouldn't worry," he returned, trying to downplay the situation. But he knew whoever had made it up the ridgeline hadn't done so by mistake.

"You said it was gated."

"It used to be, but that was years ago when your grandma was alive," he said, clearing his throat. He didn't need to sound concerned or alarmed. "You know how easy it is to get lost out here."

He wanted to comfort her, take her back into his arms, and make her feel safe. But after what just happened, touching her was out of the question.

"Yeah," she said, hesitantly rubbing her arms as she stared out into the dark night. "I guess so."

The vehicle made a turn, and the lights disappeared as it drove back down the road. "See, they're gone," he said, stepping out from under the pavilion and into the dark.

"I guess I should go," she said from behind him.

Jess raked both hands through his hair. "Yes, you should."

From the corner of his eye, he watched her backtrack across the yard. "Oh, by the way," she said, stopping just shy of the stable door. "I think I won that dare."

The woman was driving him insane. "Go to bed."

"Don't be a sore loser," he heard her yell.

He wanted to grab her and kiss her and show her just how sore he was. But he wouldn't because nursing an aching cock was a hell of a lot easier than nursing a mistake.

He took another chug of whiskey and screwed the cap back on. If Rex was around, he needed to be sober.

CHAPTER 13

"But I don't want to go," Mallory whined, adjusting the strap of her bag higher on her shoulder as she jogged down the stairs.

"I don't feel like arguing," he said, taking the lead to his truck. "You're going if I have to haul you over my shoulder and put you in the seat myself."

He had stayed awake all night keeping watch on Mallory's apartment. She was safe at Promise Point, but those headlights had been too close for his comfort. At dawn, he had gone home for a quick shower and changed his clothes. Then he had texted Logan and arranged their meeting with the mayor. The easiest way to get through the day was to keep busy and with as many people between him and Mallory as possible.

Having talked sociably to Harry more than once, Jess knew the meeting would eat the better part of the morning. The man was thorough and long-winded.

After the meeting, he would swing by the sheriff's office and inform Finn about the headlights up on the ridge last night.

He opened the passenger door and waited for her to climb in.

"Can you at least tell me where we're going?"

"I have a meeting with the mayor, and I'm not leaving you here alone."

She sighed and climbed in.

He shut the door and walked around to the driver's side. After getting in and buckling his seatbelt, he started the truck and backed into the loop.

She shoved a pair of dark aviator sunglasses on and adjusted her seat belt over her breasts. "So you don't think whoever it was on the ridge last night was just lost?"

"I think it never hurts to be cautious," he said, thinking he should have been alert instead of sipping bourbon and indulging in a game of Truth or Dare. If he had seen the headlights first, he would have taken the truck and the rifle up the back road and caught whoever was prowling around.

He turned onto Clearview Road and drove towards town. A few miles down the road, he slowed for the yield sign at the intersection by the old Jericho Mill.

"It's hard for me to remember anything about Santa Camino other than the restaurant that used to sit on the corner. I'm not even sure what the name of it was."

She hadn't mentioned the kiss, and they were back to flirting and acting like nothing had happened, which was okay with him.

He was all for pretending they hadn't kissed.

"The Bentley Café," he answered, slipping on his sunglasses to shield his eyes from the morning glare bouncing off the pavement.

The bass drum pounding to the beat of a heavy metal tune inside his head could be cured by coffee and quiet. He could come by the coffee easily. But he knew he wouldn't find quiet anytime soon.

"Is there a craft store or a place I can buy art supplies?" Mallory asked. "The lighting in the apartment is wonderful for painting."

"Rayleen Sawyer has a little craft store a couple of buildings down on 2nd Street. We can stop by there on our way back to the Rescue."

"Yes, please."

He made the turn into town. "Any thoughts about applying to the art school?" he asked, thinking she might want those supplies to work on her portfolio.

She shrugged. "I don't know. Maybe."

"I think you should," he went on to say. "Oregon is a beautiful place."

She kept her eyes on the window. "You wouldn't be trying to get rid of me, would you?"

"No," he said, though he had thought about calling Jules for a favor.

"Good," she said, passing a smile his way.

He drove past the Turquoise Moon Thrift Store and Wild Willie's Barbeque Pit before breaking for the red light at the corner of Main and 4th Street.

The light changed, and he turned onto Main. "The meeting isn't until ten. Do you drink coffee?" he asked, parking by the curb in front of Pixies.

"Only if it's accompanied by a chocolate doughnut."

"I think we can manage that."

He stepped from the truck and was thankful his leg felt close to normal. After he drank his latte, he might almost be in a good mood.

The sun was bright. The sky was clear, and the day would be over before he knew it.

He waited by the curb for Mallory and walked a step behind her until they neared the door. He made it a point to open the door for her and smiled politely as she passed by him.

The morning crowd was dwindling, and there were a few empty tables near the back. Jess motioned her toward one. "Do you know what you want?"

"I don't care about the coffee, but don't forget the doughnut," she said, walking towards the table. She sat and kept her eyes trained on the window.

Violet was nowhere to be seen, but Joel — the guy she had hired last year to fill in when she was needed at the ranch — handed Bob Setzer his coffee. He gave a gesture in Mallory's direction. "New girlfriend?"

"No," Jess said, surveying the glass case of assorted doughnuts. "I'll have my usual. She'll have a black coffee and one of those doughnuts with the chocolate frosting."

Joel gave the counter a light tap with his fist. "You got it."

"Has Finn been in?"

"Yeah, you just missed him." Within minutes, Joel placed the coffees in a carrier and set them on the counter. His eyes darted to Mallory as he used tongs to retrieve the doughnut from the case. "What's her name?"

Jess calculated the cost of the coffees and doughnut and reached into his back pocket for his wallet. "Mallory."

Joel laid the doughnut on a paper plate. "Is she single?"

He stopped filing through the money in his wallet long enough to cut the man a hard frown. He knew from Lou and Eleanor that the only reason Logan and Ty let Joel work side by side with their baby sister was that Violet had told them he was gay when she hired him.

Not that it was any of Logan and Ty's business. Violet

was a grown woman who was more than capable of making her own decisions about her business, employees, and men.

But the fact remained. Logan and Ty were overprotective of their little sister. And as tough and buff as Joel appeared to be, he was unprepared for two country boys who had cut their teeth on backstrap and bulls running him out of town on a rail.

And Jess was equally unprepared to give a man — any man — updates on Mallory's relationship status.

Jess tossed a ten down on the counter and shoved his wallet into his back pocket. "Why do you care? You're gay, remember?"

Joel's grin weighted towards a frown. "Right."

He snatched the plate from the counter, picked up the carrier, and walked to the booth where Mallory was sitting.

"Thank you."

"You're welcome."

She picked the doughnut up and bit in. "Mmmm…"

"Good?"

"Delicious." She licked the chocolate frosting from her bottom lip and held the doughnut out to him. "Want a bite?"

Jess wanted more than a bite. He wanted her whole mouth. He wanted to feel those silky, lithe lips meet the dare of his kiss just the way they had last night. "No. Those things will kill you."

"While the doughnut may be bad for you, research has shown that chocolate is excellent for the libido." She wiggled her fingers at him in a spellcasting manner. "It stimulates the pleasure centers in our brain that control orgasms."

Grasping the cup with both hands, Jess leaned in closer

as if he were about to share a secret with her. She did the same, biting her smile with her front teeth. "My pleasure centers don't need stimulating. You know that."

She let go of a chuckle and grinned before lifting her cup to her mouth.

Mallory had an energy that was refreshing and exhilarating and stirred his senses and he found himself laughing too.

He had never given much thought to the color of a woman's eyes or the way they changed with her emotions until he met her.

When she was like this, teasing and full of fun, the amber in her eyes brightened with the vibrancy of cottonwoods in the fall.

"God." Her face puckered as she forced the liquid down. "This stuff is awful."

"You said you didn't care, so I ordered you a straight black."

She lay the doughnut down and licked her fingertips. "What are you drinking?"

"A salted caramel mocha latte."

She raised an eyebrow and pointed to his cup. "May I?"

He knew there would be the temptation of Mallory and chocolate on the lid when he got it back. But he couldn't refuse her.

"Be my guest," he said, watching her lift it to her mouth and cautiously taste the salty, sweet treat.

Delight sparked in her eyes, and a soft purr eased up her throat. "I'll have that next time," she said, licking her lips before she handed the cup back to him.

She'd said that like they were going to make drinking morning lattes together a thing. He supposed that wouldn't be too bad if they didn't make sharing bourbon, kissing, and almost having sex a thing too.

Yesterday, she'd had on brown eyeliner and a dusting of beige eyeshadow on her lids. But this morning, Jess had rousted her from what must have been a deep sleep.

It had taken three hard knocks and a loud whistle to wake her. She had opened the door with that same sleepy-eyed yawn as yesterday, turned on her heel and disappeared into the bathroom, leaving behind the diffused scent of flowers and honey.

She had looked so warm and soft and ...

Damn it.

Jess closed his eyes, fighting an unexpected jolt of desire firing through his groin, and pressed his finger and thumb to the bridge of his nose.

"Headache?" she asked.

"No," he sighed. "I was thinking that all of this might be easier to deal with if I knew what Rex was after."

"I told you. I can't tell you until I've had a chance to talk to Eleanor."

"Okay, after the meeting, I'll take you back to the hospital, and you can talk to her. Then you can tell me —"

She shook her head. "No."

"Why the hell not?" he snapped.

"Because what I have to tell her can't be blurted out for your convenience."

"But my life has to be put on hold for yours?"

MALLORY WAS GOOD AT PRETENDING THINGS DIDN'T HURT. She had a hard shell, an outer coating of impenetrable armor created from years of living with Rex Montgomery. Usually, words rolled right off her back like a cold rain.

But this morning she and Jess had been talking about chocolate and sex and orgasms... And she hadn't been prepared for a verbal clash. His question, spoken in that cross tone she hated, hit her hard, split her armor, and lodged itself in the vicinity of her heart.

"There you go," she said, sinking her teeth into the doughnut. "Getting all moody again."

His bottom jaw shifted, but he didn't say a word.

With the passion of last night's kiss still swirling around inside her, Mallory had thought things might be different between them this morning. That today might involve another kiss, but Jess was behaving like a grumpy ass again.

"I didn't ask you to put your life on hold, and I don't need your protection," she rebounded, picking at a purple sprinkle decorating the top of her doughnut. "I can take care of myself, so feel free to go on with *your* life."

"And explain to El why I left her sister unprotected?" he asked, shifting his shoulders uncomfortably. "No thanks, Beautiful."

She wasn't under any illusions about their relationship. It wasn't like this was a coffee date. Jess was here because of duty, not because he gave a damn about her.

But the demeaning tone he used for her nickname pricked at her temper. "How does a man who was practically born on the back of a horse not ride?"

His brows snapped together. "Excuse me?"

"You heard me. How?"

"He gets thrown through the air and trampled by one."

"See," she said, resting her elbows on the table. "That's the part I don't get. You grew up working your parents' cattle ranch, so I think it's safe to say that wasn't the first time you'd been thrown or hurt by a horse."

His eyes iced over. "No."

"You knew the dangers —"

"I knew," he cut in, "that when I drew Dirteater there was a chance I might get hurt."

"But you rode him anyway because doing what you love and taking risks was who you used to be."

His bottom jaw opened and rolled to one side as he looked away.

It took years of dedication, hard work, and commitment to be a professional athlete, and Jess had been the best. "A man doesn't call it quits on his life-long dreams after a fall as long as he has legs. And you have two fully functioning ones," she pointed out. "Nor does he make it all the way to the top of his profession by playing it safe, and after watching you compete, I can't fathom how you could give up riding so easily."

"It wasn't easy," he gritted out. "But the doctors made it clear I would never compete again."

Mallory imagined his body was littered with dozens of scars associated with the sport. Injuries that might have had the same consequences, so Jess's decision not to ride again must have come from something more devastating than a fall.

"I understand not competing, but not riding at all?"

The muscles along his square jaw contracted tight, signaling umbrage, but she forged on.

"I know there's more to being a cowboy than wearing the hat." She glanced around the table and down at his booted feet under the pink tabletop. "And the boots and the Wranglers. But without the horse, how can you work the ranch? Drive cattle or do a hundred other things a real cowboy does from the back of a horse?"

His eyes narrowed with her insult. "A real cowboy?"

"Well, yeah," she said, unwilling to retract her words. Branding Jess a counterfeit cowboy was a bit childish. But Mallory wanted to goad this petulant cowboy onto a horse. She wanted to see him back in the saddle, holding tight to the reigns of an animal as fierce and untamable as she knew he was. "Isn't there some cowboy creed about getting back on a horse after you've been knocked off?"

His scoff was low, his smile scathing. "I had that drilled into my head from the first time my ass hit the saddle, and I did. I got back up no matter how bad it hurt, no matter what was busted, bruised, or broken. I got up."

Was Jess just a proud man who was unable to accept his life without a sport that had once been everything to him? Or were his reasons for not riding based on something deeper?

Could it be that Jess had been hurt by more than the stomp of a bucking horse? He'd been engaged once but was now vehemently opposed to falling in love. And he was living alone in a house with empty bedrooms that had been built for his future wife and children.

"Because that's the cowboy way," she added, her heart aching for him. "You get up, dust yourself off, and pretend nothing got hurt."

Jess's jaw was fixed mulishly in place and unwilling to do anything but grind. He was done with the conversation. But Mallory wasn't because she had been where he was now.

Afraid and hiding.

She'd cut her hair, tossed her makeup into the trash and worn baggy clothes to conceal her curvy figure. She'd become someone she didn't recognize; someone she wasn't in order to protect herself.

She didn't want to ruin their coffee or their growing relationship by dishing out her version of the truth. But fear was like a dirty rag on a fresh wound. It made healing impossible. And that was part of Jess's problem.

His body had healed, but the emotional injuries he had suffered had been shoved down deep and silenced.

Mallory mentally braced herself for the repercussions of what she was about to say. "I don't think you got up, Jess, at least, not all of you. I think a part of you is still lying in the dirt, wondering what the hell happened."

His eyes turned tempestuous and his head cocked back a fraction as the truth of her words hit the broken part of his spirit. "You don't know what the hell you're talking about."

Oh, but she did.

"I've never been knocked off a horse, but I've been knocked on my ass more times than I want to count," she admitted. "But I never stayed down."

Jess didn't say a word. He just sat there staring a hole through her. She stared back, daring him to say she was wrong.

The storm in his eyes cleared, giving way to lust. His gaze fell to her breasts and appraised them with a hunger that made her shudder. "Don't kid yourself. If you had gotten up, you wouldn't shrink into a ball of fear every time a man comes near you."

Jess's words sliced through Mallory, insulting her, humiliating her, and blasting her with the cold reality of how he saw her.

Damaged and afraid.

"Shit," he sighed, regret closing his eyes. "That was uncalled for."

Mallory had fought hard to break the bonds of her past. She walked tall, smiled through her insecurities, and pretended like she had it all together. But Jess had seen through her front. She wasn't fooling anyone but herself. "I stuck my nose where it didn't belong," she said, shakily. "I deserved it."

"No, you didn't," he said ruefully and dug four fingers into his forehead. "But I've had my fill of half-ass psych evaluations over the years."

It had been a half-ass psych evaluation that she should have kept to herself. But it was too late to take back her words. The damage was done.

CHAPTER 14

MALLORY WASN'T THE FIRST WOMAN TO VENTURE DOWN the road leading to Jess's past. But most, when they saw that it was a dead end, didn't go past the warning signs on his face.

She had just breezed on by and pressed him for answers. Answers he didn't owe her or anyone else. It should have been that simple.

But it wasn't because maybe, just maybe, Mallory was right. A part of him was still lying flat on his back that damn arena.

The part of him that had been manipulated and used by a woman he had loved. The fall had broken his body, but Hallie's betrayal had damn near killed him.

Jess watched as she quietly collected herself, slid from her chair, and hurried out the door. He sat there for a few seconds, debating on whether or not he should go after her.

If she was so determined that she could take care of herself, he should let her. He should let her walk right out that door and do whatever the hell she wanted.

But Jess had promised to protect her, and he would.

He grabbed his cup and hurried out the door. She was halfway down the street, and he had to jog to catch up with her. His hurtful comment about her fear of men hadn't been deliberate or accurate. She didn't shrink, flinch, or run. She was a resilient woman who stood her ground.

She had issues, and he shouldn't have thrown them in her face. He owed her an apology. "People who try to dissect me and my reasons for not riding tend to tread on my patience."

That wasn't an apology, but it was the best he could do right now.

"I've been taken apart a few times myself," she said, stopping near the corner of the sidewalk. "It sucks."

Most women he knew would have been angry and harboring a grudge for days after an argument like the one they'd just had. But Mallory had already forgiven him. She wasn't afraid of wearing her heart on her sleeve where he was concerned.

It was an ingenuous quality that niggled Jess's already guilty conscience. "I think we should just agree that the conversation, like the kiss, took us in a direction we didn't want to go and leave it at that."

"A direction we didn't want to go?" she repeated, looking taken aback.

"Well, yeah," he said, shifting from one leg to the other. "We both said things we regret and last night, we were drinking —"

"Agreed," she said, holding out her hand for a shake. "We both said things we shouldn't have."

And the kiss? How did she feel about that? He wouldn't ask.

He stared down at her small hand, outstretched and waiting for him to accept. The heart couldn't be mended with pins and made to trust again with therapy. When the heart broke, it splintered, leaving jagged shards in its wake. Those shards were still inside him, ready to catch on the tender parts Mallory threatened to expose.

He wasn't in love with her, but he was attracted to her in a way that petrified him. He didn't want to be in the same room with her, spend the day with her, and he sure as hell didn't want to touch her. But the sincerity in her eyes left him little choice.

He gently clasped her hand and gave it a shake. It was a sweet and platonic gesture that shouldn't have been arousing. But it was. Everything about Mallory Montgomery's touch was arousing. There was something about the woman that tied him up inside. Something that tempted him to grab hold of her and chance a wild and dangerous ride.

"I've made great progress," she said, nervously sliding her palm over her thigh after he let her hand go. "Six years ago, that handshake would have been impossible."

Jess hadn't taken the first step towards getting back on a horse or building a long-term relationship with a woman.

He spent a limited time with the Rescue horses, watching them from afar to assess their personality so he could help find permeant homes for them.

But that was it.

And finding that woman to settle down with…?

He took a deep breath and let it out slowly. That was never going to happen.

"Intimacy isn't easy for me. I gave my virginity to a surfer who called me babe because I wanted to feel normal." She let out a half-hearted laugh that ended with a little sigh. "It didn't work."

It had taken two long and lonely years after his last surgery for Jess to get back into the sexual swing of things.

He had gone to a bar in Dallas, sat down beside a woman he didn't know, and started a conversation. They'd gone to her place and had sex in the dark because he had needed that same normalcy as Mallory had.

It hadn't been great sex, but it had given him a release and the reassurance that he was still a man.

Mallory had needed that same validation and proof that she was a "normal" woman. The surfer had been no different than his stranger at the bar. But it pained Jess to know she'd experienced lovemaking for the first time under those circumstances.

"Something must be really wrong with you if having sex with a beach bum didn't make you feel normal," he said, shooting her an overly dismayed frown. "I hope you insisted that he wear a full body condom."

She burst into laughter. "Xander wasn't a beach bum. He was a sweet guy with a bright future in board wax."

"Ah," he nodded, feeling a little tingle in his stomach when she laughed. "Family business?"

"You guessed it," she said, chuckling. "We were friends in high school, and I liked him. I mean he was attractive and…"

"Safe?" he supplied, reading her thoughts.

"Yeah. I thought that would make it easier." Another sigh left her.

"It didn't?"

She shook her head. "No. Thank God, it didn't take long."

He wanted to keep their conversation going with the same relaxed pace. He didn't want to pry or dissect. But he had questions. Maybe by gently nudging her along, he could uncover the reason why she was so leery of men and how Aiden fit into the picture. "What happened after the surfer dude?"

"I concentrated on work and my art." She shrugged a shoulder and grimaced slightly. "Sex with Xander wasn't the great event I thought it would be. I closed my eyes and it was over, so I guess I figured, why try again?"

The sum of Mallory's sexual involvement with men had begun and ended with surfer dude, a teenage kid who obviously hadn't known a damn thing about pleasing a woman.

Jess tried like hell not to think about all the ways he could please her, satisfy her, and give her that great event she deserved.

They continued down the street, walking like two friends out for a casual stroll

"But even after the Xander encounter that kiss you gave me last night would have gotten you punched in the junk."

He shielded his crotch with a hand, thinking they should talk, and he should explain. "About that kiss…"

She stopped abruptly to face him. "Yes, about that kiss. Was that a spur of the moment thing or were you hoping to get laid?"

Her crude analogy irritated him, and it shouldn't because if they'd had sex last night, it should have only been "getting laid" and nothing more.

But still, the indelicate words spoken by the woman with her arms crossed protectively over her breasts, vulnerability in her eyes, and a need that went beyond sexual gratification, was unsettling to him.

He should have changed the subject or walked away. But he couldn't help rebounding with a question that would probably haunt him until the day he died. "Why? Are you offering to finish what we started?"

She never blinked. "Would you accept if I was?"

Jess wanted to answer her with another kiss, forget the

meeting, drive back to his house, undress her slowly, make her shudder with orgasms, and have satisfying sex until neither of them had the strength to move. He wanted to forget all his rules on dating and distance with women.

But Mallory was a lovemaking woman, plain and simple. A woman with a soft soul and delicate emotions she tried to conceal behind a tough and sassy exterior. She was also a woman who deserved a man who would be there after the feel-good wore off.

He wasn't that man and he wouldn't risk his heart or hers for a few hours of pleasure. "No."

A flash of rejection passed across her face before she dropped her arms and rotated around on her hip. "Then I'm not offering." She took off down the street like an invading army. Stride wide. Arms flailing. "Which way are we going?"

Groaning inward, he followed her. "Straight. The mayor's office is in the white building."

They crossed the street, and Jess saw Logan's truck parked near the building. The brothers were probably already inside, waiting for him to arrive.

"But." She stopped abruptly near the entrance, swung around and dug her finger into his chest. "I do have to point out that it was you who kissed me. It wasn't like I forced you to do it. You didn't dare me to kiss you. You just took it upon yourself to kiss me." She leaned closer to further her scrutiny and scrunched her nose. "So if you weren't interested in getting laid, why did you kiss me?"

"Why, indeed?" came the question from behind them.

Jess turned around to find Logan and Ty standing a few feet behind them. Both had a Pixies coffee cup in their hands.

Logan held his hand out to Mallory. "I don't believe

we've been properly introduced. I'm Logan Gates, and this is my brother Tyler."

Ty licked whipped cream from his upper lip and hitched his grin higher as he stepped forward to do the same. "At your service, Ma'am."

Mallory ignored their introduction and stared at Ty's outstretched hand with deep-seated aversion. Then spun around, yanked the door open, and disappeared inside the office building.

"You look like hell, man." Logan laughed, raising a questionable eyebrow at Jess. "I would ask what happened, but I think Beautiful explained it."

Ty moved in front of the glass door and watched Mallory's backside as she hurried down the hall to the mayor's office. "Have you lost your ever-loving mind?"

"Maybe," he sighed.

Logan widened his smile and rocked back on his boot heels, patiently waiting for Jess to say something.

"It's a long story," Jess said.

Logan laughed. "Oh, I bet it is."

"You can start by telling us why you aren't interested in getting laid by that stunning creature," Ty said.

He used the only excuse he thought they would understand. "Because Mallory is El's sister."

Logan's smile vanished. "You're shittin' me."

"I shit you not," Jess said, stepping to the door.

Ty frowned. "I don't see the problem."

Logan lifted a shoulder. "To be honest, neither do I."

Ty pushed Jess away from the door. "But you boys feel free to stay out here and discuss it. I'll be inside with that splendid creature."

"There's nothing to discuss," Jess said as the door closed behind Ty.

Logan's smile returned. "We better get in there. You know what happens when Ty gets cocky."

Seconds after Jess's eyes adjusted to the fluorescent lighting inside the building, he saw Ty walking back towards the door holding his nose. A trickle of blood oozed its way onto his upper lip. And since Lauren and Mallory were probably the only women inside, Jess could guess what had happened.

"Goddamn it, Ty," he cursed. "You touched her, didn't you?"

"Since when is putting your arm around a woman's shoulder a crime?" Ty carefully moved his nose, wincing as he did. "I think it's broken."

Before meeting Mallory, Jess had had different ideas about what was and wasn't inappropriate behavior towards a woman. He would have had the same confounded look on his face as Ty because he had thought to touch a woman's hair, shoulder, or hand was perfectly acceptable behavior.

But Mallory had redefined those ideas.

"This is the twenty-first century, you barbarian," Logan taunted, smirking at his brother's pain. "Ever hear of personal space?"

"This isn't a fucking joke," Jess said, coldly.

The grin on Logan's face melted.

"Did you notice the bruises on her wrist while you were groping her?" Jess asked Ty.

"I wasn't groping—bruises?" Ty dropped his hand, his cockiness deflated by the question. "No, I —I didn't see…"

Jess tossed his cup into a nearby garbage can. "As boys, we were taught that women weren't objects that could be taken on a whim of a man, played with, and then discarded. That there are boundaries we don't cross."

Logan shook his head, defending his brother. "Ty would never −"

"But he did." Jess cut in. "We all did. When Mallory stopped and asked us for directions, we saw her as an object. A beautiful thing we could talk about, bet on, and touch. Not as a person or a woman with who might have been through something traumatic."

Logan's face went blank. "Point taken."

"Look, man, I'll apologize," Ty said.

"You've done enough damage," Logan said, pointing him towards the door. "Go nurse your nose in the truck."

MALLORY SAT IN THE CHAIR ACROSS FROM THE MAYOR'S door and began chewing her thumbnail, her heart sinking to her stomach from Jess's rejection.

She didn't have one regret about punching Tyler Gates in the nose. The man was a pompous cretin who needed to be sterilized before he could reproduce.

Her regret lay with thinking she could pretend she wasn't damaged, that something deep down inside of her wasn't still broken, and that a man like Jess wouldn't see it or be appalled by it.

She watched Jess walk down the hall toward her. He'd dressed in a pair of light-colored jeans and a blue button-up shirt. Even in his battered brown hat and worn boots, he looked sophisticated and opulent and so far out of her reach.

His eyes were a mixture of worry and anger as he looked at down at her hand. "Let me see."

The gritty tone of his concerned voice resonated deep within her like the hard clamor of thunder. It vibrated her inner core and made her heart do a little flutter as he hunched down in front of her to look her hand.

His fingers gently inspected her knuckles like they had her wrists. He had made it clear that he wasn't interested in anything physical. His touch would always be soft and tender and with great concern. But it would never be passionate like it had been last night.

That fact was too bittersweet.

Logan dropped her a quick glance on his way to the receptionist desk but didn't offer her the smile he had earlier.

Mallory withdrew her hand from Jess's and tucked it under her thigh. "I don't need petting or cooing. I'm fine."

She had punched his buddy in the nose and made a spectacle of herself in front of the mayor's administrative assistant because she didn't like being touched.

Tyler's arm around her shoulder wasn't the same as a slap on the ass or a hand down her pants. It was something friends did. But damn it, they weren't friends. And when he touched her… she hated it.

Without the bourbon, Jess wouldn't have kissed her and wasn't the least bit interested in taking things farther. And why would he want a woman like her when he had a woman like Brandi? A woman who Mallory knew — by reading the texts — didn't have a single hang-up about sex or intimacy.

Nausea hit her, causing her to hold her belly. "I would have been perfectly fine at the apartment. Dragging me to town with you was a mistake."

"Yeah." He stood with an unreadable expression on his face. "I think it was."

Logan came back to where they were. "Harry's ready when we are."

"Stay put," Jess told her. "I'll be out as soon as the meeting is over."

The door closed, but the paper-thin walls allowed her to hear everything.

Jess made his opening points. The rodeo could bring in significant revenue and help attract tourists. He explained most of the work could be done by community volunteers. He had talked with several people who were more than happy to help with the rodeo.

But the mayor wasn't sure they had the resources to make a full-scale rodeo a success.

"I've been in contact with Winsor Rodeo," Jess said.

"The staging company out of San Antonio?" the mayor asked.

"That's the one," Jess said. "I was supposed to meet with Brandi, the owner, this weekend but something came up. We're working to reschedule."

"You think they could help us pull this off?" the mayor asked.

"Brandi was a fierce barrel racer up until a few years ago when she hung up her saddle to take over the family business," Jess answered, his voice confident as he talked about the woman.

"I don't know," the mayor sighed heavily. "There are other rodeos out there with bigger cash prizes that could make it difficult for us to draw competitors."

"We don't have to offer a giant purse to draw them in," Logan pointed out.

"He's right," Jess agreed. "When I first started out, I was happy just being there. It was a way for me to get some experience and make connections."

Brandi was one of those connections, a successful businesswoman and a skilled horsewoman whom Jess had admiration for.

He had admitted that their business meeting wouldn't be all business, and now he was rescheduling their meeting.

Mallory slumped in the seat, ready to bawl her eyes out. But she didn't because what she was feeling was ridiculous. They'd shared one kiss, and she shouldn't feel so overtaken and consumed by one kiss with a man she barely knew.

She was in Santa Camino to fulfill a promise to her mother. After she talked with Eleanor and her mother's ashes were scattered, she would be on her way.

"Men are something, aren't they?"

Mallory raised her eyes to the blonde woman sitting behind the desk. "They sure are."

"They haven't a clue how strong we really are," she said, stacking papers into a pile.

Or how deeply they can hurt us, Mallory added silently.

"Ty's a little rough around the edges but otherwise safe," the woman assured her."

Mallory had to admit that she'd probably hit Tyler to help vent some of the hurt and frustration she was feeling over Jess's rejection. "I guess I shouldn't have punched him so hard."

"You didn't hurt anything but his pride. Let him stew a while. Maybe next time he'll heed your warning." The woman moved from the desk to the small refrigerator in the corner. She took out a bottle of water and handed it to Mallory. "I'm Lauren Ritter."

"Ritter?" she asked, accepting the bottle. "As in Colton Ritter?"

A shadow of sadness passed across the woman's face, but she kept her smile. "I'm Colton's wife."

"I'm sorry it came out like that," Mallory said, thinking how weird she had just sounded. "Jess gave me a tour of the Rescue and well…"

"Colton and I are very proud of the work that's being done there."

"I can see why. The place is amazing." She held out her hand. "I'm Mallory."

Lauren accepted her hand. "Yes, I know. I visited Eleanor in the hospital yesterday, and after you came walking in with Jess, I figured you must be the sister she was telling me about."

The doors opened, and Jess and Logan walked out of the office. Both turned to shake the mayors' hand.

"I think this is a step in the right direction," the mayor said with a bright, campaigning smile on his face.

"So do I," Jess agreed.

Logan turned to follow the mayor into his office, pitching ideas of how the rodeo could be tied into local folklore and legends, the search for gold and outlaw hide-outs. They could organize guided horseback rides to Ravorn Caverns and spin the Ledged of the Lady Outlaw into it.

"Well?" Lauren prompted Jess. "How'd it go?"

His face was hopeful. "I'm going to pull together a list of committee members to get everything started."

Lauren smiled. "I knew you would convince him."

"I was beginning to have my doubts," he admitted.

"Harry is a sweetheart and a great boss, but he doesn't always see the bigger picture. He's retiring next year and is looking for a way to go out with a bang. Those are his words, not mine." Lauren gave them a wink. "I told him that being the first mayor to establish a rodeo in Santa Camino would put his name in the history books."

Jess laughed. "You are a clever woman, Lauren. You should run for mayor."

Her eyes widened. "Do you think I'd win?"

"I'd vote for you."

"Oh," she waved him off. "Don't put the notion in my head."

Jess tucked the paper he'd taken notes on into his front shirt pocket. "Have you been to the hospital yet?"

"I went by last night. Tucker is beautiful." Lauren put her hand over her heart and sighed. "Seeing him makes me want another baby. But you know how that is…"

"How is Colton?"

Lauren's face became impassive. "The same, I guess. We haven't spoken since the charity auction last year. Little Jack will be back from Montana in a couple of days, and I'm sure he'll tell me all about how his dad is doing."

Jess cleared his throat. "Harry wants me to email you that list."

Lauren's polite smile returned. "I'll be watching for it. Bye, y'all."

CHAPTER 15

MALLORY WALKED ALONGSIDE JESS AS THEY HEADED OUT the door and up the street. But she was more standoffish and less perky.

"If Lauren lives here and Colton lives in Montana, how does their marriage work?" she asked.

"It doesn't." It was the most straightforward answer Jess had to one of the most complicated relationships in Santa Camino.

"Then why do they stay married?"

"Beats the hell out of me," he answered grimly. "Maybe for Little Jack."

"Or maybe because they still love each other," she said, stuffing her hands into the pockets of her jeans.

Colton and Lauren had been happily married until his battle with PTSD caused them to separate. They'd had a unique marriage of unconditional devotion and love for one another that was rare. And now, they were a reminder of just how miserable love could be if it went wrong.

It was clear that Lauren wanted another baby, and Jess

knew that it was only a matter of time before her commitment to her marriage overpowered that need.

He made a turn at the crosswalk and headed towards
the sheriff's office.

Mallory came to a full stop when she saw where they
were headed. "Uh-uh. No cops."

"Why?" He took her arm and gently pushed her up the
steps and through the doors. "Is there a warrant for your
arrest or something they can lock you up for?"

She ran her tongue over her teeth and gave him a
sultry, but scornful smile over her shoulder. "You'd miss
me, and you know it."

"No, I wouldn't because El would send me right back
to watch over her little sister. With my luck, we'd be
cellmates."

"And that would be awful for you because I'm not
Brandi."

"It would be awful for a lot of reasons," he answered,
walking towards Finn's office. "You not being Brandi isn't
one of them."

"Then what are they?" she asked, stopping in the
middle of the hallway.

"You're never still, you have kick-ass self-defense moves,
and I think I heard you snoring through the door this
morning. You'd be a horrible cellmate." He was teasing,
but she didn't seem to find humor in it.

"Look," she said, watching nervously as a deputy
walked by them. "I knew exactly what I was doing and
where that kiss was going."

Last night, he had been the one who had gotten
carried away. The one leading the charge, instigating that
game of Truth or Dare and the one blaming whiskey for
his recklessness. But for Mallory, there hadn't been
anything erroneous about their kiss.

"Like I said, intimacy isn't easy for me. When a man touches me or steps into my personal space, I panic and usually end up throat punching him. But it's different with you."

Jess was broadsided by culpability and a responsibility he didn't want.

"Why is it different with me?" he asked, keeping his voice low and out of earshot of the employees and visitors.

"I don't know. I wish I did. Maybe then I could be just like any other woman." She dropped her gaze and began picking at her thumbnail. "I understand why you don't want to be with a woman like me —"

"A woman like you?" he asked.

"A woman who shrinks into a ball or punches men in the nose when they touch her." She swallowed hard. "A woman with hang-ups."

Those were the exact reasons Jess wouldn't have sex with her. By Mallory's own admission, *he* was special. *He* could touch her and kiss her. That made her susceptible to all sorts of emotions, including love.

Hell. Maybe he was overreacting. Maybe she wanted it to be just sex too. But if she didn't, Jess didn't want to be the man who taught Mallory one of life's hardest lessons.

Sometimes love wasn't love at all. It was just sex and satisfaction. Desire and lust. Moving on and forgetting.

"Christ, Mallory," he swore under his breath, drawing several glances their way. "Can we just forget about the kiss for now and have this discussion when the whole town isn't watching?"

She looked around, innocently unmoved by the people or their speculating chatter. "What discussion?"

His mind stalled because there shouldn't be any further discussion about that damn kiss. He had said he wasn't interested in finishing what they had started last night, and she had bought that lie.

End of story.

But Jess wouldn't add to Mallory's insecurities by letting her assume he wasn't interested in sex because she had complexities regarding intimacy and men.

He took her by the arm and drew her to the little corner where the water fountain was. "There are things we need to talk about, things I need to make clear before anything else happens between us."

Interest darkened the autumn gold in her eyes. "What kind of things?"

"Things that can't be said here. Okay?"

She agreed with a hesitant nod.

He pulled her alongside him as they moved down the hall to the sheriff's office.

Mallory resumed her preserving stance, crossed her arms over her chest, and leaned against the outside wall of the office. "I'll wait out here."

He knocked on the door, trying to center his mind on the danger Mallery might be in and away from sex. "You busy?"

Giving his eyes a hard rub as he raised his head from the paperwork in front of him, Finn leaned back in his seat and motioned Jess inside. "No. What's up?"

McCrea and Finn had graduated high school together and were about the same age. But the last three years as sheriff had given Finn a few more wrinkles around the eyes and added a couple of gray hairs to his dark blonde hair.

"We may have a situation."

Finn dipped his head in Mallory's direction, a slight smile curving his lips. "Is she part of the situation?"

"Yeah, she is," Jess answered and then proceeded to explain who Mallory was and that Rex might be stalking her. He also told Finn about the lights up on the ridge. "This guy's trouble. He has a history of violence, and though she'd never admit it, she's scared."

Finn leaned forward, taking notes as he spoke. "Do you know what the altercation was about? Did she press charges?"

"No, I didn't press charges," Mallory butted in. Moving from the wall to the doorway, she glared at Jess. "Can we go now?"

"It would help if I knew what your father was driving," Finn said.

"A red Dodge pickup with a Carlos Casino bumper sticker on the back."

Finn's pen stilled. "Is that in La Claire?"

With her jaw welded tight, she nodded.

"Is your family from there?" he asked without a trace of indifference.

Mallory's face washed pale. "I don't see what that has to do with any of this."

"I'm just trying to be thorough," Finn explained. "If your father has a criminal background and is involved in anything in La Claire, it might help us find him or at least turn up a lead or two."

She lowered her eyes to the floor with a timid expression that made Jess hurt. "We moved there when I was eight."

Finn wrote it down. "I'll contact the authorities in La Claire and send out a couple of deputies to patrol the ranch and Rescue tonight."

Mallory backtracked her way to the office door. "I'll be outside."

Jess moved to the window. Still holding tight to her midriff as she exited the building, Mallory closed her eyes and leaned against a streetlight. She looked ready to vomit. "How did you know the casino was in La Claire?"

A weighty sigh eased from Finn's lips. "La Claire is a real shit hole. The only thing that's kept it from becoming a ghost town are the drugs from the casino. Six years ago, Durant Drilling had a rig a few miles east of the casino. The boys weren't picky about their beer or women and would go there to blow off steam after their shift was over."

Finn had worked his way up the ranks of Durant Drilling after he graduated high school, and Clayton hadn't made it any easier on him because he was his son. He had sweated, hurt, and gotten as dirty as any of the men working on the crew. His work ethic and no-nonsense attitude had been a part of his campaign for sheriff and had played an essential role in him winning the election.

"The story goes that one minute they were neck deep in beautiful women and cold beer, and the next, DEA agents had them in handcuffs and on their way to jail. They questioned them, but hell, it wasn't hard for the agents to see that they were just a bunch of roughnecks looking for a good time."

Jess massaged the back of his neck. "Do you think Rex has a connection to the illegal activity at the casino?"

Finn hesitated with a hard look out the window, then tossed his pen onto the desk. "Maybe."

Jess moved to the door. "Let me know as soon as you find out something."

"Don't take this into your own hands. If the guy shows up, call 9-1-1. We'll take care of it."

That wasn't going to happen, at least not until Jess repaid Rex for the bruises on Mallory. "I'm not making any promises."

When she saw him walk out the door, she headed up the street toward the truck. He preferred those wide angry strides she had taken earlier over the short and guarded steps she was taking now. She was clutching her stomach so tight he thought she might implode.

After walking around the truck, she opened the door and climbed in.

"McCrea messaged me while I was in the meeting. Eleanor and the baby will be home in a little while. I thought we'd swing by there before I dropped you off at the Rescue."

"Okay," she said, keeping her head towards the window.

She stayed concreted in that position by the door until they reached the ranch.

He had wanted peace and quiet this morning, but right now, all he wanted was for her to talk to him. First the incident with Ty and now this silence that had started when Finn mentioned her father and the casino.

Jess felt uneasy and unequipped to deal with whatever was going on. He didn't know what to say or do, so he just sat there behind the wheel, looking like a dumbass.

He brought the truck to a stop beside the metal garage. Mallory opened her door and was out of the cab before he had time to put it in gear. She hurried up the sidewalk and waited for him to disarm the alarm and unlock the door.

When he did, she went straight for the guest bedroom and closed the door behind her.

"Damn it," he whispered, fearing he had done more harm than good by talking to Finn.

He snagged his phone from his pocket and opened his email, took a seat at the table, and used the quiet time to work on the list of committee members Harry wanted.

～

ONE BY ONE, JESS MADE CALLS TO PEOPLE WHO HAD expressed an interest. With the committee members notified, he emailed Lauren about possible dates for a meeting. She would arrange it and send out invitations to the list of members.

A little after three, the front door flew open, and Sophie burst into the house. "We're home!"

Jess laid his phone down, feeling his freedom had finally come. "It's about time," he said, teased when she came running into the kitchen. "I thought you found yourself a cowboy and had gone off and gotten married."

She giggled with a contagious smile that deepened the dimple in her cheek. "I can't get married. I'm only five."

Jess set her on his knee and planted a kiss on the top of her head. "Where's Tucker?"

Her little finger pointed outside. "Daddy's bringing him in."

Eleanor walked in, carrying a vase of a dozen red roses, undoubtedly from McCrea, and her purse. "God, I'm glad to be home."

Jess took the vase and gave her a quick hug. "Hello, Momma. How do you feel?"

"Like I could sleep for a hundred years," she answered, looking past him to the kitchen. "Where's Mallory?"

"In the bedroom, I think." He sat the vase on the table and stuffed his phone into his back pocket. He was ready to hit the road. After he visited with the baby and caught McCrea up on what had happened with the lights, he'd drop Mallory off at the Rescue and be on his way.

Eleanor tapped on the door. "Mallory." No answer. She knocked again and again, calling her name each time.

"She might be asleep," he said, watching Sophie sneak from the kitchen, lugging Pocket Change up the stairs. "I had a hard time getting her awake this morning."

Eleanor cracked the door to peek inside. "Mallory?" She opened the door wider. "She's not in here or the bathroom."

"I was busy making calls," Jess said, annoyed he hadn't seen her slip past him. But then he heard her voice coming from outside. He met her at the front door. "Where have you been?"

The dash of anger hit her eyes. "I went for a walk, not that it's any of your business."

He followed her into the living room. "It is my business. After what happened last night —"

"What happened last night?" McCrea asked, sitting the car seat on the couch.

"Bourbon," Mallory said, matter-of-factly. "Bourbon is what happened."

Jess ignored her. "We saw headlights up on the ridge."

"Did you get a look at the vehicle?" McCrea asked.

"It was too dark to see," Jess answered. "But I talked to Finn this morning. He's sending someone out to patrol the area tonight."

"Even so," McCrea said. "I think we should take a look around tomorrow. Whoever it was got through the gate. There's no livestock up there, but I don't want to leave it accessible."

Eleanor shook her head. "McCrea, I will not have that man snooping around my land."

"We don't know that it was Rex," Jess was quick to say.

"It was him," Mallory said and tossed an empty cigar pack down on the coffee table. "That's the brand he smokes."

"Where did you get that?" Jess questioned.

She shoved her hands into her pockets. "Out by the road."

"You weren't supposed to go anywhere without me," he reminded her.

Mallory ignored him. "Eleanor, we really need to talk."

Tucker let out a cry, calling Eleanor's attention to him. "Let me feed the baby, and I'm yours until supper."

"Don't worry about supper." Sitting the diaper bag down beside her, McCrea hit Jess on the shoulder as he walked by. "We got it covered, right?"

"There are steaks in the freezer," Eleanor added.

Mallory crouched in front of the baby and unlatched the buckles. "Hi, baby boy."

Tucker answered her with a kick and a small shriek.

"Oh, no," she crooned with a soft as silk laugh. She lifted the baby from the seat and cradled him in the crook of her arm. "Don't cry, buddy."

Jess took a step toward the kitchen but was unable to draw himself away from Mallory.

Everything about her changed the second she touched Tucker. Her smile, her skin, and even her hair had been transformed into that unmistakable glow. An iridescent sheen of happiness only a baby could produce.

"You look like you know what you're doing," Eleanor said, positioning a blanket over her shoulder as Mallory handed her Tucker.

"I've had some practice."

Jess wanted to ask how she had gotten that practice, but he was already in too deep with this woman. Expressing an interest in her baby experience would make all kinds of trouble for him.

"I'll defrost the steaks," McCrea said. "You wash the potatoes."

Jess followed him into the kitchen. "You wash the potatoes. I'm out of here."

McCrea's lips drew into a wily smile. "Darlin'," he called out, to his wife.

"Yes?" she answered back.

"Jess has volunteered to run into town for ice cream after supper. What kind would you like?"

"Vanilla."

"Strawberry!" Sophie yelled.

"I'll have chocolate," Mallory added.

Eleanor laughed. "Jess, you're a sweetheart."

"That's me," he yelled back then silently mouthed, *you sneaky bastard.*

McCrea handed him a bag of potatoes. "Now, wash the damn spuds."

Jess jerked the bag from his hands. "I had plans for this weekend."

McCrea opened the freezer door, and white fog billowed out as he spoke. "With Brandi Winsor. Logan told me. Did you explain why you couldn't make it?"

He identified five large potatoes big enough for baking and set the bag aside. "That I was forced to babysit a woman who just happens to be gorgeous and flirty? No. I didn't think she'd understand, so I improvised by saying El had gone into labor on my watch."

McCrea's mouth quirked up at one corner. "How did she take that?"

"She got all weird."

"Define weird," McCrea said, shutting the freezer door with his shoulder.

He turned the sink faucet on and waited for it to warm. "She started talking about how she loved babies and that she wanted one."

McCrea's eyes widened.

"Yeah, it scared the hell out of me too," he said and heard his brother laugh. He found the brush Eleanor used to wash vegetables. "Lauren got all dreamy-eyed with baby fever too when I mentioned Tucker. Maybe the old wives' tale is true."

McCrea tore open the packets of steaks. "Which one?"

He tossed the potatoes into the sink and started scrubbing. "The one about when one woman gets pregnant, they all do. That's it's something in the water."

McCrea let out another laugh. "God, I hope not. Making babies is something special."

Jess envisioned that tender, moment when love created life and felt a sharp stab of loss hit him in the chest. He had given up on that dream a long time ago.

He reached for a clean dishtowel to dry the potatoes with. "I wouldn't know."

"That's your own damn fault." McCrea's face became solemn as he piled the frozen steaks onto a plate. "Sooner or later, you're going to wish you'd stopped roaming, committed to a woman, and had those kids."

Jess had spent most of his rodeo years bouncing from one woman to the next, never letting himself get attached. The only exception had been his two-year commitment to Hallie.

He opened the top cabinet over the refrigerator, knowing exactly were Eleanor kept the aluminum foil, and started wrapping the potatoes. "I'd love to have what you have. But one try is enough for me. I've learned my lesson."

McCrea put the steaks in the microwave and punched in a defrost time. "That was a long time ago. You and Hallie were both just kids. Neither one of you were ready to settle down." He opened the back door and motioned Jess outside.

Jess gathered the potatoes into his hands, balancing the fifth one on top and followed him down the steps and onto the new deck.

"Mallory, on the other hand, looks more than willing to drink water with you."

"That's not funny."

"I didn't say it to be funny. Do you really want to spend the rest of your life going from one woman to the next, weekend after weekend?"

He wasn't a man who let the opinions of others direct his life. But he had a reputation to protect. And he wasn't about to tell McCrea that several of those weekends he spent out of town had been by himself. Mainly because he didn't want to feel like a curmudgeonly cowboy who couldn't get a date.

He could get a date, lots of them. But hooking up with a woman like the one at the bar in Dallas, a woman he didn't know and had left alone in the middle of the night, wasn't as appealing as it had been when he was younger.

But neither was digging his heels into a long-term romance even if it didn't involve love. It was a lonely life, but Jess didn't have to worry about being hurt or hurting someone else.

He laid the potatoes on the patio table and frowned. "Let me remind you that Mallory is about the same age as Hallie was when I proposed."

"She's a lot wiser than Hallie, surely you can see that. She's not a spoiled girl looking for attention from any man who walks by."

"She's also El's sister."

McCrea lit the grill and closed the lid. "So?"

Jess gave his brow a hard rub. "What if we drink water together and it all goes to hell? Have you thought about that?"

"Then we'd have a little Jess or Mallory running around for Sophie and Tucker to play with. My wife would love that."

Jess pushed that image from his mind. "The babies, yeah, but what about me, McCrea? How would El feel about the man who fathered those babies?" There was a small part of him that genuinely worried about how Eleanor would feel about him if he slept with her sister.

More importantly, Jess worried that he might become addicted to making those babies and lose his heart to the mother.

McCrea gave him a solid stare. "Eleanor knows you'd never run from your responsibilities as a father even if it didn't work out between the two of you. Besides, what if it doesn't go south? What if the two of you fall in love?"

Jess turned towards the hills, gripping the deck railing with both hands as he set his eyes on the horizon. Last night, he and Mallory had shared a kiss, and today he had learned things about her and himself he never imagined could be true.

And he was considering what falling in love with her would be like and if he could ever allow himself to trust another woman with his heart.

He found all that damn upsetting because just two days ago, he had been on his way to San Antonio for a wild, three-day weekend with Brandi. Now all he wanted to do was go back inside and have dinner with Mallory.

She was spontaneous, flirty, and unpredictable, a beautiful woman he desired. But she was also haunted by a something that had made her punch Ty in the nose and cautious of Finn.

She was hiding something that might blow up in his face or reveal a different person entirely, so he wasn't ready to think about drinking water with Mallory. "How's the horse?"

"Not so good. He'd suffered multiple injuries before we

got to him and was shoved into a holding stall the size of a bread box that kept him confined."

"How long had he been there?" Jess asked.

"Probably a few months," McCrea said, grimly. "He's a wild one, bred for buckin'."

"He's a bronc horse."

"Without a doubt. There's a bucking stock brand on him. I'm guessing he was sold and whoever bought him tried beating it out of him. I'm waiting for a detailed assessment from Doc. I'll know more in the morning." McCrea made a glance towards the house and lowered his voice, his eyes tinted with humor. "What happened last night other than the lights?"

Jess folded his arms across his chest, unwilling to divulge anything. "You're worse than the old gossips around town, you know that?"

"Oh, hell." McCrea laughed. "I'm not asking for details, just a broad summation."

Jess hesitated then said, "We drank bourbon together."

"Oh." Confusion then shocked registered on McCrea's face. "Oh, you mean…"

"Yeah," Jess drawled. "That's what I mean."

McCrea chuckled. "The whole bottle or just a couple of sips?"

"A glass."

McCrea slapped his shoulder. "That's just enough to wet your whistle, not quench your thirst."

"Speaking of quenching my thirst," he said, dropping his arms. "I think I'll head to San Antonio for a few days and try to salvage my plans with Brandi. You have everything under control here."

The humor in McCrea's eyes faded. "Are you sure you don't want to stay around for a while? Things could get interesting between you and Mallory once you get to know each other and −"

"Don't start."

"All I'm saying is, water is a lot more satisfying than bourbon."

"I won't drink water with any woman," Jess said. "Not now, not ever."

McCrea's eyebrows pushed into his hairline. "Never say never. I thought the same way, and now I'm a daddy of two."

CHAPTER 16

MALLORY WATCHED FROM THE DOORWAY OF THE NURSERY as Eleanor lay Tucker in the crib and stroked his head, giving him the maternal attention every child deserved.

This house was full of love, and the children conceived and raised here would always be cherished. They would always know affection. They would always be protected and sheltered from the evil of this world.

She hugged her stomach, feeling empty and misplaced. Had there been the tiniest notion of love involved in her creation? Guile inched its way up her throat and rested on the back of her tongue as the answer to her question seeped into her mind like dark, murky floodwater.

"What's on your mind, Mallory?" Eleanor's question burst into her thoughts.

She stepped into the hall and waited with her back against the wall as Eleanor quietly closed the door behind them.

She regretted mentioning that damn bumper sticker. She needed more time to arrange her words, but after the sheriff talked to the cops in La Claire, she might not have much time to say what needed to be said. "Lots of things changed after you left home."

The concern in her sister's eyes deepened. "How?"

Mallory rested the back of her head against the wall and stared up at the ceiling. "Rex lost his job and Mom…" She closed her eyes, remembering the isolation that came with her mother's deep depression. "Mom got worse. We lost the house and moved from Santa Fe to La Claire a few months later."

"I guess that's why all my letters came back," Eleanor reasoned and moved to take a seat on the stairs.

Mallory sat down on the step above her. "We moved into this rundown trailer park, and Rex got a job as head of security at a local casino."

"I worried about the two of you," Eleanor confessed. "Rex was so controlling and abusive."

She thought back to all the times her father had been those things, and there were many. But only one made her want to double over and disappear. "We managed. In between the bouts of depression, Mom got a job as a waitress, and sometimes, life was almost tolerable."

Eleanor placed her hand on Mallory's arm. "What happened? Why were the two of you fighting? Why is he here?"

She bit her bottom lip as she struggled for the right words. "I knew Rex would follow me, but I honestly thought that all of this would be over by the time you and the baby came home."

"What would be over?"

"Eleanor." McCrea appeared at the bottom of the stairs. "Finn is here, and he wants to talk to you."

"Tell him to wait," Mallory said, quickly.

"It's important, Eleanor," Finn replied, obviously hearing her comment.

"It'll be okay," Eleanor patted her hand before starting down the stairs. "I'll be right back."

"No," Mallory said, hurrying down the steps behind her. "There's something I need to tell you —" She froze when she saw the sheriff standing just inside the front door.

Finn Durant was broad through the shoulders like he had wrestled many a man and steer. But it wasn't his size that made her feel threatened. It was the authoritarian face under the hat, the hard jawline, and the badge on his belt.

Talking to law enforcement had always done more harm than good for Mallory. When they came to the house asking questions, she had been the one who paid the price.

As a kid, she had learned to be rebellious and unfriendly to anyone in uniform when her father was around. She put on a good act that had kept her and her mother mostly unscathed.

But the horrible feeling that settled into the pit of her stomach when the sheriff locked eyes with her and made pretense impossible.

"There are steaks on the grill," McCrea said. "You want one?"

He scrubbed a hand over his jaw. "No, thanks."

"What's up?" Jess questioned, setting his brow to a hard frown that added to Mallory's uneasiness.

Finn moved the gun holster at his hip back a few inches and hooked a thumb through his belt. "After you two left my office, I did some digging and made a few phone calls."

Mallory wanted to fade away into the shadows the way she had as a kid. She wanted to jump on her bike and never look back. No one would notice, and after a while, no one would care that she was gone. That's the way it always was for her. No one cared enough to come after her, and Mallory didn't expect that would change once Finn was finished talking.

But she had made a promise to her mother. One she was fulfilling step by step. She had come back to the little town her mother once called home and found her sister. That had been the easy part. That had been the part she could control.

Eleanor and McCrea had welcomed her with open arms. And for now, she was a part of their little family. But she feared that was about to change.

But she knew she had to go the distance; however short it might be. That meant she wasn't going anywhere until her sister knew what had happened to their mother. She would leave Redemption, knowing she'd done all she could to fulfill the promise.

When Finn respectfully removed his hat, she knew he was about to say what she'd been trying to say since she had arrived. "Rex Montgomery is wanted for leaving the scene of an accident and for," he hesitated, glancing down at the floor before his eyes settled on Eleanor, "vehicular manslaughter."

"Jesus," McCrea replied.

"He killed someone?" Eleanor asked with a voice as thin as paper.

"I'm afraid so," Finn said, his face dismal. "Witnesses reported that he was driving recklessly before the crash. Eleanor, I hate to be the one to tell you —"

"Don't," Mallory stopped him. "She should hear it from me. Not you."

"Tell me what, Mallory?" Eleanor asked, reaching for McCrea's hand on her shoulder.

Her sister favored their mother, and as a little girl, Mallory had had the same eyes, nose, and hair coloring as Rex.

Right now, her sisters' eyes were wide and full of apprehension, just the way she suspected her mothers had been seconds before the crash.

And that thought, this memory, would be forever burned into Mallory's mind. Would it be the same for Eleanor? Would she always associate the tragedy of this moment with the part of Mallory that was Rex?

Would Eleanor ever see *her* again?

Mallory took a deep breath and let it out. "Mom was in the car with him. She sustained multiple injuries….and didn't make it through surgery."

When she saw Eleanor's eyes fill with tears, Mallory dropped her head. She wanted to mourn and cry. But there were no tears for a woman who hadn't been much more than a shadow during her lonely childhood.

She stood there, unable to react with anything but silence as she closed her eyes and waited for the worse.

But instead of lashing out at her, Eleanor embraced her. "Oh, Mallory. I'm so sorry. "

Relief flooded through Mallory. "I wanted to tell you when I first arrived, but you were in labor and then Tucker was born… I didn't want to ruin his birthday."

Eleanor hugged her tighter. "I should have known something was wrong by the way you were acting and by the bruises. I should have listened, and I shouldn't have let you carry this terrible burden around for so long."

"Why is Rex here, in Santa Camino?" Jess asked Finn, his voice low with rile. "And not in jail?"

"He was taken to a local hospital and treated for a broken wrist," Finn explained. "He was headed to jail, but he was able to slip past the authorities at the hospital."

Jess sat on the couch arm and turned his attention to Mallory. "I think it's time you told us the whole story."

The whole story? Jesus, if he only knew.

"Rex has a gambling addiction. That's how we lost the house in Santa Fe. When we moved to La Claire, it only got worse."

"Did you know the Carlos Casino is a front for a major drug operation?" Finn asked.

The gunmetal gray of the sheriff's eyes sent a chill up Mallory's spine. "You can't live in La Claire and not know that."

"The authorities confiscated a significant amount of heroin and money from the trunk of your mom's car after the wreck," Finn continued as if he were conducting an interrogation. "Do you know anything about that?"

She knew more than any of them suspected. "It's how Rex pays his debts."

"By being a mule," Finn surmised.

"I don't understand how you play a part in all of this," Jess cut in, looking more confused than ever.

"Before I left home, Mom gave me the key to a safety deposit box and told me that if anything happened to her, I should take what was in it and come here, to the ranch." Mallory reached into her back pocket, pulled out the paper she had taken from her bike and handed it to Eleanor. "She left us a half million-dollar life insurance policy. You and I are the beneficiaries."

"Shit," Jess hissed. "He's after the money."

Eleanor unfolded the policy and looked it over. "But if we're the beneficiaries, he can't touch it."

"Legally, no," Mallory said, fighting through the horrible memories of what happened to her before she and Aiden left La Claire. "But the last time Rex owed these people money, he blackmailed someone into being the mule for him. Extortion is his forte. He finds what you love the most and uses it against you. When Mom died, he found out about the policy. I don't know how, but he did.

He had her cremated and was trying to blackmail me with her remains, so I went looking for him."

"By yourself?" Jess asked, unbelief in his eyes.

"Mom had to have scrimped and saved to pay for that damn policy," she told him. "And after the hell Rex put her through, I wasn't leaving La Clare without her."

"What happened next?" Finn asked, getting the conversation back on track.

"I found him in the back of a dive bar on the south side of town. He was so damn smug sitting there with her urn next to his beer. He thought I'd be the same frightened kid who left home when I was sixteen." The look on Rex's face when she walked into the bar was priceless. Shock, disbelief, fear... "He didn't expect a fight, but he got one. When he grabbed me, I fought back. That's how I got the bruises. I took the urn, ran for the door and headed for Texas with him behind me. I thought I lost him. But then he showed up outside my hotel room in Fort Sumner."

Jess scrubbed both hands over his face as he rose to his feet.

Mallory knew now that coming to the ranch had been a mistake. "If I leave town, Rex will follow me."

"You're not going anywhere," Jess said.

"He's right," McCrea agreed. "We can protect you here."

"I don't need protecting," she said, but knew she stood a better chance of making through this mess unscathed if she stayed.

"There is strength in numbers, Mallory," Eleanor said. "Mom wanted you here because she knew you'd be safe. You can't leave."

"I'll double the patrols." Finn said, stepping towards the front door. "Call if you see, hear, or need anything."

Jess now understood why Mallory had exploded in Pixies and why she had been so sad when he had mentioned her mother coming for a visit.

But it didn't explain why she shied away from men. In fact, her going into a bar full of them to retrieve her mother's remains didn't make a damn bit of sense. There had to be more to the story.

As the fight in the bar between her and Rex played out inside his head, chills raced up Jess's spine. There were a hundred ways that could have gone wrong. A hundred horrible things that could have happened to a woman in a sleazy bar.

Mallory had just fought a battle most men would have cowered away from. She was a hell of a lot tougher than she looked and braver than any woman he had ever known.

Her California plates and assorted beach t-shirts told him she had been living on the West Coast. But how had a teenage girl survived on her own?

Jess wasn't sure he wanted to know. Keeping an emotional distance to a woman he was attracted to gave him better odds of walking away unscathed.

But, hell, who was he kidding? That wasn't going to happen because Mallory had gone from a sizzling hot passerby to a woman Jess wanted to hold and needed to protect. He wouldn't be able to walk away until he knew she was safe.

He followed Finn and McCrea onto the porch. Through the screen door, he watched her pick up the bag whose contents had been very dear to her. The bag she had trusted him to carry. The bag containing a small white urn with her mother's remains.

He felt lower than a boot heel.

Every time he took a step with this woman, it was in the wrong direction. He had never felt more incompetent or more like an insensitive prick then he did right now.

Finn rested a hand on the pistol at his hip before walking down the porch steps. "I hate delivering news about death."

"There's never an easy way to do something like this." McCrea held out his hand, and Finn accepted it. "I wouldn't want your job."

"It has its days," he agreed, giving McCrea's back a slap. "By the way, congratulations."

"Thanks."

They followed Finn down the steps and to the police cruiser parked in the loop.

Finn took a few steps towards the cruiser then turned to briefly point a finger in Jess's direction. "I meant what I said about taking things into your own hands. If this guy shows up on your watch, call me."

"What happens then?"

Finn paused at the door. "I arrest him, he goes to jail, and we let justice do its job."

Jess gave his teeth a hard grind. "So far, justice has done a piss poor job of protecting Mallory from that son of a bitch."

"The system isn't perfect," Finn said, propping his boot on the step rail of the cruiser. "But taking it into your own hands isn't the answer."

"Neither is turning him over to you and your men so he can escape custody again."

Finn gave Jess a deadpan expression through the space between the cab and the open door of the cruiser. "He didn't escape *our* custody, and I won't take offense at that remark because I know you're worried about her."

"Damn right, I'm worried," he agreed.

"We'll call you," McCrea intervened, shoving a hand against Jess's chest before he could disagree.

The muscles in Finn's jaw flexed tight as if he were trying to decide on saying more or remaining silent.

"You found something else, didn't you?" Jess asked, taking a glance at the front door to make sure Mallory wasn't within hearing distance of their conversation.

Finn pulled his hat off and tossed it on the dash. "Most of it you already know."

Jess leaned against the fender and crossed his arms. "What don't we know?"

"The casino in La Claire is run by a group of local drug thugs who call themselves the Pack."

"As in wolves?" Jess asked.

"Yeah. The DEA uncovered a major drug and prostitution ring the night I told you about. Several people were taken into custody for questioning, including Rex. A twenty-three-year-old named Aiden Reynolds was also arrested and charged with drug trafficking."

McCrea and Jess exchanged glances.

Finn raised his eyebrows. "Do you know him?"

"No," Jess answered, feeling his stomach churn.

"You think this guy might be helping Rex?" McCrea asked.

"Maybe. The charges against Reynolds were dropped a few days after the arrest was made which says he probably made a deal." Finn climbed inside the cab and started the cruiser. "It's too early to jump to conclusions. I'll do some more digging. But don't leave the women and kids alone."

As Finn pulled out of the drive, Jess swore under his breath. "The guy's a fuckin' drug trafficker."

Mallory had defended Aiden Reynolds, a criminal, and gone so far as to have his name inked on her arm. Jess felt like a goddamn fool as old memories of betrayal edged their way to the surface and took hold.

McCrea gave him a warning look. "Finn is right. It's too early to jump to conclusions. You don't know what her relationship to this Reynolds guy is. She was an impressionable teenager when all this happened. It would have been easy for her to have gotten caught in the crosshairs or thrown into something ugly."

"She has his name tattooed on her arm for Christ sakes."

"Tattoos mean different things to different people, Jess."

"What do they mean for impressionable teenage girls?" he asked, heading back up the sidewalk.

McCrea stopped him before he made the steps. "If you go in there with guns blazing, asking questions about her relationship with a man you don't know a damn thing about with that accusing snarl on your face —"

"I'm not snarling." And he wasn't — yet.

"Yes, you are, enough so that Mallory might start to cry."

"I doubt that," he said, wishing like hell he had walked away from her and this whole damn situation days ago. "She didn't drop a single tear when she told El that their mother was dead."

"My wife is going to be pissed," McCrea continued as if Jess hadn't spoken. "And jump to her sister's defense. Do you want to spend the evening eating steak and potatoes or dodging dishes?"

Eleanor didn't throw dishes or vent by having hissy fits. Mallory? He wasn't so sure about. But he was willing to dodge a few bowls if it would get him the truth about her relationship with Aiden Reynolds.

"Give it a couple of days. Let them grieve for their mother. Then ask your questions."

"Just one tear," he said, through clenched teeth. "That's all it would take to ease my mind."

"Mallory has been through hell, and people process grief differently. You should know that."

Jess did know that. He had talked with several of the clients going through the equine therapy program. Some had a hard time expressing grief and chose to keep it all in as a way of coping.

"Just because she isn't swimming in a puddle of tears doesn't mean she isn't hurting or that she won't crash sometime soon." He gave Jess's shoulder a firm squeeze. "When she does, she'll need someone to help her through it."

There was a chance his brother was right. If so, Mallory would break down and everything would come crashing in on her.

But what if he were wrong?

Taking a deep breath to calm himself, Jess took McCrea's advice and went back into the house as though nothing had happened. He would eat the damn steak and potatoes and try to keep his snarling to a minimum.

The weight of their mother's passing and the circumstances surrounding her death made for a quiet dinner. Jess found himself wanting to snarl less and less.

It was hard for him to be incensed with Mallory when she looked so frail and alone sitting across from him.

She had only picked at her food, rearranging pieces of steak throughout the meal, but never taking a bite.

When dinner was over, she gathered her bag and safely lay the urn inside. She said her goodbyes and disappeared out the door.

Jess cleaned the table and washed the dishes before he ventured into the living room to say his own goodbyes.

Sophie and Pocket Change were asleep at one end of the couch. At the other end, McCrea had his back to the armrest with Eleanor situated between his legs and the baby cradled in her arms.

There was something deeply intimate about the moment, about the intensity of their relationship. The baby feeding at its mother's breast, the father holding them both in the safety and love of his arms.

Jess felt his throat tighten. He had wanted kids, lots of them. But he and Hallie had agreed they would wait until they were stable in their careers before they tried to conceive.

There had been nights when they had lain out under the stars and dreamed about those babies, their names, who they would favor, and what great parents they would both be.

Jess had lain awake some nights by himself, counting the years until those dreams would come to fruition and that baby would be in his arms. He'd be thirty in a couple of years, and his arms were still empty.

But his solitary life was his own damn fault. Not Hallie's and certainly not Mallory's.

It was his.

"I'll swing by in the morning before work and go with you to check things out up on the ridge."

McCrea never looked up. "See you tomorrow."

"Goodnight, Jess," Eleanor said softly.

He stepped out onto the porch, overcome by loneliness. He made his way down the steps, reluctant to head home after he dropped Mallory off. He dreaded going home to an empty house. He loathed the silence and the ache of knowing he would never have what he had just witnessed.

CHAPTER 17

As Jess drove to the Rescue, Mallory stared out the window. Both arms were wrapped protectively around her bag.

He wanted to hold her, console her, and offer her words that would help her through the grief. He wanted her to share more details about her life like the Xander experience, and he wanted her to trust him with her past like she had with her body.

But Mallory wasn't ready to talk.

He parked behind her bike and killed the engine. "I'll walk you up."

At the top of the stairs, she numbly fumbled with the key.

"Here," he said, taking it from her. "Let me do it."

She stepped back, allowing him to unlock the door. "The lights are on in the clinic."

He glanced over his shoulder. "They're probably working with the horse McCrea brought in this morning. It was in bad shape."

He opened the door and handed her the key. Without a

word, she moved inside and closed the door behind her. There was no 'goodbye,' or 'I'll see you tomorrow,' just the door in his face. He waited until he heard the chain slide across the door before he started down the stairs.

The question of who Aiden was and Mallory's relationship to him rankled him. The man had been twenty-three to Mallory's sixteen when the drug bust went down. That was a seven-year age difference at a volatile time in a young woman's life when sex was often rushed, and true love was rarely true.

Jess reminded himself that he shouldn't care about what had happened or why the guy's name was inked on her skin.

This afternoon had been emotionally draining for her, and he knew sleep wouldn't come easy. He should have helped her, offered her a comforting word or an arm to cry on. But instead, he'd been angry with her and for what? A tattoo? An old boyfriend?

Guilt ate at him because this wasn't about the man in Mallory's past. It was about the woman in his. The woman he had loved, trusted, and been betrayed by. It was about all those dreams he had given up on and all the risks he wouldn't take.

But Mallory wasn't Hallie. She wasn't shallow or vain. She was classy in her own way and beautifully rough around the edges. She was loving and caring and didn't deserve his wrath or bitterness. And she damn sure didn't deserve his judgments.

She hadn't lied to him about why she needed to see Eleanor or about anything else that he knew of. She hadn't said Aiden wasn't a drug trafficker only that she couldn't talk about him.

He couldn't talk about Hallie, so why was he

condemning Mallory for not being able to talk about Aiden?

Because he was a goddamn hypocrite. That's why.

He climbed inside the truck and slammed the door, his eyes going to the living room window.

Again, loneliness took hold, draping over him like a heavy coat. It sank in deep, so deep that he could feel it in his bones like a cold wind.

He rolled his window down and backed out of the parking spot, then drove around the stables. As he turned the wheel towards the main gate, a whiff of wild prairie roses caught his nose.

The flowers had been growing up on that ridge for as long as he could remember, and a faint aroma often caught the wind and traveled down through the valley. But tonight, their floral scent was unusually strong.

The piquant peach and honey rose fragrance mingled with the warm earth and night air, reminding him of Mallory and that first kiss.

In the distant, the howl of a coyote cut through the night air, embedding the lonely wail deep inside of him.

As the truck neared the gates, Jess slowed it to a crawl and then stopped dead-center of the road. After he passed through those iron bars, there was no place for him to go but home.

He couldn't bear the emptiness of that place tonight. He hadn't called Brandi, and he wasn't going to. He didn't want to go to San Antonio. He didn't want to have dinner and talk business or do anything else with Brandi.

He should have parked his ass on Mallory's couch and refused to move. At least then he wouldn't feel so damn alone. He could go back, but what excuse would he give?

He turned the truck into the parking lot, remembering

there was a left-over gallon of strawberry ice cream in the freezer from Sophie's birthday party.

After parking the truck, he hurried to the building, unlocked the main office door, and rushed to the kitchen. Shoving aside Brody's homemade chili and Kara's nugget meals, he grabbed the container and ran across the lawn to the stables.

He was almost midway when he glanced up and did a double take at Mallory's bedroom window. The light from her nightstand was on, giving a soft glow to her bare shoulder. The rest of her body was hidden behind the privacy shrubs.

Jess had never believed the phases of the moon had any influence on human nature. Civilized men didn't rip their clothes off and transform into wild and crazy beasts. And they didn't squeeze themselves between shrubs to gawk at a nearly naked woman wrapped crudely in a bath towel.

But there was something strange in the air tonight. Something that lured Jess closer and closer, in between those shrubs and to the bottom of the window. A magical force that kept him spellbound and made him forget about the consequences of what he was doing.

But it wasn't the moon or the sweet tang of wild prairie roses. It was the remnant of that damn whiskey kiss they had shared last night.

From this vantage point below her window, nothing was hidden by the shrubs. His eyes followed the line of her bare hip up to the gentle curve of her narrow waist. He swallowed, feeling fire shoot to his groin. He was mesmerized, his body tight and so hard that he couldn't have moved if his life depended on it.

He was thinking about how wrong this was, about how he should just take the damn ice cream back to the office and bury his head in the bucket. But his head wasn't the problem, at least not the one that usually did his thinking.

Jess swallowed again, ready to take control. He willed his legs to move, his eyes to blink... nothing. There was nothing but this beautiful temptation standing in the window.

When the towel covering her breasts fell, so did the bucket of ice cream. And Jess just stood there, gazing at her body like a horny teenage boy.

His eyes followed the downward slope of her left breast as she lifted her hand to release the clasp holding her hair. His gaze traveled lower over the small rise of her stomach to the dip of her belly button and lower to the dark tuft of hair at the apex of her thighs.

He drew in a shaky breath.

This was wrong, so damn wrong. He was in plain sight and the moon would give her a full view of him. If she looked up and saw him, what excuse would he give for being a peeping tom?

He would have to move quickly and dive behind the shrub. But Mallory wasn't looking up. She was looking over at the bed. Maybe for a robe or a shirt that would end his suffering.

She leaned forward and reached across the bed, hitching her bare, round bottom up for him to see. "Oh, hell," Jess choked out and felt his lungs lock after the words.

This was it.

This was how his life was going to end. Not by a horse or a bull, but by a beautiful ass. And he was going to hell on the short road for being a peeping tom.

Jess tilted his head to the side, knowing that if Mallory's ass was the last thing he saw, he was going to enjoy it.

She sat on the bed, lifted her feet into her shorts, and

pulled them over her bare bottom. Grabbing the 49ers shirt, she whipped it over her head and slipped her arms into the sleeves. The light went off, and Jess was left standing alone in the bushes.

Dazed and so rigid he hurt, he came to his senses and glanced down at the bucket of ice cream on its side, oozing its way onto the ground. "Shhhhiiiiitttt," he hissed between clenched teeth as he scrambled to pick up the bucket.

He replaced the lid, and ran a finger around the rim, wiping away grass and gravel, then dashed around the building and up the stairs.

He paused at the top, trying to catch his breath and collect himself before he knocked on her door. He set the bucket down, snatched his hat from his head, and ran a hand through his hair before he set it back in place.

Jess drew in one more deep breath and let it out with a swoosh, picked up the bucket and knocked on the door. "It's me, Mallory."

He heard the soft thump of her bare feet against the hardwood floor and the chain slide and drop before she opened the door.

She blinked a couple of times, her eyes falling to the sweaty neckline of his t-shirt. "I didn't hear your truck pull up."

"It's it at the office."

She squinted one eye. "Are you okay? You seem a little...flushed?"

"Ah... yeah." He tried to smile like he hadn't just seen her naked. "I jogged across the lawn. Didn't want the ice cream to melt."

Her face gave way to surprise. "You brought me ice cream?"

He held the bucket up like it was a prize bass. "I thought it might help to cheer you up."

She motioned him in, smiling quizzically at the bucket. "That's sweet of you."

"It — ah, slipped," he tried explaining.

Holding a hand under the bucket, he hurried to the kitchen sink before the rivulets of melted ice cream could hit the floor.

With a finger and a thumb and a somewhat amused grin, she picked a blade of grass from the side of the bucket. "You drove all the way into town to buy me ice cream?"

"No, it was left-overs from Sophie's birthday party last month. And it's strawberry, not chocolate. But ice cream is ice cream, right?"

Her mouth curved higher, pinching that little cleft on her cheek. "Definitely."

He adored that dimple. He adored that shy smile and those dark, gentle eyes.

She reached above him and opened the cabinet. "I haven't taken stock of the kitchen, so I'm not sure if there's anything to eat it with."

He knew Eleanor had bought dinnerware and cook-ware for the apartment because he had helped her carry everything up. He had also helped her unpack and stock the kitchen. "Bowls are in this cabinet," he said, reaching around her to open the door adjacent to the one she was rummaging through.

"You're handy to have around," she said, smiling up at him. "How about spoons?"

Mallory wasn't asking for much. But something about her needing his help even if it was just for bowls and spoons made him feel good. "Second drawer on your right."

She followed his directions and selected two spoons.

"Looks like we're eating ice cream." Peeling the cracked lid from the bucket, she began scooping it out.

He took his bowl and motioned to the door. "It's a nice night. Want to take a walk?"

"I'd love to. Let me get my shoes." She set her bowl on the counter and hurried into the bedroom.

"I'll meet you downstairs." Considering what he had just seen, Jess knew he should probably say his goodbyes and be on his way home without going near her.

But today had been emotionally exhausting for her. She needed ice cream and a friend.

At the bottom of the stairs, he shoved a weighted dollop of ice cream into his mouth. Some friend he was. He had just come damn close to jacking off in the bushes outside her bedroom window.

He laid his arms over the railing and stared up at the sky, shoveling more ice cream into his mouth. Against a thousand twinkling lights, the moon hovered high over the ridge.

Jess tried steering his mind away from the sight of her bare skin, the shape of her form and that thatch of hair at the apex of her thighs. But Mallory was permanently imprinted on his brain, seared into his skin like a hot branding iron. He would see her, smell her, and want her until the day he died.

He shoved the last bite into his mouth and sighed. That was a long time for a man to be haunted by a woman, a long time to wish he had done more and said more.

When he heard the apartment door close, he turned to watch her descend the stairs.

Bowl in hand, she bounced to the bottom. "It's beautiful out here," she said, gazing up at the sky.

The pale blue moonlight cast light onto her freshly showered skin. She looked so happy and unburdened right now, so elated and alive. A totally different woman from the one he had dropped off earlier.

Mallory could put on a front and say she could take care of herself and that she was fine on her own. But Jess knew otherwise. He knew she was scared, and he knew she didn't like being alone with Rex out there, so maybe this bubbly, exultant expression on her face was because of him. That made his heart plummet to his stomach and land with a beat-skipping thud.

Jess cleared his throat. "Ah…yeah, it's the biggest one I've seen in a while."

But the trouble with Rex wouldn't last forever. Finn would catch him, or the people he owed money to would collect. Mallory would be safe, and he wouldn't have an excuse to sleep on the couch or bring her ice cream in the middle of the night.

"Did you bring me ice cream for a reason, or did you get lonely and want someone to look at the moon with you?" she asked, topping off her questions with a smile and a quick raise of both brows.

He wasn't about to admit he was lonely.

"I was worried about you," he said, setting his bowl on the stairs. "What happened earlier…was intense. El was right. Death is a horrible burden to carry."

"There are worse burdens," she said.

Jess suspected there was a much heavier load resting on those delicate shoulders. "My point is you should have told me."

She kept her eyes on her bowl. "Mom's death, every-thing Rex is involved in…it's all a part of the ugliness of my world and not something I feel comfortable sharing with a man I'm attracted to."

He started walking, taking slow steps across the lawn, and she followed alongside. He wanted to tell her that she could share anything with him, but that would thrust their relationship to a whole new level of intimacy, one that went beyond sex.

Jess cleared his throat again. "We have a therapist here —"

"No thanks," she answered abruptly and was quick to offer him a thin smile. "I'd rather not talk about my parents. I'm fine, really, I am."

Following a woman who he'd just seen naked back to the place they'd shared a scorching first kiss was risky business. But here he was, under the light of a big white orb that transformed oceans and made people do foolish things.

He guided her over to the fence and propped an elbow on the top rail.

She shoveled a strawberry onto the spoon and held it up to him. "Want a bite?"

If she knew where his mind went when she asked him that question, she would probably run for the hills, especially now when he was tempted to eat more than that chunk of frozen red berry.

Jess should have refused the ice cream like he had the doughnut, but the dirty part of his mind wanted to feel her slide the creamy treat into his mouth, see the satisfaction on her face, and fantasize about how he could do the same with more than ice cream.

He opened his mouth to accept the spoon, watching the soft dark centers of her eyes expand as she pushed it past his lips. This was more than dairy pleasure to her too.

This was the sexiest kind of foreplay. A dangerous kind that tossed gasoline onto a fire that was already burning hot.

She eased the spoon free and waited for his reaction. "It's good?"

When the ice cream melted, he swallowed. Then he crushed the berry against the roof of his mouth, savoring her wanton response more than he did the creamy treat. "Very tempting."

Biting her lower lip, she licked the back of the spoon and smiled.

Jess drew in a long breath and continued down the fence line.

She followed, glancing up at him as she spoke. "You hardly said two words to me after the sheriff left."

At least she hadn't accused him of snarling.

"I thought you needed some space," he said, evasively, aware of how abrasive and lustful his voice had become.

"I thought when you showed up at my doorstep, we'd be having that conversation you mentioned earlier this afternoon."

Mallory wanted answers about that kiss, and Jess needed to lay things out about what she could expect from him if things between them went beyond that.

She needed to know that sex was all he wanted and that he was a man who walked away after the satisfaction was over. But if he told her that now, she might tell him to take his what-to-expects and go straight to hell. And he'd be left with an empty bowl and a hard on. Worse than that, he'd be alone again.

"I lied," he blurted out. "I want to finish what we started last night."

The spoon stopped in midair just short of her lips. "But I thought —"

"That I turned you down because you aren't comfortable with letting men you don't know touch you?" He frowned. "Hell, no. That only makes me want you more."

Her eyebrows arched. "It does?"

Nodding, he ran his finger along the underside of the

spoon to catch the glistening cream before it could drop. He brought it to his lips with a gentle suck. "Your ice cream is melting."

"Oh, yeah." Her laugh was tight, constricted by desire. "I think I dished out more than I can handle."

She hadn't yet, but if she kept licking that spoon...

"So," she said, stirring the frothy puddle in the middle of the bowl. "What happens now?"

Tell her it's just sex...

"That's entirely up to you," he said, toying with a silky strand of her hair. "We can look at the moon and eat ice cream, or we can finish that kiss."

His words caused her throat to flex with a subtle pause of indecision.

When she dug the spoon into the ice cream and lifted it to his lips, he let his empty bowl fall to the ground.

"Do you want more?" she asked, her eyes heavy with desire.

Absofuckinglutly.

"I'll take as much as you want to give."

CHAPTER 18

MALLORY LEANED IN CLOSER AND JESS OPENED HIS MOUTH, anticipating the juiciness of the red-ripe berries, the sweetness of the cream, and the moment when this was no longer foreplay.

With her eyes focused on his mouth, she pushed the spoon in. A faint moan escaped her throat as his lips closed over it.

He curled his fingers around her wrist and slowly slipped the spoon from his mouth. With a slow, lascivious lick, he removed what remained of the ice cream from the back but didn't let her hand go.

An involuntary shudder rippled through her body. Desire pooled in his lower stomach and swarmed lower.

Jess took the bowl from her hand and tossed it and the spoon to the side.

Cupping her face with both hands, he drew her closer. God, she was mesmerizing. A flushed face, dark sedated eyes and sweet, glossy lips that were trembling.

Mallory wasn't a virgin who needed coaxing. She was

ready for this, for him. But she wasn't a brash, corporeal female either.

She was nervous and so was he.

He smiled and gently caressed her cheek, trying to sooth her uneasiness.

"Why are you smiling?" she asked, with questioning eyes.

"I was just thinking about how pretty you."

Her mouth twisted up at a corner. "Pretty is special?"

"Very special," he confirmed, feeling something strong and powerful pull at his heart as he lowered his lips and kissed her.

Without the bourbon clouding his mind or dulling his pallet, it was like he was kissing Mallory for the first time. It was the same explosive kiss they had shared the night before. The hot sensuality of the beautiful woman he had seen naked in the window.

The sweetness of berries and cream mixed with the pureness of hungry lips.

Moaning, Mallory slid her arms around his neck and timidly arched her body into his. Her shy reserve was refreshing, oddly sensual, and wildly arousing.

His hands slid to her waist and moved down to the tantalizing flare of her hips. Those hips he had seen bare just minutes ago.

Jess wanted her lying against him the way he had up on the ledge. He wanted her crying his name as she orgasmed. He wanted to take his time with her and enjoy the scenery as much as he did the destination. He wanted to sightsee and take in all the beautiful curves, bends, and hollows of her body.

But damn, it was so hard not to push her up against the fence and satisfy himself inside her.

Suddenly, amid the passion, came the faint echo of a past conversation.

I'm very picky about who touches me…

Jess was damn happy she was.

Her hands moved up the back of his head, plowing through his hair. Off came his hat, and another moan left her lips as she curled her leg around his. With that prompt, he took a step forward, pressing her into the railing.

He felt her stiffen and drop her leg. She took hold of his shirt and swung him around until he was the one against the railing.

I like being in control…

Jess didn't care. He was up for whatever position got the job done. But there was a reason Mallory needed to be in control and like her Look But Don't Touch rule, he didn't need to know why. That was the beauty of non-committal sex. He only had to respect her and her boundaries.

He didn't have to care about the bruises on her wrists, why Rex had followed her to Texas, or why she needed to be in control.

But damn it, he did. He cared because there was a reason Mallory didn't trust men, a reason she shied away from a simple handshake. A reason she had cleverly disguised her virtue behind chrome, leather, and a quick tongue.

And there was a reason she was letting him kiss her.

I trust you…

Those words made something inside of Jess buck, hard and unexpected. It tossed him up in the air away from sensitivity and gentleness, swung him around and landed him dead center in the middle of the truth.

Fuck.

A truth Jess didn't want to accept. This woman, in his

arms, under his lips, was his to take. Body and heart. That earth-shattering revelation sliced him clean to the bone, dousing him with guilt.

And suddenly the voice in his head wasn't Mallory's, it was his.

This isn't your world. It's mine, and no one will ever hurt you here, in my world.

She was gifting him something fragile and precious, something he didn't deserve. Dragging his lips away, he rested his forehead against hers.

"Jess?"

He pulled her hands away from his neck and held them as he took a deep breath to help settle the flames shooting through his body.

When he was sure he could speak with the iciness needed, he dropped her hands and moved away from her. "Next time, make sure your blinds are closed before you go dropping that towel."

"What?" Her eyes widened, and her mouth gaped open. "You were spying on me?"

"I'd hardly call it spying. The blinds were open." Jess needed to distance himself from her, make her hate him. He needed her to run away and never speak to him again.

But this was Mallory. She didn't move, didn't flinch or run away. She stood firmly planted in place, watching him, reading his face like she had outside the sheriff's office when he'd said he would never fall in love again.

He knew if he wasn't convincing, she would forgive him, and this would happen again.

"So be forewarned, Beautiful," he said, adorning a haughty smile. "I'm not the only man around this ranch that can be tempted by a little flirting and a peep show —"

A splash of cold water doused him in the face. He gasped and spit then blinked, trying to clear the water from his eyes. When he focused, he saw Mallory standing in front of the horse trough with his drenched hat in her hands.

She hauled her arm back and hurled his hat into the air, barely missing his head. Her cheeks dusted purple under the moonlight. "You don't seriously think I left that shade up on purpose."

"No." He wiped his face and gave his hand a fling. "But the warning still stands. Look next time. Brody and McCrea are in and out of here all the time at all hours of the night. It might have been one of them who saw you instead of me."

Neither of them would have crept past the privacy fence.

He snatched his hat from the ground and gave it a hard hit against his thigh. "I'm going out of town for a couple of days."

"You said you wanted more." Her fingers clenched into tight fists at her side. "Why are you suddenly pushing me away?"

"Because we won't be getting that dog together, Mallory. There won't be His and Hers bath towels, holiday photos, or keepsakes when the sex is over. I keep my relationships uncomplicated and easy to walk away from. No one gets hurt that way."

Her fingers slowly relaxed and again, she just stood there, staring a hole through him with that examining expression.

"You — ah," he cleared his throat. "You have everyone's number, right?" He set his hat on his head and gave it a hard tug, situating it lower on his brow. "And if something happens while I'm gone —"

"Stop," she said, taking a step back. "Just stop. I'm not your responsibility. I never have been."

But she was. She had been since she'd rolled up looking for directions. And like that day, fear was causing him to do stupid things.

"My heart and my body are a package deal, Jess." She looked down at her thumbnail and then back up at him. "Don't darken my doorstep again unless you're there because *you* want to be. And don't kiss me again unless you're prepared to offer me more than sex."

THE NEXT MORNING, MALLORY RODE HER BIKE INTO TOWN for art supplies. She found Rayleen's little craft store charming and surprisingly well stocked.

She chose a variety of oil-based paints, cleaning solutions, rags, and brushes.

"Thanks," she said, taking the bag from the counter as Rayleen handed her the receipt.

"You're welcome." The woman offered her a friendly smile. "You can expect Brian around six."

She'd arranged for Rayleen's son to deliver the easels and canvas to her apartment later this evening. "I'll be watching for him."

Standing just inside the store door, she slid her sunglasses on and was about to walk outside when she glanced up and saw Rex's red truck roll down the street.

Mallory had hoped and prayed he'd given up and gone back to New Mexico. But he hadn't. He was still in town, still waiting and lurking in the shadows. Anger bubbled inside of her, overtaking any fear she had, just the way it had when she walked into the bar.

She wasn't going to wait for him to make the first move.

When he stopped for the red light, Mallory dropped

the bag, shoved the door open, and headed down the street towards him.

The light flipped to green and Rex pulled out, slowing when he saw her bike parked a few blocks down from the craft store. He whipped the truck into the empty parking space in front of it, and she picked up her pace.

She hurried to the passenger side window before he could get out of the truck. "Hello, Rex." She gave him a venomous smile.

The lines in his face deepened, and he scowled as he often did when he was angry. "Where the fuck have you been?"

"You know exactly where I've been. I saw your head-lights up on the ridge."

His lips pulled into a snarl. "You think you're safe at that Rescue, but fences and gates won't stop me from getting that money. Hand it over and I won't hurt your new boyfriend."

Mallory's anger burned red-hot. "You're not going to hurt anyone, you worthless piece of trash. No one in this town is afraid of you, least of all my new boyfriend. You're a coward. Go back to La Claire before the sheriff finds you."

Rex's snarl inched into a hideous smile as he scratched his arm just below the dirty cast on his hand. "I can't leave town without seeing Sophie and Tucker."

Fear spiked through her. "You bastard," she choked out, hitting her palm against the door. "You stay away from Redemption!"

His husky smoker's laugh cracked the air. "Oh, baby girl. You know I can't do that."

The fake endearment he always used for a warning made her want to vomit. "I hope the Pack kill you this time."

"Mallory?"

She looked around and saw Rayleen standing a few feet away holding the bag she'd dropped by the door. "Is everything okay?"

Rex rolled up the window and pulled out, quickly disappearing down a side street.

"Yeah," she said, adopting a smile. "Everything is fine, Rayleen. Thanks."

After packing the bag into the side compartment of her bike, she called Eleanor and learned that McCrea had taken the week off to be with her and the kids. She didn't mention her run-in with Rex. With McCrea at the ranch, the three of them would be safe for the time being.

Brian delivered her supplies and Mallory went to work setting up her studio. She spent the next couple of days working on her portfolio. Each day she took breaks between sketches to visit Redemption.

She'd been slobbered on, peed on, and given a complete cosmetic makeover, and she'd enjoyed every minute of it. In between naps and playtime, she and Eleanor had talked about Aiden and her move to California. She'd shown Eleanor the pictures of the portfolio she'd been working on and told her about how she wanted to apply for art school.

Today they were planning their mother's memorial service.

"Does that mean you'll be leaving us for Oregon?" Eleanor said, moving a box of old photos from the kitchen table to the living room floor where Mallory was sitting.

She leaned against the couch. "Not likely. There's a waiting list for the Kramer Art School. But I've always wanted to travel. Paris is on my Bucket List."

"So you are leaving?"

When her mother's ashes were scattered, her promise

would be fulfilled. She had no plausible excuse for staying in Texas. "I can't live at the Rescue forever."

"I have a friend who's in real estate," Eleanor said. "We could talk to her about finding a house nearby."

"I don't know. Buying a house is so," she scrunched her face. "Permanent."

"And you don't want permanent?"

Mallory loved the laid-back little town and having her sister close. She had Cassie and her friends from the gallery. But she had family here that she wanted to get to know. Her heart longed for that connection. That kinship and belonging.

But permanent here in Santa Camino without Jess would be a slow death. "I don't know what I want."

Eleanor sat beside her and wrapped an arm around her shoulders. "As much as I like having you close by, I understand if you don't stay. You do what's best for you."

If *she* only knew what that was.

"But know that you'll always have a place here at Redemption and at the Rescue. I don't want you to feel like you can't come home," Eleanor said, looping a strand of hair behind her ear as she pulled the box in front of her closer. "Mom was miserable for believing that."

"Me and Mom…" Mallory's words fell short because she couldn't explain the complexity of the feelings she had towards her mother. "We weren't close. But I know she loved me, and she loved this ranch."

During one of their long talks, Eleanor had told her about the fight her mother and granddad had the night he died and about how their mother blamed herself for his death.

"I never really questioned why she was the way she was," Mallory said, feeling she understood her mother more now that she was dead than she ever had while she was alive. "I guess I should have asked more questions."

Eleanor began pulling out photos. "I feel the same way. And now that she's gone, I can't tell her I'm sorry for resenting her all those years."

Mallory picked up a framed photo of a little girl in cowboy boots and a hat. "Is this Mom?"

"Yeah, I found it in the attic last year when I came back to sell the ranch."

"You were going to sell Redemption?"

Eleanor answered her with a sad smile.

"But why? You're all so happy here."

"Things weren't always good between me and McCrea. I had a lot of issues that caused me to run away from how I felt about him."

"What kind of issues?"

"He broke my heart and married another woman. I didn't think I could ever trust him again." Eleanor lifted another picture from the box. The photo was of her mother in her late teens with a man Mallory didn't recognize.

"Is this your father?"

"Yes, that's James." Eleanor smiled warmly. "He's the one who told me about Mom and Granddad."

Her mother often talked about the ranch, the land, and a young man she had known when she was younger. Mallory hadn't put the pieces together until she was older: The young man was Eleanor's father and her mother's first love. "Mom called him Jimmy."

"I'm surprised she talked about him."

"She did," Mallory said, remembering the gleam of light in her mother's eyes when she spoke of the boy and a smile on her lips that stayed long after her words stopped. A smile her father envied and never understood.

"We call him Ed." Eleanor reached under the table for a photo album, flipped it open, and pointed to a photo of her, Sophie, and a gray-haired man. "This is a more recent photo."

Mallory smiled. "He's the bartender who gave me directions to Redemption. If it hadn't been for him, I probably wouldn't have found my way to the ranch. God knows Jess was useless."

It had been four days since Jess had left town, and every day that passed was worse than the one before. Mallory missed talking to him and hearing his voice, seeing the sexy slant of his lips when he smiled, and the sparkle of a tease in his blue eyes. She missed the sound of his boots as he climbed the stairs to her apartment, the gentle touch of his hands, and his kiss.

Mallory cradled her face in her hands to hide the threat of tears in her eyes. "Have you heard from him?"

"No," she heard Eleanor say. "He's turned his phone off and didn't tell Kara where he was going or when he'd be back. He's never done that before."

Why couldn't she have just given in and said yes to his sex without strings? "He's in San Antonio."

"You don't know that."

But she did. Jess had rules for the relationships he had with women and plenty of experience at calling it quits. He had ways of protecting his heart.

Mallory didn't.

She'd never been in love. She had different boundaries that kept her physically safe. But not one clue as to how to keep her heart from being shattered once he decided it was over.

Why couldn't he take the risks? Why couldn't he just let go and trust her?

She raised her head, feeling animosity when the answer came to her. "What was his fiancée like?"

"Hallie Collett? Oh, she was something," Eleanor said, reaching for another box. "She was a barrel racer from Nebraska. Pretty but so damn superficial. The woman didn't even say goodbye. She left him high and dry. After surgery, he woke up to an engagement ring lying on his chest."

Mallory felt her mouth drop open. "That's how she ended it?"

"Yup," Eleanor returned. "He wasn't in the spotlight anymore. His career was over, and she didn't need him. Three months later she was engaged to a bull rider from Washington. Jess hasn't had a meaningful relationship since."

"I don't think he ever will," she said, feeling broken to the core. "No wonder he's so bitter."

Eleanor tucked the photo back into the box. "He's better than he was. He dates lots of women, but never brings them home to meet the folks, if you know what I mean."

"I do. 'I keep my relationships uncomplicated and easy to walk away from. No one gets hurt that way,'" Mallory said, wearily. "Those were his exact words to me."

Eleanor laid the pictures down, giving Mallory her full attention. "And what did you say?"

Before Cassie came along, she hadn't had another female to confide in. But after she learned to trust Cassie, she had gone to her for everything, even to vent about how overprotective Aiden was.

Cassie had always given her unbiased advice because she loved them both. She knew Eleanor would do the same concerning Jess. "That he couldn't kiss me again unless he was willing to offer me more than sex."

A tender smile quirked at the edge of Eleanor's lips. "Good for you."

Watching Jess drive out the gate was one of the hardest things Mallory had ever done. Each kiss had brought them closer. If he hadn't broken the kiss and pulled away, they would have made love. And as much as she wanted that, she couldn't abide by his No Strings rules.

She loved him.

She had cried all night, wrestling with her decision, but she knew she hadn't been wrong in laying down her terms. She wouldn't be a go-to for his sex, and she wouldn't play second fiddle to Brandi.

It was all or nothing.

Jess had chosen nothing.

"It doesn't feel good. It feels horrible."

Her sister's eyes softened with understanding. "You're falling in love with him, aren't you?"

Mallory let her shoulders fall. "Is it ridiculous for me to think I might be in love with a guy I've only known for a couple of days?"

"Not at all," Eleanor was quick to say. "Love doesn't know a time or a place. It only knows the heart. I fell in love with McCrea when I was eight years old and have loved him ever since."

"Jesus," she groaned. "That must have been awful."

Eleanor chuckled. "At times, it was. Love is full of growing pains, that's for sure. But it was all worth it. I've never been happier."

Mallory wanted that happiness and that same in-love visage her sister had. "How did you get over McCrea hurting you?"

"It didn't happen overnight." Eleanor pulled out more photos. "He was patient and loving."

"I try to be both, but Jess bucks and pushes me away when things get serious."

"It's hard to trust someone after you've been hurt."

Again, Mallory could relate. But her hurts were on the outside, not imprinted across her heart by hoofs and high-heels.

"McCrea had done all he could to show me that he loved me. But I couldn't let myself believe. I couldn't get past that hurt and fear."

Mallory knew all too well how paralyzing fear could be. "So what happened?"

"I had to see for myself what I was losing, so I left the ranch and went back to Austin. I was miserable."

Jess was used to walking away. But Mallory was determined. If he wanted her, he would have to give in to whatever was holding him back, push through those fears of his past relationship with Hallie, and trust her like she trusted him, with her whole heart.

"I read a poem once," Eleanor said while looking down at the photo of Ed and her mother, "that said love is like water. It can carve out a path through the hardest stone and bring life to the most barren land." She brought the photo to her chest, her eyes filled with faith in that unseen intensity. "Love is a powerful force that heals all wounds. I believe that with all my heart."

Mallory knew that if she wanted a life with Jess, she too would have to believe. Blind faith was better than no faith at all.

"Jess spends a lot of time with the horses when they first come to the Rescue," Eleanor said, nibbling uneasily at her bottom lip. "Not hands-on like Brody and McCrea. He's more of an observer. He watches how they interact with the other horses and staff. He learns their tempera-ment and has a gift for pairing horses with people."

I have an Aztec gelding that's as gentle as a lamb. He'd be perfect for a beginner like you.

"But he hasn't ridden a horse since his accident," Mallory said, groaning.

"No," Eleanor agreed. "And there is something you should know. The horse Jess was riding that night he fell —"

"Dirteater."

Eleanor nodded. "He's at the Rescue."

Uneasiness washed over Mallory. "Oh, God. Does Jess know?"

"No. The poor horse was in such bad shape, McCrea wanted to wait until he was in stable condition before he told Jess."

Jess said he didn't blame Dirteater for what had happened, but given his surly mood lately, Mallory wasn't sure how he would handle the news. "Is he stable now?"

"Physically, yes. But Brody isn't sure he'll ever be able to rehabilitate him."

"Meaning?"

"The horse may have to be put down."

Mallory felt her heart break. "Is there anything I can do to help?"

"You're already helping." Eleanor smiled as she reached for her phone on the coffee table. "Jess's desk is stacked with paperwork and overdue bills. He hasn't even thought about logging the horse into the database."

What would happen when he came back from San Antonio and she wasn't there to distract him?

CHAPTER 19

WHEN ELEANOR SUGGESTED THEY HAVE COFFEE WITH HER friends, Mallory had no idea one of those friends would be Tyler's sister. "I feel horrible about punching your brother in the nose," she admitted.

"Don't," Violet said with an entertained expression plastered across her face. She handed Mallory a plate of macadamia nut cookies across the counter and used a knuckle to shove her straight-browed glasses to a more comfortable spot on her nose. "In fact, consider this a small token of my appreciation."

Mallory carried the plate to a corner table where Louisa, Sage, and Eleanor where sitting. "I should apologize."

"No, you shouldn't," Louisa said, reaching for a cookie. "Ty can be a cocky little turd. It's about time a woman put him in his place."

"I'll second that." Violet hurried around the counter and locked the front doors. "And can I suggest that we start addressing Logan as Big Turd?"

"Oh," Sage said, cutting Violet a harsh frown. "You

don't know how lucky you are to have brothers like Logan and Ty."

Violet flipped the counter lights off and turned the Open sign to Closed. "You can have mine. Just show me where to sign, and they're all yours."

"Brothers can be a pain in the ass," Mallory said, trying to soothe Violet's frustration because she understood how overbearing brothers could be. There'd been times when she wanted to scream at Aiden for being so overprotective. "I'm surprised mine didn't wrap me in bubble wrap."

"Bubble wrap was acceptable when I was five," Violet said, sighing. "But I'm a grown woman with needs."

"Aren't we all," Sage mumbled under her breath.

"Y'all don't understand the gravity of my situation." Violet sat down and plucked a cookie from the plate. "Last night, Logan met Bobby Grainer at the door with a shotgun."

A chorus of groans sprang up from around the table.

"Yeah." Violet rested her elbow on the table and propped her head up with a fist. "That's the second date in a month he's ruined for me."

"Sorry. I can't offer you advice on brothers," Sage said with a sympathetic frown.

"Me neither." Eleanor motioned towards Mallory and Louisa. "But you two might."

"Oh, Jesus," Louisa said, a besmirching scowl on her face. "Don't get me started on McCrea and Jess."

"Enough with the bitchiness," Sage scolded. "Offer the poor woman something."

Shooting Sage an exasperated roll of her eyes, Louisa gave in. "You want advice? I'll give you advice. Find Logan and Ty a woman."

Violet waved her hand, shooting down that suggestion.

"Logan says he's too busy for dating and Ty… well, you know how he is."

"All I know is, once McCrea and Jess had their own relationship problems to deal with, they didn't give a damn about mine."

The dull edge to Louisa's voice brought a hush to the table and an intense exchange of looks from the other three women.

Eleanor cleared her throat. "Your turn, Mallory."

"Well…" She thought for a moment. "For my twenty-first birthday, a few of my friends from the art gallery took me to a bar in Monterey. It was a quiet little out of the way spot and nothing extreme happened. But Aiden was furious. Thank God, his fiancée was there to talk some sense into him." Cassie had been Mallory's greatest ally in her battle for freedom against her overprotective brother.

Violet used her tongue to dislodge a piece of cookie from her back tooth, all while looking less than excited. "I don't handle alcohol well."

"She's not telling you to get falling down drunk," Sage went on to say. "Start small and work your way up."

"I'd rather start big," Violet said, her eyes suddenly glued to the blue Chevy truck that had just pulled up across the street at Nash's Saddle Shop. "With something that takes to the saddle and spur but has a gentle hand on the reigns."

Eleanor laughed. "Violet, what in the world has gotten into you?"

"She's been hanging around Louisa too much," Sage answered.

"Hey," Louisa said. "I resent that."

The truck door opened, and a large boot emerged. After stepping out, Brody turned, slammed the door, and walked to the bed. He reached in and pulled up a saddle, causing his hard biceps to ripple under the weight.

"Damn, that is big," Sage said, sinking her teeth into a cookie with the voraciousness of a starving woman.

"Get a grip, Sage," Eleanor whispered, glancing cautiously at Louisa.

"Sorry, Louisa. I lost myself there for a moment." Blushing, Sage turned her head away from the window. "I'm a divorced mom who hasn't ridden a bike in so long I don't know if I'd remember how to peddle."

Failing an indifferent guise, Louisa made a *piff* sound. "The man is nothing to me. Peddle away."

"Jumpin' Jim Bowie on a wounded horse," Violet said. "We all know you've been sleeping with Brody. Why hide it from us?"

"I have not!" Louisa shouted.

"Such colorful cursing." Sage fabricated a smile. "Maybe Lily and I were lucky not to have brothers."

Mallory and Eleanor couldn't stop laughing.

"I'm not the least bit interested in Brody Vance," Louisa argued, tearing into another cookie. "And I'm sure as hell not climbing under the covers with a cowboy."

"Uh-huh," Violet said grinning. "So, if I go over there and plant a big ol' wet kiss on Brody's lips, you wouldn't think a thing about it?"

Louisa shrugged a shoulder. "Go right ahead."

Violet rolled her eyes and stuffed a chunk of the cookie into her mouth. "You're so full of crap, Louisa."

It was evident from the patchy shade of pink dusting Louisa's cheeks that she and Brody weren't as involved as everyone thought.

Sage gave Mallory a wink. "Louisa has sworn off cowboys."

"Damn, right, I have," she concurred, firmly. "Something always gets broken when they're around."

Mallory wasn't going to argue with that. Thinking Jess might be with Brandi was breaking her heart in two.

"Whoa," Violet said, sitting up straighter in her chair as the sheriff's cruiser pulled up behind Brody's truck. "Forget Brody Vance. If I cross the street to kiss a cowboy, it'll be that roughneck with the badge on his chest."

Sage puckered her lips with a deep, "Noooo…"

Eleanor gave Violet a wince. "I have to side with Sage on this one. Finn is too close to family for kissing."

"He's Ty's brother, not mine," Violet informed her. "That makes him fair game for a mutiny."

Mallory wanted to know what that was all about but wasn't going to ask questions about the Gates family tree when she barely knew Violet.

"You wouldn't?" Louisa asked, shocked by the mention of a rebellion involving the sheriff.

"Oh, I would," Violet answered, watching Finn with a keen eye. "In a heartbeat. Logan was pissed at me for weeks after I bid on Finn at the bachelor auction last year. Something must be done to show my brothers that I'm not a kid anymore."

"Having a fling with Finn Durant would prove that," Eleanor said, with a quick raise of her brows.

"Beyond a shadow of a doubt," Sage murmured into her cup.

"Imagine that." Louisa gently elbowed Violet in the ribs while grinning nefariously. "Our sweet little Vi sexing it up with the sheriff."

Everyone, including Violet, burst into laughter and more teasing and talk followed.

Mallory sipped her latte and watched the lighthearted antics between the friends. Their playful ribbing was refreshing and kept her mind on something other than her problems.

They were strong, independent women who embraced each other's flaws and fears with love and support.

They undoubtedly knew why Mallory had come to Santa Camino and why she was staying at the Rescue. But they had greeted her without judgment or questions, accepted her and made her feel welcome among the sisterhood.

JESS PULLED INTO THE RESCUE PARKING LOT AROUND NINE. He took the strong, black coffee he'd brewed at home from the console cup holder and walked towards the double glass doors of the office, ready to bury his head under a mound of paperwork.

It had been six long agonizing days since he had seen Mallory naked, and the fire inside him was still burning blue. Six days since she had laid down the law and said it was all or nothing.

For seven long nights, he'd barricaded himself in a house that felt as empty as his heart and knocked back bourbon until he could sleep. It was a ritual he would repeat tonight and every other night until he either drank himself to death or took her to his bed.

His liver was doomed.

Brody met him just outside the door. "Well, look what the cat drug in."

Jess knew he resembled that comment, feeling mangled and chewed on by something feral and toothy. "Did anything eventful happen while I was gone?"

"Nothing I care to discuss with you," Brody said.

Brody's answer galled his already raw mood. "What the hell does that mean?"

"You'll find out soon enough."

Jess stared at the man he considered a friend. What was Brody not telling him? What would he find out? That he and Mallory had taken that ride?

Brody gave him a long, measuring look. "You know my eyes are on another woman."

Jess knew, but still. "Lou swears there's nothing going on between the two of you."

"Then there isn't."

"What are you saying?"

"That I don't kiss and tell," Brody said before walking away.

Pushing through the doors, Jess greeted Kara with a, "Morning."

"Hey, boss," she said, not bothering to look up until she was done the writing. She snapped the end back on the magic marker and shoved it back into the Rolling Stones cup she used as a pencil holder. "How was your trip?"

He took the mail from the bin above her desk and went into his office without answering.

"There's paperwork on your desk about that horse they brought in a couple of nights ago."

"Thanks, I'll look at it later."

"I'm leaving at twelve to babysit the kids for Eleanor and McCrea." Kara continued. "But I made a sign for the front door saying we were closed for a funeral."

Jess had turned his phone off and hadn't opened an email in days. This morning, he'd skipped through his voice mails and found one from Eleanor.

The sisters had planned a memorial service for their mother, inviting only a small group of friends and family for the scattering of her ashes.

He wasn't attending. He had quarterly reports to work on and an agenda to finalize for the upcoming rodeo committee meeting. He had called Brandi and asked if she could pull together a presentation on what Winsor Rodeo could offer. She emailed that to him before he left the house.

His parents were going to the ceremony, and Louisa would be there too, so Eleanor and Mallory had plenty of support.

"Don't bother with the sign. I'll be here," Jess said, tossing the mail and his sunglasses onto his desk.

"No, you won't," she said, walking around the reception desk and into his office.

His hat joined the mail and sunglasses as he scrubbed a hand over the stubble on his jaw. "Why won't I?"

"McCrea called about an hour ago," she said, handing him a note. "You're someone's ride."

He read it and swore under his breath. His brother had volunteered him to drive Mallory to the ceremony. "Can you get me some Tylenol?"

A minute later, Kara came back into his office, lifted his hand, and placed two white pills in his palm. "Helping you cure a hangover isn't in my job description."

Jess popped them into his mouth and took a sip of coffee. "Neither is surfing the internet for jeans on company time."

She frowned but didn't dispute it. Instead, she set Jess's hat back on his head and tucked his sunglasses into the pocket of his t-shirt. "Go home and take a hot shower."

"I took a shower this morning." A long cold one.

She pulled him to his feet. "Then shave that garbage off your face and put something on that doesn't have holes in it." She pushed him towards the front door. "And don't be late."

His life was in a sad state of disrepair when an eighteen-year-old was telling him not to be late.

Jess showered, again. This time in hot water, shaved, changed, and drove by the barbershop for a haircut. By one-thirty – half an hour before the service was to start – he was standing on Mallory's doorstep in his best shirt and jeans, with polished boots and a clean hat.

The last time he had been this gussied up was at McCrea's wedding. He had sworn then that sparing a death in the family, he wouldn't be this uncomfortable again.

But death had come, and he shouldn't think it much of a chore to pay his respects or offer a grieving woman a ride.

He gave the door a couple of knocks.

"It's open." The sound of Mallory's voice made his stomach tighten into a hard knot.

He stepped inside and closed the door behind him. The wisp of a white curtain blowing in the breeze from an open window drew him to the next room. He pushed the double doors open and stepped into a world of canvas and paint.

Brilliant and intrepid sketches of the Rescue and the horses with a unique style that conveyed all the emotion Mallory had admired in Jules's work.

He moved around the room, examining each piece. He stopped to kneel in front of a large painting situated in the corner. The soft, gentle way she'd captured Eleanor and Tucker made Jess's throat tighten.

He rose and continued his walk around the room, spotting a painting of Sophie with the pink boa around her neck. Her soft brown eyes were a bright breath of sunshine and life. The next one was of McCrea with a countenance of complete devotion and admiration as he held his son.

There were several sketches of Hope and Filly in different poses and one of Brody that disturbed him.

The painting was as detailed and moving as the other two. Brody was sitting on the ground with his leg drawn up and a hand draped over his knee. There was a lead rope in his hand and a touch of sadness on his dirty face.

How had Mallory observed such a moment if she hadn't been near the man?

Jess took a step back and turned, ready to exit the room and leave that question behind, when he bumped a table loaded with paint and brushes. He cursed and moved quickly to steady it before everything went plummeting over the edge. After setting the can of brushes upright, he caught a glance of another man.

Drafted in charcoal, Jess barely recognized himself. His eyes were hard, his jaw rigid, and his face fixed tight with a scowl as he sat across the table from her the night she'd come to town.

Jesus, was that how he had looked?

He picked it up and saw another sketch, one of a man sitting on a rocky ledge. With a cockeye-eyed grin, a tilted hat, and a gleam in his eyes, he bore a close resemblance to the man Jess had been in his younger days of the rodeo.

The man who had ridden horses and taken risks.

When he heard footsteps, he laid the sketches down and quickly made his way back to the front door. Shifting from one boot to the other, he waited for Mallory to make an appearance.

Minutes later, the bedroom door opened, and she walked out wearing a simple, off-the-shoulder white dress he knew was Eleanor's.

Jess tried hard to breathe and even harder not to stare at her long legs and shapely calves that disappeared into the also borrowed brown square-toed boots.

The mid-thigh dress decorated with tiny blue flowers fit her perfectly and accentuated her feminine form. She had styled her hair so that it hung in long, loose curls over her shoulders. She looked soft, delicate, and more vulnerable than any woman should.

Neither of them bothered with a hello. They stood apart, bearing the sound of the loud silence created nights ago. Today was going to be so hard. "You shouldn't leave the door unlocked."

She ran her palms over the lower portion of the dress. Her lips pulled displeasingly to one side when she looked down at it. "Eleanor told me you were coming."

Jess shoved his hands into the pockets of his jeans. "Are you ready to go?"

"As ready as I'll ever be." She drew her booted foot up and over the opposite knee, rubbing vigorously at the scuff on the heel. "I should have packed more clothes." She let her foot fall with a heavy sigh. "But when I got the call that Mom had been in an accident, I didn't know..." Her voice failed.

He wanted to close the distance between them, take her into his arms, and hold her until that brokenness in her eyes was gone. "The dress is flattering on you, and no one will mind a scuff on your boot. There's no one to impress. These people are coming because they loved your mother."

"You're right." She picked up her keys from the kitchen counter and started towards the door.

Jess opened it and waited for her to walk through it.

She stopped in front of him, her eyes glossy and mournful. "I don't know if I can do this."

Her face buckled, and as the tears rolled down her cheeks, he couldn't fight the urge to touch her any longer. Bringing his hands to her shoulders, he gave them a gentle squeeze and eased her closer. "It will come in waves, honey. That's the way grief is."

She pressed her forehead against his chest. "I — I thought I was okay, but I…"

He palmed the back of her head. "Today will be hard. But it will get better. I promise."

"I'm so tired of death." Her voice trembled. "So tired of having to say goodbye to the people I love."

"You can do this, Mallory. You're a strong woman. You fought for her, and you won. You traveled all the way to Texas to bring her home, and I have a feeling you did it without shedding a single tear."

Her arms slid around his waist, tightened as tears flowed. "But you can now, honey. Cry until there are no more tears left in you, and I'll be beside you all the way."

Hearing Mallory cry physically hurt him. Her broken sobs reached a hidden cord inside of him, and each shake of her shoulders pulled the most protected part of his heart closer and closer to the surface.

When her tears subsided, she lifted her head and offered him a faint smile. She slid her hand over his shirt. "I've cried all over your pretty shirt."

He didn't care about the shirt or the streaks of makeup where her face had rested against his chest. He would gladly take mascara runs if it helped erase the sadness in her eyes.

He raised his hands to her face, placed his thumbs under her eyes, and gently wiped the tears away. "The shirt will dry."

She took a deep breath and widened her smile. "Thank you, for letting me…" She made a motion towards his chest. "You know, letting me fall apart."

Jess leaned over and planted a kiss on her forehead, fearing he was the one who was falling.

CHAPTER 20

The Mackenna land was beautiful, stretching for miles before it rolled into hills in the distant horizon. Mesquite, oak and maple trees lined the creek they crossed and tapered off as the land rose into craggy rocks and cliffs.

She chanced a glance at Jess and wondered if his recent haircut had been for Brandi. His cleanshaven face was dour as he guided the truck onto the gravel road behind the barn and drove east.

Once again, obligation had brought him to her. He had comforted her with understanding words and forehead kisses. Something he would have done for Sophie or Eleanor.

Mallory wouldn't think about what was happening between them. She couldn't. Not until the ceremony was over.

She took a deep breath, trying to fortify herself against what was to come when they reached the cemetery and she said goodbye to her mother forever. Frances Mackenna wouldn't have won any mother of the year awards, but the world was a different place when the woman who birthed you wasn't in it.

She held tight to the urn as the truck bounced and bumped along the gravel road. A half mile later, Jess turned right and followed a narrower road past a small wooden sign that read Mackenna Family Cemetery.

Her chest tightened, and so did her hold on the urn. While her mother's ashes were inside, she was here with Mallory. But there was a finality to scattering them.

There were several vehicles parked near the top. Jess guided the truck into a spot near McCrea's and parked.

Mallory opened the door and stepped out onto the dry grass. People had gathered around the newer gravestones near the top of the hill and were waiting for her and Eleanor to join them.

Sage, Violet, and Louisa were standing within reaching distance of Eleanor, ready to give support if needed.

Mallory recognized Ed immediately. He had his arm around Eleanor and the shine of unshed tears in his eyes. Louisa, Sage, and Violet were standing near a man and a woman who looked to be in their late fifties. The man, tall, broad, and Texas as the Alamo, had dark hair, blue eyes, and was the perfect mesh of Jess and McCrea. The woman had the same stunning features as Louisa, but with a touch of elegance and refinement to her pose.

Jess rested his hand on the small of Mallory's back, adding to the tension in her chest. He stayed behind her until they reached the top of the hill. Then he stepped aside to let Eleanor join her.

The service started with a prayer and reading of Psalm twenty-three by the minister from a local church.

After Eleanor read a poem by Dorothy Parker, she looped her arm through Mallory's, and they walked farther up the incline to the spot her mother had talked about. It was in the middle of a small grove of pecan trees with a beautiful view of the Redemption.

Mallory held the urn, and Eleanor removed the lid. Together they spread her ashes, giving their mother to the winds of Texas and to the ranch she had loved so dearly.

They stood together there, watching the wind blow the trees. Eleanor took in a deep breath and let it out. "Mom is finally at rest."

She closed her eyes and felt an indescribable calmness come over her. "Yes, she is."

Eleanor wrapped an arm around her shoulder and lay her head against Mallory's. "I love you, sister dear."

Mallory smiled and wiped her eyes. "I love you too."

As they turned to walk back down the hill, Jess and McCrea joined them. Eleanor slid an arm around McCrea's waist, and he bent to kiss her on the forehead.

Mallory was envious of those tender gestures. Given from a man who loved and adored you, they were more addictive than chocolate-covered doughnuts and a million times sweeter.

Jess's face remained stoic. He was a stone pillar of unemotional support.

"Mallory." Eleanor's voice brought her attention to the man and the woman she had seen earlier. "These are my in-laws. Belle and Hardin Coldiron."

Hardin placed his Stetson over his heart and gave Mallory a small nod. "Pleased to meet you."

"Likewise."

Belle wasn't so formal. She embraced Mallory with both arms. "You were just a little thing the last time I saw you playing in the yard at Redemption and now look at you." She pulled back an arm's-length. "A beautiful woman."

Mallory didn't remember either of them, but their

kindness warmed her heart, and she was instantly fond of them.

"And this," Eleanor looped her arm through the bartender's arm and laid her head on his shoulder, "is my dad, Ed."

The man's smile widened. "I believe we've already met."

Mallory didn't bother with a handshake because she already felt like she had known him her whole life. "I believe we have," she said and adopted Belle's Texas hospitality by giving Ed a hug.

He embraced her tight with all the affection of a father. "You have Franny's smile," he whispered in her ear.

That nickname didn't suit Frances Montgomery, but Mallory was sure it had the girl he had known and loved. "Thank you, Jimmy."

He drew back with a weary laugh. "Franny is the only one who called me that."

Mallory ran a finger under her eyes and sniffed, feeling as though she had found a long-lost family member. "You were a fond memory she spoke of often."

Ed clasped her hand between his. "That's good to know."

"Mom and Dad have invited everyone over to their house for a late lunch," McCrea said, addressing Mallory when they started down the hill to their vehicles. "Do you feel up to it?"

She didn't. She wanted to go back to her apartment and end the day with a hot bubble bath and a bottle of wine. But she couldn't turn down Belle and Hardin's kindness or generosity. "Yes, that would be nice."

"We're stopping by the house to pick up the kids, but we'll meet you there," Eleanor said.

Jess dug into his pocket for his keys and followed Mallory to the truck. She climbed in and waited for him.

When he was seated behind the wheel, he started the truck, made U-turn in the high grass.

She stared at her thumb, the unsuspecting target of her anxiety. Its short nail and scarred quick were like the rings inside a tree, a record of events in her past.

Her past.

Mallory closed her eyes, trying to mentally block out all that encompassed.

The silence in the cab and the grief in her heart merged and tightened around her chest. If she could just get through this day, she would be alright. She could push everything down and seal it away forever.

But she couldn't stop thinking...

Today had brought back the bad memories of Aiden's death and funeral. He'd been her rock, and now that he was gone that resilient person she had been was beginning to crumble. Sometimes she felt as though she were in limbo without a firm footing. Other times she found her feet planted perilously close to the edge of darkness, her shoulders heavy, her legs weak and ready to buckle.

Jess was quiet and unreadable, and she couldn't take his silence any longer. He wasn't going to give, and she wasn't going to keep nudging him along.

It was time to pack up her bags and move on. "On second thought, drop me off at the apartment. I have packing to do."

She saw him glance her way. "Packing?"

"I've done what I came here to do, and now it's time to leave. Rex will follow me. You'll be free from the burden of being my bodyguard and chauffeur, and Eleanor won't have to worry about her family."

"Damn, it, Mallory," he swore, gruffly. "You are her

family. You're not a burden, and I am here because I want to be. Not because of El. If you left, she'd worry herself sick."

She curled her leg under her and twisted around in the seat to face him. "Can we just forget for a second that I'm Eleanor's sister? Can we pretend that I'm a woman and you're a man? Two people who are attracted to each other."

With thin lips and a set jaw, Jess removed his hat and tossed it onto the dash.

"Tell me how *you* would feel if I left."

"I can't."

"Why?"

He let off the brake and pushed the gas down. "I have my reasons."

She crossed her arms and sat back in her seat. "I wish you'd share them," she snapped but was terrified of what those reasons might be.

He didn't share. He just kept on driving with both hands on the wheel and his eyes fixed on the road.

"Where did you go when you left town?"

His fingers tightened around the wheel.

"Were you with Brandi?" She hated the rattling sound of her voice, hated that she sounded weak and hurt. But she was. God, she was so hurt.

Again, he answered her with silence.

"Please, talk to me! I'm not asking for a June wedding, just honesty."

Without warning, Jess braked, jerking her forward until the seatbelt caught. The truck skidded to a halt in the middle of the road.

He guided the truck off the road and down a path that led to a pumpjack in the nearby field. He pushed it into Park and propped his arm on the back of the seat, looking over the console at her. "I didn't leave town. I've been at home, emptying every bottle of bourbon I have. I haven't been with Brandi or any other woman because you're all I think about. Your breasts, your naked body tempting me in the window," his teeth clenched together. "Fantasizing about your lips wrapped around parts of me that would make you blush beet red. "

Mallory felt her jaw drop and that beet red flush spread across her cheeks.

"Do I want to fulfill those fantasies? Hell, yes, every one of them. But I won't because you made it clear you want more." Jess pointed his finger at his chest. "And I can't give you more. Sex is it. That's all I have to give." He dragged his hat from his head and threw it to the dash.

She sat there, stunned by his confessions. Sparks of excitement burst inside of her and skidded across her skin. He'd told her he wanted to finish their kiss and she knew that meant sex. But what he was describing…her lips around his body. The heat scorching her cheeks spread down her neck and lower.

The tension in the truck grew thick, and Mallory found herself struggling to breathe.

How did she respond?

What did she say?

It was on the tip of her tongue to tell him that she'd take the sex because the other option was to walk away without anything.

Taking several deep breaths, Jess raked a hand through his hair. "And don't you dare sit there and lecture me about honesty when you have the name of a known drug trafficker tattooed on your arm."

The sensual burn of desire inside of Mallory was suddenly saturated with a bone-chilling wave of reality. Oh God. Mortification enveloped her. She crossed her arms over her stomach, feeling raw and exposed like she had that night.

The muscle along the upper part of his jawbone flexed tight as his gaze dropped to the wheel. "What happened when you were sixteen?"

His question sent Mallory spiraling back to a moment that was so dark, so dangerous, so frightening…a time when there were no pretty ribbons to hold onto.

She'd been right all along. The sheriff had told Jess about Aiden's arrest. He knew. He knew everything about her, Rex and the Pack, and the darkness of her world.

But Aiden had saved her, and she wouldn't let Jess belittle him. "Aiden wasn't a drug trafficker."

"Then who was he?"

Mallory unfolded her arm, holding the tattoo out for Jess to see in detail. "US Army Sergeant Aiden S. Reynolds was my brother. And what happened to me when I was sixteen is none of your damn business."

J ESS STARED DOWN AT THE TATTOO, SEEING IT CLEARLY FOR the first time. The heart situated above the I in the name Aiden had the single word brother tattooed in the middle.

Shock numbed his body. "Aiden Reynolds was your brother?"

The answer to his question had been right there in the middle of that heart. But Jess hadn't seen it. He hadn't wanted to look. He had only wanted to accuse and find an excuse to distance himself from her.

"He was killed by small arms fire on deployment a year and a half ago."

Under the bold letters of Aiden's name were two dates. The year he was born and… the year he had died.

I'm so tired of death, so tired of having to say goodbye to the people I love.

He had not only insulted her, he had offended her brother. A veteran and a man who had given the ultimate sacrifice. The people he and the Promise Point Foundation strove to serve.

She kept her eyes fixed on the pumpjack. "I'd really like to go back to the apartment now," she said, her voice undisguised and constricted.

The numbness evolved into a hot, searing pain in the middle of his chest. "Mallory —"

"I'm not talking to you, and I don't care where you take me. Just shut up and drive. The sooner I'm away from you, the better."

Her words cut him. He had seriously screwed up, and there wasn't a damn thing he could do to make amends if she left town. If he took her back to the apartment, she would pack her bags and be gone by sundown.

He needed to fix this, and he couldn't do that until she was talking to him again. Being with Eleanor and the others might help calm her down. "Everyone is expecting us. I'll make an excuse to get us out of there."

"I don't need you to make excuses for me."

He pulled the truck into reverse and backed out onto the main road. The trip to his parents' house a nearly a mile away was taxed with silence and remorse on his part.

Mallory sat anchored to the door handle.

He turned into the drive and pulled next to the attached garage. He knew she would spring from the truck the moment the wheels stopped rolling and she did, slamming the door behind her with a force that rattled his teeth.

He parked and went up to the walk after her. A few people were standing in the foyer, but he didn't see her

269

anywhere. He was polite with a brief greeting as he moved into the kitchen.

"Where's Mallory?" McCrea asked, looking around him.

"I don't know. I lost her after we came inside."

"Oh," McCrea lowered his voice. "Aiden Reynolds is Mallory's half-brother. Eleanor didn't know about him because he'd been in the foster system and didn't come into the picture until after she was living with Rose. He showed up looking for Rex when Mallory was in her early teens."

"Thanks for the heads up," Jess said, reaching for a glass of something fruity from the buffet his mother had spread out on the kitchen island.

"Damn, it, Jess," his brother groaned. "You didn't?"

"I did," he said, smacking his lips together in distaste at the non-alcoholic concoction. "What the hell is this stuff?"

"It's called punch," McCrea answered, dryly. "I hope you were subtle with your questions about Aiden."

He dumped the punch into the sink and set the glass on the counter. "I need a real drink."

McCrea sighed. "That bad, huh?"

"Yeah, that bad." He saw their sister coming through the foyer. "I see Lou made it."

"Yeah, and judging from the drool dripping from her fangs, she's pissed about something," McCrea said, his face more humorous than his tone.

"Is Brody here?" Jess asked, knowing that nowadays, Brody was usually the cause of her teeth gnashing.

"I saw him earlier." McCrea downed the last of his punch and grimaced. "God, this stuff is awful."

"Just think of how pleasant life will be when Lou takes over for Doc Tolbert."

His brother's face went grim. "If she takes over for him, we're going to need whiskey in the punch."

Louisa had always been a double shot of fire and brimstone. Even as a child, she'd been plain spoken and strong-willed with a touch of sarcasm thrown in.

But she hadn't been a hellcat who liked chewing up and spitting out every cowboy who thought they had a chance with her. That had happened around the same time a cocky horse trainer named Chris Keegan left their dad's employment at the Coldiron Ranch to strike out on his own.

Louisa had been a sophomore in college and too young for a summer romance with a man like Keegan. Though she never talked about the man or what had happened, Jess knew she'd been hurt.

Louisa hadn't committed to taking Doc's place once she finished school. But they were all hoping she would. Her love and devotion to animals would make her one hell of a veterinarian, and she would be a tremendous asset to the Rescue when Doc retired.

Jess suspected that whatever had happened between her and Keegan was interfering with her relationship with Brody. And that might keep her from coming home permanently.

"I thought after they slept together, things might be a little quieter around here," McCrea said, with a half-smile. "But nothing is easy with Lou."

"Oh, hell," Jess cursed when Lou saw them. "She's found us."

"Be forewarned." McCrea eased around the counter, preparing to run if necessary. "Eleanor introduced Mallory to the tribe on Tuesday, so whatever is going on between the two of you has been thoroughly discussed with Sage, Violet, and Lou."

"How lovely," Jess mocked.

"Here she comes," McCrea said, heading in the opposite direction. "You're on your own."

"Coward." He snatched a bottle of water from the counter, twisted the cap off, and took a long swig.

"What did you do to Mallory?" she asked, her face pulled tight with a poisonous glare that was entirely her own. "She's in the upstairs bathroom crying her eyes out."

Anger and guilt matted inside of him. "Stay out of it, Louisa."

"No." She crossed her arms over her chest and cocked her hip to one side. "I don't know what "it" is but you need to get your ass up those stairs and make things right with her."

Was it possible that Mallory hadn't confided in the tribe? Maybe, or maybe this was his sister's way of fishing for more information. Louisa could be shifty when she wanted to pry.

"How about you crawl back on your broom and stay the hell out of my business?"

She snorted and scratched her forehead with her middle finger, giving him silent directions as to where he should go.

"I mean it," he put a warning in his tone. "I didn't interfere with you and Keegan."

Disdain marbled with the brown in her eyes, confirming Jess's suspicions about the end of that relationship. "And I won't say a word about you being in Brody's bed. What you do is your own damn business."

Her face went lax. "I haven't been in Brody's bed."

Jess hoisted a haughty smile, knowing he had hit a nerve with that bit of gossip. "Rumor has it, you have."

He waited for the argument he could always rouse from his sister. But it didn't come. Instead, her face paled, and she swallowed. "I see," she said, taking a step back. "I wonder who started that rumor?"

"It wasn't Brody," Jess said, jumping to the man's defense because he knew Brody wouldn't say or imply anything that might be detrimental to his sister's reputation. He wasn't a man who would spread immature bragging stories about any woman. Brody truly cared for Louisa. "The rumor came from Cody Peters."

Anger reddened her cheeks, and Jess almost felt sorry for the young cowhand. She spun around and marched out of the kitchen with her sights set on the bunkhouse. Poor Cody would be walking funny in the morning if he could walk at all.

CHAPTER 21

Jess made his way through the people and took the stairs two at a time until he reached the top. He paused when he heard muffled cries coming from the bathroom three doors down.

How was he going to apologize? What could he say that would make her stop crying? Nothing. Not a damn thing.

He raked his hands through his hair, squared his shoulders and headed down the hall. He was going to go into that bathroom and take whatever punishment Mallory thought he deserved.

The rug muffled his footsteps and drowned out the sound of his approach. He eased his hand around the antique knob and gave the door a soft knock.

"It's occupied," came her sobbing reply.

He wiggled the knob, knowing that if he moved it just right, it would open. His parents hadn't bothered fixing it after the three of them had moved out. Guests used the one downstairs.

He eased the door open. "Mallory?"

She was on her knees in front of the toilet with her arms folded across the lid. Her small body shook uncontrollably against the tears.

Grief was a merciless emotion that couldn't be eradicated by a single bout of crying. The pain of losing her brother and her mother in such a short period had finally caught up with her. And he hadn't made the loss any easier by accusing Aiden of being a drug trafficker.

"God, honey," he said, sighing heavily. "Don't cry..."

"D—don't tell me what to do," she barked between hiccups. "Get out! I don't want you in here with me!"

"I'm sorry I said those things about your brother."

"I don't care! Get out!"

Jess slid past the sink and closed the door behind him, then crouched down on his haunches next to her.

The bathroom was narrow, with just enough space for a shower, toilet, and pedestal sink.

He and McCrea had outgrown the shower in their early teens and had to use the one adjacent to Louisa's bedroom which made most mornings a standoff of who showered first.

Louisa was an early riser. Consuming the hot water in a twenty-minute shower was a vindictive part of her morning routine, so he and McCrea usually wound up in a tangled mess of fists and fury, fighting over the meager trickle that was left in the pipes once she had finished.

"I'm not leaving. Not until we've talked." He reached to brush wet strands of hair from her face.

She sprung to life, knocking his hand away, eyes cold and angry. "Don't touch me."

He studied her from a second or two, surprised by her reaction. "Okay," he said, moving back to give her room. "Your rules. Your space. I won't touch you unless you want me too."

Jess wasn't sure how long he could abide by that. Seeing her in this crumpled mess of tears and mourning made him want to pull her into his arms and never let her go. It was a disturbing revelation he didn't want to give much thought too, right now or in the future.

"I understand you're pissed at me. You have every right to be, but why are we back to the Look But Don't Touch rule?" He sat and leaned his back against the door. "You know me. Remember those kisses we shared?"

"But you don't know me." She moved to the small space between the toilet and shower, drew her knees up, curled her arms around her legs and hid her face. "So don't pretend that you do and that everything is okay. Just don't. Don't look. Don't touch. Just go away. Please. Please, go away."

Her exhausted plea cascaded over Jess like a wave of icy water that damn near broke him in half. "I can't do that, honey. I can't leave you here to cry your eyes out all by yourself. So." He positioned his back against the door and stretched his leg out in front of the toilet. "I guess I'm here until you're done crying."

"Then what?" she asked, her voice muffled and broken.

"You start to heal."

"If you know about Aiden's arrest," she hiccupped, keeping her face hidden from him, "then you know what happened to me that night."

He thought for a second, trying to recall anything Finn might have said that he had overlooked. But he couldn't think of anything. Their conversation had been about Aiden, and Mallory hadn't been mentioned.

He didn't have a clue as to what she was talking about, but he wasn't going to let her know that. Whatever had happened had been so distressing that it had transformed a fearlessly strong woman into a ragged mess of tears.

"How," multiple hiccups foiled her attempt for a deep breath, "can someone heal from that?"

This wasn't grief and it wasn't anger over what had transpired between them in the truck. This was something else, and Jess wasn't sure how to respond. He only knew that he had to help her.

He decided the best way to do that was to shed some of his pride and admit that part of her half-assed psych evaluation hadn't been so half-assed.

If he were going to get Mallory out of this bathroom, he would have to give a little. "You and I are a lot alike, Mallory."

Her head shook in a disagreement. "Nothing alike."

"Yeah," he said, inching closer. "We are. We both have one night that changed everything for us. One night we can't talk about."

She sniffed.

He scooted closer and put an arm on the toilet lid. "One night we've let define us."

She raised her head just enough so that he could see her glance up at him.

Seeing those red-rimmed eyes of hers gave him hope and made him smile. He reached over to touch her arm but paused, remembering that he had promised not to touch her. "Can I?"

"How can you want to—to touch me?" Her eyes darted down, her lips bending up in the middle with the threat of another wave of tears.

There were a thousand carnal reasons why Jess wanted to touch her, a thousand ways he could ease the physical ache building between them over the last two weeks.

But here, now, in this small room, desire wasn't moving

him. He needed to comfort her, hold her, and sooth every fear she had.

"My world," she rested her forehead on the top of her wrist. "Is so ugly, so horrible…"

"Honey, that world is gone. You left it. It's behind you." He scooted closer and gently hooked his finger in the shank of hair hiding her eyes without any protest from her. "And as for me touching you…" He drew the hair back and tucked it behind her ear without any objection on her part. "Nothing makes me happier than holding you in my arms, hearing you laugh, seeing you smile…"

He paused, giving his words time to sink in and they did, all the way to his bruised heart.

"Jess?" Louisa's whisper followed a knock on the door.

"Yeah?"

"People are concerned. Should I tell them she'll be down soon?"

"No," Mallory whispered, her eyes panicky. "I can't face all those people."

He stood and held out his hand for her to take. "We'll go down the backstairs."

Hesitantly, she took his hand and pulled herself up. Sliding one arm around her waist and the other under her knees, he lifted her into his arms.

She curled her arms around his neck and huddled closer to him, hiding her face in his shirt.

When he opened the door, Louisa's worried face fell to sympathetic. "Poor thing."

"She's in no condition to face all those people. Tell El not to worry. She's with me."

"You take care of her." His sister had the disposition of a jackal and the protective instincts of a lioness. "She's in a vulnerable state. Don't you dare take advantage of that."

Jess took the narrow stairway leading to the sunroom.

The Spanish-style ranch house had been built before the Civil War by his great-granddad. A founding father of the town and an abolitionist. There was more than one way to leave the house unnoticed. If this stairway had a crowd at the bottom, then he'd try another one.

He slipped past the kitchen and continued down the back hall toward the garage. From there, he hurried down the gravel drive to his truck.

Brody had just pulled up and was walking towards them. Concern pulled at his face when he saw Mallory. He hurried to Jess's truck and opened the passenger door. "The lady looks like she could use a friend."

"She's got one." After safety depositing Mallory into the seat, Jess reached for the seatbelt, then closed the door and started around to the driver's side. "Lou took a bite out of Cody," he said, jerking his door open. "You might want to stay clear of her for a while."

Brody's smile was one of anticipation. "What's the new gossip? Have we eloped yet?"

"I'll let her fill you in," Jess said, climbing into the cab. "She's dying to sink her teeth into you."

"Hot damn." Brody rubbed his palms together and headed for the house.

Jess was sure he would never understand the relationship Brody had with his sister. And he didn't need to. If Louisa was safe and happy, he was okay with whatever craziness worked for them.

Mallory curled herself into a ball and closed her eyes. Within the time it took them to reach the main road, she was asleep.

He drove slowly, careful of all the potholes and dips in the road. He parked in the garage and was careful as he unbuckled the seatbelt and lifted her out of the truck.

She whimpered once and snuggled closer to his chest.

He carried her into the master bedroom and laid her on the bed. She stirred, shifted, and curled back into the ball she had been in the truck.

He eased the boots free from her feet and chose a thick blanket from the linen closet in the hall to cover her with. After tucking the blanket around her, he pulled the door to a crack and walked to the kitchen out of hearing range.

He dialed Finn's cell and tucked the phone between his shoulder and ear as he took stock of the food in his pantry.

"Hello," Finn answered against the shuffling sound of papers.

"Did you find out anything else about Aiden Reynolds' arrest?"

The shuffling stopped. "Like what?"

"Was Mallory involved?"

Finn went back to shuffling papers. "Her name didn't come up in any of the research I did on Reynolds. But she would have been a minor back then, so finding out might require more digging. Why?"

"She broke down after we came back from scattering her mother's ashes."

"That's a reaction I'd expect from a grieving daughter."

"This wasn't grief. This was something else." Jess braced a hand on the counter. "Something traumatic."

"How do you know it happened when this Reynolds guy was arrested?"

"He was her half-brother," he clarified, remembering the dull sheen that came over her eyes when he had pressed her further with what happened when she was sixteen. Sixteen. That had been the trigger that unlocked everything. "She referenced the night of his arrest."

A deep sigh left Finn. "I see."

"She's asleep now, but I don't know what's going to happen when she wakes up."

"Don't crowd her. If she trusted you enough to share that something happened, then, she might tell you more. But," there was a pregnant pause to Finn's words, "you should prepare yourself."

"For what?"

"Horrible things can happen to a young woman in a town like La Claire, especially when their father is a major player in a casino that deals in drugs and prostitution."

Revulsion slammed into Jess's stomach, pitching his insides into a sickening state that almost had him dry heaving.

"Sheriff." Jess heard Carla, Finn's assistant, in the background. "A cattle truck has overturned just past Meyer's Road."

"I've got to go."

Jess laid his phone on the counter and cupped his hand under the sink faucet. Bringing the cold water to his mouth, he pulled it between his lips as McCrea's words came back to him. *She was an impressionable teenager when all this happened. It would have been easy for her to have gotten caught in the crosshairs or thrown into something ugly…*

Something ugly. Jess's mind began to wander to dark down alleyways, into back rooms of casinos where filthy, drunken men lurked.

What happened to me when I was sixteen is none of your damn business…

A thunderous boom rattled the windows and jerked his eyes towards the hills. The dark blue clouds clashed with the deep green colors of the tree line, kicking up wind and rain. Judging from the direction of the clouds and the speed in which they were traveling, the storm would be here within the hour.

Remembering the anxiety Mallory had about storms, Jess manacled his thoughts and walked back to the bedroom.

She hadn't moved, and her breathing had settled into a soft rhythm.

He sat in the chair near the window and removed his boots, then placed them beside hers.

He tried focusing his mind on what he should do and say. That was harder to do because, with every shudder, every tear, pain shot through his body with the temperament of a tornado.

Jess turned his phone to vibrate and laid it on the nightstand. Then he crawled in beside her, settling in. The storm arrived. Thunder clashed, lightning sparked, and rain pelted the windows, rocking her awake. "It's just a storm," he said, pulling her closer.

Her hand clutched the front of his shirt. Holding on to him, her breathing leveled, and she fell back to sleep.

The storm passed, and night darkened the room.

Jess felt the soft rise and fall of Mallory's breasts against his chest. He tightened his hold and rubbed his cheek across her head.

She felt safe enough to fall asleep in his arms and trusted him enough to cry her heart out without repercussions.

But what would happen in the morning?

Mallory sat up in bed, holding her head. Her eyes felt like rubber balls inside her skull that burned every time she blinked.

She wasn't in her bed at the apartment or in the spare room at Redemption. She was in Jess's bed.

"Oh, Jesus," she whispered, remembering everything that had happened yesterday.

She'd broken down when Jess asked her about Aiden. She hadn't been strong. She hadn't put on a brave face or tried laughing past the pain.

She'd just let go, free-falling into the darkness of Aiden's death, and with the tears of grief, came the memories. Terrifying memories of what had happened the night Aiden was arrested. Fear, bitterness, sorrow, and disgrace had all come rushing in.

She had tossed and turned, fending off horrible dreams. But every time she opened her eyes, Jess had been there. Holding her, reaching out to pull her back into his arms, murmuring soft words.

Groaning, she rubbed her face. Jess knew. The sheriff had told him, and there was no use pretending.

She kicked the blanket back and shifted around until her feet fell over the bed. She raked both hands through her hair and stood, putting one foot in front of the other. That's all she could manage. There was no grace, no dignity, and not one ounce of coordination in her steps as she walked from the bed to the door.

She caught a glimpse of her reflection in the dresser mirror. Puffy eyes, red nose, sleep creases on her cheeks, messy hair, a wrinkled dress — she wiggled her toes — and bare feet.

She sighed, thinking that she could run out the back door. If she had known where it was, she probably would have. But the house was too big, and her head hurt too much to forge forth with that expedition.

She would have to face Jess just like she was.

She walked out of the bedroom and down the hall but stopped short of the foyer when she heard Kara's voice. "There's extra cheese on the pizza and a box of chocolate-covered doughnuts in the bag. And," she swung the plastic shopping bag that was over her shoulder around and onto Jess's desk. "I found these on sale." She dug into the department store bag and pulled out a pair of buttercream cowboy boots.

"I told you the cost didn't matter," Jess said, reaching over the four other bags on his desk to inspect the boots.

"I know. But I love a bargain. Oh, hi." Kara smiled brightly when she saw Mallory.

Jess rose from the chair. "You're awake."

"I'll be going." Kara handed Jess a credit card. "Here."

"Thanks, Kara," Jess said, shoving the card back into his wallet as he walked around the desk and over to where Mallory was standing.

"No problem, boss man." She winked at Mallory. "He has my number if you need anything."

"Thank you."

Jess had on those gray pajama bottoms Mallory loved so much and a white t-shirt. He looked disastrously handsome from the top of his mussed hair to the soles of his bare feet.

With Kara gone, the house was silent, and Mallory felt uncomfortable in her own skin. Naked and exposed. She hadn't felt this way in a long, long time, and it was hard to stand here in front of this man she loved and hold her composure now that he knew about her past.

"So," she said, rubbing her forehead. "Can I get a ride back to my apartment?"

"Ah…sure, if that's what you want." A smile was on his lips, but there was uncertainty in his eyes. "I'll take you back whenever you're ready."

Mallory looked down at her dress and bare feet. "I could use a hot shower and a change of clothes. And Eleanor is probably worried."

"I called her last night to let her know you were spending the night here," he was quick to say. "She called back this morning to check on you."

The throbbing in her head was getting worse. "What did you tell her?"

"That you were fine, and you'd call her later."

"She was okay with that?"

He shrugged. "Seemed to be. I told her we were working on a project."

The air conditioner kicked on, and Mallory felt a chill. "A project?" she asked, wrapping her arms around herself.

He moved his hands to her bare shoulder and slide them down her arm, causing a cascade of goosebumps. "You're cold."

"I usually am when I first wake up."

"You are a hard critter to keep under a blanket," he said grinning.

The feel of his hands on her arms alleviated the chill and warmed the most inner parts of her body. But his careful attention to her wellbeing also added to her guilt over what had happened yesterday. "I'm sorry," she blurted out because she didn't know what else to say.

A bolt of confusion flickered in his eyes. "About what, honey?"

Honey. He had called her that in the bathroom. Not Beautiful or Mallory.

Honey. It was special, like pretty.

"For being so rude when you asked me about Aiden," she said. "And for the meltdown."

His eyes softened. "You have nothing to be sorry about. I'm the one who jumped to conclusions about you and your brother," he said, lowering his lips to kiss her head.

She let her forehead rest against his chest. "You deserve an explanation about what happened —"

"No," he cut her off. "I don't. Whatever happened with Aiden is none of my business."

With Aiden? She looked up at his smiling face. There wasn't an ounce of disgust or pity in his eyes. But how —?

Oh...her heart sank. *He doesn't know.*

CHAPTER 22

THE SHERIFF HADN'T TOLD HIM ABOUT THE PACK AND what happened in La Claire. But they'd talked about that one event that had defined them both?

"Are you hungry? Kara brought pizza and doughnuts."

Should she tell him?

He was calling her honey and offering her food. He was smiling and laughing and holding her in his arms.

She couldn't ruin that.

Rattled and unsure of what she should do next, she laughed. The hollow sound was a mixture of relief and indecision. "You allowed junk food into your house? What will the Brussels sprouts think?"

His chest vibrated with a gravelly laugh that tightened the muscles of her lower abdomen. He gave her arms a final rub and a little pat before stepping back into his office. "I don't think the junk food will make it into the refrigerator. Besides, what kind of host would I be if I didn't give my guest what she wanted to eat?"

That made her reminisce about the first day they met

out on the road. Her first impression of him had been so wrong.

Jess was a tender and caring man.

Her heart ached with guilt. He deserved that honesty she'd preached about in the truck and a woman without issues and hang-ups and secrets in her past.

She loved him and wanted him. God, how she wanted him, in her life, forever, smiling and laughing just like he was now. She longed to wake up to those cool blue eyes every morning and fall asleep wrapped in those muscular, protecting arms every night.

But she would never have that. She was already fighting Jess's past; once he knew about hers, they wouldn't have a chance at a future together.

Mallory was dying inside, but she wouldn't show it. She clamped hold of her tears and smiled. "That just caused me to have déjà vu and some serious concern about your motives behind the junk food."

His eyes sparkled just like they had when he had given her wrong directions, only not quite as mischievous. He tried not to grin as he held up his right hand as a sign of amity. "Consider the junk food a peace offering."

She swallowed, holding tight to her sorrow, and eyed him suspiciously. "I'm not sure I should accept that offering when you haven't told me what project you've volunteered me for."

"Ah, yes," he said, reaching over to take a doughnut from the box on his desk. "The project." He held it out to her, using the pastry as bait.

She would never be able to eat another doughnut. Hesitantly, she took it and waited for Jess to explain what the project was.

But he didn't. Instead, he licked the chocolate glaze

from his thumb, walked back to his desk chair, and sat down.

She smiled, expecting nothing less from a man who was her match at teasing quarrels and flirty wordplay. "And the project …?"

"It's a hobby of mine, and I can't explain it," he said, simply.

"You horrible man," she accused. "You know I have a weakness for chocolate-covered pastries, and you used it to trick me into accepting the white flag."

His grin faded into a soft smile. "Grab a shower while I finish up what I'm working on, and I'll show you the project."

She took an exaggerated bite and swung around in a vexed fashion that made him chuckle.

Numbly, she headed back down the hallway to the master bedroom. Misery clawed at her throat, demanding to be expelled, but if she started crying now, she wouldn't stop until Jess knew everything.

She padded across the wood floor to the bathroom. *Keep it together for just a little while longer.*

The soft neutral tones of the bathroom walls gave the room an airy feel and added to the natural light. The large window over the creek rock garden tub gave a spectacular view of the hills behind his house. It was perfect for sunsets and relaxing with a bottle of wine.

Her apartment over Aiden's garage hadn't had a bathtub, only a shower with a head that was equivalent to a garden hose.

She was tempted to crawl in and watch that sunset. But there would be no more of that, at least not in Texas. No more climbs to the top of Promise Point or learning to ride a horse. In a couple of hours, she would be back on her bike, headed out of town and away from everyone she loved.

Again, her throat tightened, and again, she fought through it. She was stronger than this. Stronger than the temptation to let it all out.

She stepped to the glass door of the shower and turned the faucet to hot. Then moved back to the double bowl copper sink to undress. Between the bowls was a basket filled with a pink and white bottle of soap, matching lotion, and a loofah sponge.

Mallory held it to her chest. Jess had bought her a loofa sponge.

Tears sprang to her eyes. It wasn't like a loofa sponge was a sign of unrelenting love and devotion. But it was a small touch that showed just how much he cared.

"God, Mallory," she scolded herself. "It's a tropical cucumber that exfoliates dead skin."

She shed the dress and laid it on the sink. Taking the sweet-scented soap and the loofa with her, she stepped into the shower.

Steam clouded the room, and as she hurried to wash her hair, the sweet smell of honeysuckle and vanilla lofted through the mist.

She turned the water off and reached for a towel. She wrapped it around her and stepped onto the mat. Wiping fog from a mirror with a washcloth, she gazed unhappily at her reflection.

She was such a fraud and a weakling.

"Did you find the basket?" Jess asked from the other side of the bathroom door.

She secured the towel around her and opened the door. "Yes, I found it."

"Kara picked it out, so I hope it was okay."

"It was nice. Thank you."

He took a few steps back and motioned towards the plastic department store bags he'd placed on the bed. "She also picked out the outfits and the shoes." He paused to wince. "I'm horrible at matching clothes, which is why I mostly stick to jeans and t-shirts. My mother swears I'm color blind."

He gave the back of his head a nervous scratch. "And I've never bought ladies underwear, so you can thank Kara for that too."

First the loofa now underwear and outfits. "Jess, you really shouldn't have."

He waved her rebuttal aside. "I knew you'd need something to wear, and Kara loves shopping. Get dressed and meet me in the workshop." He stopped shy of the door. "Go through the kitchen. It's the second door on your left."

When he was gone, Mallory discarded the towel, and snatched a light pink set of panties and bra from the clothes on the bed.

They felt soft and luxurious against her skin. She should have bought new underwear months ago, but who did she have to impress?

She half-heartedly sorted through the bags looking for something that matched. Kara had outdone herself. Mallory cringed when she thought about how much money Jess had spent on the clothes.

There were several outfits and matching shoes, plus a Boyfriend style nightgown. The black, button-up, mid-thigh garment had a curved hem and a modest neckline. There was nothing risqué or revealing about it. The gown was a practical alternative to her 49ers t-shirt she knew Jess hated.

She folded the gown and laid it to the side and chose a pair of baggy blue sweatpants and a white off the shoulder, wide-collar sweatshirt.

She slid her feet into a pair of open-back sandals and ran a comb through her hair, then followed Jess's directions to the workshop.

She paused before turning the knob and heard the blaring voice of a local radio station cut through the door. "WKBR, home to Hill Country's best classic rock." As the guitar intro to AC/DC's "You Shook Me All Night Long" began playing, Mallory opened the door.

Jess was sitting on a stool. Behind him on a high position rack was a Shovelhead Harley. Large matte black tool chests sat along the wall next to him, and an assortment of tools hung neatly on panel racks over them. Diamond-plated cabinets sat on the far wall. Over them, were vintage garage signs.

On the worktable in front of him was the carburetor he'd had on his desk. His bare foot tapped in rhythm to the drum, and his lips moved to the words.

Was there any place the man wasn't at home? Did he ever look unattractive or ugly?

She stepped down from the main house and planted her feet on the concrete floor of the workshop, prompting Jess to look up.

He turned the volume down on the radio, did a quick appraisal of her new clothes, and smiled. "Very nice."

She tucked her hair behind her ear and crossed her arms over her breasts. Looking down at her bare toes, she returned Jess's smile. "Thank you, but really, you shouldn't have."

He patted the stool next to him. "Take a seat."

She hoisted her bottom onto it, spread her legs out, and placed her palms on the seat between them.

He scooted a steaming cup of chartreuse liquid in front of her. "It's a new blend of herbal tea Kara brought from a local shop."

She dared a closer sniff and rubbed her nose. "It smells... horsey."

His soft chuckle filled the air and mingled with the aroma of the tea. "It has Ashwagandha in it along with raw cacao and a few other ingredients. Try it," he prompted and scooted the cup closer. "I added sugar to yours."

Hesitantly, she lifted the cup to her lips and took a sip. The sweet and spicy blend was surprisingly good. "Not bad."

"So, what do you think about my hobby?"

Smiling, she looked around the room. "This is more than a hobby. It's an obsession."

He chuckled. "I've always had a need for speed and danger, so when I couldn't compete anymore, I turned to bikes."

She pointed to the one behind him. "Is this Shovelhead our project?"

The corner of his mouth quirked up. "Aiden taught you about bikes?"

She smiled. "They were his obsession too. He took me to trades shows and a few rallies with him. On nights I couldn't sleep, he would stay up with me, teaching me everything he knew about bikes. He said if I was going to ride them, then I needed to know how they run.

Taking the carburetor with him, he swung around and removed himself from the stool. "He was right."

"He was right about a lot of things," she said, remembering the night he told her not to be afraid, that he would take care of her.

"Ready to get your hands dirty?"

"Normally, I'd say yes, but right now, I think I'd rather just sit here and watch you."

He hunkered down near the bike and pointed to the top of the worktable. "Can you hand me that socket?

"The nine-sixteenth?"

"That's the one."

She reach it to him.

"Can you hold the carburetor until I get the bolts started?"

She crouched down beside him, holding the part in place like she had a dozen times for Aiden.

"I thought we could ride it to the fundraiser tomorrow," he said, screwing the bolts in with his hand.

She had to tell him she was leaving and that she wouldn't be here tomorrow. She needed to stop delaying the inevitable.

"Mallory?" He had stopped ratcheting the bolts and was looking at her. "What's wrong?"

"You shouldn't have done this."

"Done what?"

"You shouldn't have bought me clothes and pizza and doughnuts…"

"Sweatpants and comfort food aren't a big deal, honey."

"Don't," she said, shaking her head as she dropped her hands. "Don't call me that. Don't call me honey."

"Why can't I call you, honey?"

"You don't understand."

"I'm trying to."

"I can take wrong directions to some godforsaken land-fill, and I can take a lewd remark about a ride. I can take us bickering and kissing and you telling me all you want is sex."

She sat back on the floor, raised her knees and wrapped both arms around them. "But I can't do nice and sweet. And if you call me honey one more time, or kiss me on the forehead one more time, I'm going to fall apart. And I don't like falling apart. Argue with me, flirt with me, offer me Brussels sprouts or some other gross food...but don't," she choked back tears, "bring me doughnuts and sweatpants because I don't deserve them or...you."

She knew he must think she was crazy. What woman wouldn't like a man bringing her doughnuts and sweatpants? It was a processed food and cotton-polyester fantasy.

"Why don't you?"

"Because —" her words faltered. This was the last time Jess would see her, the woman on the Chieftain, pretty, strong, and brave. "Bad things happened to me."

His eyes became steely, and the muscle in his jaw flexed tight. He was thinking hard about something — about her, about if he really wanted to know about those bad things.

She thought he might get up and walk away, that he might spare her the humiliation of introducing him to that beaten and broken sixteen-year-old girl.

He sat next to her and began pulling up his right pajama leg.

Then he gathered the material between both hands and yanked it up past the scar on his thigh, baring the wounds of his fall.

His face was pained as if he were about to be ripped open by a sharp knife. "This is the ugly part of my past. It's off limits. I keep it hidden. I don't let anyone near it. Not even the women I've slept with could touch it."

He took her hand and placed it on the scar. "But now you have. You've seen it, you've felt it. I've shared it with you."

He put his finger to her heart. "I know my scar may not be the same as yours. But scars are scars, Mallory. It doesn't matter if they're on the outside or the inside.

They're there. They can tell us truths about ourselves we didn't know. But they can also lie to us and make us believe were not good enough, not deserving of good things. They can be bullies if we let them. Don't ever feel like you have to keep whatever is in your past a secret. Nothing that's happened to you could ever change the way I feel about you." His finger moved up to brush her cheek. "Do you understand?"

Oh, those beautiful, wondrous words. Mallory's heart had never been so full or so close to breaking. She wanted to dive into her unanswered questions about how he felt about her, She wanted to bare all her secrets, cleave open her soul, and let the ugliness spill out.

But doing that wouldn't be as easy as laying Jess's hand on a part of her body. She had to relive that night, those memories, and she had to say the words, but like the tears of her grief, they wouldn't come.

～

JESS WATCHED MALLORY WAR WITH HER PAST. HE DIDN'T know if he was ready to hear what had happened to her. He only knew she needed to share the burden, and he needed to be the person she shared it with.

She dropped her head and rested her forehead against her knees like she had in the bathroom at his parents' house. "I can't talk about it. The therapist tried — I couldn't."

He understood not wanting to talk about how bad you were hurting. He hadn't wanted to talk about the fall, almost losing his leg, or Hallie. That hadn't changed, but if talking about all that helped her, then he would try. "The doctors wanted me to see a therapist while I was in physical therapy, but I just couldn't cotton to telling a total stranger what was troubling me. How does pouring your heart and soul out to a person you don't know help solve your problems?"

He went back to bolting the carburetor onto the bike. From the corner of his eye, he saw her head lift. "I felt trapped in my own head, confused, angry...and scared," he went on to say. "I was more than scared, I was terrified. I felt so damn lost and alone. Isolated and like no one would understand how I felt even if I could put it into words."

He motioned for her to hand him the other bolt lying on the floor near her foot. "But then a few of the older guys I'd rodeoed with came to see me. Some of them were like me, lucky to be alive. Sam Rawlings was bucked in the chute and was almost paralyzed from the waist down. He came to see me every day for almost a month." The guys hadn't talked about their injuries, but knowing they were there had helped him to go on.

Mallory handed him another bolt. "How did Hallie handle your accident?"

Jess wasn't surprised she knew Hallie's name. The woman wasn't a big secret, and she wasn't an unbearable pain that Jess couldn't talk about. But there was something bizarre about hearing Mallory say her name. Something that connected her to his life before the fall. He wasn't comfortable with it, but he couldn't close the door to his past when she was so close to opening the door to hers.

"She ran off with some bull rider from the Northwest, Washington, I think." He twisted the bolt into the thread until it caught and then placed the socket over it. "The same bull rider she'd been sleeping with for months and a man I thought was my friend."

"She never came to see you after the fall?"

"Nope, just left her engagement ring on my chest and disappeared," he said, flatly because that's how he felt about it. "I'd proposed, and she'd accepted. We were building the house. The first year we were together was great. I was climbing the ranks and making a name for myself. We were both happy. I *thought* I was in love."

"You thought?" she asked.

Hallie was a scar. He knew that but sharing her with Mallory had revealed a new truth. What he'd felt for her wasn't love.

"I was hungry," he admitted and felt a part of that scar disappear. "I needed something real in my life. A person that would be there after the crowds had gone home. I thought Hallie was that person. But in the second year, everything went to hell. It was the best year of my rodeo career. I won competition after competition. I had sponsors lining up at my door, reporters calling me for interviews. I was at the top and winning. But the more I won, the more strained our relationship became."

He motioned for the last bolt. "First she wasn't happy with the size of the house. It had to be bigger and better. I needed to want more, be more. I gave her everything she wanted. The week of the finals, she told me she wasn't happy with her engagement ring. She wanted a new one with more diamonds."

He laughed, amused by that stupid kid he had been. "She'd worn that ring for nearly two years, and suddenly it wasn't enough. It needed more diamonds. Everything was about style and status with that woman, so I gave in. The day before the last night of the finals, we went to one of those expensive jewelry stores on the Strip in Vegas, and she picked one out. It needed to be sized, and the owner told me he'd call when he had it ready."

Jess rested his forearms on his knees. "He called the next day, and I rushed out to pick it up because I wanted that night to be perfect. I knew I was going to win and when I did, I wanted Hallie there with me."

"Wearing that big diamond ring," she added, her voice low and empathetic.

"Men aren't prideful about diamonds, at least I'm not. I just wanted her to be happy."

"So what happened?"

"I went after that ridiculous rock when I should have been preparing for the ride. My mind should have been on it, not chasing a diamond in Sin City for a woman who didn't give a damn about me."

Jess stood to his feet and laid the ratchet on the table. "I knew Hallie was sleeping with someone else. A man just knows, so I don't know why I was shocked when I found her in bed with that bull rider minutes before I mounted Dirteater."

"Oh, Jess," she whispered. "I'm sorry."

"Don't be. I'm not." And he wasn't. He'd thought that losing Hallie was the only good thing that had come from the fall. But now, he wasn't so sure.

If he hadn't fallen, his career would have continued, and he wouldn't have had time to help McCrea with the Rescue or been on that backroad helping Logan and Ty.

Mallory was Eleanor's sister, so they would have probably met sooner or later. But it would have likely been just an exchange of brief introductions. So without the fall, there was a possibility he wouldn't have gotten to know the beautiful soul sitting across from him.

Jess cleared his throat and continued. "Everything that happened that night was my fault. I was over the swell, not spurring high, or getting a good drag. The horse was jumping high, kicking hard, and switching leads. He did everything he was supposed to do, but I lost my grip."

It was also bizarre that he was sharing this secret with

Mallory. His family and friends had been there with him through his accident and recovery. They'd watched the horse break him.

But no one knew the details about what had happened minutes before the ride, what had caused him to lose his hold or why Hallie had left without saying goodbye.

He'd never told anyone about it, never had to say the words, so this almost felt like a confession. His soul felt a little lighter and his heart... well, he didn't want to think about how it felt.

Mallory needed a safe zone, a place she could let down her guard and talk about what had happened to her. He wanted to give her that security, help her to heal and move past whatever had hurt her.

Jess wanted that for himself too. But moving forward together meant they might move closer to something he feared worse than losing his leg.

CHAPTER 23

JESS SLOWLY DIVERTED THE CONVERSATION FROM HIM BACK to the Shovelhead They spent the next couple of hours working on the it and the rest of the day in the garage, looking at the older ones he'd restored. Mallory had hung to every word, listened to all the stories of how and when he had acquired each one.

They ate cold pizza and drank beer out on the terrace and took a walk up to the top of the hill to watch the sunset. They laughed and talked like they had been friends for years. It was the happiest he'd been in a long, long time.

He sat on the ground, leaned back on one of the limestone rocks nestled near the start of the downslope, and pulled her down beside him.

The jeans he had changed into helped conceal his body's blatant reaction to having Mallory so close. That too was part of the safe zone. He didn't want sexual tension to distract or hinder the steps she was taking toward talking about her past.

She crossed her legs and picked at the grass as she

stared out over the horizon. "Aiden had been tossed into the foster system when he was just a baby. He'd been searching for his biological father for a couple of years when he showed up on our doorstep. Rex denied Aiden was his son, but we both look just like the bastard." She smiled sadly. "I miss him so much."

Since he had learned Aiden was her brother, his mind had sifted through the conversations they'd had after her arrival. Aiden had been the soldier she had mentioned when they were touring the Rescue. He had been the kind and caring man who didn't condone violence, the man she might never be able to talk about. The man, the brother, and the fighter who had been influential in Mallory's life. A man of character whom Jess wish he could have had the privilege of knowing.

"You mentioned the name Mally Cat when you zoned out on the tour," Jess said, watching surprise cut through the grief in her eyes. "Did he call you that?"

"Yeah. I used to take a shortcut on my way home from school through an alley behind one of the bars there in La Claire that led straight to the trailer park we lived in. After Aiden moved in with us, he got a part-time job at one of the grocery stores. He didn't want me taking that shortcut alone, so he would wait for me after work, and we'd walk home together. That's how I became his Mally Cat."

Before adult problems had complicated their lives, Louisa had been the quintessential baby sister that he and McCrea had sheltered and adored. They'd had cute and sometimes teasing nicknames for her like Button and Pinto.

Jess missed that little girl and the close relationship he once had with her. Seeing Mallory mourn for her brother made him want to find Louisa, give her a big bear hug, and tell her just how much he loved her.

"He told me not to take that shortcut without him,"

Mallory continued her story, staring bleakly into the evening light. "But a storm was coming, and I wanted to get home before it hit. The rain started, and I didn't hear the man walk up behind me until it was too late."

Dread centered in the middle of Jess's chest and spread outwards. He wrapped his arms around her, and held on for whatever was to come.

"It all happened so fast… I fought back, but he was too strong. He dragged me into the back of the bar."

"The bar where you confronted Rex?" he asked, realizing that's how she had found him.

She answered him with a quick nod. "When Rex wasn't at the casino, he was there, so I kept thinking that he would see me and help me. But no one saw me. No one helped me. The man blindfolded me, bound my hands and feet with duct tape, and shoved a dirty rag in my mouth. Then he threw me into the back of a van and drove me to another place. I didn't know where I was, who had taken me, or what was going to happen to me. I was terrified."

Her body tensed, and she started trembling with the memories. "I must have blacked out. When I woke up, I was so cold. I found a corner to huddle into and started thinking about how I could escape. I could hear slot machines and voices, but I didn't recognize any of them."

"You were at the casino."

Again, she nodded. "I lost all track of time. I couldn't think, couldn't feel my hands or feet. I had almost given up on ever being found. But then, I heard Rex's voice through the door. I thought, "He's here to save me. He'll save me because he's my father and that's what fathers do. Even the bad ones protect their own flesh and blood." He felt a hard shiver overtake her. "But he didn't. He was there to settle his debt. He told them to keep me. A young girl like me could make them triple what he owed."

Bile rose to Jess's mouth. "Christ," he whispered as her words grabbed hold and birthed a cold, steel rage inside of him.

"But Rex wasn't in the position to make deals. The Pack own his soul. They get what they want and that night they wanted a new mule and me."

Suddenly, everything fell into place, and Aiden's arrest made sense. "Rex used you to blackmail Aiden into being that mule."

"He knew Aiden would do anything to save me, and he did. But they had no intentions of letting me go after he made the run. They were about to throw me back into that van and ship me across the border into Mexico when I broke free and started running. I got as far as the foyer when they caught me."

She rubbed her side. "I had two broken ribs and a concussion from being kicked around, but I was lucky. If the DEA hadn't raided the casino, I would have never been found."

Jess wrapped his arms around her shoulders and pulled her closer, thinking how close he'd come to losing her. Anger and fear clamped around his throat so tight he thought he might strangle to death.

"Rex and the others got off, and the man who kidnapped me was found dead in his car a few days after. When the authorities dropped the charges against Aiden, he left La Claire and joined the Army."

All loose ends had been neatly tied up or done away with. The men running the casino were pros, and Rex would be desperate for that life insurance money.

"I was so afraid of everything. I had nightmares and anxiety attacks. I couldn't go to school or even to the grocery store with Mom. Four months after I was released from the hospital, she put me on a bus to California." She laid her head on his chest. "Aiden and his girlfriend, Cassie, took me in. He taught me self-defense and empowered me until I wasn't afraid anymore."

Aiden hadn't wanted his sister to spend the rest of her life being a victim.

"The story made the national news," she said, her voice low and a little frail. "I was sure the sheriff had told you all about it. You acted differently after he left. You were so quiet."

"No," he said, softly, wishing he had done things differently that night. "Finn didn't say anything to me about what happened. I wish you had trusted me enough to share what happened to you sooner."

"I do trust you. You know that, but I was ashamed." She pulled back and shifted around to look up at him with chagrin in her eyes. "I was terrified my father was going to kill me. That's the kind of ugly world I come from. How could I share that with anyone? I have the man's DNA, his blood running through my veins."

That was the disgrace? The stain on Mallory's soul and the darkness she could never outrun? Who her father was was such an insignificant thing to him, but to her, it was a shameful burden. "You also have your mother's which makes you a Mackenna," he said, smiling proudly as he combed back her windblown hair. "Your grandparents were some of the finest people around. They were loyal, trustworthy, and had hearts of gold. The Mackenna bloodline is strong. You hold tight to that and leave what happened with Rex and La Claire behind you. You are a strong woman with a beautiful and giving soul who deserves donuts and sweatpants..." He saw her lips teeter with amusement. "Don't let Rex Montgomery or any other man cheat you out of happiness and love."

The moment that four-letter word parted his lips, Jess

knew it was too late to throw up his guard or run. This sharing of their pasts, the breaking down, the tearing apart and the healing, had been as he suspected it would be, more intimate than any sexual encounter he'd ever had.

He was falling again, head over heels, into the air. But this wasn't the same kind of falling it had been with Hallie. This was deep. It was a consuming, passionate, and scary falling because this was an authentic and rare, once-in-a-lifetime love.

And he knew that Mallory was falling too.

"I'm exhausted," she said, smiling up at him "Can we go home now?"

Home. Not his house. But *home.*

Jess propped his hand on the rock and lifted himself up. Dusting his jeans, he held his hand out for her. "Yeah, it has been a long day."

She took it, rose, and laced her fingers through his. There was a calmness about her that hadn't been there before. The tranquility of serene waters and blue skies that said she had finally found peace.

Under the light of the setting sun, the sky blazed orange and splintered the sky with shafts of gold.

Jess had seen a thousand sunsets, but this one was different.

He was different. Something had happened to him. He felt strange, light-headed, and dizzy. He felt confused and out of sorts.

He couldn't shake the elated feeling in the pit of his stomach. The one caused by him thinking of having sex with her.

The feeling was like those three or four seconds when his body was catapulted into the air by a bucking horse, and he was weightless. It was an exhilarating, free-fall ride that ended with a hard, sometimes bone-breaking landing that knocked the wind from his lungs and left him senseless.

Falling in love with Mallory could have the same consequences.

On the walk back to the house, Mallory paused to pick a Brown-eyed Susan from a clump growing near the base of a rock. "I've talked to Sage Parsons about buying a house here in Santa Camino."

He'd assumed when Rex was caught, she would go back to California. He hadn't once considered that she might want to make Santa Camino her home.

Mallory embodied the essence of everything he hungered for in a relationship: companionship, compatibility, and desire. He wanted her. But she wouldn't be placed into that small compartment where all the other women who had walked in and out of his life were neatly stacked.

There would be no closing her off and no walking away if things went wrong. And if they took this relationship to the next level, a physical level, she would want all of him.

As they neared the house, Jess moved in front of her and opened the back door. The dizziness inside his head changed to panic with that thought.

She twirled the flower stem between her finger and thumb, watching the bright yellow petals spin. "You're quiet again."

"I'm just surprised."

She walked inside. "Why?"

"Santa Camino isn't Monterey," he said, following her. "There's not a lot of entertainment here, no art galleries or beaches. Nothing that's recreational to a single lady like yourself."

"Maybe," she paused, lifting her lips in a sexy smile, "I'll find a cowboy to marry."

He felt caught in the crosshairs of a lethal weapon, not knowing if he should stand still or run. His body went tense.

"I'm kidding, Jess." Her smile broke into a laugh. "I'm not looking for a husband."

Relief washed over him. He sure as hell wasn't marrying her and Santa Camino was a small town. If she stayed and found herself that husband...

"But I am serious about the move." She dropped her head to pick at her nail. "Aiden's gone, and I want to be close to the family I have left. Eleanor and the kids, they're all I have now."

"Yeah." He sighed. "I can understand that."

"Well." She started toward the master bedroom. "It's getting late. I'll get my things."

He was still addled from her marriage joke, so it took him a second or two to understand that she thought he was taking her back to her place.

Driving her back to the apartment so she could spend the night was probably for the best. But Jess wasn't set on giving in to a night without her.

"There's no need for me to take you all the way back to the apartment just for you to sleep." He shoved both hands deep into the front pockets of his jeans as he studied the floor. "I'd have to come back in the morning to pick you up unless you wanted to take your bike to the barn raising."

An element of confusion darkened her eyes. "I thought we were going together..."

Why had things between them suddenly gotten so awkward?

"Yeah," he said, giving her a nod. "So, just crash here in my bed or in one of the others upstairs."

Sharing his bed with Mallory had become as natural as

holding her hand. But tonight, Jess didn't want to just hold her. He wanted to make love to her.

"Okay," she said, wielding a shy but expectant smile at him. When she started for the master bedroom, the breath he'd been holding came out as a low whoosh.

"Are you coming?" she asked, hesitating when he didn't follow. There was an open invitation in her eyes that Jess wanted to accept. His body needed to be with her. He yearned to be inside of her, loving her with all the power and passion she deserved.

But the part of him that was still lying in that arena dirt wouldn't let him give in. He could give Mallory every material thing her heart desired. But he couldn't give her the lasting kind of love a woman like her was worthy of.

He gave his jaw a rub. "I have some work to do before I turn in."

Her smile wavered. "I can wait—"

"No," he said, clearing his throat after the abrupt word. "You go ahead."

She dropped her gaze to her finger, her lips pulling to one side before she nodded. "Goodnight, then."

"Goodnight." He watched her walk down the hallway and into his room, feeling destroyed by the decision he'd just made.

There was a woman — whom he had spent his life waiting for — in his bed. A gorgeous woman who was undoubtedly willing to fulfill every sexual fantasy he'd ever had. A beautiful and courageous woman who trusted him with her body and heart. A woman he would always love and want, but one he would never allow himself to have.

Jesus. Where did that leave him?

Alone in an empty house with fear and regret to keep him company.

He walked to the liquor cabinet in the corner of the

living room, mulling over that damn depressing fact. After opening a decanter of his favorite bourbon, he poured himself a shot and downed it. Then he closed his eyes and waited for the soothing kick of the alcohol to hit.

When it did, he let out a long sigh, refilled the glass, and headed into his office. He had plenty of things to keep himself busy and his mind off Mallory.

Sipping the bourbon, Jess went to work on foundation reports and answering emails. He made a few minor changes to the agenda Lauren had sent him for the rodeo committee meeting and then confirmed the date.

By midnight, he stood and started to switch off the lamp when he saw the folder on the horse McCrea had rescued. Kara had brought it over in the files he asked for.

He picked it up and pulled out Doc's report. Reading over it, he saw the horse had severe lacerations on his hindquarters, some were infected and needed stitches. He pushed the paper back into the folder and reached for the pictures that documented the report.

The horse's flaxen coat was lathered and dark. Abused horses were fearful, sometimes aggressive, and often worked up a sweat during rescues. Beads of blood lined the whip marks across the animal's flank and hip.

For the second time tonight, anger rolled over Jess like a rogue wave. Icy cold and overpowering. How could people be such a willing conduit for brutality?

He slipped the photo to the back and picked up the headshot, recognizing the face of the horse instantly. The blaze mark with flesh color on his snip near the right nostril was unmistakable.

The horse from Dallam County was Dirteater.

"Son of a bitch." He stared down at the photo, recalling the fall. He pain had been so intense and relentless that he'd floated in and out of consciousness. Some parts were foggy, others still vividly clear. The sound of his bones snapping under the weight of the horses' hooves clashed with the sound of the noise of the crowd and Louisa calling his name as they rushed him into the ER.

As the taste of blood and dirt overpowered the residue of bourbon in his mouth, he moved his fingers along the deep gash in his thigh.

He'd given Mallory that uplifting speech about how he didn't hate Dirteater. But that was a lie. A part of him hated the animal, but not for the injury to his leg.

He hated the horse because when he looked at Dirteater, he saw the rider he'd been, the strong, fearless man who hadn't shied away from a challenge.

A cowboy who always got up no matter what was broken or busted.

Jess drained what was left of the bourbon in his glass then tossed the photo onto the desk. He'd sworn to keep women and horses at a healthy distance, but now that distance was closing in on him.

His life had gone in a full circle, and the two destroying forces that had nearly killed him eight years ago had found their way back into his life.

CHAPTER 24

Taking his empty glass, Jess walked back into the living room for more bourbon.

If he drank enough, the horse and the woman would disappear tonight. But in the morning, they would both be there, waiting for him to confront.

He could ignore the horse, stay in his office, and let McCrea and Brody deal with it. But he couldn't push Mallory aside so effortlessly. She was buying a house and sleeping in his bed.

After refilling the glass, he lifted it to his mouth for another sip and caught sight of the oil painting hanging next to the fireplace. Jules had donated the Comanche maiden wrapped in a red blanket to the Promise Point Silent Charity Auction a few years back.

Jess thought back to the way Mallory had reacted to the Worrier painting above his desk and the longing in her eyes when she talked about going to art school. It was a dream he could make come true with one phone call.

She was so talented and spinning her wheels in a small

town like Santa Camino, waiting on a man like him to fall in love with her... He couldn't let Mallory waste her gift or her love on him. And if she did decide she wanted a cowboy to marry, Oregon was full of them.

He hooked his forefinger around the decanter neck and headed across the foyer towards the stairs, intent on sleeping in one of the guest rooms upstairs.

But like the night he saw Mallory naked in the window, his feet refused to move when he came to the hallway leading to the master bedroom.

This was his fork in the road, a pivotal point in his life where clear thinking was required.

He leaned a shoulder against the wall and glanced down at the amber liquid inside the bottle with a doubtful lift of an eyebrow. He wasn't plastered, so alcohol couldn't be blamed for whichever path he chose.

The ache that had been gnawing at him since Mallory's arrival was eating him alive. Bourbon wouldn't slake it and a cold shower wouldn't douse it. Because he'd fallen in love with her days ago.

There was only one way he was going to soothe that ache and if he did, he was afraid he might not be able to walk away afterwards.

And that was the root of his problem.

He was afraid.

Dirteater flashed in front of him and again, he was reminded of why he hated the horse. The man he'd been before the fall wouldn't have thought twice about bedding Mallory or falling in love.

But Jess wasn't that man anymore. He never would be, no matter how hard he tried. He'd always have those scars.

He pitched the last of the bourbon into his mouth and swallowed, feeling the burn go soul deep. He knew what he had to do.

He'd give Jules a call in the morning.

But the question about where he was sleeping remained.

He could go upstairs, drink until he passed out, and forgo the temptation of Mallory's curvy body pressed against him all night. Or he could spend the night giving in to that temptation and make love to her just once before they parted ways.

Hell no. That wasn't happening.

Resigned to having a dark, soul-eating oblivion with a skull-crushing hangover in the morning, Jess pushed himself upright and took a step towards the stairs as a third option came to his mind. An option that would leave him painfully unsatisfied but with the memory of Mallory reaching that great orgasmic moment in his bed, in his hands.

Turning on his heel, he walked down the hall to the master bedroom, opened the door and moved to the bed.

Moonlight filtered through the sheer curtains, allowing him to see Mallory's face. She was lying on her back with her head turned toward the window. One hand was folded under her chin. Her long lashes were fixed peacefully in place and her lips parted with the soft breath of sleep. And that dark hair was just how he had imagined it: tossed wildly over his pillow.

God, she was beautiful.

He set the decanter and glass on the nightstand and reached for his t-shirt. He slid it over his head and tossed it to the floor, then eased into bed with his jeans on.

He slid one hand under her pillow and moved over her, kissing the spot just under her ear.

She stirred with a faint moan and her lids fluttered open with a sleepy smile. "There you are," she said, her voice husky from sleep.

"Yes," he answered, moving farther down her neck as he spoke. "Here, I am."

Jess knew Kara had bought her a nightgown and he expected to run into that black garment the moment his lips reached her collarbone. But when she lifted a hand to curl her fingers through his hair, the comforter shifted, and he saw nothing but skin on those shoulders.

He had imagined her bare body in his bed for so long, he wasn't sure she was really naked until she shifted, and her nipple grazed his forearm.

His dick, already swollen and hard, began to throb against the tight restraint of his jeans.

"I was afraid you weren't coming," she said, raising her head to look at him with those soft bedroom eyes that almost made him forget why he was holding back.

"I wasn't."

"Why?"

Mallory was his to touch, taste, explore, and please. His to love if only for a night. He couldn't tell her he was afraid of losing himself to the hardcore moment of making real love to a woman for the first time. "I don't want to talk. I don't want to do anything but enjoy you."

And make a memory that will help me through the lonely nights ahead.

He kissed her deeply, savoring every inch of her mouth. She gave him her lips like he knew she would her body, willingly and without limit. It was the most passionate kiss of his life.

Shifting his weight to the other knee, Jess slid the comforter from her breasts.

A deep groan curled its way up his throat. Full, bare, and with a dusting of bronze darkening the centers just the way they had been in the window.

He brushed his fingers up her hip, across her ribcage to the underside of her breasts. The smooth fullness of that firm mound in his palm triggered a heated rush of adrenaline inside of him.

He skimmed the taut surface with the pad of his thumb. When Mallory's back arched, he dipped his head and took the nipple into his mouth. The sweetness of her skin and reaction to his touch ignited a trail of fire through his body.

Jess wanted more, so much more. But he wouldn't take, only give. Without releasing his lips from the nipple, he eased to the bed beside her. She held his head with both hands and curled her leg around his hip. The heat of her body burned through the denim, blanketing him in her temptation.

He could take her right now, and the release would be phenomenal. But this wasn't just about gratification. It was about cherishing every moment, every sensation and flavor that was Mallory. He wasn't her first lover, but he wanted to set a precedent for all the other men who might follow.

And there would be others.

Jess discarded the sharp stab of pain in his chest and immersed himself in this moment.

Mallory's moans grew shorter and higher with every teasing lick. His hand caressed her body, recording the slope of her hip, the well-rounded curve of her backside, and the softness of her midriff to his memory.

When his palm moved over the slight rise of her lower belly, her hand clamped around his arm. The slight scrape of her nails and the decadent whimper of pleasure as his fingers slipped into that soft, wet thatch of hair almost drove him over the edge. He gently teased her swollen flesh, bringing her body to a fever pitch.

She reached for the zipper of his jeans. "Now," she pleaded, arching into him. "Please, now."

He caught her hand and drew it to his chest, knowing if she touched him, there would be no holding back, no saving himself.

When he plunged his fingers into her, her chest heaved, her head arched back, and her mouth opened in a gasp. He loved her with his hands, with his mouth, and with his whole heart until her pleasure shattered and she cried out his name.

"Remember this. Remember me." His words were breathless, broken whispers against her neck and barely audible to his own ears.

THE SKY WAS BLUE, AND THE WIND WAS WARM AGAINST HER face. For the first time in her life, Mallory felt at peace with who she was, where she came from, and where she was going.

She'd Mackenna blood running through her veins. She'd always known that, but something about the way Jess had said it made her feel renewed and stronger than she'd been before.

She had a family heritage she could be proud of. Her ancestors had deep origins in Santa Camino and in Texas.

She had roots and people who loved her.

Letting Jess see the ugliness of where she'd come from and her past life hadn't been as awful as she thought it would be. He'd been right. Those scars of hers were bullies. She deserved happiness.

She deserved him.

She laid her cheek against Jess's back and tightened her

arms around his waist. He moved one hand from the handlebar to hers and grasped it firmly.

Last night played over and over in her mind. The passion in those hands and the tender way they had made love to her flooded her with love and desire.

She felt whole.

From a distance, Mallory could see the wooden framework and green metal roof of the Gates' barn. Several black bulls grazed the lower fields, and country music blasted over the roar of the motor as Jess throttled back and slowed the bike for a turn onto the gravel road where they first met.

So much had transpired since that day. She'd found her sister, said goodbye to her mother, and…fallen in love.

Jess guided the bike up the hill to where a nearby field was being used as a parking lot, popped the kickstand out, killed the engine, and then waited for her to dismount before he did the same.

"Just in time," Eleanor said, passing them with two covered casserole dishes in one arm and a fussy Tucker in the other.

"Let me take him." Mallory relieved her of the baby and began bouncing him.

"Jess," Eleanor tilted her head to one side. "There are more dishes in the crossover. Would you mind getting them?"

"Don't mind at all." He reached into his back pocket for his ball cap turned, the bill to the back, capped it over his head and walked towards the crossover.

He'd dressed in a faded pair of blue jeans, a gray t-shirt that fit him tight through the chest and those scuffed up boot's he loved so much.

It was strange seeing him in a ball cap. Without that brown, battered Stetson he looked like a different man.

The hat was as much a part of him as the scar along his thigh and the fear in his heart that kept him from giving in to love.

Mallory wanted to spend the rest of her life with this man, healing and loving all his hurts away the way he had hers. But even after all they had shared, there was a distance between them.

Eleanor squinted her eyes against the bright morning sun as they walked towards the barn. "How are you?"

"I was great until this morning," Mallory said, glancing over her shoulder to make sure Jess wasn't close by. He was stacking casserole dishes on an arm with that same considering, granite face he'd had all morning.

"What happened this morning?" Eleanor asked, keeping her voice low.

Like the night before, Mallory had fallen asleep in Jess's arms. But he'd left her just before dawn. She found him in the living room doing one of those stretches that resembled a pushup and her new clothes packed neatly into the side compartment of his bike. It was a subtle but clear sign she wasn't going back to his house tonight.

"Nothing really." Tuckers' fussiness turned into a full-blown cry. "He's just... different."

Eleanor propped the dish in her right hand onto the one in her left, dug into her pocket, pulled out Tucker's pacifier and popped it into his mouth. "The file on Dirteater is missing. McCrea thinks Kara accidentally picked it up with the paperwork she took to him yesterday. And the horse was logged into the database early this morning."

"Then he knows," Mallory said, hearing the hatch of the crossover close.

"It could explain why he's so different," Eleanor said, leading her inside the barn.

"Hey!" Louisa climbed higher on the ladder and gave her a quick smile before pinning one end of a brightly colored banner to a rafter. "Look who's here!"

She faked a smile. "Here and ready to work."

After placing a sleeping Tucker into his carrier, Mallory busied herself with helping Eleanor and Belle spread table clothes and arrange the food dishes while McCrea and Jess helped Tyler carry more tables and chairs from the truck.

Violet helped Logan set up the area were a local band would be playing, and Brody filled the metal beer tubs Ed had donated with ice. Hardin was manning the giant grill out back.

Everyone was doing their part to make the event successful for the Gates's. By noon, the smell of wood smoke, spices, and cooked meat wafted through the barn.

Soon, Hardin and Jess were carrying in trays of barbecued meat from the cooker as more and more guest arrived. Tables began to fill with hungry guests and plates of homemade food. There was hardly sitting room. When the band started playing, the couple sitting at the table with McCrea and Eleanor moved to the dance floor.

Mallory sat down next to her sister.

"I need a refill.' McCrea took his empty plate and left the table in search of seconds.

Eleanor switched Tucker to her other arm. "Aren't you eating?"

She scanned the crowd in search of Jess and found him standing near the back of the barn. He was leaning against one of the center poles talking to another cowboy.

"I had a slice of cold pizza for breakfast." She should be starving by now, but her stomach was filled with an uneasiness that wouldn't let her eat.

"Has he mentioned the horse?" Eleanor questioned,

cutting a glance at Jess as she sucked her sweet tea through a straw.

"We haven't had a chance to talk." They'd both been so busy helping with the set-up and food that they'd only exchanged passing smiles. But Mallory knew it was more than Dirteater's arrival that had Jess avoiding her.

She held her bottom lip tight between her teeth until the urge to cry eased. "Things happened last night. Intimate things."

"Oh…" Eleanor said, after swallowing the tea.

"Things I know he regrets now."

Her sisters' face fell sympathetically. "Jess just needs time…"

"I don't think so," she said, seeing him look over at her. There was a worried slant to his usually smiling lips and a dullness to his bright blue eyes. "You should have seen the panic on his face when I mentioned buying a house."

Remember me. Remember us.

Last night, those jagged words he'd whispered in her ear as she climaxed had worried her. But right now, they were tearing her heart out because she knew they were the words of a man saying goodbye.

"Where's Sage?" Louisa came packing a chair and her plate to the table.

"She's showing a house," Violet answered, setting her plate on the table next to Louisa's before taking the other unoccupied chair next to Mallory. "She'll be here later."

"Where did you find that chair?" Eleanor questioned while eating on a fry.

Louisa licked barbeque sauce from her thumb and reached for her plastic fork. "I stole it from the Peters' kid."

"Sounds about right," Violet said, washing her food down with a sip of beer.

Louisa stuck a finger in her right ear, the ear closest to

the speaker, and winced. "I think this shindig is going to be more successful than the last one."

"I hope so," Violet yelled back. "Logan is a turd, but I don't like seeing him worry himself to death."

Jess moved from the pole to one of the tubs and pulled a bottle of beer from the ice. They weren't lovers, yet. But after last night, Mallory had hoped...

It had all been so beautiful and magical. She wanted to move on to that fulfilling moment when their bodies merged completely. She wanted to feel him inside her, holding her and loving her with the passion he'd had last night.

Jess had helped her to heal and sheltered her in his arms. Their time together had been deeply intimate. He knew things about her, things no one else knew. He had touched hidden parts of her, pain and passion alike.

He had loved her and healed her.

At the same time, he had opened the door to his past and allowed Mallory to see the brokenness he'd suffered by Hallie's betrayal and the loss of his career.

And now... she didn't know.

After a long chug, he wiped his mouth and started toward the table.

Tucker cracked a cry, shoved both of his tiny fists into his mouth, and let out a wail that could rival a banshee.

Mallory reached for him. "Let me have him."

"Are you sure?" Eleanor questioned, taking a quick look towards Jess.

"I need something to hold on to."

JESS KEPT HIS EYES FIXED ON MALLORY AS HE MOVED through the crowd and over to the table. Throughout the day, his mind had ventured back to last night. Her hot, wet body tightening around his fingers, the caressing cries of her rapture, and the glossy sheen of tears in her eyes as the pinnacle of her pleasure ebbed.

She was killing him — slowly.

He'd sent Jules photos of Mallory's artwork this morning along with a message saying he wanted to secure a talented artist a spot as soon as possible.

Though Jules hadn't replied yet, he knew Mallory's spot was as good as confirmed. But her acceptance into the school was far from being a solution. He still had to break the news to Mallory and be convincing about his reasons for doing it.

He paused to let a couple leaving the dancefloor walk to their seats, then he quirked his lips into a challenging grin as he locked eyes with his sister.

He moved behind her and braced his hands on the back of her chair. Then, he gave it a playful shove forward.

Louisa looked over her shoulder, lifted a rib to her mouth, sank her teeth in, and ripped away a chunk of meat from the bone.

If that wasn't a sign that she was still pissed at him about the Keegan comment, he didn't know what was.

He drew in a fortifying breath, knowing he'd have to deal with Louisa's sharp tongue before he could get to Mallory. "Afternoon ladies. What's the hot topic of gossip?"

Louisa snorted. "How men can't master the art of cunnilingus."

Violet covered her mouth to keep from spewing beer across the table, Eleanor bit her bottom lip to keep from laughing, and Mallory's cheeks turned crimson.

"Oh, well," Jess said, keeping his face serious with

mock concern as he searched the crowd. "That sounds like a Brody issue. Let me get him over here."

Violet began to choke.

"You've done it now," Eleanor said, her attempt at composure foiled by laughter.

"Jess put your hand down," Louisa seethed, smacking Violet on the back as she tried making a grab for his raised arm. "Stop waving at him."

"Too late," Eleanor said, watching Brody make his way across the crowd.

"Brody," Jess said, clamping a hand over his shoulder. "My sister would like to voice a complaint."

Brody crossed his arms over his chest, frowning slightly at the mystery of Louisa's said complaint. "About what?"

Jess turned his head and discreetly spoke low near Brody's ear.

Brody's eyes went wide and then dark. "Far be it from me to ever leave a woman unsatisfied. Please," he said, a lecherous smile broadening his lips as he stared down at Louisa. "Let me make it up to you."

"Oooo, girl," Violet coughed out in a raspy voice, trying to catch her breath. "Let him make it up to you."

"Shut up, Violet," Louisa gave her a warning glare, jerked to her feet, and stomped away with Brody in hot pursuit behind her.

"That was mean," Eleanor said with the remnants of humor clinging tight to her lips.

"But effective." Jess gave his sister-in-law a wink and eased around the table to lay a hand on Mallory's shoulder as a slow song started. "Care to dance?"

Without answering verbally, she stood and with Tucker in her arm, followed behind him.

Jess took her hand, pulling her to the dancefloor. With

his hand on her lower back and the baby nestled in between them, he led her around the dance floor.

The sight of Mallory with Tucker lying gently at her breast quickened his pulse and stirred a longing in him that was more than desire.

The captive image of woman and child pulled at him and for a moment, Jess allowed himself to pretend they were his. Mother and son. The conception of love and life with Mallory.

He lifted his hand to Tucker's cheek and gave it a gentle rub with his finger. "You have a special touch."

A glossy sheen of happy tears cloaked her eyes. "When I first moved to California, the lady down the street from Aiden and Cassie had a newborn. Aiden talked her into letting me watch him for a couple of hours every day while she was cleaning the house or just needed a minute to breathe. I didn't know the first thing about babies, but I learned. That baby helped me to focus on something other than what had happened to me."

She drew Tucker up to her lips and planted a soft kiss on his forehead. "It's hard to think about all the wrong in the world when you have a miracle in your arms."

After all she had been through, Mallory should have been a cold and callous person. But she had so much love to give. "You'll be a wonderful momma someday."

Her smile turned jovial. "Yeah, maybe. Someday."

Jess turned his head, knowing that if he didn't end whatever this was between them, someday might be exactly nine months from now.

The words of the ballad resonated inside of him. Bitter memories, fears, hurts, and love told the story. He listened to the slow hiss of the drum brushes, the bass guitar, and that low, buttery voice of the woman crooning out the ballad. The song was about two lovers, one was damaged and the other was in search of a soft place to fall. Both dreaded the dawn when the sun would rise, and they would part.

Jess felt those words resonate inside of him. When the song ended, he didn't move. He was fixed in place by a sudden bout of indecision until a shout jerked him lose.

He blinked and dropped her hand.

"The sheriff is here," Eleanor said, appearing beside them to collect Tucker. "You'd better find Logan."

CHAPTER 25

IN FINN'S HANDS, THE LARGE ALUMINUM-COVERED container he'd relieved Sage of appeared to be the size of a tapas bowl. The two of them were walking down the hill from where his cruiser was parked and towards the barn.

Mallory assumed everyone's panic about the sheriff's arrival involved the complexity of the Gates' family tree.

That was confirmed when Logan came steamrolling through the crowd, looking like he could chew through a locomotive. "Who the hell invited you?"

Jess clamped a hand over Logan's shoulder. "Calm down."

Violet ran to Finn's defense, planted herself in front of him, crossed her arms over her chest, and raised her chin in full-force rebellion mode. "I did."

"Oh, lord, Violet," Sage whispered. "Don't. Not now."

"She didn't invite me." Handing the bowl back to Sage, Finn eased Violet behind him and faced Logan. "I was just helping Mrs. Parsons —"

"Miss," Sage quickly corrected him and blushed.

"Miss," Finn restated for clarity. "Parsons with her potato salad. I'm here on official business."

"What kind of official business?" Ty asked, not nearly as angry as his brother.

Finn turned his attention to Mallory. "I need to speak with you privately."

There were a few tense seconds where Mallory thought punches would be thrown, but when Finn planted his hands on his hips and shot Logan an are-we-going-go-do-this look, Logan swung around and stomped off.

The crowd quickly dissipated. But Jess stayed by her side.

SHE KNEW WHEN FINN TOOK OFF HIS HAT THAT HE WAS here to deliver bad news. "There was a wreck yesterday afternoon involving an overturned cattle truck and a red Dodge truck."

"Is he dead?" Mallory asked, hoping the accident had ended Rex Montgomery.

"No, but he was pinned for hours. The doctors say he'll never walk again."

The violence and abuse, the kidnapping, the trauma she'd gone through, her mom's death, the blackmail, Aiden... It wasn't fair the that people she loved had been destroyed, but Rex was still alive. The punishment didn't fit the crimes.

"Being confined to a wheelchair for the rest of his life is hardly recompense for all the things that man did to me and everyone I loved."

A slight flinch darted across Finn's chiseled features. "I realize that."

"And the casino?" Jess asked.

"I talked to the authorities in La Claire this morning,

and they're sure they can link him to the Pack. He might make a deal and testify against them for a lesser sentence, but he's facing multiple charges. Your father will be going away for a while."

She stood there, unmoved by all that had been said, feeling numb to her core.

Her journey to this point in time had been a hard road to travel. But so much had been gained along the way. She hadn't come to Santa Camino expecting to find love and security, but she had.

She and her sister had been reunited. No matter what happened between them, Eleanor and the children would always be a part of her life.

Jess wrapped his fingers around her upper arms, consoling her quietly.

Satisfied that she was in good hands, Finn situated his hat back in place before turning to walk back to his cruiser alone.

It might have been the shadow cast by the low branch trees near the fence that made his shoulders appear slumped, or perhaps it was the gravity of what had happened between him and Logan.

Whatever the reason, Mallory felt empathetic towards the large, quiet man. Finn had played a small, but significant part in all she had gained. "Wait!"

He stopped near the end of the fence and waited for her to catch up.

"Why didn't you tell Jess?"

His eyes narrowed. "Tell him what?"

"You knew I was the kidnapped girl authorities saved from the casino that night. You knew Rex used me to blackmail Aiden into making that drug run."

"I didn't know you were that girl," Finn denied. "Not for certain."

"But you could have put two and two together and told him. Why didn't you?"

He looped a thumb through his belt and tilted his head to one side. "Whatever Jess knows about that night should be because you told him, not because I was speculating. He's a good man who cares about you. What happened when you were kidnapped won't change that, but he needs to know."

Finn Durant had a heart that superseded the power behind the badge he wore and the office he held. And Mallory had a new respect for the man.

"He does." She held out her hand and smiled. "Thank you, Finn, for everything."

Surprise flickered across his face as he returned her smile and accepted her hand with a gentle shake. "Ma'am."

When she turned around, Jess was there. He leaned over and gave her forehead a kiss. "Are you alright?"

"I will be," she answered, summoning a small smile for his sake. "Once I have time to process everything."

The evening after Jess dropped Mallory off at the apartment with a reserved goodbye, she took her half-empty glass of wine and ventured from her studio to the balcony overlooking the stalls.

As he did every evening, Brody was making his rounds. She acknowledged him with a raise of her glass. He responded with a single wave and went back to checking the horses.

She'd sketched him from up here. The quiet times between man and horse. The sadness in his eyes during those moments when he didn't know she was watching felt like an invasion of his privacy. But the emotion on his face had moved her.

She was going to miss Brody's noiseless presence, the soft whinnies of the horses at night, and her little apartment that had quickly become a home.

When Brody exited the stables, the horses settled, and the space fell quiet. Oddly, the silence didn't bother her. She no longer needed to turn on the television or plug in her earbuds to calm her mind.

Mallory had gone through a mental growth spurt. Her heart and her mind had changed.

She walked back to her studio. The drop cloth she used to protect the hardwood floor felt rough against her bare feet, much like her eyes did every time she blinked.

Having worked through the night and most of the day on the painting, she hadn't changed from the nightgown Kara had bought for her.

A spot of white paint comet-tailed across the bottom of the black material, but it didn't matter. There was no one here to notice.

Disappointment stabbed at her heart so hard she thought she might buckle into tears. Jess hadn't been by and she'd be gone by morning.

She examined the painting as she sipped her wine. Sitting on the stool, she picked up her palate knife, mixed a dark shade of blue and with a fine-tipped brush, and added the finishing touches to the eyes. Then she dipped her brush into a mineral spirit solvent and dragged it over the paint - speckled rag lying next to the glass.

Giving the brush a few whisks in safflower oil to clean the remaining pigment, she dried it before placing it in the plastic box with the others.

She uncapped a pen and quickly sketched out a carica-ture on a blank notecard, then added a single word under it. After folding it in half, she added Jess's name to the front and set it beside the painting as the unmistakable sound of his boots hit the stairs.

As it always did when Jess was near, her heart began to race. She grabbed her glass, hurried out of the room, and closed the doors behind her as he tapped on her door. "Mallory?"

Twisting the knob, she gave the door a yank. "Hello, stranger."

Frowning slightly, Jess rubbed his neck. "I've been busy."

That was always his handy excuse for ignoring her. Leaving him alone to close the door, she walked into the kitchen and emptied the wine bottle into her glass.

"How's Dirteater?"

His bottom lip pulled tight, his chin dipped lower, and he answered her with silence.

"I get why you're ignoring me," she said. "But not the horse."

Jess's head snapped up. "I'm not ignoring you. I've just been *busy*," he reiterated.

She shook her head and let out a laugh. "So we're not going to talk about the horse at all?"

"I have good news."

She jerked her head sideways. "I guess that's a no."

Leaning a hip against the counter, she eyed him unexcitedly. "Okay, what's your good news? Did you bring me a dog?"

His frown deepened. "What? No, why would I bring you a dog?"

Oh, so now he's going to play dumb.

He flipped open the paper in his hand and held it out to her.

She snatched it from him. "What's this?"

The creases along his forehead disappeared with his broad smile. "I called in a favor to Jules."

Mallory skimmed over the paper, feeling every nerve in her body rise to anger. A few weeks ago, being accepted into the Jules Kramer Art School would have made her the happiest woman alive. But now...

She set her glass on the counter so she wouldn't be tempted to hurl it at his head like she had his hat because this time, she wouldn't miss.

She pressed her knuckles to her hip and focused on the light above the island. This was their last night together, and she was done with tiptoeing around his denial. And she was done playing nice. "I understand why you don't ride and why you're afraid to love me, really I do."

Jess rolled his jaw to one side and paled as if he'd been punched in the chest.

"You're afraid of taking risks." She held the paper up and gave it a shake. "But I never in a million years figured you for a coward."

He pulled in a deep breath that expanded the hard muscles of his chest. "Mallory," he started in a voice that spoke of controlled patience.

"No!" she yelled, slamming the paper down on the counter. "You don't get to walk in here and hand me a one-way ticket out of your life. We need to talk. You need to face what's happening. I know you love me."

Jess targeted a piece of flooring and scrubbed it with the toe of his boot as he spoke. "You're wrong, honey. I'm sorry."

His face answered differently. Those blue eyes of his always gave him away.

Her unexpected grin made him scratch his jaw and look away. "Don't quit your day job to play poker, Hoss. You'll lose your ass."

With the pretense gone, Jess turned on a heel and started for the door.

"And don't you walk away from me."

Her order brought him to a boot-skidding halt. He whipped around and took two long strides back to her. "That's what I do, Mallory. I walk away. Whether it's now or in a few months." He pointed at himself. "I walk away."

"Not tonight you don't." Without batting an eye, she grabbed the front of his shirt, spun him around, hooked her leg around his, and pushed him towards the white leather chair.

Caught off guard, Jess lost his balance, stumbled back and fell into the chair with a thump. His angry eyes bit into her. "Don't think those self-defense moves are going to keep me from walking out that door."

"I'd be a fool to think I could hold you here with brute strength," she said, straddling his thighs like she did her bike. Confident and in control of the road ahead. "And I'm no fool, Jess Coldiron. I *know* you're in love with me."

He tried shaking his head to voice his disagreement, but she silenced him with a long kiss that left them both breathless.

"You brought light into my dark, dark world, Jess," she whispered softly against his lips. "You healed my wounds. Only love can do that. I took a chance. I trusted you and you healed me. Trust me to do the same."

"I—I," he closed his eyes and fought for words.

She raked her fingers through the top of his hair, loving the silkiness of those sun-kissed strands. "I know you won't make love to me because you're afraid. Afraid you won't be able to walk away after, and it'll all end in disaster."

He looked away, disarmed by her intuitiveness.

She smiled again, pushing his hat up higher on his

forehead. "But no matter what happens between us, my heart will always be safe with you, here in Texas."

The ice in his eyes melted into a lustrous blue. "Don't say that."

"What? That I love you? I do. I think I have since I helped you up the porch steps."

When her hand moved to the buckle of his belt, he caught it. "Don't."

"I'm not asking for anything past tonight. No commitments. No morning after. Just this."

The ridge along his throat moved with a hard swallow. "I can't."

"You can. Take that risk. Show me how beautiful we can be together. Make love to me."

"Honey," he choked out. "You don't know what you're asking."

Holding his face with both hands, she rested her forehead against his. "Oh, but I do," she whispered and gently brushed her lips over his.

He groaned and wrapped his fingers around her upper arms, pulling her closer for a deeper kiss. Under her hands, the wide slope of his jaw moved with the motion of his lips and Mallory was reminded of more things she would miss. Those strong, masculine features, those piercing blue eyes…

God! She loved this man! Tears welled in her eyes, but she fought through them. This was their moment. Their time to be together. And she wouldn't let tomorrow's sorrow stomp out the fire she'd ignited.

She slipped her hands over his shoulders, down his chest and to the pearl snaps of his blue western shirt. One by one, she popped them loose and slid her palms over his chest. That dusting of golden blond hair felt wonderful. He was so warm and hard and all beautifully male.

Breaking the kiss, she let her lips wander along his jaw and down his neck to the cleft between his pecs. The sounds he was making in response to her touch made her dizzy, breathless, and fearless.

Mallory had never wanted to taste a man like she did Jess. She had never thought herself brave enough or open enough to do what she was about to do.

But with this man, all things were possible.

She popped the button of his jeans loose and drew his zipper down. He sucked in a breath between clenched teeth as her fingers coiled around the hard length of his erection. The thin blue material of his briefs darkened with dampness, prompting a rush of warmth and wetness between her thighs.

When she shifted to her knees in front of him, fear sparked through his desire-filled eyes. "Honey, please, don't," his voice was rough and pleading.

Hooking a finger in the waistband of his briefs, she slowly unveiled him, and he was magnificent. She ran the tip of her tongue over the head of him and tasted the salty dampness she'd seen earlier. Keeping her eyes on his face, she opened her mouth and took him in.

A gasp of air escaped his throat. Biting down on his back teeth, his jaw tightened as his eyes closed and his head fell back. His fingers fisted her hair, gently holding her in place as his hips thrust up.

Her breasts felt heavy. Her nipples budded and the ache inside her grew painfully tight.

"God, honey." Jess's raspy voice cut through the air. "Stop or —" With a firm jerk, he freed himself from her and sat up. Taking gasps through his teeth, he stared down at her. "No more."

Mallory gave his shoulders a hard push, propelling him back against the chair. "Yes, more." She straddled him and guided the top of him to her swollen folds. "All," she breathed out and slowly lowered her body over his.

The size of him stretched her body to its limits and beyond. Pain and pleasure opened her mouth. With a low moan, she sheathed him to the hilt.

His body tensed tight as his fingers bit into her hips. He was holding back for her.

"I won't break," she said.

"I can't —" As if against his control, his body flexed hard inside of her.

Her breath hitched from the pleasure and she rotated her hips. His body convulsed, tightened then released with a hard thrust into her.

She gasped and dug her fingers into his biceps as a burst of pleasure spiraled through her. He thrust again and again. Her ears began to hum, and her heart fought to find a rhythm. Arching her neck, she let her head fall back. She rode the building wave, losing all reference to time and place.

Every minute of every day, every touch, every kiss, had been building to this moment. Teasing foreplay and delicate kisses were tossed aside and replaced with rough, hot, pulsating sex.

Pleasure turned into shimmering sparks of fire that rippled from the center of their joined bodies and spiraled outward. She could feel herself climbing higher and higher toward the point of that scorching peak. When she reached the top, her body tightened, and a breathless, high-pitched whine escaped her throat that ended with a bite to his shoulder.

Jess made a low-growling noise, and she felt his body spasm, spilling heat inside her.

Mallory fell against him in a puddle of steaming satisfaction.

"Jess."

"Yes."

"Don't go. Not yet."

He wrapped both arms around her waist and hugged her tight. "I won't. Not tonight. Not before I've had you at least a dozen more times."

He kicked his boots off and stood to his feet, taking her with him to the bedroom. They made love twice more and each time, love and contentment overtook her.

Mallory slipped from his arms in the early hours before dawn, collected her bags from beside the bedroom door, and took one last look at the man sprawled out face down and naked in her bed.

She knew she was taking a chance by leaving, but it was the only thing she could do. Maybe, just maybe, he'd realize what he was losing by not taking that risk.

CHAPTER 26

Something roused Jess from a deep sleep. Not the presence of a noise but the lack thereof.

He rolled onto his back and opened his eyes. Staring up at ceiling, he reached for Mallory. But didn't find her.

The sheets were cold.

He turned his head, taking in the empty spot beside him. He knew without looking that she was gone from the apartment and from him.

With the heaviness of dread pressing down on him, he rose and looked around the room.

Nothing.

Untangling the sheet from his legs, he placed his feet on the floor and reached for his underwear and jeans. He zipped his fly, buttoned the button, and snagged his shirt as he headed into the living room.

Again, nothing.

Jess didn't call to her. He couldn't bear the empty echo he knew would answer. Finding his socks and boots, he sat in the white leather chair where they'd first made love and slipped them on.

He stood and started to the front door but was struck by the portrait staring back at him through the open door of her studio.

It was from the sketch he'd seen earlier, the one of him at Vera la Luz. The one resembling the man he used to be.

He walked to the room and moved to the table where the portrait was siting. In front of it was a single notecard, folded neatly in half with his name written across the center.

He looped a finger through it and flipped it open.

The cute puppy eyes of a sketched dog caricature stared back at him. Under it was the name, Archie.

"Jesus," he whispered and rubbed his eyes.

Tucking the card into his back pocket, he walked back to the living room, picked up his hat, and slammed the front door behind him.

He hurried down the stairs, tucking the ends of his shirt into his jeans with hard jabs.

At the bottom of the stairs, he paused when he heard the sharp whinny of a horse. Through the dusky light, he saw Dirteater standing in the round pen.

He took the distance across the lawn with less speed. Brody stood on the opposite side of the pen with his arms folded across the rail; in his hand was a silver coffee mug.

Coffee. Damn, he needed a pot.

Under the arms of Brody's gray cotton shirt were dark circles of perspiration and his arms were smeared with dirt, both signs that his morning had started hours ago.

Jess rested his forearms over the rail and gave into a long sigh.

"I'll gladly give you the ass-kicking you deserve," Brody said, his eyes still firmly fixed on the horse. "Hell." He grinned with a wooden smile. "We might even enjoy it until one of us loses a tooth."

There wasn't a doubt in Jess's tangled mind that Brody wouldn't try jerking a knot in his tail. He and Kara and everyone else at the Rescue had grown fond of Mallory. They'd adopted her into their work family, and she'd be missed.

He groaned inwardly. Eleanor would probably never speak to him again. He'd drunk water with her sister and hadn't used a condom. Memories of last night flooded his mind, impaling his body with a stab of desire and pain. There was a chance that next spring there would be more than calves arriving.

Jess closed his eyes and scrubbed a hand over his face. He *would not* let his mind go there. "It's too late to take my teeth."

"Yep," Brody agreed. "She slipped out of here before sunup."

"Did she say where she was going?"

"Nope." Brody lifted the large plastic, see-through bag sitting next to his feet. It was the canvas portrait she'd painted of Brody. "She said it was an early Christmas present. That woman is talented."

Jess dropped his eyes to study his dusty boots. "That talent would have been wasted here."

"That wasn't for you to decide," Brody said, cutting him a hard, split-second stare. "She was happy here with you."

He looked up at the tangerine-colored backdrop of the eastern sky, feeling those words stab deep into his heart. "She'll be happier in Oregon."

Brody silently shook his head and took another drink of his coffee.

Jess made a motion towards Dirteater. "How is he?"

"Not good," was the in-depth answer. "I had a hell of a time getting him in the pen this morning."

"He'll come around," Jess said without an ounce of faith that the horse would. The animal was as doomed as he was. "He just needs time."

"He refuses to give in," Brody said, narrowing his eyes as he considered the horse. "I've never seen anything like it. He won't let me or anyone else within a few feet of him. And he won't eat. At this rate, he'll be dead in a couple of weeks."

As if cued, the horse raised its head and started a slow course for Jess. Head down, ears forward, Dirteater stopped just shy of his hand.

"Well, I'll be damned," Brody said. "Look at that. I think he remembers you."

Jess doubted that. Dirteater was a stock horse with a career that spanned hundreds of events and riders. The probability of him remembering a single cowboy that hadn't stayed on his back more than five seconds was slim to none.

He extended his fingers, letting the horse take in the scent of him. Dirteater sniffed, raised one ear and gave the other a flick, then let out a high-pitched whinny.

"Maybe you should try working with him," Brody said, raising one eyebrow to a high peak. "He might respond to you."

Or he might just finish him off. Jess dropped his hand and walked away.

FOUR MONTHS AFTER HIS REUNION WITH DIRTEATER, JESS assumed his usual spot in the white leather chair he'd carried into Mallory's studio, dropped his hat onto his lap, propped a boot heel on the railing overlooking the training pen, and crossed his ankles.

It was mid-November and the trees had begun to

change. The air had a chill and everyone, but Jess was looking forward to the holidays.

After making sure Mallory had arrived safe and sound in Oregon, he'd settled into a routine that closely resembled the one he'd had before her arrival.

Only now, instead of going home to an empty house, he came here, to the apartment. Surrounded by her paintings, he felt a little less lonely.

Dirteater had become more and more restless and now bordered hostile. Characteristics that, according to Kara and his family, were similar to his own.

Brody had managed to get a saddle on the horse. This afternoon, the Dirteater stood on the far side of the training pen with his head down looking rowdy and ready to do damage.

Jess lifted the glass of bourbon to his lips and sipped, listening to the conversation below.

"He's making progress," Louisa said, throwing a hand towards the horse. "His wounds have healed and he's eating. Look at him. He's strong as an ox."

"A restless ox who's easily agitated and refuses to interact with any of the other horses," Brody countered. "I hear him at night grunting and pawing around in the stables."

Jess wondered if he was talking about him or Dirteater because even with the bourbon, sleep wasn't easy. Most nights, he paced the apartment like a corralled horse yearning for the freedom of open pastures.

"If being cranky and anti-social is cause for euthanizing," she scoffed and swung her hand to the balcony, "Jess should have been put down months ago!"

With that jab, Jess lowered his boots to the floor, stood, and walked back inside.

"He doesn't trust anyone, Louisa," he heard Brody say

and felt another jab. "He bucks and rears anytime someone gets close."

Another jab.

He was just as miserable as Dirteater. And if he stayed on the path he'd been on for the last eight years, he was going to die a slow and lonely death.

He downed the bourbon and set the glass on the table next to the painting of him at Vera la Luz. With those bright, brilliant colors swirling around in his head, he hurried out the door and down the steps.

"Someone is going to get hurt," Brody declared.

"McCrea," Louisa snapped. "Tell him we are not euthanizing this horse."

"Lou..." McCrea answered her in a hushed tone of dread as he clamped a hand over his eyes.

When Dirteater saw Jess, he dug his hind feet into the ground, raised his head high, and let out a trumpeting sound of anger. The sound vibrated through Jess, prompting a surge of adrenaline through his veins.

"Where are you going?" he heard McCrea shout.

Jess planted a boot on the lower rail, clamped his hands around the top, and hoisted himself over. He hit the ground and locked eyes with the horse.

The horse grunted and pawed the earth, declaring a challenge. Then he lowered his head and released a hard blow that rustled a cloud of dust and stomped his right hoof.

He might never be the man he had been before the fall, but he was tired of being the man he was now. Impassive, alone and unhappy.

He was ready to ride, ready to take a chance and damn it, he was ready to love.

As Jess moved in, Dirteater took a step to the side and began circling the pen.

Jess matched his steps.

It was a showdown between horse and rider, Jess's past and the future he wanted. If the horse didn't kill him, he'd go to Oregon and beg Mallory for forgiveness.

From the corner of his eye, he saw Louisa start over the railing. "Get out of there!"

"Sweetheart, no," Brody said, clamping an arm around her waist to secure her beside him. "You can't help him now. Let him go."

Again, Jess wasn't sure who Brody was referring to, him or the horse. All he knew was he wasn't leaving this pen until he finished the ride he'd started eight years ago.

Running full force, Jess grabbed the saddle horn and hoisted himself onto the horse. The ligaments in his thigh pulled tight and burned from the stretch.

The instant his ass hit the saddle, Dirteater bucked and nearly pitched him off.

He took hold of the reigns and held on for the fight. Throwing his back legs up for a kick that could have moved timber, the horse twisted his body around and lunged forward.

Jess pitched frontward and back as the horse spun around and kicked again. He raised his spurless heels and made a drag down Dirteater's neck. The horse let out a whinny and kicked again.

Suddenly, everything he thought he'd forgotten about the sport came rushing back and he was in control.

He held his free arm out. He hadn't been on a horse in eight long years. But he wasn't going to pull leather. Staying behind the swells, he extended his body and allowed the horse to buck.

And he did, hard, fast, and in every direction.

Jess's body popped and cracked. His leg hurt, his teeth

ached, and his head was pounding with every beat of his heart.

But the ride was exhilarating. The power and fluidity of the horse beneath him was pure poetry in motion. If this had been a competition, they'd be taking home the purse.

He felt free, renewed and alive.

Just when he thought Dirteater had given up, the horse reared back on his hind feet, gave the air a hard paw with both front feet, and lunged forward again. This time Jess came off. Up and over the horse's head he went, shooting through the air and landing hard against the rail.

"Jess!" he heard Louisa scream.

The force of the ground knocked the wind from his lungs. He drew a breath and pulled in nothing but dust.

"Brody, get that goddamn horse!" he heard McCrea say as he slid to his knees beside him.

"Oh, God! His head is bleeding!" Louisa's face appeared above him, her eyes wide and full of fear like they had been the night he fell. "Jess? Can you hear me?"

He knew his arm was broken. He'd heard it snap when he hit the ground, and it was beginning to throb. He blinked, trying hard to focus on anything but the pain.

Somewhere in the muddle muck of dust and broken bones, Jess saw Mallory. She was smiling at him, forgiving him… loving him.

Coughing, he cleared his lungs and let out a laugh of sheer happiness. He'd ridden Dirteater and hadn't died. He was going to Oregon. "Where's my truck?"

"He's talking out of his head," Brody determined from somewhere above him.

With his good arm, Jess pointed in the direction of Brody's voice. "Don't touch that horse! He's mine!" He raised his head, searching for Dirteater. "Do you hear me?

He's mine..." he yelled again as those bright, brilliant colors fired behind his eyes and the blackness closed in around him.

It was amazing how a hard hit to the head could make a man open his eyes and see. Really see the truth around him, the people who loved him, and the second chances he'd been given.

Jess saw all of that now with clarity and humility. He shifted his eyes to the woman sitting on the side of his hospital bed.

Shoulders bent, head bowed, Louisa wiped her face and sniffed, causing his chest to tighten. He'd been such a shitty brother for so long.

He moved his hand to her arm and gave it a gentle squeeze.

Her head popped up and relief flooded her face. "Thank, God," she said through tears. "What were you trying to prove? You could have killed yours —"

"I'm alright, Pinto," he reassured her softly.

Her face buckled and more tears rolled down her cheek. "You haven't called me that in years."

"I haven't done a lot of things," he confessed with a long sigh. "I'm sorry. I should have kicked Keegan's ass," he said, shooting straight for what was on his mind and hoping he could make amends for not being there when she needed him the most. "You were too damn young to know what was going on."

Her eyes dropped to the Kleenex in her hand. "I wasn't a kid. I knew what I was doing."

"What happened wasn't your fault," Jess said, giving her hand another squeeze. "It was Keegan's."

With a small nod of her head, more tears dropped to

his hand and another piece of his heart cracked. "Brody isn't—"

"Oh, God," she laughed, raising her head. "Brody and I aren't engaged. I'm not sleeping with him and I'm not pregnant with his baby."

He gave his eyebrows a quick rise and winced from the discomfort of what he knew were stitches in his forehead. "I hadn't heard the one about the baby."

"Regardless of what you have or haven't heard, there is nothing going on between me and Brody Vance."

"And why is that?" he questioned, already knowing the answer.

She rolled her eyes, brushing his question to the side with her own question. "You're trying to give me relationship advice?"

"Yeah, well," Jess sighed and let his head lay back against the pillow. "You do have a point, but I plan on making a trip to Oregon just as soon as this cast comes off."

"It was a clean break, so I'd say it will be off in six to eight weeks," she estimated.

Maybe by then, Jess could figure out what he needed to say to Mallory.

Louisa wiped her eyes. "But you don't have that long. Mallory's flight for Paris leaves in two days."

He raised his head. "What?"

"Did that fall do something to your ears?" Louisa asked, sniffing. "Mallory is leaving art school. Jules called Mom this morning because you wouldn't answer your phone. She was worried about losing one of her prize students."

Panic bolted through him. If Mallory got on that flight, he might never have the chance to tell her he loved her. He sat up and threw back the blanket.

"Where are you going?"

Throwing both feet to the floor, he stood. "To Oregon."

"Are you taking that with you?" she asked, pointing to the IV in his arm.

"No." He jerked it free and ignored the draft on his backside as he spun around looking for his clothes. "Have you seen my jeans?"

"Whoa!" Louisa clamped a hand over her eyes and blindly went for the cabinet beside the bed. "They're in here."

He pulled them out and shoved his feet through the legs. "Where are your truck keys?"

"You can't drive to Oregon with one arm," she said, tossing him his dirty t-shirt.

He tugged on his boots and grabbed the t-shirt. "You're right. You drive. I'll hold the dog."

"Dog?" Louisa asked, following him out the door. "What dog?"

FLUFFY WHITE SNOWFLAKES CAUGHT IN A FUNNEL OF winter air and spun in a whimsical globe outside the studio window. Through the gray clouds of early morning, Mallory could see the lights of Bentwood Falls.

Against the twilight of the morning, the rooftops of shops and businesses glistened pearlescent, and she could almost smell the pastries from the bakery.

Oregon was beautiful and she'd learned so much from Jules. But Mallory was homesick for her little apartment and Hill Country. She missed her sister, her niece and nephew, and Kara.

And she missed Jess. She felt empty inside like her

physical heart was really in Texas with him and there was a big gaping hole in the middle of her chest.

She'd risked her heart and lost.

She drew her knees up and hugged her legs as she stared at the Christmas card scene, wishing things could have been different.

She'd been gone for four months and she hadn't heard a word from him. No phone call, texts... nothing.

He wasn't in love with her and he wasn't coming for her.

Moving from the window seat, she walked to the kitchen and made herself a cup of Ashwagandha tea. After adding honey, she walked back to the window to lose herself in the memories invoked by the tea.

With the others gone, the studio and living quarters were as quiet as a tomb. Thanksgiving was next week, and the other students had left to spend the holidays at home. But Mallory had nowhere to go. Cassie was flying to Alaska to be with her parents for the holidays. And Jess was in Texas with the only family she had left.

She was along again.

Feeling the cold fingers of loneliness settle into her bones, she set her tea down and rubbed her arms.

But in the silence, she heard a sound. Faint at first, then loud. Chill bumps spread across her arms and up her neck when she recognized the unmistakable sound of Jess's boots tapping up the hall in a familiar saunter.

She froze, unable to let herself believe he was really here. The tapping grew louder and louder as it neared the studio door. Finally, it stopped, and Mallory held her breath.

"Excuse me, Ma'am," Jess's soft voice cut into the silence and floated around, melting the cold. "I'm lost. Can you help me?"

Holding a hand to her mouth to keep from crying hysterically, she swallowed and cleared her throat. "W—what kind of lady would I be if I didn't help a cowboy in need?"

"I made a wrong turn and lost my way." His words grazed across her skin like silky sheets. "I fell in love with an amazing woman and then," his voice faltered. "I let her walk away."

Tears spilled from her eyes. Her gamble had paid off. She hadn't lost him.

"I love her and can't live without her."

Mallory couldn't hold back any longer, spun around, laughing through tears until she saw the cast. "Oh, God!"

The blue of his eyes was bright with emotion as he smiled at her. "It's nothing."

"What happened?"

His lips twisted up at the corners and he ducked his head. "Dirteater and I came to an understanding."

She couldn't believe what she was hearing. "You rode him?"

"We had a good go at it and then he bucked me off."

She moved closer and touched a finger to the bandage on his forehead. There was something different about his eyes. A tranquility that hadn't been there before. "You fell?"

"I did," he said, taking her hand in his. "But this time, I got up."

Her heart fluttered and skipped. "All of you?"

His eyes glossed over and he swallowed. "All of me," he assured her. "I'm sorry, honey. You were right. I was afraid. But I'm not anymore. I'll risk everything for your love." He curled a finger under her chin and tilted her head up for a kiss. "Please forgive me."

Mallory flung both arms around his neck, knocking his hat to the floor. "I always do."

Jess kissed her with all the passion and love of that first bourbon kiss. "I brought you something."

"It's not a ring, is it?" she asked, impishly, but really couldn't wait for the day when he proposed.

Pulling away with a seasoning of mischief in his eyes, he turned to the door, tucked his finger and thumb into his mouth, and whistled.

The soft scramble of uncoordinated paws hit against the floor and out popped a basset hound puppy from the hall.

"Oh, Jess," she said and went to her knees. "You brought me a dog."

The pup tripped over his ear, rolled to a stop, barked, and started for her again.

She picked him up and nuzzled him close. "Hello, Archie."

He knelt beside her. "Cancel your flight to Paris."

"Paris?" she questioned as the pup licked her face. "I didn't book a flight to Paris."

Jess closed his eyes and summoned a deep breath. "Lou…"

Louisa appeared in the doorway, looking uncharacteristically sheepish. "I couldn't let you ruin Thanksgiving."

Laughing, Mallory took Jess's hand. "Can we go home now?"

JESS WATCHED MALLORY PACK HER BAGS AS ARCHIE JUMPED and growled at her ankles. For now, she had the dog, but one day soon, he was going to marry that woman and they were going to have a tender moment where love created life.

He snatched his faded brown Stetson – a hat that was older than any of his relationships — from the floor and smiled as he scrubbed a thumb over the hoof print near the back of the brim.

He and the old hat had plenty in common. They'd both seen a lot of airtime, been knocked around, stomped on and reshaped.

Nowadays, it kept the sun from his eyes, his hair in place and reminded him of everything he had gained.

BREAKING THE COWBOY

Chapter One

Louisa Coldiron could buy her own drinks, saddle her own horse, and drive herself to the chapel without any assistance from a cowboy.

Yet she desperately needed one to ride to her rescue.

The fully restored, midnight black 1979 Chevy truck was her baby and she loved it. But right now, she wanted to roll it into the weeds and let it sit until the tires dry rotted.

She'd always wanted a vintage truck, something classy and sexy, so she'd traded her little sports car for a practical work vehicle when she'd started her veterinary internship.

But as she felt under the hood for the release handle, she realized that her purchase had been based on a zealous and impractical wish from her adolescent years, not a pragmatic decision for her career. After finding the handle, she gave it a squeeze and then raised the hood. Placing her boot on the front bumper, she hoisted herself up to get a better look at the engine.

She fidgeted with the battery cable, hoping a loose

connection might be the problem. *That can't be it.* If it were, the headlights and dash gages wouldn't work. Too bad, the truck didn't have all the bells and whistles a new vehicle had to warn her when something wasn't right under the hood.

Normally, she wouldn't have needed them. Having been raised on a cattle ranch with two older brothers and a father who insisted she be self-sufficient had given Louisa a common knowledge of basic automotive care and taught her how to notice telltale signs of engine trouble. When she was twelve, McCrea let her help change the brakes on one of the ranch's flatbed diesel trucks, and thanks to Jess, she could change the oil in any vehicle. But neither of those lessons would help her now.

There hadn't been anything wrong with the truck's performance last night on the way home from the wedding rehearsal or this morning when she'd driven it into town to have her hair and nails done. That meant whatever had gone wrong had done so after she got home.

The problem could be something simple, a loose wire or bolt or just a faulty part. There was no need for her to worry. Engines failed, vehicles needed upkeep and repairs. Just because her truck wouldn't start didn't mean there was foul play afoot. Still, she couldn't shake the familiar uneasiness stirring inside of her.

She stepped down from the truck, slammed the hood closed, and dusted her hands, careful not to chip a nail. After climbing back inside the cab, she held her breath as she gave the engine one more desperate crank.

Nothing, not a sound nor a click, just silence.

Frustration bubbled up her throat, rousting a sharp, ear-splitting scream that frightened a nest of scrub-jays from a nearby tree. A frenzy of fluttering wings and squawks rattled the air as the birds took flight.

She gave the steering wheel a couple of hard yanks for good measure, then snatched her phone from the seat beside her. Using her thumb, she scrolled down her list of contacts to find the only uncalled one on her list.

She stopped when she came to the photo assigned to Brody Vance's personal cell phone number. He had collar-length, chestnut hair, assertive blue-gray eyes that glittered when he smiled, and a cleft chin that did crazy things to her stomach.

Louisa remembered, in detail, the hot summer day she'd taken the photo. Brody had been working in the paddock with a rescued colt. He'd been covered in dirt and grim, sweaty and shirtless, she'd wanted to enjoy the moment longer than the seconds it took for her to pass from the veterinary clinic to the horse stables. So, like a teenage girl stalking her first crush, she'd darted behind the head-high bales of hay stacked to the side and hoped to secretly capture a few shots when he wasn't looking.

But Brody had swung around to look directly at her just as she snapped the picture. She'd been mortified, of course. He, on the other hand, had loved every minute of her red-faced excuses and salty curses as she'd lost her balance and pitched forward into the hay bales. They'd tumbled over and she'd been caught standing with her proverbial pants around her ankles. He'd chuckled and given her a wide, sexy grin before she'd hurried inside the clinic.

In a few hours, she'd be holding onto the arm of Mr. Hot Ass himself as he escorted her down the aisle. They'd be close, their bodies touching like they had been last night at rehearsal.

How was she going to make it through this wedding without melting into a puddle?

Damn the man for making her feel out of sorts and

damn her truck for leaving her stranded. Unwilling to throw in the towel and make the call to Brody, Louisa scrolled up and hit the call icon beside her friend Violet's name.

Louisa was four months into her veterinarian position at the Promise Point Horse Rescue, a non-profit organization her brothers had started six years ago. Not only did the Rescue save horses, but its equine therapy program had helped hundreds of veterans suffering from Post Traumatic Stress Disorder.

It was immensely rewarding to know that she was saving horses and helping to make a difference in the lives of people. And it felt so good to be home with her friends and family. But so much had changed in the years since she'd left home for college. Three out of four of her closest friends were either married or involved in a serious relationship. Eleanor, her best friend since the second grade, had married McCrea two years ago and they'd recently welcomed their second child. Last Christmas, Sage announced her engagement to Carter McDermott. Today, everyone in the small town of Santa Camino, Texas, was piling into the Tall Oaks Winery for Mallory and Jess's wedding.

She and Violet were the last remaining bachelorettes of their five-member sisterhood, and right now, Violet was her only alternative to Brody. "Come on, Vi. Please, answer your phone."

But Violet didn't pick up. Like a dozen times before, her phone rang three times and cut straight to voicemail. "Howdy, this is Vi. Leave a message."

Groaning, Louisa flipped the phone face down and planted her face in her hands. She was not calling Brody for a ride.

Nope.

No.

Ah-uh.

She'd just sit here and wait.

Lifting her head, she drew in a steadying breath. When her family realized she was late, they'd check their phones, see her missed calls, voice mails, and text, and call her back. She just needed to relax and be patient.

"Right," she mumbled.

Blowing a stray strand of hair from her eyes, she settled against the seat and waited for her phone to ring. Minutes ticked by and like her truck's engine, there was nothing. No ring. No vibration or message alerts, only silence, and the longer she waited for someone to call, the later she'd be.

The auto repair shop in town wasn't open on Saturdays, and no one was answering the phones at the new tow truck service.

Whether she liked it or not, Brody was her last resort for getting to the wedding. Gritting her teeth, she flipped the phone over and scrolled back to his number.

Heat swept over her body, causing Louisa to inhale a shaky breath before hitting the call button beside Brody's number. It was June in the Texas Hill Country. When she'd carried her things to the truck, the outside thermometer had read seventy-five degrees, but she hadn't felt the rising heat until she'd started thinking about Brody.

As his cell started ringing, Louisa wedged the phone between her shoulder and her ear and began fanning her face with a coloring book she'd snatched from the dash. At seven, her niece, Sophie, was infatuated with anything remotely related to fairytales and princesses. *Aladdin* was one of her favorite stories.

She slid from the truck and headed towards the cool comfort of her air-conditioned Airstream travel trailer, thinking that if she could magically summon Brody like a genie from a bottle, it would spare her the task of asking him for a ride. Simply rub the lamp and her wish would be his command.

A snarky grin pulled at her lips when she thought about her chaps-wearing nemesis as a mythological shapeshifter.

"Imagine that," she said and snorted through a laugh.

Brody Vance popping out of a lamp riding a magic carpet, ready to grant her three wishes. No way. If that cowboy popped out of anything, it would most likely be a bottle of whiskey, and he wouldn't be sitting cross-legged on a rug. That was too tame for a cowboy like Brody. He'd be riding a wild stallion.

His chest, tantalizingly tan and smooth with a well-groomed spread of dark brown hair covering his pecs and abs, would be bare. Her daydream deviated to naughty as she stripped those dusty chaps from his firm, sculpted thighs. There Brody stood in all his magnificent male splendor, completely naked in her mind's eye.

Holy Moses.

Nearly tripping at the bottom step of the trailer, Louisa tried to remember how many rings had passed since she'd dialed Brody's number. She'd lost count but knew he should have answered by now. Two more rings and she started to worry. He always answered when she called.

Always.

The next ring was interrupted by a deep and winded, "Hello."

That single word spoken sensually jerked the air from her lungs. "T—there you are."

"Here I am." The husky tone of his voice intensified the burn that was gathering between her thighs.

"W—what were you doing? Wait." She grimaced and was hit by a nauseating surge of jealousy in the pit of her stomach. She'd suspected that Brody was secretly entertaining a woman on his mysterious weekend trips out of town. But she'd never had a shred of proof to back up her claim.

So, had Brody brought his lady friend to Santa Camino? Had she caught them in the middle of something? And did she want to know the answer to either of the above?

No, she did not. "Forget I asked. I assumed you were alone."

"I am alone," he drawled, his voice velvety soft.

Her nausea eased and another hot flush rushed over her skin as her mind latched on to an activity a man like Brody might be doing alone. Something that would leave him breathless. Flustered and aroused, she spoke in broken syllables. "Oh…I, ah. That is…I…"

"Shame on you," he scolded, his voice dipping lower. "For thinking of me doing that."

"How'd you kno−" She stopped in mid-sentence when she realized he'd tricked her into confessing her dirty assumption. "Damn you, Brody."

That deep laugh of his, the one that made all her lady parts applaud and whistle, rumbled up his throat. "Don't clutter your innocent mind with such thoughts of me. I'm not a five-finger, one-handed kind of guy."

Louisa's mind was far from innocent and the mental picture of Brody's wide hand fisted around himself had her nearly taking a bite out of her bottom lip. "Can we just stop the bullshit and get back to why I called?"

"Okay, sweetheart." The tender humor in his voice made her want to hang up and walk the twelve miles to Tall Oaks. "What can I do for you?"

Louisa hadn't been intimate with a man in quite a while, and after that little stroll down Dirty Lane, her body was more than eager to jump in with a long and detailed list of what Brody could do for her.

But this wasn't a wicked fantasy where sex wouldn't have repercussions. This was reality and that sexy voice on the other end of the phone belonged to a man with a sensibility and gentleness about him that had made Louisa want to reconsider her rule about dating cowboys.

That unsettling fact, plus Brody's mysterious trips out of town every other weekend, had her throwing up barriers left and right. Experience had taught Louisa that cowboys weren't worth the risk. Wild and reckless, they often left a trail of shattered hearts behind as they rode off into the sunset in search of another naïve heart.

Having been that credulous conquest six years ago had given Louisa a proactive and unsparing attitude towards shooting down Brody's advances. "My truck won't start. Can I catch a ride to the wedding with you?"

"Let me guess." There was a short pause for effect. "No one else is answering their phone?"

Brody had a real gift for reading horses. It was like he knew what the animal was thinking. It's what made him such a good trainer. But he also had an unnerving knack for reading people as well. Body language, eye movements, and hand gestures were all like signals to him.

Not that a guy had to be gifted or psychic to know when Louisa was giving him the cold shoulder. She was damn good at pushing men away. But nothing had worked on Brody. She'd tried every way in the world to detour him, but nothing seemed to affect his determination. He simply sauntered past or sidestepped whatever she threw at him. Angry words and sharp-tongued insults were nothing to the man. His course was fixed on her and so far, nothing had slowed him down.

Brody had been the Rescue's horse trainer for nearly

two years, so she'd known before accepting the veterinarian position that they'd be coworkers. She'd told herself that she could handle the attraction, and it was only a matter of time before he lost interest in her and moved on.

Boy, oh, boy, had she been wrong.

The cowboy was as persistent and patient as he was handsome, which was the most disturbing part of all. Because when Brody Vance wanted something, he got it. And it was no secret to Louisa or anyone else that what he wanted was her — in his bed.

Trying hard to dismiss the images that thought provoked, Louisa added an extra layer of iciness to her voice. "How'd you know?"

"Oh, just a hunch." He laughed, unoffended that he'd been her last resort. "I know you'd rather eat the rattlers off a snake than ask me for anything."

You got that right. "So, are you comin' or not?"

"Yeah," he answered. "Give me time to shower and change and I'll swing by and pick you up."

ABOUT THE AUTHOR

Books by Mina Beckett

Coldiron Cowboys series

The Cowboy's Goodnight Kiss
(ebook prequel novella only available on Mina's website)
The Heartbreak Cowboy
The Fallen Cowboy
Breaking the Cowboy

Rough Creek series

A Cowboy Charming Christmas

Coming soon

Hollywood Cowboy
A Cold Montana Christmas: a Coldiron Cowboys inspired novel

For more book news, visit minabeckett.com

Made in the USA
Middletown, DE
06 December 2021

54374369R00224